~~~~ance novels— because writing is ~~~~ ...assion, along with her family and church. Rebecca loves to hear from readers. If you wish to email her, please visit her website at www.cleanromances.net.

A career Air Force officer, **Merline Lovelace** served at bases all over the world. When she hung up her uniform for the last time, she decided to try her hand at story-telling. Since then, more than twelve million copies of her books have been published in over thirty countries. Check her website at www.merlinelovelace.com or friend Merline on Facebook for news and information about her latest releases.

FALLING FOR THE VENETIAN BILLIONAIRE

REBECCA WINTERS

MARRY ME, MAJOR

MERLINE LOVELACE

MILLS & BOON

First Published in Great Britain 2018
by Mills & Boon, an imprint of HarperCollinsPublishers,
1 London Bridge Street, London, SE1 9GF

Falling for the Venetian Billionaire © 2018 Rebecca Winters
Marry Me, Major © 2018 Merline Lovelace

ISBN: 978-0-263-26503-3

38-0618

MIX
Paper from
responsible sources
FSC™ C007454

FSC
www.fsc.org

This book is produced from independently certified FSC™
paper to ensure responsible forest management.

For more information visit: www.harpercollins.co.uk/green

Printed and bound in Spain
by CPI, Barcelona

FALLING FOR THE VENETIAN BILLIONAIRE

REBECCA WINTERS

To my darling daughter, Dominique,
who lived and studied in Italy in her late teens.
Like Lord Byron, she fell in love with it.

PROLOGUE

AFTER A MORNING of driving his ski boat for his sister and her friends, thirty-year-old Vittorio Della Scalla, finance director of the Della Scalla Shipping and Passenger Lines Company in Venice, Italy, announced he had to get back to the office.

His twenty-four-year-old sister, Maria, padded up to the front. "Please take Paola one more time," she begged out of earshot. Maria's best friend, Paola Coronna, was the same age as Maria, and both of them worked at the Della Scalla travel agency. "She's been practicing on her slalom ski and is dying to show you her front flip."

Very few skiers could manage it, but Paola and her brother, Dario, who was a year younger, had always been a handful, if not willful at times. He shook his head. "I'm late for work now."

Maria's gray-blue eyes pleaded with him. "Do it for me, Vittorio. Paola is crazy about you and wants to impress you."

That was the last thing Vittorio wanted to hear, but it was the end of vacation for everyone. Since it was September, he wouldn't be coming out to the family villa on the Lido di Venezia again this year. Before he spent more time here, it would probably be late spring of next year when the weather started to warm up.

Letting out a groan, he murmured, "*Bene*, but this is the final run. You and Dario are the spotters, remember. Don't take your eye off her for a second!"

"*Grazie.*" Maria kissed his bronzed cheek and walked back to tell the others.

Fifteen years ago, Vittorio, along with three friends, had been out here skiing and goofing off. Drinking had been involved. But there'd been an incident. He'd been the driver and no one was watching carefully enough, including Vittorio. When the girl fell while skiing, they didn't realize it in time for another boat to almost run over her after she'd fallen.

The owner of the other boat happened to be a neighbor who lived on the Lido. He stopped and waited for Vittorio to pull alongside. He gave him a lecture he would never forget and called the police. Apparently, he'd been keeping track of the Della Scallas' younger son and his antics with his other friends from high-profile families.

This time he reported the drinking and negligence, and it made the newspaper as well as the news on TV. Vittorio's father had to live with the bad press because there'd been other reports from locals that the privileged teens on the Lido, including Count Della Scalla's younger son, were a menace. It brought out the paparazzi who followed Vittorio around for a long time.

Vittorio's father was a kind man, but he didn't spare the discipline when it came to his younger son. Thus followed several years of humiliating pain for Vittorio, and his privileges were severely curtailed. No more partying on the ski boat, no more scuba diving, no more being allowed at the villa on the Lido without adult supervision.

It didn't matter that Vittorio hadn't been the one drinking. He'd been driving the boat and had acted totally irresponsibly. In a vulnerable moment, his father had said that Vittorio's older brother, Gaspare, would never have brought embarrassment to the family like Vittorio had done.

His father's disappointment in him, plus the offhand remark, had made a deep impression on Vittorio, who swore never to let anything like that happen again. He turned his life around, threw himself into his studies. In time, he made enough money to buy a sailboat and develop a plan to make money on his own. Even after his father put him to work in the company, Vittorio managed his own business on the side, determined to make his father proud of him.

"She's ready, Vittorio!"

Brought back to the present, he turned on the engine. After looking around to be sure, he accelerated the throttle, then felt the tug of the rope. Soon he could see she was up. Paola was a good skier and a definite show-off. She did several wide arcs back and forth.

He brought Paola around for the last time and headed to shore, watching her through the rearview mirror. She got in position to do her flip. But suddenly her body flew forward and hit the water at an odd angle.

"Stop the boat!" Dario and his sister yelled at the same time.

With his adrenaline surging, Vittorio swung the boat around and raced toward Paola. When he came alongside her, he put the transmission in Neutral and helped Dario pull her into the boat. That's when he spotted two slalom skis bobbing in the water. Where in the hell had the other one come from?

Once they'd laid a groaning Paola on the banquette, he saw blood dripping from her ankle. In trying to perform the flip, she had to have hit the other water ski hard for so much damage to have been done. He reached for one of the towels to stanch the flow. Already he could see swelling.

"Hold her still, Dario. I'm calling for an ambulance."

Within a few minutes he saw the blue flashing lights of a water ambulance coming toward them with its siren blaring. Maria had hunkered down to comfort her.

"You're going to be fine, Paola. We're getting you to the hospital."

Vittorio leaned over her. "I promise to take care of you, Paola."

While his sister tried to comfort her, he pulled both skis out of the water. Maybe someone skiing behind the other boat he'd seen in the distance had dropped it trying to get up on one ski. The wake could have brought it in their direction. Or it could have fallen off the transom at the back of a boat. Perhaps it had been out here for a long time. He stored both skis to get them out of the way.

Nothing like this had ever happened before. As the medics put her in the ambulance, he phoned the Coronna family to let them know about the accident. Dario got on board with her to go to the hospital. Maria rode back to the villa with Vittorio, who had to phone the office and tell his private secretary that he wouldn't be in.

Two hours later Paola had been taken into surgery and put under a general anesthetic. The doctor made a cut on the skin near the ankle. Then special screws and plates were used to put the bones together and hold them in place. Finally a plaster cast was put on below her knee to the toes. After ten weeks an X-ray would be taken to see how the bones were mending.

Vittorio talked with the doctor who explained that the sheer force of hitting the other ski had twisted Paola's ankle in such a vulnerable spot, it was enough to cause the break. He hoped for a good outcome, but it was too early to tell.

The bad news came when she suffered more pain in January and had to go in for a replacement of some screws. The second surgery, followed by physical therapy, fixed the problem and Paola eventually recovered. But she couldn't walk on her foot the same way as before the accident. The doctor advised her to wear flats from now on, no high heels.

Maria felt awful and wished she hadn't asked Vittorio to take Paola on that last run. Naturally he was horrified that there'd been an accident at all. But for it to have happened on his watch, the same way a near accident had happened out here fifteen years ago…

His father wasn't going to be happy about this. Vittorio had spent years making recompense for his foolish behavior. He'd done everything in his power to preserve the family honor.

Though he wasn't responsible for this accident today, guilt put a stranglehold on him more intense than before.

CHAPTER ONE

Eight months later

NOW THAT IT was nearing the end of May, Ginger Lawrence's work in Italy was drawing to an end. She had a laptop bulging with files. Some contained her work writing a series of stories about children around the world. Others contained the research on Lord Byron she'd amassed. The early nineteenth-century British romance poet and writer had been her reason for coming to Europe.

Yesterday she'd come from Genoa, Italy, where Lord Byron had lived in his last Italian home. Today she'd met some researchers in Ravenna, Italy, among them Dr. Welch and Dr. Manukyan with a group known in literature circles as the International Lord Byron Association.

They'd asked her if she'd like to join them for dinner aboard the *Sirena*, one of the passenger ships on the Adriatic docked outside Ravenna, Italy. She'd been pleased to be invited.

Their group had spent the better part of the day sharing new information on Lord Byron, who'd traveled and had lived in this region. It was here he'd turned to drama and wrote *The Two Foscari* and one of her favorite plays, *Cain*, his slant on the biblical Cain.

This evening they met with one of several other board members who'd be presenting material at the Byron Conclave in Armenia in July. Unfortunately, by then Ginger and her coworker friends would be back in California, preparing for fall semester.

Ginger admitted to the group seated with her that she was upset for not having allowed enough time to go to Venice and really explore it. She needed another month, but that was impossible. Her one day in Venice would have to count!

Dr. Manukyan, the Armenian professor and host, smiled at her. "Just remember that Byron's most important time in Venice was spent at the Armenian Monastery during his San Lazzaro period in 1817."

Ginger nodded. "I plan to spend the whole day there engrossed."

"As you probably know, the island of San Lazzaro was named after Saint Lazarus, the patron saint of lepers," he explained. "The four-hundred-year-old leper colony existed from the twelfth to the sixteenth centuries. At the end of that time, Mechitar, an Armenian monk, escaped from the Turks and arrived in Venice, where he was given the island for his Dominican congregation.

"Now there are a dozen-plus monks and Armenian students who come to study Italian and are in charge of its precious museum and library. During his travels in Europe, Byron turned to a new intellectual amusement to supplement physical pleasures and decided to learn Armenian."

"That's what I want to learn more about," Ginger exclaimed. "I know he worked on an English-Armenian grammar book. I'm fascinated by the way Byron's brain worked and what motivated him."

Dr. Manukyan nodded. "Byron set himself a project to study the Venetian dialect, too. In truth, Lord Byron had one of his most productive periods in Venice. Besides his work at the monastery, he wrote the first half of *Don Juan* while there."

Ginger couldn't get enough of learning about Byron, while they enjoyed a delicious seafood dinner followed by dessert and coffee. Afterward, Dr. Manukyan announced some other Byron conclaves being held in the future. Too bad she would have to be back in California teaching during those dates and would have to miss them.

With her thoughts on her friends, knowing she would be with them soon, Ginger sat back in the chair pleasantly tired and drank her coffee. Since January, Ginger had been in Italy digging for any fresh information on the life of the poet. Before Christmas her department head at Vanguard University in Costa Mesa, California, where she'd been teaching, had approached her.

Would she like to attend a workshop in Los Angeles on a new academic project about Lord Byron for the famous Hollywood film director Magda Collier? Her revered mogul friend would be producing it, and research was needed to supply original material for the screenwriters.

Ginger would have to leave the university for a semester and travel to Europe. After having lost her husband, Bruce, to cancer over two years before, Ginger had jumped at the opportunity to work in Italy, hoping for new experiences that would help put her pain behind her.

No man could ever replace Bruce. Her pain was doubly excruciating because he'd died before they could have children. Ginger had wanted children more than anything. Her therapist had suggested that since she'd dabbled in writing over the years, she should work on a children's story, something her own children would have loved.

After so much sorrow and anguish over broken dreams, Ginger knew she needed to concentrate on something else and took her therapist's advice.

At the seminar she'd met Zoe Perkins and Abby Grant, who'd also been hired. All three had obtained master's degrees in literature from UCLA, San Jose State University and Stanford respectively, focusing on the romance poets and writers.

Abby had been sent to Switzerland and Zoe had been assigned to Greece, but all three of them had kept in touch through Skyping and phone calls. Her travels and theirs began to feed her imagination, and she got the idea to write about children around the world when she couldn't do her research.

As Ginger had explained to the others at the table aboard ship, tomorrow she would take the train to Venice and spend time at the monastery in the afternoon. That evening she'd meet Zoe at the airport and they'd take the night train to Montreux, Switzerland, where they planned to pick up a hire car and then join up with Abby at Saint-Saphorin on Lake Geneva, where they'd begin their vacation.

Magda had rewarded them with a month's stay on a

vineyard there. They could use it for their home base while they did whatever they wanted.

Ginger turned to ask Dr. Manukyan a few more questions, but he suddenly said, "Excuse me for a minute," and got up from the table.

Surprised, she watched him walk toward a thirtyish-looking man with raven black hair who'd just entered the dining room. Everything about him, including his elegant dark blue suit and tie, shouted sophistication and an aura of authority he probably wasn't even aware of.

He stood tall and was the most gorgeous, virile Italian male she'd ever laid eyes on in her life. Every feature from his olive skin to his powerful jaw mesmerized her.

Her heart thumped as the two men walked over to the table. "Everyone," Dr. Manukyan began, "I'd like to introduce you to Signor Della Scalla. He's not only responsible for the souvenir menus you've all been given, he's the one who made it possible for us to have dinner aboard ship this evening."

"I hope you're enjoying it." The striking man spoke excellent English with an enticing Italian accent.

Della Scalla. The name was synonymous with one of the most renowned shipping and passenger lines in Italy, let alone Europe. But there were probably hundreds of Italians with the same last name.

Ginger listened while their host introduced the five members of their party to the stranger. When it came her turn, she found herself captivated by a pair of black-fringed cobalt-blue eyes the color of handblown Venetian glass.

Those penetrating orbs seemed to take her all in, as if he were searching for the very essence of her.

For the first time since Bruce's death, another man had managed to take her breath away. Who was he?

"It's a pleasure to meet you," he spoke to all of them, but his gaze remained focused on her.

"Won't you sit with us for a moment?" Dr. Manukyan asked.

"Thank you, but I'm afraid I'm pressed for time. If you're finished with your meal, does anyone need a ride back to Ravenna? It'll be on my way. You're welcome to come in the limo."

Dr. Manukyan looked pleased. "We're staying at the Palazzo Bezzi Hotel and were going to call for a taxi. But we'd love a ride, if it isn't too far out of your way."

"Not at all."

"We appreciate your kindness for everything."

"Let me escort you out."

Ginger couldn't credit that they'd be driving back to town with him. She stood up and followed the others to the elevator. It took them down to the deck, where they walked through the covered passageway to the dock.

A black gleaming limousine stood parked right there. Ginger was the last person to climb in. She decided this man had to be an important person, but she couldn't ask Dr. Manukyan because they weren't alone.

When Signor Della Scalla came around to help her in, she felt his arm brush hers by accident. A shiver of awareness ran through her.

He rode in front with the chauffeur. Before long they arrived at the hotel near the old town where she'd gone exploring early in the morning before meeting the group. Again, he was there to open the door. Everyone thanked him and said goodbye. Then it was her turn.

"Signora?" She looked up at him before getting out. She found herself drowning in his gaze once more. "How long are you going to be in Ravenna?"

Ginger's heart was still overreacting, especially when she noticed he didn't wear any rings. She wasn't wearing any rings either. Whoever he was, Ginger couldn't believe she felt such an instant attraction to him. Though she'd been coming to terms with her loss, she wasn't sure about loving another man again. "I'm leaving tomorrow morning."

He'd put both hands on the frame of the door, blocking her exit though she knew it wasn't on purpose. "Where are you going next?"

"To Venice."

"For a long visit?"

"Don't I wish, but no. I only have one day before I leave on vacation."

He cocked his head. "Only one? Couldn't I convince you to stay on several more? We could meet at your hotel and I could show you around."

A tremor shook her body. Ginger couldn't help but be flattered by his interest. Other men had flirted with her while she'd been in Italy, but she'd never been tempted. Not until now. This Italian's charisma was so overpowering, she couldn't believe a man like him existed.

"I won't be in Venice long enough to get a hotel." Ginger's heart was in her throat. "There isn't enough time. I have to spend a good part of the day at the monastery where Lord Byron spent so many hours. It's part of my job and the reason I'm here at all."

For some reason the revelation caused his eyes to gleam. "Then be sure to ask for Father Giovanni. I know him well. He's the resident expert."

Dr. Manukyan hadn't mentioned the monk's name. "Thank you for the information. I'll remember."

"Where will you go next?"

He really wanted to know? "My friend and I will be taking the night train to Switzerland."

His gaze played over her. "I see. He's a lucky man."

Ginger sucked in her breath. "No, no. I'm going with my friend Zoe, who's flying in from Greece. She and I will be meeting another friend at a vineyard on Lake Geneva."

Good heavens. Ginger had practically told him her life story and had found herself babbling like a schoolgirl. "Thank you for giving all of us a ride. Do you live here in Ravenna?" She found she wanted to know more about him.

"No. I'm a Venetian," he said in his deep voice. "Unfortunately I have to get back to Venice tonight on business. But perhaps our paths will cross again."

He moved aside to help her out of the limo. She felt his touch on her arm once again, and felt fingers of delight dart through her body.

"*Alla prossima*, signora."

Until next time? There couldn't possibly be a next time. In two days' time she'd be in Switzerland with her friends. But the thought of seeing him again made Ginger's pulse leap. Deep down she didn't want to say goodbye to him.

Since Bruce had died, Ginger hadn't paid attention to other men or encouraged them. She couldn't. The thought of falling in love again only to lose that person in such a terrible way frightened her.

She'd told Zoe and Abby that she didn't want to give her heart a second time to another man, only for it to end in tragedy. In fact Ginger had never expected to meet a man who could ever help her get over the pain of having to say goodbye to her beloved husband. Only a miracle could cause that to happen.

She didn't believe in miracles like that. But something shocking had happened for this stranger to take over her thoughts like this. It made no sense that for once she wasn't thinking about Bruce.

Ginger's legs felt insubstantial as Signor Della Scalla walked her inside the foyer of the hotel.

"*Buona notte*, signora," he whispered.

"*Buona notte*, signor." She sensed his eyes still on her until she rounded a corner to take the elevator to her room.

To her dismay when she finally got in bed, Ginger's thoughts were still haunted by one incredibly handsome Italian male and the way she'd felt when his gaze swept over her at the dinner table. It was as if every cell in her body had been ignited by a bolt of electricity. She'd never lay eyes on him again, but that didn't mean his image would go away. Not ever.

At nine o'clock the next morning, a showered and shaved Vittorio, wearing a black suit, left the centuries-old Della Scalla palazzo on the Grand Canal. Last night he'd flown back to Venice in the helicopter with a plan in mind to meet up with Signora Lawrence the next day at the monastery.

But this morning, after his flight home from Ravenna

last evening, he'd awakened to the gut-wrenching news that his father had passed away early in the morning.

Overnight Vittorio's world had changed forever. After leaving his grieving family with the doctor, he drove his speedboat out to the lagoon toward the nearby island of San Lazzaro two kilometers away.

Many boats crowded the canal. He passed by the boat ferrying passengers who intended to visit the Armenian monastery, the sole feature of the island. After pulling up to the jetty, Vittorio alighted and hurried past the welcoming signs printed in several languages to the main building. A plaque had been placed there commemorating the famous English writer and poet Lord Byron, who was known as a "Faithful friend of Armenia."

Since it was always open in invitation, Vittorio entered the doors to the cloister that enclosed a garden. Beyond it lay the incense-filled chapel covered in mosaics. He hoped to find his brother, Gaspare, who was known among the brothers as Father Giovanni, but only a few monks were present in here. That meant he was probably in the famous museum, which had many treasures, including a mummy and a bust of Napoleon's son.

But further exploration didn't lead Vittorio to his thirty-four-year-old brother. If he wasn't in the private enclosure for the monks, then he had to be in the room designated as Lord Byron's studio.

Vittorio's brother, who'd studied in England before joining the priesthood, had a passion for Byron. Vittorio entered the studio with a reproduction of a painting of Lord Byron above the door.

In the early 1800s the poet had studied the Armenian language here over a two-year period while he'd been in Venice. Prized books and manuscripts in this library drew crowds of tourists as well as serious scholars at all seasons of the year.

Vittorio scanned the room and saw his brother in his brown habit at the other end, talking to some visitors. Their backs were toward him while they were discussing a manuscript under glass.

Vittorio moved closer with a heavy heart, knowing their father's death would come as a great blow.

"Gaspare?"

His brother looked around, having been taken by surprise. "Vittorio—"

After a pause, he turned back to the visitor. "I must ask to be excused," he said in English. "I'll send Father Luca to assist you." On that note, he joined Vittorio and they moved out of earshot.

Since Gaspare had become a monk, the only consolation for Vittorio had been the ability to visit his brother here on occasion and confide in him. Just three years separated them. They loved each other and had been close growing up.

"Something tragic has happened. I see it in your countenance."

Vittorio stared into the same blue eyes of his sibling. The two bore a superficial resemblance to each other in height and their black hair. Both were taller than their father. His throat tightened in fresh pain.

"Papà died early this morning," he spoke quietly. Vittorio could still visualize the scene at the palazzo a little while ago.

Dr. Farini, the longtime physician of the family, had examined their father before sliding the sheet over his face. Count Mario Goretti Della Scalla, beloved husband, father, brother, friend and CEO of the Della Scalla Shipping and Passenger Line Company, was officially dead.

The doctor had stared into Vittorio's eyes. "*You* are now Count Della Scalla. Your father has been blessed to have a son like you ready and able to step into his shoes."

There was another son Vittorio felt should be taking his place, but that wasn't possible. Soon the news would be out. The bells would toll throughout Venice for the loss.

"How did he die, Vittorio?"

"Dr. Farini said it was a heart attack. It happened quickly, the only blessing I can see."

Gaspare's eyes glistened with unshed tears. "He was too young."

"No one expected it."

A deep sigh of pain escaped. "How are Mamma and Maria?"

"I'm sure you can imagine."

He bowed his head. "They worshipped him."

"We all did," Vittorio whispered. "I left a message with Uncle Bertoldo's maid. He and Aunt Miah are due back from Rome before the day is out. The doctor is with the family and will stay until you and I arrive. Being with you will help all of us get through this."

His brother stood stock-still, but Vittorio saw the mask of sorrow that had already settled. "Wait here for me. I have to talk to the abbot and gather a few things. I'll be back in a few minutes."

While Vittorio waited, Gaspare walked back to the visitors and said something to them before he left through a side door. The action reminded him that Signora Lawrence would be coming to the monastery before long seeking out his brother. The image of her had been constantly in his thoughts.

Vittorio had determined that the woman who'd caught his interest last night had been maybe twenty-four, twenty-five, dressed in a summery blue and white print suit. As he'd moved closer to the dinner table, he'd been stunned by her beauty. She'd possessed such exquisite features, he hadn't been able to look anywhere else.

Her glossy short black hair of soft natural curls made his breath catch. He couldn't remember the last time he'd seen an hourglass figure like hers. Luminous gray eyes fused with his.

Vittorio had felt her appraise him with unexpected candor before she got up from the table with the others. In his opinion the gorgeous creature looked too young to be a professor, yet she'd been with a team of experts on Lord Byron. It was for this group he'd arranged the dinner on board one of the Della Scalla passenger liners.

Vittorio had instructed the captain of the *Sirena* to make a special stop in Ravenna. He'd done it as a special favor for Gaspare, whose birthday would be celebrated in a few days, an early present. His brother had been longtime friends with Dr. Manukyan, who was from Yerevan State University in Armenia and had been visiting Ravenna.

But when Vittorio had made the arrangements, little did he know there'd be a woman like Signora Lawrence attached to this group. Had he realized, he could have flown there earlier to eat dinner with them and get to know her better.

He was still thinking about her when he heard Gaspare's voice. "I'm ready."

His head swung around. "I didn't see you come back in."

Gaspare stood there carrying a suitcase. "I'm not surprised. None of us could imagine this day arriving this soon in our lives."

Shocked to have been caught distracted while their father's death was on their minds, he headed for the doorway to the museum. Gaspare caught up to him, and they left the monastery for the boat.

There were many things to discuss, not the least of which was the planning of the funeral. No one had expected their father to die for at least twenty more years.

But even with so many weighty matters to consider, including the running of the company, Vittorio had a difficult time putting the enticing American woman out of his mind. How incredible was it that she'd planned to come to the monastery today and he would miss her by only a few hours!

The fact that he might never see her again shouldn't matter to him, but it did… He couldn't understand it.

Vittorio had enjoyed several intimate relationships with women in his adult life. They'd been important to him, but he hadn't fallen in love with one of them to the point that he wanted to be married.

Maybe it was the burden of the family name and title, plus all the expectations that came with it, that had prevented him from wanting to settle down yet. Growing his side business had taken up any free time Vittorio had away from the company.

If an affair of the heart was going to happen, Vittorio hadn't felt it.

Until last night…

Just looking at her had caused something to come over Vittorio—an indescribable feeling that had pulled at all his senses and more. Vittorio had been so drawn to Signora Lawrence, he'd invited the whole group of scholars assembled to ride to their hotel with him in the hope of talking to her for a while longer. But it had increased his guilt over Paola, who still thought he would marry her. How was he going to let her down gently?

Once he and Gaspare reached the jetty, they climbed on the boat and Vittorio headed toward the bell towers of San Marco and San Giorgio Maggiore in the distance. As the island receded behind them, his mind was still on a certain gorgeous woman who would be arriving there soon.

But before long they reached the palazzo, where their devastated family was waiting for them to arrive. Once again Vittorio felt the dark cloud of sorrow descend, knowing their father was gone and he was now the head of the family. He felt the heavy weight because already the family looked to him for everything.

CHAPTER TWO

THE NEXT DAY nothing went the way Ginger had planned. First of all, when she arrived in Venice and went to the monastery, she discovered that Father Giovanni, the resident authority on Byron, had been called away for the better part of a week.

One of the other monks showed her around, but he didn't have the information to certain questions only an expert could answer. Disappointment swept through her before she took a water bus back to Venice. By five in the afternoon she met Zoe's plane.

Ginger was thrilled to see her friend. They ate dinner and headed for the train station, excited to meet up with Abby and enjoy their month in Switzerland. But another disappointment awaited all of them the next day when they arrived in Switzerland and found out the vineyard where they'd be vacationing had been sold.

Magda's friend had died.

Though they could stay on while the caretakers ran the place, the girls decided they would prefer to go somewhere else and not be a burden. They were planning to travel to Europe together to make the most of their last few weeks. Then came another shock—Abby had met an attractive French relative of the previous owner staying at the vineyard, and he invited her to travel to Burgundy with him.

The invitation had included Ginger and Zoe, but they didn't want to intrude if something of a romantic nature was happening to their friend. Instead they agreed to go back to Italy and Greece, where they could spend a week in each place.

After taking the morning to visit a chocolate factory in Switzerland, Ginger and Zoe bid Abby goodbye, wishing her luck, and left in a rental car for Italy with Ginger doing the driving.

A sigh escaped Zoe's lips en route. "Our famous vacation at the vineyard in Switzerland fell apart fast, didn't it? Trust a man to ruin our plans."

Ginger nodded, but to her chagrin, her thoughts weren't on Bruce. Instead she'd been thinking about Signor Della Scalla. He was constantly in her thoughts. "In all honesty you have to admit that Raoul Decorvet wasn't just any man," she reminded Zoe.

"No, I suppose not, but it's hard to trust someone so attractive."

Zoe's unfaithful husband had done a lot of damage. Given time, and hopefully a wonderful man, love would come into her life.

As for their friend Abby, she'd been smitten, an old-fashioned word that seemed to suit. The more she thought about it, the more Ginger began to realize the same thing had happened to her.

Since that unforgettable moment at dinner aboard the passenger liner outside Ravenna where she'd met the gorgeous Italian, Ginger had a lot more insight into why Abby had accepted Raoul's invitation to travel to France.

"It'll be interesting to see how that turns out," she murmured.

"After what Nigel did to her heart, Ginger, let's pray this Frenchman doesn't end up breaking it."

There were a lot of ways a heart could be broken, as all three women had found out. Ginger had been trying hard not to dwell on the fact that in losing her husband, she had lost her chance of happiness. There'd never be a man she could love as she had Bruce. Thanks to his death, Ginger hadn't had the chance to have children. It had raised the fear that she might never have them, not without a remarkable husband. Ginger couldn't believe one existed.

Being an only child, Ginger had longed to raise a family with Bruce. They'd talked about it from the beginning, but his death had ended that hope.

Perish the thought of meeting a man she could fall in love with a second time. If something ghastly were to happen to him, Ginger knew she'd never be able to handle it. Ginger shivered as the image of Signor Della Scalla passed through her mind.

On Zoe's mournful note, they drove on. By the evening they'd arrived back in Venice and had checked in at the Hotel Arlecchino. It was one of the hotels where you could park a car in their garage.

They immediately began exploring the area called Frezzeria, a part of Venice where Byron had lived above a merchant's textile shop. It was no wonder the poet had chosen to stay here. This was one of the most famous districts of the city and included the Piazza San Marco with its cluster of restaurants, shops and museums frequented by the glitterati of Venice. Perhaps some detail would come to light they could send on to the writers working on Magda's film.

But the next morning, Zoe broke down and was honest with Ginger. "Venice is fabulous, but as long as I have a little more free time before going back to California, Greece is where I want to be."

Zoe had fallen in love with Greece, but Ginger knew something else more important was propelling her to go back. So far, Zoe hadn't told Ginger what was really on her mind. That was all right. Ginger had been entertaining a few private thoughts about the gorgeous Italian that didn't bear scrutiny.

"I understand completely, Zoe. The trouble is, I hated leaving Venice when I was here before. Now I have a chance to finish up some more research for Magda's project." Maybe she'd find that Father Giovanni was back at the monastery.

"Thanks for understanding." Zoe immediately phoned the airline to make a reservation for an evening flight. After dinner Ginger drove her to the San Marco airport in their rental car. They pulled up outside the terminal. "I wish you'd come to Greece with me, Ginger."

"After I finish up my research here, I'll probably fly to Athens and join you. I know you loved it there and it was hard for you to leave."

"Only time will tell. Are you sure you're all right if I leave you?"

"Positive. Who knows?" Father Giovanni still might not be there. "I could be joining you sooner than you think."

"I'd love that," Zoe exclaimed before getting out of the car with her suitcase.

Ginger smiled at her. "Text me when you arrive so I'll know you got there safely."

"You know I will. Enjoy Venice to your heart's content. Before long we'll all be back in class lecturing again and dreaming about days like this."

At the moment Ginger couldn't comprehend being anywhere else but here. She watched until Zoe disappeared, then she headed back to the hotel to park the car.

As she passed the front desk at the hotel, Ginger made arrangements to visit Burano, a place Byron loved for its color. The film being made on Byron would be enriched by some scenes from there. After she got back to her room, Ginger had a surprise phone call from Abby.

"Abby? Hey—what are you doing phoning this late?"

"I'm sorry, but I'm flying to Venice tomorrow and will try to plan a flight that fits in with your and Zoe's schedule."

"You're not staying in Burgundy?"

Ginger heard Abby release a shuddering sigh. "No."

"So the 'come and see my notebook' thing turned out not to be for real."

"Actually there was a notebook with a poem, but it wasn't an authentic signature of Byron's."

"But he really had something to show you?"

"Yes. I met his grandparents and they showed it to me."

"Then he was on the level."

"Yes."

"You sound odd. Are you okay? What's going on with you two?"

"It's been a very full day with a funeral and a dinner. He's a very important man. Don't let me keep you up any longer. Shall I come early or late? You'd better check with Zoe."

"She's not here."

"What do you mean?"

"Zoe decided to fly to Greece early, so I took her to the airport this evening and now I have the car. Tomorrow is Sunday and I'm going to Burano Island for a couple of days. I've already paid for travel and the hotel room for two nights on a special deal. Why don't you check flights for Tuesday and I'll meet you whenever you say?"

Ginger heard a hesitation, then, "That sounds fine. I'll call you Tuesday and we'll plan from there."

"Perfect."

Ginger realized something had gone wrong with Abby's plans. What a shame for her.

The next morning Ginger left on a water bus for Burano and explored the island. The bright colors of the houses were remarkable, and she was glad she had come. After another productive day, Ginger returned to the hotel in Venice, tired and happy.

The next evening, she was getting ready for bed when she received a text from Abby rather than a phone call.

I won't be flying to meet you after all. Maybe you should be sitting down. Raoul and I are going to be married in two days in a civil ceremony. We don't want to wait. I adore him and I know it's forever. We'll

have a church service later on and I hope you and Zoe
will be able to come. I promise to tell you everything
later. Love, Abby

Ginger read the text three times. How absolutely
amazing and wonderful for their friend. Zoe would
have received a text, too. But Ginger was worried
for Abby. Wasn't she nervous about getting married
so fast when her engagement to Nigel had ended so
painfully?

Abby hadn't even known that Nigel was married
and had children back in England. Now she was going
to marry a Frenchman after such a short period of
knowing him? It sounded very scary to Ginger. But
at the same time she had to admire their friend who'd
decided to take the plunge anyway and not let fear
prevent her from following her heart.

Ginger got up from the side of the bed, realizing
that's what she was doing, following her heart by
wanting to return to the monastery. Of course, she
desired to talk with Father Giovanni, but she now
knew he was friends with Signor Della Scalla. The
monk was her link to the dark-haired stranger who'd
mesmerized her.

She could still hear what he'd whispered. "*Alla
prossima*, signora." Did he really hope to see her
again? After asking her to spend another day with
him, Ginger had to believe it.

Her heart pounded painfully to imagine seeing him
again. The possibility gave Ginger the impetus to follow through with her plan. Abby's decision had given
her a little more daring.

By the next morning Ginger was up early to drink

coffee and eat a roll, unable to sleep any longer. She checked her hair and makeup in the mirror.

Today she teamed a short-sleeved pink-and-white-striped blouse with a summery white skirt. After putting a small notebook in her purse, she left the hotel at nine thirty and took a water taxi to the island.

A semicloudy sky covered the lagoon with its boats and ferries. The temperature would be a little warmer today.

Father Giovanni ought to be on the island. He just *had* to be.

For the last seven days Vittorio had spent all of his time with family while they dealt with the funeral and interment. Now he had to attend to business. But with his father gone, Vittorio wasn't prepared for the pang of loss he felt as he arrived at the Della Scalla Shipping and Passenger Line Company.

As Vittorio's uncle Bertoldo was the general manager, he'd asked the executive secretary to call a June meeting of the fifteen-member board set for 9:00 a.m. His father's successor would have to be voted in as chairman. Everyone needed to be here, no exceptions.

Vittorio was the financial director for the company. He would prefer to stay in that position. But with the funeral over, it was necessary to restructure the business. Now there would have to be changes. One by one the board members arrived and took their place around the conference table.

Vittorio was the youngest board member and was probably resented by some of the older men. Maybe a few of them, like his uncle, had a hard time realizing he was the new Count Della Scalla. He despised the whole title business. Bertoldo, two years older than Vittorio's father, never had children.

There were other problems. Bertoldo had his own ideas on how the company should be run. The two brothers had argued over the company's direction for a decade, but it had never been full-out war.

Long ago Vittorio's grandfather, the former Count Nunzio, had secretly influenced the board to vote in his son Mario instead of Bertoldo when he'd stepped down because of ill health. Of course, it didn't stay a secret, and Bertoldo had always carried a grudge.

As Vittorio grew older, he recognized the wisdom of putting Mario in charge. His father had vision and knew when to take the necessary risks. Which is why he'd kept the business in the black at a time when Italy was going through economic crisis.

But now the situation had changed. Vittorio knew Bertoldo hoped to be made chairman. Both Vittorio and Gaspare liked their uncle well enough despite his view of limiting company expansion beyond Italy's borders. His ideas would have held them back. In that regard, Vittorio had his own ideas about venturing further afield and knew his father had been in agreement, as well as Renaldo Coronna, his father's friend and Paola's father.

With Mario gone and their grandfather no longer alive to influence the vote, it was possible Bertoldo would finally achieve his dream. Vittorio could live with that if he had to. But there were other men on the board perfectly qualified to run the company.

In a few minutes the executive secretary called the meeting to order. Everyone in the room took a turn to express their sympathy over Mario's passing. They'd all been to the funeral and had talked to Vittorio and his family, but he was touched by the outpouring of praise for his father.

Finally, the secretary called for the vote to elect the new chairman. Vittorio knew whom he wanted and wrote down the name Salvatore Riva, one of the directors. Within ten minutes the ballots were collected and tallied.

Their secretary cleared his throat and stood up. "Without question, the will of the group has prevailed. Congratulations, Vittorio. Please stand and say a few words."

The possibility that he could be voted in had come to pass. Vittorio's only consolation at the moment was that his father would have been happy about it.

Vittorio looked around. Nobody had jumped up and run out of the room, but he knew there were several people there, including his uncle, who couldn't wait to leave and vent in private.

"Signori," Vittorio began. "This is a great honor, but overwhelming since I'm still grieving over the loss of my father. No one could ever take his place. Please be patient and give me time to take on a mantle that could fit the shoulders of anyone in this room more qualified than I am. We'll meet in a week or so when I'll have had an opportunity to take a good look at everything. *Mille grazie*."

Now it was Vittorio who left the room in a hurry. His brother, Gaspare, had known this meeting was going to happen and was waiting for him. With business concluded, he headed for the speedboat. His brother sat on a banquette reading. When he saw Vittorio, he stood up. The two men eyed each other before he gave him the news.

"I knew you would be chosen."

"Then you knew something I didn't. I'm aware you don't want to hear me say it, Gaspare, but you should have been the one voted in to head the company."

"It would never have been me. There's greatness in you. Don't forget you have your calling. I have mine."

Yes, he did. Gaspare had known by his early teens he'd wanted the religious life. To show his approval, their father had established a perpetual fund to help support the monastery.

Still it didn't help the wrench of separation from the family, Vittorio reflected, as he started the engine and they left for the monastery. Once they reached the jetty, he tied up the boat and they headed for the building.

Because Gaspare had taken family bereavement leave, his presence had helped all of them to begin the healing process. But Vittorio needed his ideas and counsel more than ever about the direction of the company. "How soon can I visit you, Gaspare?"

"Any time."

"Then I'll come soon and plan to stay overnight so we can really talk about more foreign investments."

Vittorio also had a personal matter to discuss to do with the situation with Paola, which had grown serious. Meeting Signora Lawrence had increased his guilt and anguish because he knew he couldn't marry Paola even if it was expected. He needed some objective advice on that subject. No one had a more level head than Gaspare.

The abbot had granted Vittorio special privileges

to stay inside the *clausura*, the heart of the cloistered monastery where the public wasn't allowed to enter. He followed his brother to his room.

Gaspare lowered his suitcase to the floor and smiled at him. "I always look forward to your visits and will expect to see you when you can make it. As you know, I also need someone to confide in and have done a lot of that in the last year. I'm unworthy in so many ways, but when I'm with you, I feel better."

"I could tell you the same thing."

At that moment one of the monks appeared in the open doorway. "Father Giovanni? A tour group has arrived to speak with you. They're waiting in the museum. And there's an American college teacher from California who has been here before and is also waiting in the garden, hoping to talk to you."

"Thank you, Father."

Vittorio's head reared. *Could he possibly mean Signora Lawrence? Was it possible she'd come back from Switzerland?*

He'd already made up his mind to call Dr. Manukyan and get more information on Signora Lawrence. But if she was here at the monastery for some miraculous reason, then he didn't have to go to the trouble of contacting the other man.

His heart thundered so hard in his chest, he feared his brother could hear it. *Was* she the person outside?

After the other monk walked on, Gaspare smiled at Vittorio. "I'm afraid I have to get to my duties."

"Then I'll walk you as far as the museum." Vittorio wouldn't be leaving the monastery until he knew the identity of the woman. When they reached the doorway, he put a hand on his shoulder. "Take care, Gaspare."

"God keep you, Vittorio."

Ginger was excited because she'd just learned that Father Giovanni was here. She already knew that he was the most knowledgeable about Lord Byron's life when the poet had spent time at the monastery.

Ginger wanted to pick his brains. That's what she kept telling herself, but she also knew there was another reason. Signor Della Scalla was a friend of the monk's. Ginger wanted to know who he really was. She couldn't rest until she found out.

While she waited, Ginger took a walk around the colonnaded courtyard. A ledge with tubs of flowers placed between the columns enclosed the lush green garden where Byron had strolled during his studies.

Ginger didn't care if the monk was busy for a long time. She would stay until she'd spoken with him. After a few more minutes, she sat on the garden bench. Before long someone came and sat down near her.

When she looked up, Ginger almost fainted to see a certain unforgettable black-haired Italian male. She'd never expected to see him again. This morning he was wearing a luxurious dark gray suit and tie. He turned in her direction. His left arm slid along the top of the bench.

On the third finger of his hand gleamed a gold and red signet ring that looked *royal* for want of a better word. He hadn't been wearing it the night of the shipboard dinner. *It isn't a wedding ring.* Those fabulous cobalt eyes stared into hers in recognition. Her pulse was racing.

"We meet again, Signora Lawrence. I thought you only had one day to be in Venice."

She could hardly breathe. "My plans changed."

"So did mine," he said in a gravelly voice.

"What do you mean?"

"After the night we met, I'd intended to find you here the next day, but fate intervened."

Before she could ask him anything else, he stood up because a monk had walked out to the garden and approached them. When she turned around, she let out a quiet gasp.

The monk bore such an amazing resemblance to Signor Della Scalla, she realized they had to be brothers. But the latter had longer, wavy hair and might have been a little younger.

Both men were tall with similar features and black hair that shouted their blood relationship. They had a solid build and presence that made them stand out from other men.

"Father Giovanni? May I introduce you to Signora Lawrence. She was with Dr. Manukyan's group aboard the *Sirena* the other week and we met. I told her I knew you well."

The monk's eyes smiled at Ginger. "Good morning. I'm sorry you've had to wait. There's still another tour group ahead of you."

Ginger was so dumbstruck, she couldn't find words. In a daze, she slowly got to her feet. "Good morning, Father. I was told you might be here today."

"Please forgive the difficulties. Summer is a particularly busy time."

"I understand and it doesn't matter. If or when you're free, I'd appreciate it if you had time to discuss Lord Byron's preface to the grammar book with me."

"It would be my pleasure. I'll be available shortly and can give you an hour before I have to take charge of another tour. Until then, continue to enjoy the garden."

Ginger had just walked past it. "Thank you."

After Father Giovanni headed for the museum, she turned to his brother. Again, she felt his all-encompassing gaze study her.

"I'm afraid I'm the person who prevented you from seeing Father Giovanni the first time."

She found his Italian accent irresistible. "Why was that?"

"Our father died in the early-morning hours on the day you were coming to Venice a week ago. I drove to the island to inform my brother and take him home, where our family was waiting for him."

"I'm so sorry," she said on a rush of emotion. "How terrible for all of you."

"It's been the most painful shock of my life so far. As I look back on the events of the night before, I realize you and I weren't properly introduced." A faint smile appeared, causing a fluttering sensation in her chest. "My name is Vittorio Della Scalla."

Vittorio.

Ginger knew the Della Scalla name, but it wasn't until she'd returned to the hotel the night of the dinner and pulled the menu out of her purse that her questions were answered. They'd been honored to eat aboard one of the Della Scalla passenger liners docked in the port.

Later in Switzerland when she'd been in her room at the farmhouse watching the news, she'd heard that the head of the company, a count of the old Della Scalla aristocracy, had died recently. Suddenly the signet ring on his finger took on significance for her. Everything fit and all the pieces fell into place.

Vittorio personified the quintessential nobleman of the modern-day Italian aristocracy.

CHAPTER THREE

GINGER COULDN'T HELP staring at him. "The likeness between you and your brother is so striking, it's like two sides of the same coin."

"Growing up people thought we were twins even though there's a three-year difference in our ages. What's your first name, signora?"

"Ginger."

"Like the spice."

A soft laugh escaped. "I've learned the Italians don't use it much except in the southern part of your country."

One black brow lifted. "It sounds like you've been here awhile."

"Five months."

He studied her for a moment. "Dr. Manukyan introduced you the other week as a Californian professor who's an expert on Lord Byron."

"Maybe one day I'll attain that status once I've received my doctorate. But yes, I teach classes on the romance writers of the early nineteenth century at Vanguard University in Costa Mesa."

"I traveled to that area years ago with friends. You come from a beautiful part of the US."

"Considering where you come from, that's a generous admission."

"Not at all." He cocked his dark, handsome head. "I can tell you that you've come to the right person to learn about Byron's passion for the oppressed as well as his genius for words." Ginger couldn't have said it better. "How long are you going to be in Venice?"

The first time he'd asked her that question, it could have been an idle one. But not this time. Afraid to sound too interested—like a certain starry-eyed widow she knew—Ginger said, "I'm not sure. My research leads me many places."

"Considering we're talking about Lord Byron, it would." Something told her Vittorio Della Scalla probably knew as much on the subject as his brilliant brother. "His journeys *were* legendary. Besides all the travel, Byron accomplished a massive amount of work during his short thirty-six years."

She nodded. "Since I've been in Italy, I've decided Byron was a man with nine lives."

His eyes smiled. "A very apt description. If you're returning to Venice after your meeting with my brother, I'll be happy to give you a ride. As you already know, I live there and I'm still anxious to show you around."

The man's charm was lethal. Ginger swallowed hard. "That's very kind of you. I don't know how long I'm going to be, but thank you."

"You're welcome." He got to his feet. "*A presto,* signora."

It meant *see you soon,* and sent an adrenaline rush through her. She'd lost track of time while they'd been talking. Without waiting for his brother, who'd just emerged from the doorway, Vittorio strode down the length of the courtyard on his long powerful legs and disappeared.

Ginger knew her cheeks were flushed when Father Giovanni asked her to return to the studio with him. He made no mention of his brother.

They discussed the problem of Father Pasquale Aucher, Byron's teacher who'd instructed him in Armenian. Aucher was offended because in the preface of the grammar book, the poet referenced the Turks, who'd kept the Armenian people under their rule. Which is why he didn't give Byron credit for the book, and the poet took it badly. Eventually Father Aucher added Byron's name to the grammar, but not as a sign that he'd done an expert job.

Following that conversation, they discussed the letter Byron had written to his English publisher, John Murray, in 1817 about the time he'd spent at the Armenian monastery.

Before Ginger had to leave because the next tourist group had arrived, Father Giovanni quoted the last few lines of the letter from memory, lines that had become famous. The last line Byron wrote about life in the monastery made an impact. "'"There is another and a better" even in this life.'"

Obviously Father Giovanni, who'd come from such an aristocratic family, had found a better life here, too.

Ginger thanked him for making this visit so memorable. She'd finished her research here and left the building, not knowing if Father Giovanni's brother was truly waiting for her. She felt jittery with anticipation as she walked past another group of tourists to reach the dock.

"Signora Lawrence?" She'd know that voice any-where and looked to the right.

Vittorio Della Scalla was standing in a sleek-looking blue and silver ski boat. Despite his modern clothes, she could imagine him one of the fierce Ve-netian warriors of the fifteenth century who'd opened up the Mediterranean trade routes in defiance of the Ottomans and Spaniards.

"I'm surprised you're still here." Ginger moved closer to his boat. "Your brother and I were able to talk longer because the tour group was late."

Vittorio's gaze wandered over her. "Did he answer your questions?"

"He's a great intellect and cleared up several points that have bothered me. It was a privilege to talk to him."

"I feel that way every time I'm with him. He was my idol growing up." Vittorio's sincerity moved her. "If you'll come aboard, I'll drive you to your hotel or next destination."

Now that the miraculous opportunity had come to be with him, Ginger was excited to the point that she felt feverish. Her hope that she'd see him again had happened. It was incredible.

"That's very nice of you, but I can wait for the next water bus." Ginger didn't want to sound too eager. Oh, what was wrong with her?

He jumped on deck with male agility and undid the rope. "Don't tell me you don't trust me."

A chuckle escaped her lips. "Of course I do."

It was herself and her feelings for him she didn't trust. In truth Ginger was frightened by her intense at-traction to him. It had taken her by complete surprise.

She reached for his outstretched hand and climbed in. The warmth of Vittorio's clasp swept through her. As she sat down on the banquette opposite the driver's seat, her thoughts flew to Abby, who'd tried to explain her immediate attraction to the Frenchman.

To think they were getting married this fast! Right this minute Ginger understood her friend's initial feelings and fears after first meeting him.

They took off and headed into the lagoon at a wakeless speed. He cast her a penetrating glance. "It's past lunchtime and I'm hungry. How would you like to eat at the Terrazza Danieli near the Bridge of Sighs on our way back? Their salmon appetizer alone is worth a visit."

"Those sound wonderful. I'll have to try them." She flashed him a glance. "Do you suppose Byron ever ate something similar while he was writing the Fourth Canto of *Childe Harold's Pilgrimage*?"

"You mean you haven't uncovered that information after all the research you've been doing?"

She shook her head. "No one, no matter how clever, has ever scratched more than the surface of Byron's life. But I do love the beginning of his epic poem. He made the bridge famous."

"It's true he understood the plight of the poor prisoners. No doubt they *did* sigh one last time looking at Venice. I don't like to think of them being taken away to the dark, dank, unhealthy wells in the bowels of the Doge's Palace, never to see her again."

Ginger studied him for a minute. "Byron loved too much, felt too much. He makes *me* feel too much. You should be at the monastery teaching the tourists. Your brother's vocation is evident. What is it *you* do for a living besides send chills down my spine? Aside from working in your family's business," she added.

He gave her another sideward glance. "Chills?"

A quiet laugh escaped her lips. "I was referring to your tone of voice. For a brief moment, you conveyed emotion that took me back in time to those wretched souls in the fifteenth century who had no hope."

"Thank you for explaining yourself. You had me worried for a minute," he confided in that deep, sensual voice. "While we enjoy a meal of *baccalà mantecato* and polenta I'll tell you what I do. As it stands I now have a new responsibility with the family company, and frankly, I'm terrified."

Ginger averted her eyes. She couldn't tell if he was being serious or not. What she did know was that he was the most fascinating, mysterious, exciting, desirable man ever to come into her life.

But the second those thoughts passed through her mind, she experienced pangs of guilt. While Bruce had been dying, she couldn't have comprehended feeling the way she did right now about another man.

Maybe she was going to wake up at some point and realize she'd been dreaming. But the thought of that happening and there being no Vittorio sent her into a panic.

Vittorio had ordered a table for them ahead of time. From the terrace you could see the busy lagoon dotted with cupolas. After he'd helped Ginger to her seat, the waiter came over to pour the wine and take their order.

When he walked off, Vittorio noticed that her extraordinary gray eyes had focused on the Doge's

Palace, the subject of their conversation before he'd docked the boat.

He was aware that the gaze of every male in the place, young or old, had watched Ginger come in the restaurant and envied him. Her beauty stood out, but they didn't know there were stimulating depths to her he was just beginning to discover.

Vittorio had enjoyed several relationships with beautiful women over the years, mostly through business and travels. He had always imagined that in time he'd get married when he realized he couldn't live without *the* one, whoever she was.

His family expected a wedding with Paola soon. His mother had brought it up again after the funeral and was demanding he do something about it right away. At this point he regretted what he'd told Paola after the accident that he'd take care of her.

He'd said it to comfort her while they waited for the ambulance, little knowing she would take him so seriously. His mother's comment had angered him, and he'd confided in Gaspare about it. His brother knew he didn't love Paola and had said as much to their mother.

When she argued with him, Vittorio took her aside and told her he would settle down when he found a woman he could love the way his brother loved his life as a monk. That comment had sent her to her bedroom in angry tears.

Now chills ran up and down *his* spine remembering that conversation as he looked at the unique woman seated across from him. For Ginger to show up at the monastery again while he was there made him wonder what unseen forces were at work. It was almost as if his desire to see her again had willed her return.

"These are delicious," she said after eating the salmon appetizer, "but I'm still waiting to hear about this terrifying new job of yours. We may be strangers, but you don't strike me as a man whose vocabulary includes a word like that."

Every thought of hers came as an intriguing surprise. Vittorio lowered his wineglass. "After working as the financial director for several years, I have just been voted in as the new CEO of my family's company."

Ginger nodded. "I heard about your father's passing on the news while I was in Switzerland. What was his name?"

"Mario Della Scalla. He was only sixty-eight. His death has devastated the whole family. My mother and sister are still inconsolable."

"As you and your brother must be."

"He left us far too young."

The soft light of compassion had entered her eyes. "No one is ever prepared for news like that." A sad expression broke out on her face. "I understand how you feel. My husband died from bone cancer and the complications that followed."

Ginger was a widow?

Santo cielo! The knowledge that she was a widow shook him. "You have my deepest sympathy."

"When I realize what you're going through, Vittorio, I know you mean that. My pain was excruciating for so long, nothing could describe it. Bruce was such a wonderful man, you can't imagine. We'd hoped to have children, but it didn't happen."

"I'm sorry you were denied that experience. I've always hoped that when the time is right, I'll be a father, so I can understand your deep disappointment. I couldn't have imagined my childhood without siblings."

Vittorio studied Ginger, haunted by the depth of her love for her dead husband. It made him wonder if he could ever come to mean that much to her. Had her husband's death made Ginger untouchable? Added to which, the situation with Paola was made more difficult now that he had such powerful feelings for Ginger.

Although Vittorio was suffering the loss of his father, he hadn't yet had her experience of grief, *grazie al cielo*. He sat back. "How long ago did he die?"

"In April, over two years ago. Nothing but time has helped me, as you will find out for yourself in the days and months ahead. When I was offered a chance to do research in Italy on Lord Byron, I accepted it in the hope of losing myself in something that took me out of my grief."

"How did the offer come about?" Vittorio couldn't learn enough about her.

"The head of my department at the university told me that Magda Collier, a Hollywood film director, wanted to make a film on Lord Byron, but required a fresh look at his achievements.

"She ended up hiring me and two other women to spend time in Europe retracing his footsteps. Anything we could share that would help the screenwriters working on the film. Thanks to your erudite brother, I'll be able to pass on some fascinating information to Magda."

"How much longer are you going to be here?"

"I'm still on vacation even though my trip to Switzerland fell apart. Tomorrow I'll be leaving for Athens to join my friend Zoe, who's been doing research in Greece.

"I've enjoyed the travel with this job because it gives me fresh material for a series of children-around-the-world books I've been writing. Of course, I'll have to find an illustrator for it and can only supply pictures."

"Tell me more about them." Vittorio was fascinated.

"They're nothing exceptional, believe me. I'm featuring a brother and sister in each story around five years old. In their speech and dialects, plus their mannerisms, they depict the area they're from with the clothes worn by their ancestors. Every country, every region has so many differences, and it's fun to bring them out.

"For example, I have a pair playing outside the leaning Tower of Pisa. The brother, Enrico, is teasing his sister, Concetta, that it's going to fall down. She gets mad at him and swipes the fingers of the back of her hand under her chin to let him know she's not buying it."

Vittorio burst into laughter, enchanted by her personality and intelligence. "My sister does that all the time."

Ginger's eyes shone as she said, "I'm planning to do some Greek children while I'm with Zoe because in another week I'll be flying home to Costa Mesa."

That was news he refused to entertain.

She smiled. "By then my spending money runs out and it's back to the grindstone at the university. But enough about me. You still haven't told me why your new job has alarmed you so much."

"It isn't possible to fill my father's shoes."

"Sounds like you worshipped your father, too. I can't imagine the thought of trying to follow after my dad and do any good. He's a top businessman. My interests have been in the academic world. Now that I'm writing fiction on the side, I would be hopeless doing anything else."

"If my brother hadn't gone into the priesthood, he would be the one in charge now."

Ginger cocked her dark beautiful head. "Yet I assume you've worked with your father for a long time and know his bottom line. Now it's up to you to set new challenges that will ensure his legacy while you ease your pain. That's pretty heady stuff being the new CEO of Della Scalla Shipping Lines. Kind of exciting."

Signora Lawrence was better for his psyche than icy-cold water on a sweltering day. "How would you like to accept a job with me until you have to be back at the university?" *Like come live with me.*

Ginger's eyes played over him in amusement. "In what capacity?"

"Have I alarmed you?"

"Well…a woman on her own has to be careful. It all depends on what you have in mind." Her teasing beguiled him.

"We'll figure it out as we go." He was going to have to because Vittorio had no intention of letting her go. Already she was in his blood. Given enough time, he hoped she wouldn't want to leave him.

"There's a thought." Ginger finished the last of her wine. "Shouldn't you be at work right now?"

A chuckle escaped his throat. Since his father's funeral, he hadn't thought he was capable of anything remotely resembling laughter. But she'd brought sunshine back into his life.

"If you want to know the truth, I *have* been working. While my brother has been home, we've been brainstorming, speculating and plotting our heads off over what to do with the company. Gaspare should be running it instead of me."

Her finely arched brows lifted. "Because he's older?"

He shook his head. "Because he's a man of vision and understanding."

"Even so, that doesn't explain why you were voted in as CEO. I know how most boards work. How many members are there on the Della Scalla board?"

Ginger Lawrence was a different, exciting woman. He loved the way her mind worked. "Fifteen."

"All of them family?"

"Only one, my uncle Bertoldo."

"Then he or any one of the other fourteen members could have been elected, and I bet they're all older. That means you were the one out of the group of them they wanted, even if you are your father's son. Even if you are the new count," she added, "and some of them are jealous of you."

Vittorio hadn't seen that one coming.

"Maybe you wish he'd been able to choose someone, and you'd been his choice?"

"Maybe," he murmured, not realizing until now that he'd wanted to hear his father tell him he had his full approval. She knew how to hit the nail on the head.

"I think it's terrific everyone wanted you. Certainly no one can accuse him of nepotism," Ginger exclaimed. "If that doesn't convince you you're in the right spot at the right time, then I give up."

"Please don't!" She had erased a worry for him and was getting to him in ways he didn't think possible.

This time she was the one who laughed, delighting him.

"If you've finished eating, let's get out of here and enjoy this warm weather. We could go out in the sailboat and visit some of the villages whose cottage industries support an export business of mine."

She looked surprised. "You run another business, too?"

"For the last ten years."

"What kinds of products?"

"Anything from specialty foods, liqueurs, ceramics to embroidered linens. I'm sure we could find a spot that would provide inspiration for another story for your book series."

Ginger shook her dark head. "I don't know where you find the time to do it all. How can you possibly afford to take even the rest of the day off?"

"I need one. Since we're so close, let me at least take you on a private tour of the Doge's Palace right now. How does that sound?"

"I'd love it."

Vittorio paid for their meal before escorting her back to the boat. The desire for her was building inside him with every accidental brush of her body against his. On the way, he made a phone call so they could be shown inside and avoid the lines.

Once they alighted from the boat, they had to walk only a short distance to enter the palace. "It's so fabulous," Ginger exclaimed once they were inside.

Vittorio stood close to her. "This was the sumptuous repository of the great Venetian art and architecture of the time," he explained. "It served as a hall of justice. Come on. We'll go down to the dungeon."

When they descended, she never left his side. "It's chilly and creepy down here, Vittorio. I'm probably going to have nightmares."

He chuckled. "I've got plans for us later so you'll forget what you've seen here."

From the palace they walked to Saint Mark's church. "Look up at the ceiling. Eight thousand square feet of mosaics from the Byzantine Empire. There's not another building like it."

Ginger marveled over it until Vittorio asked her where she would like to go next.

"Hmm. Let me think about it."

"Have you decided?" After they reached the boat, he was waiting for an answer with breathless anticipation.

"Yes. I'm aware that you brought your brother back to the island this morning. I think you're too much of a gentleman to tell me you need to get home. Much as I've loved the tour, would you mind driving me to the Hotel Arlecchino off the Grand Canal?"

Vittorio's hand tightened on the gearshift. "That's near our palazzo."

"Then maybe on the way you could point out your home to me. I'd love to see where a true Venetian lives who can trace his family history back so many generations."

Vittorio would like to show Ginger a lot more than that. He'd love nothing more than to take her away to someplace private for weeks on end. He could hardly believe he was this infatuated with her when they'd spent so little time in each other's company!

Never in his life had he felt this way about a woman. When she looked at him, the thought of him having to marry Paola was anathema to him. He had to do something about this impossible situation as soon as he could.

Ginger's personality and intellect blew him away. He couldn't explain it, but he wanted to spend every minute possible with her. She spoke to him on some deeper level, and he couldn't get enough of her.

But in the last little while he'd also learned that Ginger was a widow who might never get over the loss of her husband. Vittorio needed to spend enough time with her that she longed to spend every free moment with him.

CHAPTER FOUR

GINGER DIDN'T WANT any of this to end. But she didn't want to be like a ripe piece of fruit, ready to be plucked from the nearest tree by a passerby who would soon reach for another one when he felt like eating again.

To go back to the hotel was the safest course so she wouldn't get too involved with him. Vittorio didn't have time to spend with her when he had the weight of the company on his shoulders, plus his own company. As for his private life, a man of his looks and stature had to be in a relationship with a woman. She could imagine that the females attracted to him were legion.

When she and Vittorio had been in the restaurant earlier and at the palace, she'd seen a dozen women staring at him. She could tell that some of them had wanted to scratch her eyes out so they could be with him.

Soon they headed up the Grand Canal filled with the unique gondolas Venice had always been famous for. More ideas for her stories danced through her mind. There was every type of watercraft. At one point she asked about a big boat filled with people in dark clothes.

"It's a funeral procession."

Vittorio didn't need a reminder of that as they kept moving. She found it an amazing experience to see Venice from the water with him as her guide. He had phenomenal patience answering her questions.

After rounding a long lazy curve, he slowed down in front of a fantastic, triple-tiered palazzo with its ivory and white facade. "You live here?" she cried out in sheer delight.

"The first Della Scalla moved in near the end of the sixteenth century."

"How absolutely beautiful!"

"I live in the top floor in an apartment completely separate from the family whose suites are on the lower floors. I would have moved out years ago, but after my brother entered the priesthood, my father asked me to stay so our mother didn't feel completely abandoned."

"He probably didn't want to lose you either."

"I don't know about that. Right before he died, I'd decided to move out."

Ginger stared at him. "Are you still going to?"

Vittorio nodded. "As soon as possible."

"Do you have a place in mind?"

"Definitely."

Ginger looked away. "Tell me about the history of your palazzo."

"You'll see that the inflected arches above came from the Moors. But below you'll notice the Gothic design of the pointed arches."

"What are those toppings that look like lace?"

"Crenellations like you see on Greek temples."

"It's so exquisite, I'm speechless. Thank you for letting me see where you live. Now I feel like my visit to Venice is complete." She took some pictures with her phone camera, including one of him. "This has been a day out of time for me."

"In case you didn't know, it's not over yet," Vittorio declared, exciting her because he'd sounded so fierce just now.

He drove on. She moaned inwardly when they turned down a canal where she saw her hotel. Her time with him was over. He pulled up and turned off the engine, then glanced at his watch.

"It's ten after five. Will two hours give you enough time to freshen up and do what you have to do? Then I'll come by for you. We can walk around, whatever suits you. But I'm not prepared to say good-night or goodbye to you."

Neither was she.

"Are your reservations already made to fly to Greece? If not, tomorrow I have plans for us."

A delicious shiver ran through her body. To hear him plan for tomorrow was like an impossible dream. The last thing she wanted to do was leave him. "I don't know my plans yet." She'd been going back and forth on what to do. "I have to talk to Zoe first."

"Then tell her you don't know your schedule yet. I'll be back at seven thirty and meet you out here."

Ginger couldn't resist him. "I'd like that. Thank you for the lunch and a wonderful day of sightseeing, signor."

"The name is Vittorio. I'd like you to use it."

He helped her out of the boat and squeezed her hand before letting her go. Her heart palpitated too outrageously. She turned away from him and hurried inside. But once she'd passed beyond the doorway, she looked back to watch him drive away.

Her plan to visit the monastery had resulted not only in seeing the monk's brother again, but spending the day with a man who was already bigger than life to her.

Ginger went up to her hotel room and pulled out her cell phone. She needed to call Zoe and tell her she wouldn't be flying to Greece tomorrow. Something unexpected had happened.

Again, she realized Bruce hadn't been on her mind at all. Since that night on the ship, she hadn't longed for her husband. Vittorio was the man who filled her thoughts. It made her feel guilty, as if she were betraying Bruce. Yet Vittorio was so attractive in every way, she couldn't wait to be with him again in a little while.

Even if this turned out to be a brief interlude in her life, she didn't want to miss a single second of it. Otherwise she'd regret it once she was back at the university wishing she hadn't turned down an experience that could never be repeated in this life.

As it turned out, Zoe wasn't available, so Ginger left a message that she was staying in Italy for another day or two. Could Zoe please call her back when she could?

After hanging up, Ginger took a quick shower and washed her hair. If they were going to stroll along the canals where every female would stare at Vittorio, unable to do anything else, she wanted to look good.

Ginger decided to wear her fawn-colored, jewel-necked sleeveless dress with a matching cotton cardigan. After she brushed out her hair and put on coral frost lipstick, she reached for her new gold stud earrings she'd bought in Florence after leaving Rome.

Finally she slipped on her wedge tan sandals and left the room for the lobby.

Since it wasn't time yet, she intended to examine some of the brochures, but someone intercepted her. She looked up. "Vittorio—" He'd come early, too. She felt out of breath.

Tonight he wore an elegant black silk shirt and gray trousers. He was so gorgeous and smelled so marvelous, she couldn't think straight. His blue eyes trapped hers. "You look beautiful tonight."

"Thank you." He was so handsome, it hurt. Something exciting was happening to her. A force she couldn't stop and didn't want to.

"Did you reach your friend?"

"I left her a message that I was staying in Venice for a few more days."

She heard his sharp intake of breath before he cupped her elbow and walked her outside. She was sorry when he let go of her. "Since we didn't have dessert at the restaurant, come with me and I'll treat you to some gelato you'll enjoy. What's your favorite?"

"Triple chocolate."

His deep laugh resonated deep inside her as they walked close to each other avoiding the crowds. Every so often their arms and hips brushed against each other, and those old sensations of desire surfaced.

Vittorio led her through a maze of surrounding backstreets to show her the gems not every tourist knew about. They ended up at a *gelateria* and sat down to eat while they talked for at least an hour.

"Where has your work taken you in Italy?"

"I spent two months in Rome, researching the journals of the shipbuilder Daniel Roberts at the Keats-

Shelley Memorial House. From there I stayed in Genoa for a month, where Byron owned his last home. Later I traveled for another month to Pisa, where he started a newspaper.

"This last month I've lived in Ravenna. It was there I learned a lot about him through Shelley's writings and met Dr. Welch, who was part of the dinner party the other night.

"I saved my study in Venice until last, but ran out of time. What I did know was that the most important area of research would be at the monastery. Thanks to your brother, I learned new information that should be a part of the film. I'm indebted to him."

Vittorio covered her hand with his own, filling her with warmth before letting her go. "I'll let Gaspare know. It'll mean a lot to him."

She sat back in the chair. "Now, no more talk about Byron. I want to see the Venice *you* know and love."

His eyes gleamed blue fire as he helped her up from the table. "Come with me."

For another half hour they wandered down narrow alleys and over stone footbridges, including the Rialto Bridge. They went into a shop and he bought her an exquisite lavender-white porcelain mask of a princess as a souvenir.

"Maybe you can write a story about a brother and sister who go to a masked ball at the Palazzo Cavelli we just toured. The one with the wooden consoles that allowed the upper floors to protrude from the ground. She's looking for a boy she likes behind her mask."

"What a wonderful idea. I adore this, Vittorio!" She pressed the package against her. "Thank you so much."

"Now I want to dance with you."

They wound up at a local club. Vittorio walked her down an alley to the entrance. She could hear music before they went inside. It was a great place filled with tourists and locals.

Ginger's heart got the workout of its life when he pulled her into his arms and they danced for at least an hour. She hadn't been dancing since college. It wasn't something she did with Bruce.

Vittorio was a wonderful dancer. To be this close to his powerful body and feel his cheek against hers set her on fire. By the time they left, she was trembling.

On the way back to the hotel, he put his arm around her. Like Cinderella in the fairy tale, she'd been storing up memories of an unforgettable night that would end on the stroke of midnight. But she didn't want it to end and could feel herself on the brink of something new about to happen in her life.

When she looked at Vittorio, she felt an explosion of need that had nothing to do with Bruce. In just a couple of days she realized that Vittorio had supplanted him to a degree she could never have envisioned. How could she feel like this when she'd loved Bruce so completely?

Vittorio stared into her eyes outside the hotel entrance. "I don't want this night to end, but it has to. Tomorrow I have an errand to run and would like to take you with me. The caretakers of our family villa on the Lido di Venezia have gone on vacation for the week.

"I need to check things out in case there's some kind of problem. We have our own private beach. You can swim and sunbathe to your heart's content.

Please say you'll come," he murmured in his deep, captivating voice.

Ginger knew she shouldn't give in, but the way he was looking at her and the way he made her feel broke her down. She found herself caving in spite of her guilt. "That sounds heavenly."

"I agree," he murmured, studying the lines of her mouth. She could almost feel his lips on hers before he pressed an unexpected kiss to her cheek. "I'll be here at eight thirty. We'll eat breakfast at the trattoria next door, then take off for the day. *Buona notte*, Ginger." The way he said her name in that Italian accent melted her to the spot.

"Thank you again for tonight. *Buona notte*, Vittorio," she responded, but her bad accent sounded pathetic in comparison. She turned away and hurried upstairs to her room.

For years her dad had quoted the old adage, "Beware of what you wish for, you might get it." She was reminded of it now as she got ready for bed. She'd hoped to see Vittorio again, and today he'd shown up at the monastery.

It worried her that being with Vittorio for such a short time had actually pushed Bruce's memory to the back of her mind. A mere stranger shouldn't be this important to her, let alone cause her to think intimate thoughts about him. The fact that it did proved to her she couldn't pass off this interlude as just one of those things.

Tomorrow they would be together again. Would another day convince her he was a man endowed with so many outstanding qualities, she had to take this attraction seriously? If not, she would leave for Greece and that would be the end of it.

The next morning Vittorio was about to leave the palazzo when his mother returned from mass and saw him in the foyer. She frowned. "I thought you would come to church with me today and we could light a candle for your father. Now I see you're not dressed for work yet. What's going on?"

"*Buongiorno*, Mamma." He kissed her on both cheeks.

"You haven't answered my question. Bertoldo is upset because you haven't been at work since the board meeting. He wants to discuss several issues with you, but you haven't been there!"

"I promise to meet with him before long. But the truth is, yesterday I spent time with Gaspare at the monastery talking over Papà's wishes for the company."

"Ah." Her eyes watered. "I didn't know that," she said in a broken voice. When his brother had entered the priesthood, it had devastated her. Not all mothers wanted their sons to devote themselves to the religious life. She was one of them.

Now that their father and husband were gone, her emotions were on the surface and probably would be for a long time. "Are you going into the office later?"

"Not today. I have to drive out to the villa. After the last water leak, I need to check the pipes in case it's flooding again. If you remember, Beppo and Alda are on vacation this week."

"Why don't you take Maria and Paola with you? They have the day off from work. She spent the night at the Coronnas'. Paola adores you and would come in an instant. You need to start making plans for your coming marriage."

The guilt he felt about this situation was killing him. "There isn't going to be a wedding."

"Oh, yes, there is. Today would be the perfect time to talk to her about it. She wants to spend all her time with you, but you're rarely home. You could pick them up on your way."

He shook his head. "My schedule is already full for today once I've checked on the villa. What are your plans?"

"Your aunt Gianna will be over later."

"Good. I'm glad you're going to have company. *A piu' tardi*, Mamma."

She walked him to the entrance. "Lena has invited us and your aunt and uncle for dinner tonight. It's Renaldo's birthday. Be sure to be home in time."

He knew what was going on between his mother and the Coronnas, but throwing Paola at him was never going to work. "You'll have to go without me. We went through this last week. I'm not going to marry Paola."

"She's expecting it, Vittorio. When she had her accident, you promised you would take care of her. She took that in the literal sense."

"Then she was out of her mind. I said that to reassure her at the time. She was bleeding and in pain. In no possible way could it have been construed as a proposal of marriage."

Vittorio was reaching the end of his rope. Ginger had a hold on him, which meant he needed to put an end to the situation with Paola.

"Your sister thought that's what you meant. So do her parents. They've expressly invited you to come."

While Gaspare had been home, they'd talked about this situation. Vittorio realized he needed to be firm with his mother, even if it meant there was a temporary breakdown in their relationship.

"With my new position running the company and the demands of my export business, I don't have that kind of time anymore. The Coronnas need to invite other men she can meet and not rely on my presence, Mamma." He couldn't have made it any clearer and hoped she'd finally gotten the message.

Vittorio gave her frowning brow another kiss and hurried out to his speedboat tied up at their private dock. All he could think about was meeting Ginger. They would be spending this day together, and he wouldn't let anything get in the way.

Despite the canal traffic, he reached the hotel in record time, but he didn't see Ginger. A part of him had been anxious since they'd said good-night. What if she'd decided to leave for Greece early this morning and would let him know after the fact?

If the memory of her husband was still getting in the way, Vittorio had no answer for that, no way to combat it. Naturally there was so much they didn't know about each other yet, but that would come with time. Crushed by the possibility that she'd left a note for him and it was too late to catch up with her, Vittorio alighted from the boat and tied it up before heading for the hotel entrance.

"Vittorio?"

At the sound of her voice, he swung around. Relief swamped him to see her with her overnight bag, standing by an empty table outside the crowded trattoria next door. She'd nabbed it for them.

He loved the way she looked in jeans and the short-sleeved top in a mini plaid of white, red and orange. Between her breathtaking figure and coloring, she was more beautiful than any woman had the right to be.

He walked toward her. "I thought I was on time."

Her eyes played over him. "You are. I got up early and came out to take a walk. But the tables were filling so fast I grabbed this one."

Needing to hold on to something before he pulled her into his arms, he drew out a chair for her and they sat down. "Let's order coffee and rolls. Later when we get to where we're going, I'll fix us a big meal."

"You cook, too?"

He took a deep breath. "It all depends on my motivation."

"Will you let me help? I haven't done any cooking since I left California. I can't think of anything I'd love to do more."

For the first time in his life, Vittorio knew total excitement. This divine woman wanted to be with him. He signaled for the waiter and told him they were in a hurry. After being served quickly, he paid the bill and reached for her overnight bag. They walked to his boat and got in.

"On the way to the villa we'll stop for groceries."

"What are we going to make?"

"Let that be my secret."

"As long as it's one of your favorite meals. One thing I've learned after being here this long is that most Italian men are fabulous cooks who learned from their *mamma*."

He slanted her a glance as they made their way through the canal traffic to the lagoon. "How many Italian men are we talking about?" he half growled.

She gave him a full unguarded smile under a Venetian sun with the air a perfect eighty degrees. There could be no more sensational sight.

"Oh, probably hundreds."

"I guess that's possible since you've been in my country five months. One Italian meal an evening with the cook of your choice for one hundred and fifty nights."

"That's right." She grinned. "You've been the financial director for your company a long time and know your math. I'm going to have to watch myself around you."

She had no idea...

They pulled into a grocery store that had all the ingredients Vittorio required. Ginger helped him find everything. It was fine with him if everyone believed they were husband and wife. They walked up and down the aisles, laughing and teasing while she tried to pronounce words correctly. In fact it felt so right, he knew this woman was transforming him.

After he'd grabbed a couple of bottles of red wine, they paid the cashier and left in the boat for the Lido.

Ginger borrowed his binoculars as he drove them the length of the seven-mile-long sandbar. "I've heard about this Venetian playground for years. Seeing it in person, it's everything and much more than I had imagined. I'm overwhelmed."

"I discovered there are areas on the Southern California coast to match all of this. Costa Mesa is such a place."

"I agree the Spanish influence makes it unique, but nothing matches the beauty here where centuries of other civilizations have left their mark. Byron's friend Shelley said it best. 'The temples and palaces of Venice did seem like fabrics of enchantment piled to heaven.' When I saw your palazzo yesterday, I'm positive he was describing it."

"That's a fascinating possibility."

"Oh, Vittorio—" She put the binoculars down and turned to face him. "How wonderful to be a poet with the God-given gift to capture the pure essence of something out of this world that pierces the soul!"

There were moments when she moved him with her thoughts. "You're a poet in your own right, Ginger. Being with you, I'm seeing the world I grew up in through different eyes."

"That was a nice thing for you to say."

"Not nice. Just true. No doubt your book series will bring out the delight of a child's world. I'm anxious to read them."

She looked away. "I'm talking about great literature like Byron's."

"But your research is bringing it to the world. You know what they say about the teacher who brings out the voice of the singer. Both are valuable. You can't have one without the other."

"Except those chosen few who seem to arrive from heaven in full bloom."

"Point taken." He smiled. "If you look on your left, can you see that Persian-melon-colored villa with Moorish-style windows and a tile roof?"

She turned her head and gasped. "That's where we're going to cook our meal?"

"Do you like it?"

"What a question, Vittorio."

He'd gotten his answer, and concentrated on his driving. A new happiness had come into his life. While she studied the scenery he'd loved beyond all else since he could remember, Vittorio turned into the private dock behind the villa's helicopter landing pad. His sailboat was moored there.

They were home where he'd rather be than any other place on earth. And they were alone…

This was going to be fun. Ginger had come this far with him. It gave him hope that this was only the beginning of a new chapter in his life. The most important one. Deep in his gut he knew she was the woman he couldn't live without.

But it was the fear that she could live without him that had caused him to awaken in a cold sweat in the middle of the night. The husband she'd loved might have a hold on her that made her out of reach.

CHAPTER FIVE

THE DECOR OF the Della Scalla two-story villa enchanted Ginger from the moment Vittorio let them in through the rear French doors. The luxurious nineteenth-century structure was of neo-Gothic design with five bedrooms and all the accoutrements.

The kitchen, everything, had been modernized. The villa contained every comfort of home imaginable.

Vittorio told her she could tour the whole house. She went upstairs on her own. There were three bedrooms. She particularly loved the *mansarda*—the large attic room—with its Altana terrace. This room overlooking the Adriatic was her favorite. There was a photograph of his brother on the dresser. Maybe this had been Gaspare's room before he'd become a monk.

Or, it might be Vittorio's room and he kept a special photograph there to remember his idol. She had a hunch this was the room where Vittorio slept when he came out here now, but she didn't ask.

From the main floor, you walked out the double doors of the front entrance and down two steps to the pale sand. A private beach lover's dream.

"You won't see a surf here like you do in San Clemente, for example," Vittorio explained. Ginger had surfed there with her friends many times. "The Lido rarely has breaking waves. Families with small children love it here because they have to walk out a hundred feet in shallow water before they can swim."

"Even better." She smiled. "There are no rocks or seaweed. This is definitely paradise."

They walked back to the kitchen. She looked around. "These walls must have hundreds of stories to tell about the Della Scalla children."

He started putting their perishable groceries in the fridge. "Each of us had our own sets of friends. When we were all here together, it turned into a circus."

She put the other items out on the counter. "In other words you drove your parents crazy."

"Don't all children?" he teased.

Ginger chuckled. "I was an only child, so I didn't have siblings. But I had girlfriends, and I'm sure we put my father through torture. Fortunately, he has an even temperament."

"What about your mother?"

She lounged against the edge of the counter. "I never knew her except through Dad. She died when I was born."

"Ginger—"

His shocked response revealed his concern over what she'd told him.

"You don't miss what you never had, Vittorio, but of course I always wished I'd known her. Dad remarried a wonderful woman when I was four years old. Nora is my stepmother, and I love her dearly."

"They didn't have children?"

"She couldn't."

His blue eyes darkened with emotion. "That means they both lavished their love on you."

"They still do. I've been very fortunate." Without them she would never have made it after Bruce died. But she didn't want to think about that painful period now or ever.

"Shall we go out and enjoy the beach? Later we'll come back in and prepare our own feast."

"I can't wait." It had been at least two years since she'd played like this. That was before the pain in Bruce's legs had made it impossible for him to tolerate physical activity.

"While you change in the guest bedroom down the hall past the stairs, I'll check the laundry room to make sure there's no more water leakage. It will only take a moment. A few months ago, I had to put in a new pipe."

She darted him a glance. "What can't you do?"

A solemn expression broke out on his face. "I don't know. It all depends on you."

Her heart did a kick. If she understood him, he was leaving their relationship up to her. He didn't know what was really wrong with her... She was falling for him way too fast.

Ginger quickly reached for her suitcase and found the bedroom in question. After opening the lid, she drew out the things she needed. In a few minutes she'd slipped on her green-and-white polka-dot bikini. It was one of the most modest styles she'd been able to find before leaving home.

Next came her white beach coat and white capri flip-flops. She put sunscreen in her jacket pocket and left the room. Vittorio met her in the front hall carrying towels and two lightweight folding chairs under his arm. He wore black trunks and nothing else.

Built like the bronzed Venetian warrior she'd imagined earlier with a smattering of hair on his chest, he left her absolutely breathless. "How's the pipe holding up?" She had to say or do something before she was too mesmerized to function.

His white smile told her he wasn't fooled. No doubt he could see the nerve throbbing at the base of her white throat and knew the cause of it. To make her embarrassment worse, she might be a Southern California girl, but she hadn't been out in the sun for a long time. Not like this.

"So far, so good," he answered. "Shall we go?"

She followed him out the doors to the beach. They walked a ways before he stopped and laid out the chairs side by side. Afraid to be too close to him, Ginger stepped out of her flip-flops, threw off her jacket and walked toward the water.

"This is wonderful!" she called out over her shoulder. "I didn't know there was a beach like this anywhere in Italy." After she reached the water, she kept going. He hadn't been kidding about having to walk a long way before you could swim.

Ginger had grown up a water baby and started swimming in the warm water. In another minute Vittorio had caught up to her. His black hair was sleeked back from his forehead. He was too gorgeous.

"Did you know there are sharks out here? You need a bodyguard to protect you."

His white smile and the dangerous look in his eyes caused her to scream. She dived under the water to get away from him. This might all be part of a game, but there was something about him that made her heart thud.

The next thing she knew he'd caught up to her. When he brought them to the surface, her arms were around his neck and he'd trapped her legs. The feel of their bodies sent a huge message to Ginger that she was in trouble. She wanted him.

He trod water for both of them. Those brilliant blue eyes smiled at her. "You swim like a fish, but I shouldn't be surprised."

His compelling mouth was too close to hers. "I've always felt sorry for people who don't live by the water. My father taught me how to sail and surf. We went to Mexico and the Caribbean often, where we scuba-dived. I was very lucky."

Too entranced by him to keep this up, Ginger flipped out of his arms and started doing the backstroke. Vittorio came along beside her. Ginger couldn't get away from him, but she didn't want to because he made her sick with excitement.

For a half hour they raced each other, swam under and around each other. He was such a powerful man, she couldn't dunk him.

"No more!" she cried to him when she saw his wicked grin. Summoning the little energy she had left, she did a front crawl toward shore, kicking her legs fiercely. Virtually worn out, she ran across the sand, knowing he was right behind her.

With uncontrollable laughter, Ginger sank down on the lounger. She hadn't had this much fun for so long, she'd forgotten what it was like to be happy.

"Have pity on me," she begged.

He reached for a towel and dangled it over her. His rock-hard body blocked out the sun. "Would you like me to dry you off?"

The rakish gleam in his eyes was too much. She grabbed it and snapped it at him. He let out a bark of laughter because she missed.

"Oh—" she muttered. "I can never get the best of you."

"I'll be kind...for now." He found her sunblock and handed it to her.

"Thank you," she whispered and started to put some on, but deep inside Ginger wished he were the one applying it. She loved his touch.

She would have offered it to Vittorio, but he didn't need it. Casting him a covert glance, she watched him relax on his lounger. The hot sun radiated through her, making her feel alive in a brand-new way.

After a while, she turned over, then realized she'd burn without sunscreen. But to ask Vittorio to spread it on wouldn't be a good idea because she realized she wanted to lie in his arms and be kissed into oblivion.

She had to do something quickly, so she got to her feet. Vittorio still lay there with his eyes closed while she put her beach coat back on.

"Vittorio?" she said softly, stepping into her flip-flops. "If you don't mind, I'm going to go in and get a drink."

He opened his eyes to half-mast and stared up at her. "I'll go in with you. We'll leave everything else out here. Toward evening we'll come out again and take another dip."

In one lithe move, he stood up. In a surprise gesture, he touched her face with his fingers. She felt the contact dart through her system. His dark brows furrowed. "You're flushed. You've probably had too much sun for one day. I shouldn't have let you stay out this long."

"Vittorio—I haven't lived twenty-seven years without knowing when to take cover."

A surprised look crossed over his face. "You're older than I thought."

She laughed. "Well, that makes me happy. For your information I'm fine."

"We'll see," he murmured.

"If I stayed out too long, it's not your fault."

He walked ahead of her. She could tell he was upset, but she couldn't understand it. When he opened the doors, she stepped past him, but he reached the kitchen first and fixed her a tall glass of ice water.

"Thank you."

He eyed her anxiously. "What else can I do for you?"

"Vittorio, why are you so worried?"

"Maybe because I don't want anything to happen to you that could be my fault."

She shook her head. "There's more to it than that. I *know* there is."

His chest rose and fell. "You're right. I'll tell you about it later."

"I'm going to hold you to that." She smiled at him. "Pour yourself a drink, too. I'll go take a shower and cool off. Then I'll come back out and start earning my pay by helping you fix our meal."

Ginger hurried past him to the guest bedroom and got in the shower. Not even her dad had shown this much concern over a sunburn. She would find out what was wrong before too long.

The cool water felt good. After washing her hair, she put on a pair of white shorts with the same blouse she'd worn earlier and stepped into her sandals.

One look in the mirror and she saw that she'd picked up some sun. Nothing serious. Ginger was glad to have acquired a little color for a change. All she had left to do was apply her coral frost lipstick and brush her hair dry.

When she went back to the kitchen, she found Vittorio hard at work. He too had put on white shorts and a navy short-sleeved crew neck shirt. The man looked fantastic in anything.

He shot her a glance. "That tint you acquired has made you lovelier than ever."

"Thank you." She wished Vittorio wouldn't say things like that to her because she wanted to believe everything he told her. She realized this was more than infatuation. She already cared for him way too much. "Are you ready to reveal your secret dish to me?"

"It's called braciolone, a roulade meat dish. My *mamma* taught me how to make it a long time ago. You can use any meat, but we prefer veal at our house."

"We hardly ever eat veal at mine. But since I've been in Italy I eat it a lot and love it. What can I do to help?"

"If you'll boil two eggs, I'll lay out the meat with the cheese and salami. When we have all the ingredients ready and you've diced the eggs, we'll roll it up with breadcrumbs."

"How interesting you put salami with the veal."

"When you taste it, you'll see why it's our favorite dish at home. While it's baking, I'll show you how to make the tomato sauce with parsley and garlic. The secret ingredients are the walnuts."

"I'm salivating already."

He flashed her a smile. "We'll appease your hunger with some of my signature bruschetta and a glass of wine."

Ginger loved to cook, but she'd never had so much fun cooking before. The crusty bread slices covered in olive oil and balsamic vinegar with tomatoes, basil and feta turned out to be superb. Between bites he fed to her, they sipped wine and wouldn't be able to eat the main meal for another hour at least.

"I've got to write down the recipes."

"Mamma goes by the old proverb, day-old bread, month-old oil and year-old wine."

"That should be easy to remember." She opened her mouth so he could feed her the last of another one. His fingers brushed her lips, sending bursts of desire through her. Nothing had ever felt so good or tasted so good. "This is ambrosia."

"I couldn't agree more." The seductive tone of his voice caused her to look up at him. "I think I have to kiss you."

Suddenly their bodies were touching. He cupped her face in his hands. "You're the most beautiful sight this man ever beheld." Then his mouth closed over hers, robbing her of breath.

"Vittorio—" That was the only muffled word to escape her lips before he deepened their kiss and swept her away. His arms went around her so there was no air between them.

In that first moment he created such ecstasy, she let out a cry as he sent them whirling together to a place she didn't know existed. Before she knew it, they were molded together while she tried to satisfy the primitive hunger building inside her.

This was too much, too soon, but she was helpless against the passion he'd aroused. It ignited her body until she was on fire for him. Never in her life had she known anything this powerful. With every touch of his hands clasping her closer, she found herself drowning in sensation after sensation.

At first when she detected footsteps, she was so intoxicated, she thought it was the pounding of her heart. Then she heard voices. Someone was coming.

She pulled away from him, but she could see the glaze of desire still blazing in his eyes before he turned in the direction of the people talking.

Vittorio should have been furious with his mother. Because of her, he'd been caught unaware. But since the usual three culprits, including Paola, had invaded the villa kitchen, he decided nothing could have pleased him more. In so doing they'd received a wake-up call they could never have expected.

If a picture was worth a thousand words, then the unwanted, uninvited guests had been given several hundred thousand to see Ginger here in the kitchen with him while they'd been creating their own firestorm of rapture.

He smiled at his sister. "As I told Mamma, I had other plans for today. Allow me to introduce you before you leave. This is Mrs. Lawrence from the US.

Ginger? Please meet my sister, Maria, and her friends Dario and Paola Coronna."

"How do you do?" Ginger spoke with enviable poise. "I'm so sorry about your father, Signorina Della Scalla."

Vittorio waited for his tongue-tied sister to say something. She'd lost color and looked like she was in agony. "Thank you."

"Sorry we burst in on you," Dario murmured. "The girls asked me to bring them out in our boat."

"That's all right. However, I understand your parents are having a dinner party this evening. If you leave now, you won't be late for it."

Paola stared hard at him for a moment longer before she turned away first and left the kitchen. She'd been living in denial for years where he was concerned. Though still feeling guilty, he was now relieved because what she'd just seen had removed her blinders.

Dario followed after her.

Maria was the last to leave. She shook her head. "I—I didn't realize you—"

"Don't worry about it," he cut her off gently. "There's no harm done."

Her lower lip trembled. "You know that's not true," she whispered before hurrying out of the kitchen.

When they heard the back door close, Ginger put more distance between them. "I think our dinner is probably done."

"I'm sure it is." He reached for the mitts and pulled the glass dish out of the oven.

She looked over at him. "It looks and smells perfect." After a silence, "Vittorio? Tell me what happened just now."

"You were here. You saw what I saw." He set the table that included the rest of the bruschetta and their partially filled wineglasses.

"What I saw were three people who were utterly devastated to find you in here with me. A few seconds sooner and—"

"They would have seen us thoroughly enjoying our first kiss," he broke in on her. A thousand kisses like that would never be enough for him.

The sun she'd picked up camouflaged her blush. "I think they knew what we'd been doing."

"I'm certain they did, *grazie al cielo*. It's long past time, and we have my mother to thank."

Ginger's gaze flew to his. "What are you saying?"

"I told her I was coming to the villa to make sure there were no more water leaks. She asked me to bring the girls. I explained that I had other plans. When she told me I was expected at the Coronnas for dinner with the family this evening, I let her know I couldn't make it. One way or another she must have told Maria where I was. They came anyway, knowing they weren't invited."

"Why would your sister bring her friends and come, knowing it wasn't convenient for you?"

Vittorio knew the exact reason, and it wasn't because they wanted to water ski. Paola couldn't anyway.

"Because Paola is Maria's best friend and they've been close from childhood. They work together at the family travel agency. She's always been around our family and today was their day off. They love it out here."

"But your sister looked traumatized. So did Paola."

"Paola has had a crush on me for a long time and thinks she's in love. But I've never returned her feelings and have felt badly about it. I've had relationships with women over the years and they both know it, but I've never brought one to the villa before."

"Never?"

Their eyes fused. "What you felt was their shock when they found me here with you. They'd caught me with a beautiful woman in the kitchen and could tell I'd been kissing the daylights out of her.

"You have to understand that until today, this villa has been sacrosanct to me. During my childhood it morphed from a castle, to a fort, to a hideout, to a retreat on Mars for Gaspare and me."

A hint of a smile caused one corner of her luscious mouth to lift, filling him with relief. "Mars?"

"That's right. No females have ever been allowed out here."

She chuckled. "That's interesting. I was just the opposite. My girlfriends and I always played house with imaginary husbands who came home from work carrying briefcases."

Vittorio laughed. Maria and Paola hadn't been any different, but Paola had always pictured him as her husband.

"I'm sorry if what happened was unpleasant for you, but they're gone. Let's forget about it and enjoy our meal."

"Maybe later you'll tell me what you've left out."

"I promise."

He carried the dish to the table and cut a portion to put on her plate. After eating everything with total enjoyment he said, "I want to hear what you think of my braciolone."

"Are you sure you weren't an Italian chef in another life?"

"Thank you for the compliment." He finished off another bruschetta. "Since you've been asking questions, I'd like to pose another one of my own. Why am I worried that when I take you back to your hotel, you'll disappear on me? This morning I was half-afraid I wouldn't find you waiting for me."

She averted her eyes and drank a little more wine. "Maybe it's because you know I'm on vacation. But I wouldn't leave without saying goodbye to you first."

He shook his head. "I'm talking about something else. After the way you kissed me back earlier, I know I'm not repulsive to you."

Without warning she pushed herself away from the table and stood up, clutching the chair back. "Have you considered that you've just answered your own question?"

Vittorio sat back in his chair. "What are you saying? That you wished I hadn't kissed you?"

"No," she said after hesitating. "We both know it was mutual."

Her honesty did her credit. "Is that such a terrible thing?"

"It is to me."

He got to his feet. "Have you said you're going to Greece when it's not true? I can handle the answer. I only want to know the truth."

She lifted her head. "You deserve it, but it's hard to talk about."

Vittorio rubbed his chest absently. "Are you in some kind of trouble?"

A frustrated sigh escaped her lips. "In a manner of speaking. It all started when I met you on the ship in Ravenna."

"You're not making sense."

"I know." She let go of the chair and walked over by the window to look out. "I—I felt drawn to you," she stammered. "Since my husband's death, nothing like that has happened to me before."

"You said it's been over two years."

"Yes. But I loved him so much, I knew I could never love like that again. That's why it took me by surprise to have noticed you at all. In a way it angered me. When I thought about it later, I realized that what I'd felt was guilt for thinking about someone else besides Bruce."

Guilt. Vittorio had become well acquainted with that word himself in the last eight months. Paola's accident had revived his old feelings of letting his father down. They'd been exacerbated by his death and his mother's insistence that he marry Paola.

"When I left for Switzerland, I thought I'd seen the last of Italy. I never expected to come back. But the plans with my two friends fell apart because the place on Lake Geneva where we were supposed to have vacationed had been sold.

"At that point, Abby chose to leave for France. Zoe and I decided to travel together. Since I hadn't been able to talk with Father Giovanni, I asked Zoe to travel back to Italy with me for a week. I'd hoped to go to the monastery and meet up with him again. Then I'd fly to Greece with her for the next week before we flew home to the States.

"You know the rest. Your brother did return, but I didn't know if you'd be with him. The truth is, there was a part of me that wanted to see you again. I couldn't understand why. Not until I figured out what was going inside me. Again, I felt as if I was betraying Bruce's memory."

The blood pounded in his ears as Vittorio walked over by her. "Tell me about him."

She kneaded her hands. "I don't know where to start. He was so wonderful." Tears welled in her eyes.

"Bruce was a professional tennis player who was giving a clinic at the country club my father belonged to. I met him while he was teaching my stepmother. I was crazy about him from the moment we met and took some lessons from him, too. We fell in love fast and got married."

"Were you teaching then?"

"Yes. I'd just been hired at Vanguard. I'd never been happier in my life. We had plans to start a family. But then he began getting pains in his legs."

Vittorio watched tears roll down her cheeks.

"Before long he was diagnosed with bone cancer. A year later he died because it had metastasized to the spine, causing paralysis and kidney failure."

"Caro Dio," he muttered. Much as he wanted to hold her in his arms, he couldn't risk offending her, even if he only wanted to offer comfort.

"It was slow and agonizing for him." The pain in her eyes and voice gutted Vittorio. "I adored him. For a long time after he died, I didn't want to go on living, but somehow you do."

She threw her head back. "I never want to go through that kind of agony again in my life. No one can depend on something so incredible lasting forever. I found that out much sooner than I'd expected. Because my father had lost my mother early, he helped me to find purpose in life again."

Ginger's pain had been excruciating.

"When you came and sat by me on the garden bench yesterday, I was happy yet astounded to see you again. Part of me experienced that same feeling from before of being…interested in you.

"I was flattered by your offer to drive me back to the hotel and decided to enjoy the moment for what it was. A chance encounter with an attractive man for a day or two was something I ought to be able to handle."

"But your guilt is tearing you apart," he ground out.

"No. It's more than that now. It scares me to think that I care about you, let alone anything more. Getting involved again terrifies me for fear of losing that person, too. Another kiss like the one you and I shared in here earlier and I couldn't deal with it. Vittorio," she said emotionally, "I'm not sorry I met you, but I've decided I won't be seeing you again."

That's what you *think, Ginger Lawrence.*

He started clearing the table while he decided how to handle this. "Thank you for answering my question. I'll be happy to run you back to your hotel anytime you say."

"Would you mind? I'll do the dishes if you want to bring things in from the beach."

Her lack of argument deflated him. *Give the woman her space, Vittorio.* "It won't take me long."

Leaving the house on a run, he retrieved the items and put them away. By the time he returned to the kitchen, she'd disappeared and the dishwasher was going.

He went upstairs to the bedroom and changed into cargo pants for the trip across the lagoon. When he came back down, Ginger was waiting for him in the foyer with her overnight bag. She, too, had changed out of her shorts and put on her jeans.

They left out the back door and made their way to the boat. Once he'd untied the rope, he drove them to the open water. At six at night there were a lot of boats and watercraft coming and going from the Lido.

She'd put on her sunglasses and looked at him. "Are you angry with me?"

"Why would you ask such a question?"

"You would have every right to be upset. I told you I wanted to come here with you, and now I've asked you to take me back."

"If you want to know the truth, I'm devastated for the grief you've suffered." Vittorio realized he'd been especially affected because his father had just died and his sympathy for her pain ran deep.

"I didn't mean to tell you all this."

"Don't apologize for baring your soul to me today. I'm honored that you trusted me enough to talk about your husband. He was the luckiest of men to have you in his life no matter how short the time. I'm more envious than you know over what you shared."

Ginger wiped the tears trickling beneath her sunglasses. "Thank you for your understanding, for everything." Her voice shook. "As I told you earlier, I'm not sorry we met."

It didn't take long to navigate the Grand Canal to her hotel. When he pulled up in front, he shut off the engine and helped her out of the boat with her overnight bag. He walked her inside the entrance and stared into her eyes.

"We've only spent a short time together, Ginger. It's not nearly enough for me. Surely you must realize I don't want you to leave. When your vacation is over and you're back in Costa Mesa, remember there's a man in Venice who'll never forget you."

He pressed a brief kiss to her lips. "If you want to know what I'll be thinking, look up the Byron poem that could have been written about you. I'm sure you know the one."

On that note he walked back out of the hotel to the boat. He needed to be strictly alone and headed back to the villa instead of the palazzo. The first thing to do was find out what flight Ginger was taking to Greece. He planned to seek her out at the airport tomorrow and talk her into spending the rest of her vacation with him.

CHAPTER SIX

GINGER HAD NO idea what poem Vittorio had meant!

When she reached her hotel room, she threw herself across the bed and sobbed. Two hours later her cell phone rang.

Vittorio? her heart cried. Like the fool she was, she grabbed for it, desperate to hear his voice. "Hello?"

"Hi, Ginger! I've been waiting to hear from you. Are you coming?"

Zoe's question caused another meltdown. Vittorio didn't have her cell number. He could have called her hotel room, but he'd brought her back to the hotel without persuading her to stay in Venice. It would be absurd to think he'd phone her now and ask her to reconsider leaving.

"Ginger? You're not saying anything. What's wrong?"

When she could get herself together she said, "I have to talk to you. Do you have the time?"

"Of course. This has to be about a man. The *one* you wanted to come back to Italy to see. Right?"

She dashed the tears from her face so her phone wouldn't get too wet. "It's true that I've met someone, but I said goodbye to him this evening."

"Why?"

"Because it would be ridiculous to get involved when I'll be going home shortly."

"That's not enough of an explanation. What aren't you telling me?"

Trust Zoe to dig deeper. "I don't want to go through pain again."

"How could you be in pain? You barely met him, right?"

"Yes. But if I go on seeing him, something terrible might happen and I might lose him, too!"

"Oh, Ginger, I'm sorry you've been through so much suffering. Of course there are no guarantees. Has he already told you he loves you?"

"No. We haven't been together that long."

"But it's been enough to turn you inside out. He must really be something."

She closed her eyes tightly. "Vittorio Della Scalla is so incredible, I can't begin to describe him."

"Good grief. You sound so much like Abby before she left Switzerland with Raoul, it's spooky."

"I know."

"I guess you have to ask yourself if Vittorio is really worth it."

"I don't have to ask," Ginger admitted, "otherwise I wouldn't be in this much pain after saying goodbye to him. That's the trouble."

"I wish I could help you, but it sounds like you're going to have to go with your heart and have a little faith."

A little faith if she wanted a relationship with Vittorio…

She wiped her eyes. "Thanks for talking to me,

Zoe. You're the best. I don't think I'll be coming to Greece after all." Besides, instinct told her that Zoe didn't want or need any company. Her silence had convinced her. "Whatever else happens, we'll keep in touch."

"I want to know everything when you're ready to tell me."

"I feel the same way. Goodbye for now. We'll talk soon."

After Ginger hung up, she got ready for bed and climbed under the covers, knowing she wanted a relationship with the amazing man who'd brought her back to life.

Tomorrow was a brand-new day. Before she fell asleep, she went through half a dozen scenarios trying to decide how to make contact with Vittorio. She didn't have his phone number. But since he was the CEO at Della Scalla Shipping Lines, she could phone his office.

The next morning Ginger asked for a tray of coffee and rolls to be sent to her room. While eating, she used the hotel phone to ask for assistance to call him. She was put through to the main office and told to leave her name and number. His secretary would get back to her.

But at the last minute Ginger decided against leaving any kind of message and hung up. It would be better to show up at his office and see him in person without giving warning. The second he saw her, she'd know by the look in his eyes if he was happy to see her. If she was wrong about the strength of his feelings, that would be the pain she took home to California.

With her mind made up, Ginger got dressed in a silky three-quarter-sleeve blouse. It had an all-over white-and-green print on a navy background. She wore a matching navy cotton skirt and sandals. Once she'd done her makeup and brushed her hair, she was ready to leave.

The concierge at the desk told her which water bus to take to reach Della Scalla Shipping Lines. Because of the crowds, it took an hour before she could be dropped off near the massive neoclassic building located just beyond the Grand Canal leading into the lagoon.

Ginger trembled just thinking about daring to approach Vittorio like this. But she had to be sure that when he'd told her he didn't want her to leave, he'd meant it.

When she walked inside, Ginger had to pass through security. The uniformed guard asked her the nature of her business. She told him she'd come to see Signor Vittorio Della Scalla, but that it was personal and she would rather not leave her name.

He made a phone call while she waited.

In a few minutes another man not much older than Vittorio walked toward them. His eyes shone with male interest as he smiled at her. "I'm Rico Emilio, Signor Della Scalla's private secretary. I understand you wanted to see him about a personal matter, but he won't be in today. If you would leave a name and phone number where you can be reached, I'll let him know as soon I hear from him."

Ginger felt foolish and shook her head. "Thank you, Signor Emilio, but that won't be necessary."

"You're sure?"

"Yes. I'm sorry to have bothered you."

"I can assure you it's no bother."

She smiled and left the building. For Vittorio's sake she was glad security was tight, but she shouldn't have come here. Now he would know she'd been by because the secretary would have given him her description. Any surprise had been foiled.

Once outside she caught another water bus back to the hotel. En route she got off at the stop near Vittorio's palazzo and walked past it several times, hoping she might catch sight of him or his speedboat. But after ten minutes she realized it was foolish and walked back to her hotel.

By now it was lunchtime. Ginger ate in the trattoria next door. Why hadn't Vittorio gone to work today? His company was without its CEO. Could he afford to be away so long, or had he sought out his brother at the monastery?

Disappointed beyond belief, she paid for her meal and went back to the hotel. Her only choice now was to wait until Vittorio made contact with her. But this wasn't the way she'd hoped the day would turn out. She'd taken a risk to be with him, but now there was no sign of him. What had she done?

Vittorio had suffered a near sleepless night at the villa. This morning he'd phoned his secretary and told him to hold all his calls. He wasn't coming in to work at all and wouldn't be back before tomorrow at the earliest. Vittorio had left his uncle in charge until his return.

For the next few hours he continued to check with the airport to find out what flight Ginger had booked to fly to Greece. He'd planned to intercept her, but so far she hadn't made a booking.

Between calls to the airlines, he kept phoning the hotel and was told Signora Lawrence hadn't checked out yet. On his fifth call he learned she still hadn't come to the desk to pay her bill.

What was going on with her? Maybe she wouldn't be able to join her friend for another day.

In a dark mood, he heard his cell ring around two and glanced at the caller ID. "Rico?" he said after picking up. "I thought I told you to hold my calls."

"I think you'll want to know about this one."

His stomach muscles clenched. "What do you mean?"

"You just had a visitor at your office. She wouldn't leave a name or number."

His heart started to pump like a jackhammer. "What did she look like?"

"Probably the most gorgeous woman I've ever seen. American."

Ginger had gone to his office looking for him while he'd been calling the airport? Something had kept her from leaving yet. Alternate emotions of elation and alarm gripped him. "Thanks for the update. Remind me to give you a bonus."

Vittorio hung up and flew out of the villa to his speedboat. He turned on the engine and sped back across the lagoon to her hotel. After tying up the boat, he hurried inside and approached one of the staff at the desk.

"Would you please ring Signora Lawrence's room? If she's there, will you let her know her friend is waiting in the lobby?" Vittorio didn't want to leave his own name. He would stay here until she showed up, whether it looked like he was stalking her or not.

The man rang her room. Vittorio experienced infinite relief to hear him talk to her before hanging up. "She says she'll be right down."

His fears allayed that he hadn't missed her, he thanked the receptionist and walked to the elevator to wait for her. Twice the door opened, but she wasn't among the people coming out. Again his frustration mounted.

"Vittorio?"

At the sound of her unforgettable voice, he wheeled around. Ginger had come down the stairs and moved toward him dressed in a blue outfit he hadn't seen before. The sight of her took his breath.

She stopped short of walking into his arms. "I presume your secretary told you I came by your office?"

He nodded. Rico would have had a heart attack when he first laid eyes on her. "You didn't leave for Greece today. I spent hours on the phone with the airlines trying to find out which flight you were taking."

"Why did you do that?"

"Because I planned to intercept you and talk you into staying in Venice. What prevented you from leaving?"

Her breathing suddenly grew more shallow. "I was about to ask why you weren't at work today. Your secretary said you didn't intend to go in at all."

The fact that she'd evaded his question meant she was nervous. But again he didn't know if that was a good or bad sign. "Does this mean you'll be flying to Greece tomorrow instead?"

She shook her head. "I found out Zoe has her own

agenda right now, so I'm not joining her after all. That's the reason I went to your office, to let you know."

Incredible! "Has the change in plans upset you?"

"Not at all. To be honest, nothing has been definite about our vacation since Abby went to France."

"Have you decided to go back to the States tomorrow?"

"I still have some vacation time left."

That was what he'd been waiting to hear. "What are your plans?"

"I don't have any yet."

He let out the breath he'd been holding. If this meant what he was hoping...

"Yes, you do, but I don't want to have to keep coming to the hotel for you. Why don't you go upstairs and start getting packed? I'll be back in an hour to get you. When I return, I'll tell the desk you're checking out and ask them to send up someone to bring your bags down to the foyer."

"Where are we going?" She sounded like she'd been running.

That one question settled it. "To the villa. I need a vacation, too, more than you know. We'll make it our home base for as long as you can stay. The guest bedroom on the main floor is yours."

Her lustrous gray eyes searched his as if she couldn't quite believe this was happening. "Hurry," he urged her and pushed the button for the elevator. After she'd stepped inside, their gazes clung before the door closed.

On a burst of euphoria he hurried out to the boat and headed for the palazzo. In a few minutes he'd parked his boat and rushed inside. One of the maids told him his mother and sister were up in the master suite. He was surprised his sister was home. Maybe she'd taken the day off to be with his mother. It was only two o'clock.

He bounded down the hall to her apartment, where he found them sitting on the bed talking.

"Mamma?" He walked over to hug her.

"Where were you all night, *figlio mio*?"

"At the villa." He gave his sister a kiss, but she answered with an accusing stare. "I came home to let you know I'm now on vacation and will be for the next week."

A gasp came out of his mother. "You're taking time off this soon after being voted in?"

"I've spoken with Uncle Bertoldo. He'll be in charge until I get back."

"But you've just been installed in your father's place!"

"That's exactly the reason why." He sat down in one of the upholstered side chairs. "I don't remember the last time I took time off. The point is, I need it badly before I take over. There's also something else I need to discuss with you. I'm glad you're here, Maria. This involves you, too."

Yesterday his life had undergone a fundamental change. Nothing was going to be the same again. He saw his mother and sister exchange anxious glances.

"After Gaspare went into the priesthood, we all know how difficult it was for us to lose him. That's why I've lived at home this long. But it's time for me to take hold of my life. I need a home of my own and have one in mind." He'd already discussed the idea with Gaspare.

"You're really going to move out?" His mother's alarm was palpable.

"Yes, but you mustn't worry. Maria is here, and you know how much I love you and will always be around for you. What I'm hoping is that you'll consider inviting Bertoldo and Miah to come and live with you permanently at the palazzo. The three of you love each other. They have no children and adore Maria.

"But Maria won't be at home forever. One of these days she'll get married. I'm thinking of you and your future. Maria and I don't want you to be alone. Isn't that true?" He glanced at his sister, who slowly nodded but didn't say anything.

"Papà carried a pain for years because Uncle Bertoldo wasn't chosen to be the head of the company. We all know whose fault that was. Think about how happy it might make him and Aunt Miah to live here with you. This palazzo was his home growing up, too. It could be again. But it's just an idea." Vittorio stood up. "All I'm asking is that you think about it, Mamma."

"I can't believe what I'm hearing."

His mother couldn't disguise her pain over his news. This was the hard part, but it had to be said. After what happened at the villa yesterday because he had no guaranteed privacy, Vittorio realized he should have moved out years ago.

"It's past time, Mamma. We'll talk more when I get back."

"You're leaving now?"

"Yes, but I promise to stay in touch with you."

"I see."

"Stay well." Vittorio kissed her cheek and left the bedroom.

He closed the front door of the palazzo and walked out to the boat. Within minutes he headed for the hotel, relieved Maria was with his mother. Now he was free to go on vacation and explore what was waiting for him with Ginger. Though she was still dealing with her husband's death, she hadn't been able to walk away from Vittorio. That was a start.

As soon as the hotel came in sight, he parked in front. After tying the boat up, he rushed inside the foyer to speak to the man he'd talked to before. "Please ring Signora Lawrence's room. She'll be checking out. Will you send someone up for her bags?"

"*Subito*, signor."

Vittorio would have paid the bill, but knew Ginger wouldn't go with him if he tried to take over. She was much too independent, and he wouldn't want her any other way. Within five minutes she appeared in the foyer. While she took care of it, Vittorio carried her two suitcases to the boat. Before long she was settled. He started the engine and turned to her.

"We'll stop for groceries at the same place as before."

Ginger put on her sunglasses against the afternoon sun and sat back in her seat. "This evening I'll cook dinner, but it won't match the braciolone and bruschetta you made for us yesterday. What do you feel like?"

It was a question she shouldn't have asked when her nearness was *so* intoxicating to him. "If we were in Costa Mesa, what would you fix?"

"Probably chicken stir-fry and a green salad."

"You have me intrigued."

"I promise it's nothing complicated. Are you hungry?"

"Starving."

"Then this dish is perfect. No baking. If you're ready for dinner early, we can eat in an hour."

They stopped long enough to buy the necessary ingredients before reaching the villa. Vittorio carried her bags to the guest bedroom. After putting extra towels in the en suite bathroom, he went back to the kitchen to help her.

She'd already started cooking some bacon in one of the skillets. He walked over to the sink to wash his hands. "What can I do to help?"

"Will you boil two eggs? Then separate the spinach leaves in a bowl while I brown the chicken." In a second saucepan she sautéed onions, green and red peppers and mushrooms in olive oil. Next she prepared white rice.

"For someone who hasn't done any cooking for a long time, you definitely know your way around a kitchen."

She rolled those fabulous gray eyes. "We'll see after you've tasted everything."

"What have you got there?" She was opening a packet of something.

"The pièce de résistance. Yesterday we had walnuts with your veal. This evening it's cashews." She mixed them with her own from-scratch version of sweet and spicy Asian sauce in a third saucepan.

After he set the table and poured some red wine, Vittorio watched in fascination as she broke up the bacon into bits and added them to the spinach with the diced eggs. She also made her own salad dressing and cut up avocados.

"Are we ready?"

Ginger nodded. "Sit down and I'll serve you." Within seconds she brought two plates of rice topped with the stir-fry to the table. They helped themselves to the salad.

Vittorio ate everything in sight and got up to serve himself a second helping. "This meal is fabulous."

"Thank you."

He flicked her a sideward glance. "Does it make you homesick to eat something so familiar?"

Ginger shook her head. "No. After I get back to California I'll be fixing it a lot. If anything, I'll be yearning for cannelloni and chocolate *tortas*. Only Italy could make foods so divine."

"With that kind of praise, I'm going to take you to a restaurant tomorrow where you'll be served those very items."

Excitement lit up her eyes. "Here on the Lido?"

"No. I'm taking you on a short driving tour of the Veneto region. There's a lot to see I know you'll love."

"That sounds exciting. How will we get there from here?"

He chuckled. "We'll take the boat to Tronchetto, where our company leaves a fleet of cars, and go from there. But I'll need to get some petrol here and better leave right now. I didn't realize until we were half-way across the lagoon that my second tank was registering empty."

"Oh, no—"

"Don't worry. I keep a small can of petrol on the

boat for an emergency, but I'm glad I didn't have to use it. Do you want to come with me?"

"I have a better idea. While you get gas, I'll wash the dishes since I made the mess. Then our work will be done."

He nodded. "When I get back, we'll go for a swim."

"I'd love that."

His pulse raced. "I won't be longer than a half hour. Promise me you'll still be here."

She wore a vexed expression. "Vittorio—where would I go when I'm having the time of my life?"

Ginger took the words right out of his mouth. "I'll lock the door." Before he left the kitchen, he walked over to the counter and turned on the radio to a station that played music he knew she would enjoy.

Once Vittorio had gone, Ginger hugged her arms to her waist. The voice of Andrea Bocelli singing a romantic Italian love song filled the air. It was her favorite from Puccini's *Manon*. She turned it up to capture the richness. When it was over, another song from Puccini followed. A night of Bocelli. Nothing could be more enchanting!

Ginger was so happy to be here with Vittorio she was giddy and almost forgot she'd volunteered to do the dishes. She looked around and laughed because there were no leftovers. He'd eaten everything she'd prepared!

That thrilled her heart and made the cleaning up easier. She got busy loading the dishwasher while she dreamed about dancing with Vittorio. Just as she was rinsing out the saucepans to put in the washer, the music suddenly shut off.

"Vittorio?" He hadn't been gone long enough. "What did you forget?" She turned toward the radio on the other side of the kitchen and found herself staring into the accusing eyes of an older female stranger. Ginger jumped in surprise.

"Excuse me for intruding, Signora Lawrence. I'm Signora Chiara Della Scalla. I thought my son was in here. Bocelli is one of his favorite tenors. The music was loud enough that you obviously didn't hear the helicopter."

Ginger hadn't heard anything except the glorious music. She noticed his mother was an attractive, dark blond woman probably in her mid-sixties standing in the kitchen.

Of course she had a key to the family home and could come and go at will. Like her sons, she spoke excellent English and bore a faint resemblance in features to her children. Her daughter took after her in coloring.

Vittorio hadn't told Ginger his mother was coming. It was another surprise just like the one yesterday. Something was definitely wrong.

"How do you, Signora Della Scalla? Your son is out buying petrol for the boat. We've just finished eating and I was doing the dishes. He should be back in the next few minutes."

"I think it's just as well I've missed him. My daughter told me you're a very, very beautiful American woman. She certainly didn't exaggerate."

"Now that I've met you, I understand where your children get their good looks, signora."

His mother was on a mission about something and

ignored her comment. "Vittorio told me he has only known you a short time."

"That's true. In May we met in Ravenna aboard the *Sirena* during a dinner conference on Lord Byron. Then recently I saw Vittorio again at the monastery, where your elder son gave me some valuable information about Byron and I learned about your husband's passing."

"So I understand."

"I'm so sorry for the pain you must be going through. While I was in Switzerland, I saw the news about the funeral on television. His death has to be a devastating loss for your family."

"It has been unbearable. What shocks me is to find you installed here in the villa, making yourself right at home with my second born. Only yesterday my daughter walked in on the two of you eating a meal he'd obviously prepared."

Ginger was stunned by her attitude. "Signora— have I done something to offend you or your daughter?"

His mother took a deep breath. "On the contrary, I came out here hoping to have a talk with him about his behavior. But since *you* are here, let me ask you a question. Has he told you he's about to be married?"

Married—Ginger clung to the kitchen counter, shaken by the other woman's words.

She struggled to keep her cool while she tried to take it in. In her heart of hearts she couldn't believe Vittorio would have pursued her if it were true. But equally shocking, she couldn't imagine his mother making up such a lie to her face.

"You've lost a little color, Signora Lawrence. It's obvious my son has not been honest with you. That's not your fault. For that I'm very sorry, but it's best you know the truth now before this goes on any longer. Under the circumstances, I'll leave so you can tell him I flew here, and why."

She left through the back door while Ginger still stood there in absolute agony. In the back of her mind she remembered the words Vittorio had exchanged with his sister, Maria, yesterday after she and her friends had shown up at the villa uninvited. He'd said something about no harm being done. But Maria had answered that he knew it wasn't true.

Vittorio had promised he'd tell Ginger all that was going on behind the scenes, but it hadn't happened.

What did he know? What had it all meant? And now his mother had come.

Was Vittorio a liar like Abby's former fiancé, Nigel, had been? A man who'd gotten engaged to Abby while being married to another woman and a father of two children?

Did Vittorio fear she'd somehow find out the truth about his leading a double life? Tomorrow he said he was taking her away from Venice for a few days. Had it been his plan to make love to Ginger until his lie was exposed?

Sick to the pit of her stomach, Ginger dashed to the guest bedroom. She picked up her suitcases and carried them to the living room of the villa. When Vittorio returned in a few minutes, she'd tell him she wanted to go back to the hotel in Venice immediately and get herself another room.

They would talk about his mother's bombshell on the way. Whatever the truth, or where it lay, she couldn't handle this and would be on the next plane home.

CHAPTER SEVEN

EARLY EVENING WAS the perfect time to go for a swim with Ginger. Now that the boat was ready for tomorrow, Vittorio maneuvered it down the canal to the rear of the villa, excited to get her to himself.

But when he tied up to the dock, he saw that the Della Scalla helicopter had arrived from the pad atop the office building. What in the name of heaven was his uncle doing out here without as much as a text or phone call to find out if he'd be welcome?

As Vittorio raced toward the back entrance to find out what was going on, he saw his mother leave the villa and head toward the helicopter. Maria wasn't with her. She appeared to be alone.

His *mother* was the one who'd come?

Santo Cielo! That meant she'd already been inside alone with Ginger. He'd never known such anger and stepped in her path, putting his hands on her upper arms to stop her.

"Mamma—what are you doing here? Tell me what was so vital, you flew here to see me without letting me know you were coming!"

"Would you have answered if I'd left a message that it was urgent?" she retorted. "I don't think so.

I see a son who has lost his reason and sanity over some foreign beauty who has already invaded your life and the villa. Your father was barely laid in his grave, yet here you are taking a vacation and plan to move out of the palazzo.

"When you get back from wherever you're going with this opportunist, do you honestly believe your job will be waiting for you?"

Vittorio shook his head. "I don't know you like this."

"That makes two of us. It's time you heard the real reason you were made CEO at the board meeting. I was told about it early this morning."

"You're speaking in riddles."

"Would it clarify things if I told you Renaldo talked to everyone on the board behind your back after the funeral and influenced them to vote for you?"

He let go of her arms. *"What did you say?"*

"It's true. What greater proof that he wants you for his son-in-law! He's been planning on your marrying Paola for a long time."

A sound of exasperation escaped. "His plan for the two of us to marry so he's assured of the Della Scalla fortune has never been mine. I don't love her. End of story."

"But you care for her. I know you do, and there are other things," she argued.

"More important than love?" he blurted. "You can say that to me when we all know how you felt about Papà? I'd never marry a woman unless she'd become my whole heart and soul."

"But you have a longtime friendship and compatibility with Paola. The kind of passionate love you're speaking of can grow with time."

"No, Mamma. Not even you believe that."

She clasped her hands together. "You have to understand that making you CEO was Renaldo's way of giving his blessing. Last night at the party he hoped to talk to you about finalizing the date for the wedding. He and your father had an agreement before he died. It was your father's wish that you marry her."

Vittorio fought to remain calm. "You're wrong. Papà told me and Gaspare that our lives were ours to live as we wanted. He never inflicted his will on us. If he told you that, it's because Renaldo has been holding something over him and he didn't want you upset. Rumors about Renaldo have been floating at the company for the last year. Now it's all making sense."

"What do you mean?"

"This has to do with money. The man's a big gambler. Everyone knows it. I'm beginning to wonder just how deeply Renaldo is in debt. If he could make me marry Paola, then his financial worries would be over. It's called blackmail!"

"You really believe that?" She looked horrified.

"I do." His brows furrowed. "Who told you about the vote? Uncle Bertoldo?"

"No. It came from someone who knows the truth."

Probably Paola's mother, Lena. Or maybe even Dario. He fought the sickness rising in his throat. "If that's the way I was made the CEO, then I don't want the job."

"But it's your legacy!"

"A legacy is a gift left to a family member. Being

CEO is the result of a vote. In this case one that has been tainted in corruption. I want no part of it."

"You don't mean that, *figlio mio!*"

"Watch me. I have my own business." He cupped her elbow and walked her to the waiting helicopter. "Right now I have to go inside and try to salvage my relationship with Ginger. I don't need to ask you what you said to her. It's written all over your face. I've never known you to be cruel."

"You don't understand."

"Of course I do. I have to believe Renaldo's threat to this family drove you to come out here. When you discovered I was gone, you confronted Ginger deliberately. She's more important to me than you know and deserves an apology, but that will have to wait until another time."

"What are you going to do?" At this point his mother's demeanor had turned fearful.

"I already told you I'm on vacation. I'll let you know when I'm back." He nodded to his pilot, who opened the door. "Take care of yourself, Mamma." Vittorio gave her a kiss and helped her into the helicopter.

He nodded to his pilot, Ciro, and stepped away. The rotors turned, and the helicopter lifted in the air before heading back to the office building. Maria was probably waiting for her in a private water taxi to go home with her.

Nothing could stop the hammering of his heart as he hurried in the villa and discovered Ginger sitting in the living room waiting for him. She'd put her suitcases next to her.

He stood there with his legs slightly apart. "Before

you say anything, will you do me the favor of hearing me out first?"

A minute passed. Finally, "Go ahead," she said in wooden voice. Any other woman would have raged at him the second he'd walked in.

"I ran into my mother while I was coming back from the boat and know enough to realize she's turned you inside out."

"She said you're about to be married."

He knew it. "Did she tell you I was engaged?"

"She didn't use those words."

"That's because she couldn't," Vittorio bit out. "Mamma wishes it were the case. Before I left the palazzo yesterday, she told me that up until the morning my father died, he wanted me to marry Paola."

Ginger jumped to her feet. "You're talking about your sister's friend. *She's* the woman?"

"You met her yesterday. My father and mother have always been very fond of Paola. Maria, of course, would give anything if I married her best friend, but she knows I've never been interested. It's impossible."

But their conversation brought up feelings from the past and his guilt that he'd disappointed his father.

"*That's* why she was so crushed when she saw you and me together."

Vittorio nodded. "The sad news is, Paola is her father's sacrificial lamb. Renaldo Coronna, the company's attorney, is a big gambler and has made some investments that have turned on him. I suspect he's in real financial trouble to the tune of millions of euros and needs someone to bail him out. Only a son-in-law of means will fill the bill."

She walked around for a minute, then halted. "How

terrible! It's hard to believe people still think and function that way."

"Too many unfortunately. Just now my mother told
me something I didn't know. She has indisputable
proof that behind the scenes he arranged to have me
voted in as head of the company."

"What?" Ginger put a hand to her throat. He saw
sorrow in her eyes as they fastened on him. "So that
speech I made about your being the one all the board
members wanted to run the company had everything
to do with him leveraging them for future favors?"

"Exactly."

"Oh, Vittorio. I'm devastated about this."

"Don't be. As for Renaldo's motivation, it doesn't
require imagination to guess why. That's when I told
my mother something she didn't know until a few
minutes ago. My father must have pretended to her
that he wanted me to marry Paola. It was his way of
covering for Renaldo."

"How ghastly," she whispered.

"Isn't it? But the kicker is, Papà didn't know he
was going to die. I'm positive he would have eventually found a way to help Renaldo without using me
in the process. They'd been friends for a long time.
Manipulating me wasn't my father's way. My siblings
would tell you the same thing."

Ginger stared hard at him. "What are you going
to do?"

"I'm on vacation because I need one. But whether
you want to stay with me is up to you. Do you believe
I've told you the truth? Or do you want me to take you
back to the hotel and get you checked in until you arrange for a flight to the States?"

He held his breath until he heard her say, "I want to be on vacation with you."

The clamp squeezing his lungs relaxed. "Come on. Let's take a walk outside on the beach while I tell you everything that's on my mind."

"I'm ready right now."

After removing their shoes that they left at the front door, Vittorio clasped her hand and they walked out on the sand into the glorious night.

More than ever he was thankful for his mother's interruption this evening. It gave him warning of what was coming. He was sickened by the corruption on Renaldo's part to buy votes. But he wouldn't do anything about it while he'd been given this time with Ginger.

Vittorio clung to her hand while they walked at the edge of the water. Darkness had descended. Lights from various boats flickered here and there, but they were alone and Ginger craved this time with him.

After his mother had delivered her disturbing message, Ginger couldn't have imagined being out here with him like this such a short time later. The explanations he'd supplied in the living room had come hard and fast. Truth rang from every word, every look. She believed him.

But it had convinced her that getting involved with a man like Vittorio meant he lived in a complicated world full of intrigue and made her nervous.

Was it worth it to get in any deeper?

Ginger couldn't answer that question, not while their bodies brushed against each other, causing her to ache for the contact.

"Do you have any kind of history with Paola?"

"None, but something happened last September that exacerbated a difficult situation."

"You don't have to tell me if you don't want to."

"I don't believe in secrets, Ginger. I want you to know everything. Eight months ago I took my sister and Paola water skiing. While I was pulling Paola behind the ski boat, she hit a loose water ski floating in the water. I had no idea where it came from. It turned out she broke her ankle. I was horrified and called for a water ambulance."

"That really was a freak accident, Vittorio. I've done my share of water skiing, but nothing like that has ever happened."

"She's had two surgeries. I don't know if you noticed, but she doesn't walk as normally now and can't wear high heels."

"Oh, that's too bad."

"Paola and my sister work at the company's travel bureau. While she was recuperating, Maria used to bring her to the palazzo most days after work."

"Your sister sounds like a remarkable friend."

"She is, but she felt guilty because she'd begged me to take Paola skiing one more time around the lagoon. That's one of the reasons why she was so attentive to her. Sometimes Dario came over, too, if he didn't have a date.

"The three of them tried to involve me in the evenings, but I had commitments and often stayed the night in the penthouse bedroom at the office. As time went on, I could tell Paola wanted to be with me and sought me out the minute I walked in the door. I didn't want to spend time with her, but a part of me felt guilty because I'd been the one driving the boat."

Ginger looked up at his handsome profile. "I guess it would do no good to tell you it wasn't your fault."

He put his hands on her shoulders. A slight breeze ruffled his black hair. His potent masculinity overwhelmed her.

"In the last few months I've purposely stayed at work or gone out with a woman or good friends before going home. During this period, I've hoped Paola would turn to someone else. But it hasn't worked. No one was more shocked than I when the three of them showed up at the villa yesterday."

"Doesn't she date? She's attractive."

"Maria says she doesn't like the guys who are interested in her."

Ginger smiled at him. "That's what happens when you set your sights on one man. After her knowing you over the years, I'm afraid Vittorio Della Scalla would be an impossible act to follow." The second the words came out of her mouth, she realized she'd meant them. They'd come straight from her heart.

"According to whom?"

"A certain college teacher who should have flown to Greece to meet her friend Zoe. Instead, she's walking on the beach with him. That should tell you something."

"Ginger—" He crushed her against him. "I need to kiss you again. After yesterday it's all I can think about."

She was on the verge of telling him she suffered from the same problem, but he didn't give her a chance. Instead his mouth closed over hers and once again they were communicating in the most elemental of ways. Their bodies clamored to get closer. Hers was on fire for him. Every kiss grew longer and deeper. If she allowed this to go on, she knew what was going to happen.

Calling on the little self-control she had left, she eventually broke their kiss and eased away from him. "I'm sorry, Vittorio, but I'm enjoying this too much. I—I'm not sure being on vacation with you is a good thing." Her voice faltered.

Lines darkened his handsome features. "Tell me what's wrong now."

"We've been living in a dream since we met, but for it to go on any longer is putting off the inevitable. You've shown me a day I'll never forget, but tomorrow I need to leave for home. Your life is too full of complications for this to be working."

"Don't put that on me, Ginger. I want to know the real reason why you've suddenly decided you need to disappear from my life."

"Surely I don't have to spell it out for you."

"I'm afraid you do. I've told you everything so you know exactly what is going on, but you haven't been honest with me."

"I have!" she cried. "But I've asked you to be understanding of me, and it's not fair to you."

"In what way?"

"You're the one who's made it possible for us to be on vacation together. We're staying in your family's villa. You wait on me, take care of me. If I ask you not to kiss me, you honor my wishes. I tell you I'm only in Italy for a little while and you go along with it as if it's just fine. This situation isn't real. If we part tomorrow, there's no real harm done and we'll have some special memories to savor."

"What needs to change for it to seem real?" he challenged her.

"Nothing. I need to go back to my life."

"From what you've told me, your life in Costa Mesa is full of pain."

"But it is my life, and my family and friends are there. I'm sure you think I'm being a tease, but that's not it."

Ginger heard him suck in his breath. "I know you're not. It's evident you need more time after the loss of your husband and our problem amounts to the fact you have to go back to California soon. We don't have the luxury of getting to know each other over weeks and months."

"Why aren't you a Californian?" she asked to add some levity to her turmoil.

"You probably wouldn't be attracted to me if I didn't have a Venetian accent."

She lifted her hands to cup his striking face. "I was attracted before I heard you speak. It goes much deeper, and you know it."

His hands roved over her back. "I want you in all the ways a man can want a woman," he murmured emotionally, "but I haven't lost a wife. Considering it hasn't been that long since your husband passed away, your need to hold back makes sense.

"I'm sensitive to that and won't ask for more than you're willing to give while you're still here. At least I'm saying that right now because I can't let you go yet."

"I don't want to leave you either." Ginger raised

her mouth to his, kissing him tenderly. "Thank you for being able to appreciate my situation."

Every passing moment with Vittorio meant she was getting beyond the point of no return. Whether she flew back to California tomorrow or in a week, she still had five weeks of freedom until she needed to be at the university. Vittorio didn't know that, and she hadn't told him for fear he'd talk her into staying in Italy longer. He thought she was returning to classes right away.

Before meeting him in Ravenna, she'd looked forward to seeing her father and Nora again. Ginger had other friends she and Bruce had been close to, like Cherry and Bob. They'd talked about spending time at the beach in Balboa when she got back. In fact they'd tentatively planned taking a trip to Mexico before fall semester. Yet the thought of going home right now brought her no joy.

With Vittorio's arm around her, they walked a while longer savoring the magic of the balmy night. Once again he pulled her close. "Why don't we agree to enjoy this time we've been granted and see what comes? By now you have to know I'd rather be with you than any other woman."

"It goes without saying I feel the same way about being with you, otherwise I wouldn't be here."

Vittorio kissed her thoroughly before releasing her. "Let's go in and pack our bags. I'd like to get an early start in the morning. After I make breakfast, we'll take off."

As they walked back to the villa, Ginger was aware her feelings for him had taken root to the very core of her being. To spend the next few days with him was so thrilling to contemplate, she knew she wouldn't be able to fall asleep for a long time.

They picked up their shoes before entering the kitchen. "Do you want coffee before we say good-night?"

"I'd better not." She purposely moved away from him. "Vittorio—if you should change your mind about us going away together, don't be afraid to tell me. After what your mother revealed about the vote, I would understand if you need to stay in Venice and concentrate on business."

His eyes smoldered a penetrating blue. "You're my only business. I thought you understood that. *Buona notte, bellissima.*"

Her legs would hardly support her as she hurried down the hall to the guest bedroom. Ginger knew he wouldn't follow her. Tonight he'd laid the ground rules and wouldn't pressure her. They would enjoy each other for a while longer and see what happened.

She took another shower and got ready for bed. One suitcase would be enough for the clothes she planned to take on vacation. After filling it with the clothes she'd need, she climbed under the covers.

The conversation with Vittorio's mother filtered through her mind. No matter how well Vittorio handled the news about the vote, he had to be appalled that Paola's father would go to those lengths to get what he wanted.

Gambling was a great evil in Ginger's eyes. Vittorio was up against something so ugly, she could hardly bear it. But there was one thing she knew above all else. He could handle anything. There wasn't a man in the world to match him.

CHAPTER EIGHT

VITTORIO HAD CALLED AHEAD. The black four-door Mercedes sedan stood waiting for him and Ginger at the garage on the artificial island of Tronchetto. Two of the servicemen managing the pickup area were so besotted with her looks, they didn't hear a word Vittorio said.

He couldn't blame them. She'd dressed in pleated white pants with a stunning lilac-colored button-down blouse tucked in at the waist.

While they chatted with her, he stowed the bags in the trunk and helped her in the front passenger seat. Once behind the wheel, he turned to her. "I hope you realize you've made their morning."

She laughed off his comment. "In case you didn't notice, the female cashier was all smiles and couldn't take her eyes off you."

"Donetta and I have known each other several years now."

"A former girlfriend? She's cute."

"Her husband thinks so, too."

But no one had looks like Ginger's. He turned on the engine and drove out of the garage, heading for the A4 autostrada.

"Where are we going?"

"To one of the country's most unique wine regions. Before long you'll start to notice small vineyards planted on the steep slopes. It's where they make prosecco. I think you'll find the area charming."

"I have news for you, Vittorio. There are no uncharming places in Italy."

He burst into laughter. Now that he was with this fantastic woman, he'd already thrown off his cares. "That's a quote worth publicizing. We're going to follow the Prosecco Road between Conegliano and Valdobbiadene. The hills are filled with renovated farmhouses and villas. We'll stop to sample some of the wines."

"It's a good thing you made us that delicious, filling breakfast. Now I know why you urged me to eat more bread. I'll have you know I rarely drink, especially not in the morning."

Her comments brought out another chuckle. "Don't worry. A sip here and there won't do any damage."

"I guess we're going to find out." Her wry tone amused Vittorio to no end. Being with Ginger brought him a degree of happiness he'd never known before. They continued winding into the countryside.

"These roads are so thin, they're like spaghetti. Oh, look at that darling farmhouse on the hillside! Can we stop there?"

"Of course."

Vittorio slowed down and parked the car. There was quite a crowd as they went inside. Once they were served, Vittorio watched her eyes as she sampled the sparkling wine. They lit up on cue. "Mmm. What is that amazing taste?"

Vittorio took a swallow out of his own glass. "The citrus flavor really comes through."

"That's it."

They drank a little more, then left to go out to the car. Once they were on the road again, he leveled her a glance. "I've got a treat for you." He took a turnoff that wound up another hillside.

"All of this is new to me."

"That's good. I remember your telling me that one of your favorite poems of Lord Byron's was called *Cain*."

"I marvel at your remarkable memory."

"I couldn't forget anything about you," he muttered. "We're headed for the tenth-century church of San Pietro di Feletto. There's a remarkable fresco of the Sacrifice of Cain and Abel that I know will appeal to you."

"Ooh—I can't wait to see it. I think every old-world artist or sculptor has tried to portray them."

"I know you haven't been to France, but I recall seeing a sculpture of Cain in the Tuileries Gardens. He's a tragic figure."

"His life was tragic. Byron was obsessed."

Vittorio kept following the road up to the top, where they came to the church. He parked the car and helped Ginger to get out. Before they entered, they walked beneath the fascinating medieval portal displaying five frescoes. Ginger saw one of Cain and Abel right away and took some pictures.

For the rest of the day they traveled through the different villages, ate lunch in a vineyard, sampled a little more wine and ended up at the Hotel Villa del Poggio for dinner on the terrace.

"What a fabulous view. The vines stretch as far as the eye can see. If I hadn't come with you, I would have missed all this. I'm a very lucky woman."

Vittorio eyed her covertly. "I've never enjoyed a day more, but I think you sound a little tired. We did a lot of walking today. I booked two rooms here. They overlook the valley below. Whenever you're ready, we'll go up."

"But it's a good kind of tired, don't you think?" Ginger's eyes smiled. "What fabulous sights are you going to show me tomorrow?"

"I don't think I can top the fresco we looked at today, but tomorrow we'll drive to Valdobbiadene for breakfast and enjoy another sampling of a superb vintage prosecco. From there I have a surprise."

"Now I won't be able to go to sleep."

Vittorio hadn't slept since he'd met her. She had no idea his condition was growing more serious the longer they were together without his being able to make love to her throughout the night.

They went up to their rooms. He opened her door, but didn't go in or he would never have come out again. "Let's program our phone numbers into our cells. Then I can call you in the morning."

"I meant to bring that up at dinner." She pulled the phone out of her purse and put in his number. He did the same thing.

"I'll see you in the morning, *bellissima*." After kissing her cheek, he walked down the hall to his room. She waved good-night to him from her doorway before disappearing inside.

He got ready for bed and walked out on the terrace off the bedroom in his robe. Her room had a terrace, too, but she hadn't gone out there. The situation couldn't go on like this much longer...

But the woman in the next room still clung to memories of her husband who'd died. Even if Vittorio could convince her to stay in Italy longer, would she ever be able to put the past away? Vittorio wouldn't be able to handle anything less.

Vittorio remembered what his mother had said last evening while they'd talked about Paola. "The kind of passionate love you're speaking of can grow with time."

No it couldn't. Not when he was on fire for Ginger.

If she didn't know her own mind soon, then he wanted her to leave for California. He'd put her on the plane himself and pray for forgetfulness.

Ginger put on a nightgown and got in bed, but there'd be little sleep tonight. All day they'd gone through the motions of loving being on vacation together and enjoying each other's company. Of course she'd adored every moment of it. But they hadn't acted normally, not the way they'd done that first day at the villa when he'd started kissing her. Today had been Ginger's fault.

Everything up to that time had felt real, but last night on the beach she'd ruined everything by pulling away from him. He'd gotten the message, assuming Bruce was still the reason. She'd let him go on believing it, but she'd been wrong to have done that.

At some point in the last few months she'd put her husband away along with the memories. Otherwise there'd be no way to explain why she'd fallen so hard for Vittorio. Tonight she couldn't lie to herself any longer and had paid the price.

When Ginger had first met Vittorio on the ship, she'd questioned how it could have happened so fast. But tonight she had few reservations. That trip to his office had been a test to surprise him and judge his feelings for her. She'd wanted to find out just how deeply they ran inside him.

After learning that he'd called the airport to find out when she was leaving and stop her, joy had almost given her a heart attack. But at thirty-one years of age, Vittorio still hadn't married even though he'd told her he'd had several meaningful relationships with other women.

Today she'd continued to keep her physical distance from him because she didn't want to be like one of those other women who hadn't been able to hold him.

Tonight she could have cried out in pain when he'd kissed her good-night like he might have done his sister. Her fear that she didn't mean everything to him at this point was one of the few things torturing her now. She hadn't wanted him to realize how terribly she ached for him. But that had been her mistake.

Tomorrow she wouldn't hold back from letting him know what he meant to her. Instead she would act naturally, the way she'd done when he'd driven her from the monastery to the hotel. That day had changed her life. She'd never be the same again. Vittorio just didn't know it yet.

Her cell rang at eight the next morning. She grabbed for it. When she saw the caller ID, her pulse raced out of control. "Vittorio—"

"*Buongiorno*, signora. Did you get any sleep?"

"Not much, signor. I'm too excited for today's surprise."

"That's nice to hear. I'll meet you in the lobby in ten minutes and we'll get going."

"I'll be right down."

After hanging up, she pulled on a pair of designer jeans and a light blue crewneck cotton top. They would probably be walking a lot. Once she'd brushed her hair and put on her makeup, she carried her bag downstairs.

Her heart turned over to see Vittorio waiting for her in the foyer. His eyes traveled over her with a thoroughness that brought heat to her face. But she was just as busy studying him.

He wore jeans that molded his powerful thighs and an off-white sport shirt unbuttoned at the neck. Only an Italian could look that good. He didn't know he was the world's most desirable male no matter how he was dressed.

He took her suitcase and carried both their bags out to the car in the parking area. Once ensconced, he turned to her. "We're going to be taking a helicopter ride after breakfast. Are you comfortable with that?"

"I've taken a few over the years. It's a different sensation, but exciting. I don't mind, if that's what you're asking."

Vittorio appeared relieved by her answer. "That's all I needed to hear."

"Are we going to view the vineyards from the air?"

"We're going to see a lot of things."

Their drive to Valdobbiadene took only a few minutes. He found a trattoria that served pastries, some of them meat-filled. He ordered their best prosecco wine to accompany the meal.

"Wine for breakfast is a new experience for me."

His eyes glinted in amusement. "How do you like it?"

"Too much actually." She drained her wineglass. "That fruity flavor is addictive. It's going to be your fault if I start drinking at breakfast."

Laughter rumbled out of him before they left and drove to the small airport where their helicopter was waiting. Vittorio loaded their bags and introduced her to his pilot, Ciro, before she was seated in back and strapped in.

Once there was liftoff, Vittorio reached for the microphone to talk to her. "We're headed back to Venice. En route you'll see a portion of Veneto and then we'll be flying across the lagoon."

Ginger's eyes were peeled as the helicopter flew them over the most amazing mosaic of Veneto vineyards to the water. "What a fantastic sight!" she cried. "Everyone should be so lucky to have an eagle's-eye view of your world."

"You like it?" the pilot asked with a big smile in passable English.

"*Like* isn't the right word," she answered back. "It's all so beautiful, my heart hurts."

"Signora Lawrence was born with a poetic soul," Vittorio interjected.

"Ah," came Ciro's response.

By now she could look down at the waterways and currents that led to the different islands away from Venice itself. Until you saw it from the air, you couldn't appreciate the remarkable symbiosis of water to land the way the Venetians had managed it over the centuries. The whole indescribable scene had left her speechless.

They passed over Lido island. In the distance she saw several sparsely inhabited islands totally unlike Murano or Burano. Before long another one came into view that had only two structures.

"Vittorio? What's that island coming up on our left, the one with the vineyards covering it? How amazing to see them surrounded by all this water as if it sprang up like magic! It's utterly beautiful!"

"This island is unique in this part of the Adriatic. There's not another one to compare to it.

"Do you want to take a closer look?"

"That's another question you already know the answer to."

They smiled at each other before he said something to the pilot and they began to descend. He circled it to give her a good look, but instead of flying on, he descended and landed them on an uncultivated piece of ground near a small house.

Vittorio unstrapped himself and turned to her. "Let's go exploring."

"But isn't this private property?"

"It is, but I have special permission to land." He helped her climb out.

Before she knew it, he'd unloaded their suitcases and a covered basket she hadn't noticed in the rear. He turned to Ciro. "See you at three."

The pilot's eyes twinkled. He said something in Italian, then smiled at her. "Enjoy yourselves. I envy you."

Vittorio shut the door. She took her suitcase and

followed him toward the small bungalow. The one-story house built of sand-colored rock had a tiled roof, nothing out of the ordinary.

He unlocked the front door. "Come inside."

She entered the house. The place was empty except for a wooden table and three chairs set in front of the fireplace. Vittorio took her bag and put it with his over in one corner. The basket he set on the table.

"I asked Mimi, who manages the cafeteria at our office building, to pack us enough food and drink to last for the day. Ciro dropped by for it on his way up to the helicopter. The bathroom is down that hall. We have hot and cold running water."

"All the comforts of home. You've thought of everything. Excuse me for a minute."

Ginger found the ladies' room and freshened up. Vittorio had a distinct reason for bringing her here. She was dying to know what it was. On her way back to the living room, she passed a bedroom on each side of the hallway. The house was probably a hundred years old. She wondered how long it had been standing vacant and why he wanted her to see it.

When she returned, she found him in the tiny kitchen putting away some of the perishable items from the basket into the fridge.

"You've piqued my curiosity, Vittorio. Why did you bring us here?"

"In truth I'd like your opinion of this place. What you think is important to me. Come on. I'll take you on a tour."

They left through a door leading from the back of the kitchen. Once outside they passed more uncultivated ground until they came to the vineyard.

"These vines are tall and in full flower, just like the ones at La Floraison in Switzerland. The fragrance is intoxicating."

"This is the perfect time of year to bring you here." Vittorio reached for her hand, and they walked the length of the property under a full sun. His touch sent sparks of desire through her body. If she didn't know differently, she'd think she was in a dream. To go through life with him like this would be all she could ever ask of it.

While she hoped he was feeling the same way, a couple of big bees zoomed right at her. She cried out and pressed herself against his side. He laughed and caught her around the waist. As he held her tightly, they continued to walk through the rest of the vine-yard.

Every so often she spotted a small storage shed. "This place is so well tended. Who does the work? I don't see anyone."

"A family of six living in that two-story building we're coming to. No doubt they're eating right now."

The walls were a dull yellow and an uninspiring washed-out red. Everything appeared dilapidated, but she kept her thoughts to herself. "It looks like it could house quite a few people."

"In the past, six families have lived there. At one time it held twenty-four people. Now it's down to one family."

"Why is that?"

"The latest owner of the island decided the vine-yard wasn't worth the investment and has put it up for sale. He's been keeping on a skeletal staff until some-one buys it. Over the centuries there have been many owners. Because it has its own deep, private harbor, it has been used for everything under the sun."

They walked on until he showed her where two small boats were moored. "This place could hold a dozen more."

"I get it. You're talking illegal things going on, like hiding pirates' plunder."

"What else?" He grinned and kissed her cheek. Vittorio was still treating her like he would Maria. "In our teens, Gaspare and I used to come over here all the time from the villa after our parents went to bed. We would row the old fishing boat out into the lagoon before turning on the outboard motor.

"We thought they never knew about our nightly escapades until one night when Papà asked us if he could go with us. But Mamma must never know."

Laughter burst out of Ginger. "I wish I could have met your father."

"So do I," he whispered on a husky note. "My brother and I imagined the things we would do if the island fell into our hands." His blue eyes shone as he talked about the past.

"You and Gaspare really did share an amazing life."

He looked down at her. "When he told me he was going to become a monk, it meant separation from the family. We all had to get used to it. Although I ran with good friends, no one was like him. We all miss him."

"Of course."

"About six months ago I learned that the owner of the island was putting it on the market. From that moment on I've been making inquiries and eventually met with him."

Ginger wondered where this conversation was going.

"After looking into it, I put an option on the property. But after my father died, I've needed more time to think about it. The owner has given me until mid-July to buy it, or my option will expire."

"That's not very far away."

"There's only one more thing I have to do before I make the final decision. I was hoping to enlist your help."

She blinked. "What do you mean?"

"Let's go back to the house for lunch and I'll tell you everything."

Vittorio slid his arm around her waist and they retraced their steps. The feel of their bodies touching each other turned her legs to jelly. If there'd been a bed inside the house, she would have pulled him down with her and begged him to kiss her all day long.

Once they entered the house, Vittorio washed his hands and got their food out of the fridge; ham sandwiches, pasta salad, fruit and pastries. Anything to keep busy before he pulled Ginger down on the floor with him and started to devour her. So much for the ground rules he'd set!

Mimi had done a good job of selecting their picnic food, including two bottles of water. When Ginger came back from the restroom, he excused himself. After his return they began eating.

"Mmm. I didn't realize how hungry I was. This all tastes delicious."

Vittorio agreed. After consuming three sandwiches, he sat back in the hard chair and eyed her intently. "Would you be willing to go to the monastery with me after we leave?"

"That's the help you want?"

"Yes. I need you to talk to my brother without his knowing I'm there."

"What?"

He took a deep breath. "I have private business with the abbot."

"Naturally I'll do it, but why?"

"I can't make a decision about the island until the abbot tells me what I need to know. I realize I'm sounding cryptic. The truth is, months ago I told him I would buy the island so I could donate it to the monks. The funds are my own, not the company's. Once the renovations are done, they could move in and be very comfortable.

"More than once Gaspare has told me how the brothers long to do work in the fields to offset their academic studies. Some could use this as a summer retreat, and they could trade off living at the monastery. The profits from the vineyard would help contribute to the expenses.

"When Gaspare went to live there, my father set up a perpetual fund to help keep the monastery going. Now I want to do my part. Do you think it's a good idea? I'd like your honest opinion."

Tears welled in her eyes and dripped down her cheeks. "I think it's the most amazing, generous, unselfish gift I ever heard of in my whole life."

"Not unselfish, Ginger, because I know how much Gaspare loved this island. He'd be so happy here working in the vineyard and studying in a place where we had such a wonderful time years ago.

"If the deal goes through, I'm going to have this house gutted and build another housing unit for the monks. My dream is to turn this end of the island into a garden. I know it would please Gaspare. Nothing would mean more to me than to make him happy."

He heard her soft gasp. "What a wonderful brother you are!"

Vittorio reached for her hand and kissed the palm. "Not wonderful, and don't forget the abbot has to obtain permission from the church. I'm not sure it has been granted. Today I'll find out how much progress he's made."

"Oh, Vittorio—does Gaspare know anything?" she cried.

"Nothing."

In the next breath she got out of the chair and walked over to him, throwing her arms around his neck. She pressed her wet cheek against his. "You marvelous, amazing man. I can't imagine the church turning you down. But if they do…"

"I don't want to think that way. If he's here or at the monastery, he'll be close to our family."

"It's close to your work, too."

"But I'm planning to resign, so it won't be my work much longer. The business I started will always keep me busy and financially secure. I don't need to be joined to the company any longer. In fact the idea of being on my own holds more and more appeal for me."

"You're incredible," Ginger whispered. Vittorio felt her warmth infuse him. Unable to hold back, he pulled her onto his lap and began kissing her. This time she kissed him back hungrily, withholding nothing. Her approbation meant the world to him. But there was a lot more he wanted from her.

"What will you tell my brother is the reason you've come back?" Vittorio asked some time later after kissing her senseless.

"I'll think of something. Don't worry. I won't let you down." As she covered his features with kisses, they heard the sound of the helicopter landing. The timing couldn't be worse. There weren't enough hours in the day or night for Vittorio to do what he wanted with her.

Ginger extricated herself from his arms on a moan and helped him pack up the basket. He grabbed their suitcases. At the doorway, he put them down and reached to kiss her again. She clung to him as if the pain of letting him go was killing her, too.

Somehow they made it to the helicopter, but they were both breathless. After helping her climb in, he noticed she avoided Ciro's glance.

"We're ready to be taken to the villa," he told the pilot. No one spoke during the short flight to Lido island. Not only was Vittorio on fire for her, he was anxious to hear what the abbot had to tell him.

Ginger thanked the pilot before getting out of the helicopter with her suitcase.

"*Grazie*, Ciro." Vittorio waved him off and took his things to the back door of the villa. Once inside, they put everything down in the foyer. He shot her a penetrating glance.

"Come here to me one more time, Ginger, then we'll leave for San Lazzaro."

She ran into his arms without hesitation. Maybe the miracle was finally happening. He felt she was finally with him, really with him.

CHAPTER NINE

AFTER A QUICK SHOWER, Ginger changed into her print blouse and navy skirt. Once they left for the island, Vittorio had outlined his plan. He would use a side door of the monastery to the abbot's private office while she entered the normal way.

He kissed her as if it were their last before helping her out of the boat. "I'll be in your debt forever for doing this for me."

"I'm excited to be a part of something so incredible. Now go on. Depending on what happens, I'll come back to the boat and wait for you no matter how long it takes. Bless you," she murmured.

He squeezed her arm before striding toward the building ahead of him. Vittorio had no idea he was taking her heart with him.

"Okay, Ginger. You can do this."

She followed a group of people who'd just gotten off a *vaporetto* and made her way to the Lord Byron studio. She'd never thought to be here again. So much had happened since last time, she didn't recognize herself.

The second she stepped inside the room, she trembled. There were three monks on hand helping visitors, one of them Father Giovanni. Thank heaven he was in here and hadn't seen Vittorio!

He might be a priest who'd decided to devote his life to God here, but he was Vittorio's beloved brother. She hung back to wait until he was free. In her mind's eye she saw the two Della Scalla teens sneaking away from the villa at night to head for the abandoned island.

After twenty minutes, the people Father Giovanni was talking to left the room. When he turned, he saw Ginger. She smiled and walked toward him.

"Father Giovanni—you thought you'd gotten rid of me."

"I'm very happy to see you again. I hope the information you gleaned here helped you with your work."

Ginger nodded. "That's why I'm back. I had a chance to be in Venice again and wanted to get your opinion on another aspect of Byron to add to the information I've sent to Magda Collier. Not so much about his writings as his interests."

"I'll be happy to help if I can."

"Do you have time now, or are you expecting another group?"

"I'm at your disposal."

"Thank you." Knowing what Vittorio was doing somewhere else in the monastery, she needed to concentrate and tamp down her excitement. "Stories of Byron's swimming and horseback riding exploits abound, including the trip on horseback he and his friend took to the Levant.

"In academic circles there's been an attempt recently to discuss the Levant in terms of political analysis and include it as another acceptable topic besides archaeology or literature. Do you think Byron went there purely to explore? Or do you suppose he had political motives?"

Gaspare cocked his head. "You raise a fascinating question, one I haven't given any depth of thought to. Through his writings, we know of Byron's desire to throw off the oppressor wherever his travels took him. I can only offer you my humble opinion without any proof."

"Please. I want to hear what you think. That's proof enough for me."

"You're very kind. Come. Let's look at this map over here." Just then he sounded exactly like Vittorio.

Ginger followed him.

"By 1947, the Levant meant the dozens of Mediterranean lands east of Italy. During his sojourn here, Byron—without the knowledge we have today— would no doubt have seen the whole area as the historical region of Syria with all its attendant struggles over the centuries. In answer to your question, I do believe his interest was political in nature."

She let out a sigh. "That's all I wanted to know. I happen to agree with you. He was always concerned with man's struggle. This is the angle I want the writers of the script on the film of Lord Byron to bring out."

He nodded. "I admire the producer who wants to show him in the light of a spiritual human being."

"So do I, Father Giovanni. He was a genius, and he had a side to him the world needs to know more about. I'll always be thankful my friends and I were chosen for this project.

"My life has changed since coming to Italy. Meeting you has been a privilege. I know God watches over you."

So does your brother. If you only knew what he's trying to do right now. I love that man with every fiber of my being.

"I'll go now." She could hear her voice shaking. "Other people are waiting to hear from the expert."

His eyes smiled. "Bless you in all your endeavors, signora."

"Thank you."

Another group of people were waiting for help. That meant he'd be occupied for a while longer. Relieved that Vittorio had escaped detection this far, Ginger left the monastery and walked out to the boat. No sign of him yet.

While she marked time, she texted her father to let him know she was still enjoying her vacation. They'd talk soon. She sent three more to Cherry, Zoe and Abby, telling them all was well.

If Abby was still on her honeymoon, then a text wouldn't disturb her. Ginger knew Raoul was her whole world. Before long they'd talk on the phone and catch up.

Another half hour went by before Vittorio appeared. His expression was so fierce, it caused her spirits to sink. He undid the rope and jumped in the boat, obviously anxious to get away before his brother knew he'd come.

"Sorry I was so long, Ginger."

"Please don't worry about me."

He turned on the engine, and they backed out at a wakeless speed. She knew better than to ask him questions right now. After he opened it up, they took off for the villa, passing a lot of other watercraft.

In the mood he was in, Ginger was glad they didn't have far to go. When they pulled up in back, he shut off the motor.

After turning to her, he grasped her hand. "Forgive me."

"You think I don't understand you received bad news?"

Vittorio studied her features. "How did it go with my brother? Could you even find him?"

"He was in the Byron studio talking to some people. I waited until he was free and we talked. It went very well. In fact I'm going to pass on what he told me and hope the information gets written into the script."

"At least *that* part of our visit was worthwhile."

"What went wrong, Vittorio? Can you tell me?"

"The abbot was away on church business. I was told I could wait because he was expected back. But it became clear I might have to stay there all night. I couldn't risk Gaspare seeing me, or making you sit out in the boat for hours."

"I wouldn't have minded. You must know that."

"I don't deserve you. Come on. Let's go inside where we can relax."

Vittorio helped her out of the boat and grasped her hand once more. Once they entered the villa, he headed straight for the kitchen to make coffee for both of them. Ginger used the restroom, then came back and sank down on a chair at the table. Vittorio served them mugs of the streaming brew and a plate of biscotti he began to devour.

"Do you know your brother's schedule in the mornings?"

"They have prayer and study before going about their duties."

"Then why don't you go over there early and slip in that side door. If he happens to see you, then you can pretend you were planning to visit him and he'll never know the truth."

A faint smile broke the corners of Vittorio's mouth. She was happy to see it. "You make it sound so simple, it just might work."

"I know it will, but it's *you* who needs to relax. If you'll let me, I'll fix us fritattas for dinner Costa Mesa style."

He jumped up from the table. "I'm going to take you up on that. I'll be back in ten minutes to help."

She watched him disappear and got busy cooking her favorite omelet recipe. Along with salad and bread, they would have a feast.

Ginger expected to see him in a better mood when he came back to the kitchen showered and cleanshaven. Instead he wore a disturbing scowl.

Their gazes locked. "What's wrong, Vittorio?"

He threw back his dark head. "I just got a text from my sister. She's arriving any minute in the helicopter from my office with bad news. No doubt Ciro told her I was here. Evidently Mamma gave her permission for my pilot to bring her here."

"It must be of critical importance, probably something else Paola's father has done that you need to know about."

"I have no idea."

"You're hungry and I've got dinner ready. Let's eat

until she gets here." If his sister was coming, Ginger knew this had to do with her friend Paola.

They both sat down to the meal she'd prepared. He seemed to love it and ate every morsel. After a second cup of coffee, he sat back. "I needed that. You're one terrific cook," he said before they both heard the helicopter landing.

"Since she's here, I'll go in the bedroom to give you your privacy."

He shook his head. "We'll let her in and talk together."

"You're sure?"

"Haven't you figured out I want you with me all the time?" His voice throbbed with emotion. Nothing he could have said would have thrilled her more.

She followed him to the back entrance. He turned on the lights and opened the door. When Maria appeared, he kissed her cheek. "I take it this visit is serious."

"It is. I'm sorry to barge in on you like this, but I knew it couldn't wait. Mamma agrees."

"Then come in the living room with me and Ginger and tell us what's going on."

Maria didn't look that happy about Ginger's joining them, but Vittorio had left her no choice. When they reached the other room, he drew Ginger down on the couch with him. Maria couldn't hide her surprise before she sat on a chair opposite them.

"Vittorio?" She looked horribly uncomfortable. "This is about... Paola."

"Who else?" he came right back. "You can speak freely."

"I don't know if I can. Not in front of Signora Lawrence."

"Her name is Ginger. We have no secrets."

"This isn't for her ears."

"Then you've wasted a trip here, Maria."

"All right!" She jumped up from the chair. "Tonight you and Signora Lawrence were featured on the six o'clock news! The paparazzi took pictures of your trip to Veneto yesterday and today. It showed you entering a church and walking in a vineyard as well as climbing in and out of the helicopter.

"Dario told me his father is furious because you haven't asked Paola to marry you yet, so he's taking matters into his own hands. I'm frightened for you, Vittorio. You *have* to marry Paola!" she blurted. "Or he'll ruin your life!"

"He can do his worst, but it's no use. Mamma has already had this argument with me."

"But Paola has always loved you. Since she can't walk the same way as before, her life has changed. Even if you don't love her, you owe it to her."

Ginger felt his body tauten.

"I *owe* her? Did I just hear you correctly?"

"I'm not the one who's saying it," came the quiet response.

"It was an accident, Maria!"

She averted her eyes. "I know. In fact I'm the one who begged you to take her skiing one more time. But Paola's father blames you for not being able to prevent it."

Ginger was aghast.

"Do *you* blame me, too?" Vittorio challenged her.

"No—b-but if you don't marry her," she stammered, "then—"

"Then what?" he demanded.

"He's bringing a lawsuit against you."

At this point Vittorio got to his feet. "Renaldo plans to sue me? How do you know this?"

"Dario told me."

"When?"

"The day before yesterday on the way back from the villa in the cabin cruiser. After we'd walked in the kitchen and saw you with Signora Lawrence, it hurt Paola so terribly she ran out to the boat and went below sobbing.

"Later Dario said that their father was furious. When I told Mamma, she admitted that Renaldo fixed the vote so you would become the CEO. She's afraid you'll leave the company. It's bad enough that he's planted fake news on TV, but what if he turns on you for not doing what he wants?"

"I'm not worried about that."

"But Vittorio—Dario said his father is so angry with you, he has threatened to ruin you if you don't propose soon."

"Renaldo doesn't know what real anger is." Vittorio hissed the words. "For the man to be this desperate for his daughter to marry me means he's in deep financial trouble. Does our mother know about this latest threat?"

"Yes, because I told her. Dario says you need to be prepared to be served with a warrant soon, forcing you to appear in court."

"Don't let this alarm you, Maria. I'll take care of it in my own way. I'm glad you came to tell me." He hugged his sister. "Come on. I'll walk you back to the helicopter. When you get home, you tell Mamma to stop agonizing over this."

Maria gave Ginger a sheepish glance. "I'm sorry to have intruded."

"You did the right thing."

Ginger was thankful his sister had warned Vittorio. Now she'd been warned, too. While they were gone, she went back to the kitchen to wash the dishes, knowing what she had to do.

Five minutes went by before Vittorio joined her. She heard the helicopter lift off. Their eyes met. Unspoken messages passed between them.

"Do you think Paola knows what her father has been doing?"

He nodded. "Just now Maria confided that Paola found out through her own mother what Renaldo has planned to force my hand. She had to tell Paola because she and Dario will be summoned in court as witnesses. He's planning to turn the accident into a scandal, hoping I'll cave. Paola is ashamed and embarrassed."

"That poor girl."

"I don't believe Renaldo has a prayer of a chance taking me to court. His case doesn't hold water. It's too frivolous, but if he coerced the members of the board into voting the way he wanted in return for certain favors—and it can be proved—then that *is* something that needs to be addressed."

"What are you going to do?"

"Hire an attorney."

With those words the bell tolled for Ginger, bringing her excruciating pain. A lawsuit meant weeks of pressure for Vittorio, who didn't need any extra complications. She'd wondered how long her happiness with him would last. Now she knew. Their idyll was over. It had to be!

She struggled to keep her voice steady. "Do you know someone who can take on her father? Didn't you say he's the lawyer for your company?"

"He's a corporate attorney and was my father's choice, not mine. I need a criminal attorney, someone I trust implicitly. I know the one I want and may be on the phone half the night if I reach him."

"Why don't you try now. I'll make us some fresh coffee." Already her mind was forming her own plans for tomorrow—ones that would take her away from him.

An hour later Vittorio had contacted Casimiro Melchiorri in Rome, probably the most renowned criminal attorney in Italy. The man had been a good friend of Vittorio's father and had come to the funeral. Vittorio gave him the facts as he knew them.

After hanging up, he got to his feet and found Ginger in the kitchen.

She eyed him anxiously. "You were on the phone a long time. I couldn't follow your Italian. Tell me what he said."

"Casimiro is interested in Renaldo's gambling problems and the fixed vote at the board. As for Renaldo trying to prove negligence on my part while we were out water skiing, he scoffed at the idea.

"But in order to be prepared for anything, he'll obtain a judge's warrant for me to go to the water ambu-

lance office as well as the hospital to get full copies
of the paperwork on Paola.

"He'll come to the palazzo tomorrow at three and
wants Maria there so he can take her deposition. There
won't be any meetings at the shipping office. He needs
as much information as possible when we meet to
talk business. Depositions from the board members
will follow."

"Thank heaven he's taking the case."

He nodded. "Only Casimiro's friendship with my
father over the years could have made this possible
on such short notice."

"You must be so relieved."

He pulled her against him. "This isn't the way our
vacation was supposed to turn out."

"So far I've enjoyed every second of it, Vittorio."
I adore you and love you desperately. "But now that
you've retained this attorney, you've got to get busy
fighting for your life. It means my vacation has come
to an end. I can't stay in Italy any longer."

Ginger heard his sharp intake of breath. Vittorio
shook her, not ungently. "You're not going anywhere!"

Ginger eased out of his arms. "I have to leave so
you can concentrate. Do you remember what you said
to me a few nights ago on this beach? 'Why don't we
agree to enjoy this time we've been granted and see
what comes?'"

Frustration and pain had turned his eyes a slate
blue. "You knew damn well what I really meant!"

"But you didn't see anything this ugly coming."

That was true. Renaldo had revived the original
story in the press about Vittorio's behavior as a young
man, and had now made him out to be a billionaire

playboy. The idea that this could affect Ginger was killing him.

"Your life as Count Vittorio Della Scalla is being ripped apart by an unscrupulous, flawed enemy who is tearing his own family apart and threatening yours.

"Because of your position as CEO of one of Italy's economic mainstays, you're not only dealing with a horrendous situation, you're still in negotiations with the abbot that could affect your plans for the island. You can't afford to spend time with me that will create scandal and grief for you while your whole world is going up in smoke!"

A long silence ensued. "I thought you wanted to be with me," his deep voice grated.

"You *know* I do!"

"But I've been rushing you."

"No you haven't." A tremor shook her body. "I hope you're listening now. Bruce will always have a place in my heart, but my reason for leaving has nothing to do with my memories of him."

"Then prove it and stay with me!"

"Vittorio—don't you realize how this looks? By now Paola's father has to know about you and me. He'll use it to twist our relationship into something tawdry. I can imagine the headlines he's planning everyone to see. *CEO of Della Scalla Shipping Lines keeps opportunistic American widow in hiding in his luxury villa on the Lido di Venezia, where he caused the tragic accident of his would-be wife, Paola Coronna, last year.*"

Vittorio's face looked like thunder. "Those won't be the headlines, Ginger. Casimiro and I talked things over. It doesn't matter if Paola's father has already sent his spies out here to the villa—knowing we've been here—I've decided you should go back to the hotel and stay where you've been comfortable doing your research on Byron."

"You really think that's a good idea?"

"Yes. The front desk knows you went to Burano and the monastery because they helped make the arrangements for you. Your business in Venice has had nothing to do with me. Renaldo may want to bring me down, but any paparazzi working for him won't know where to look for you in order to connect us further."

"But Vittorio—"

"No *buts*. I want you with me right now while I see this thing through."

Vittorio knew he was in love. He wanted her in his life forever. After all these years, it had finally happened. "How long can you extend your vacation? We need more time together, Ginger."

Ginger wanted that, too, but there was a problem with his plan. "If I stay a little longer, I don't dare check in to that hotel."

"Why?"

A hand went to her throat. "Because of something that happened while I was checking out."

"Tell me," he demanded.

"I didn't plan to tell you about it, but under the circumstances, I have to. The concierge kept smiling at me and said all the staff were excited because they'd seen Count Della Scalla coming and going with me quite a few times. The truth is, you're too famous for me to be seen with you in public. He told me I was very fortunate to have such a renowned escort showing me around Venice."

"Diavolo!"

Ginger smiled. "I've been the luckiest woman I know."

A strange sound escaped his lips. "When we've got all night without worries, I plan to tell you just exactly how I feel about you. Sadly for now we'll have to keep you out of sight. Since that hotel is off-limits, we'll get you installed at the Colombina Hotel near the Rialto Bridge.

"It's only a few minutes away from the palazzo. Tomorrow I'll drop you at a water taxi stop. From there you can take one to the hotel with your luggage. It will work."

"In that case I have another idea, too! I'll sign in as Ginger Montague."

His dark brows lifted. "Montague? Though I've spent time with you, this is the first I've heard it."

"There's so much we haven't talked about yet. My father's name is Wallace Montague. Everyone calls him Wally."

"You love him, don't you? I can see it in your eyes."

"I'm crazy about him. It's no different from the way you felt about your father. I'm thinking that when they check my passport, they'll see Ginger Montague Lawrence, but I'll sign in as Signora Montague.

"If they say anything, I'll tell them my husband died and I'm going by my maiden name. When some photojournalist is snooping around for Paola's father, he won't recognize it."

"I like the way you think." In the next instant Vittorio drew Ginger into his arms. His hunger for her was too great. He couldn't stop kissing her, but he had to so she could breathe.

"I know I can get through anything if you're with me. Much as I want to devour you for weeks on end, I have to get this problem of mine out of the way first. I'm afraid I'm going to be up for a while longer compiling some information for Casimiro on my computer. As you can see, if you stay in here with me, I won't get anything done."

"I've gotten the hint and am going to bed." Ginger rose up on tiptoe and kissed him passionately before leaving the kitchen. She paused at the doorway. "Are you going back to the monastery tomorrow?"

He nodded. "Even if the paparazzi follow us. We'll go first thing in the morning."

"I'll pray it's good news."

"It may be too much to ask."

"I don't believe that."

"I'll hold that thought. No matter what, after our visit we'll do several errands and have lunch. Then I'll drop you off so you can settle in at the Colombina. Depending on when my meeting with Casimiro is over at the palazzo, you and I will enjoy a night of dinner and dancing at a quiet place along the coast."

"Mmm. That sounds like heaven."

CHAPTER TEN

VITTORIO PASSED FATHER LUCA on his way to the abbot's office. That was too bad. The other monk would tell Gaspare. That meant Vittorio would have to seek out his brother after meeting with the abbot, but it couldn't be helped.

He knocked on the door and was told to go in.

The abbot, a kind man in his seventies, sat behind his desk. "Vittorio. Come in and sit down."

"Thank you."

"I'm sorry you waited in vain for me yesterday. I was held up."

"Please don't apologize. I know how busy you are."

He let out a little laugh. "Yes. Busy on Della Scalla business."

Vittorio held his breath, fearing a negative outcome. "Do you have news, Father?"

The older man nodded. "We recognize that the love you have for your brother is rare and commendable. The gift of the housing and vineyard would be a great blessing to our congregation."

Those words were gratifying, yet Vittorio heard the *would* in his comment. He knew why, and it prompted him to speak. "Father? I recognize that this is a self-ish desire on my part to stay close to my brother."

A beaming smile broke out on the abbot's face. "On the contrary. If we have any reservations, it's because your offering is so generous. We're all very touched you would spend so much of your own money when it's of no benefit to you."

"That's not true. It would mean the world to me to know it would help the congregation of which my brother is an integral part."

He sat forward. "In that case the congregation accepts your generous offer with all our hearts."

"Nothing could make me happier, Father." It was the truth. His brother would love it on the island where the two of them had spent so many wonderful hours. Gaspare had found his life many years ago, but this would bring him so much joy.

And now, Vittorio, too, had found his life. Ginger had everything to do with the dramatic change in him.

"I'll make sure the renovations on both buildings are started right away. By September the island will be ready for occupation. We'll keep in touch. As a final favor, I would appreciate it if you don't tell my brother."

"Something tells me he'll know one day. But be assured my lips are sealed. Bless you for your good-ness, my son. We won't put up a plaque in honor of you that says 'A friend of the Armenian people.' But be assured it will be there in our hearts."

Vittorio's throat swelled so he couldn't talk. Anxious to find Gaspare, he left the abbot's office and made his way to the museum. Not seeing him there, he headed for Byron's studio. When that produced no results, he went outside to the garden.

His brother sat on the bench reading. No doubt he was waiting for a tour group. Vittorio approached him. "Gaspare?"

He put the book down and got to his feet. "I heard you were here."

"I was looking for you."

Gaspare studied him for a minute. "There's something different about you this morning."

"You think?"

"I know. It's finally happened."

His pulse picked up speed. "What do you mean?"

"You've met the woman you're going to marry. What pleases me is that I've met and talked with Signora Lawrence. I've seen into her soul and totally approve of her. Lord Byron could have written 'She Walks in Beauty' with her in mind. You're a very lucky man."

"Except that I haven't proposed yet."

"Why not?"

Vittorio sucked in his breath. "I couldn't bear it if she turned me down."

"Why would she do that?"

"She's still trying to recover from the death of her husband over two years ago."

His brother chuckled. "No. She has put her pain behind her. After you'd been talking with her on this bench, you didn't see her eyes or the way they followed you when you left for the boat. It was the look of a woman who'd appeared as dazed as you. No shadows, only light.

"I saw two people who'd found each other if you'd

but known it. Don't make the mistake of losing her out of fear. There's no finer man in this world than you, Vittorio. I plan to come to your wedding."

Too filled with emotions to talk, he gave his brother a fierce hug before hurrying toward the boat dock where his raison d'être was waiting. She stood up in the boat when she saw him coming. Gaspare was right. Her eyes were full of light for him.

He untied the rope and leaped in. Without giving her a chance to breathe, he leaned over and kissed her luscious mouth. She looked up at him. "It must be good news."

Vittorio felt jubilant. "The very best. By September the congregation will have a place of retreat."

"Your brother won't believe it!"

"I don't think he will. I'll be starting the renovations immediately." She sat down while he turned on the engine and they moved out into the lagoon. "Now I have the luxury of planning my own house at the same time."

"What do you mean?"

"My life is going in a new direction. I can't live at the palazzo anymore and need to find a new place to live."

"Do you know what kind of a house you want?"

He darted her a glance. "I know exactly." They headed across the water for Venice. "I'm now on the brink of making exciting changes in my life." He reached for her hand. "After we make some important stops, I'll tell you everything over lunch."

"Does your brother know about the lawsuit?"

"I haven't told him anything."

"I bet you wish he could be with you through all the trouble coming."

Vittorio shook his head. "He chose his own world a long time ago. I know that now. Besides, I have you."

"You mean you have to figure out a different place to hide me so Paola's father can't use me to destroy you."

She wasn't listening to him.

"We already have a plan, Ginger. Our next stop is the Piazzale Roma Law Court building. I'll pick up the warrants. Once I'm able to retrieve a copy of the medical reports on Paola for Casimiro, I'll grab some food at the deli and we'll eat on the boat."

Vittorio's change of mood was a mystery to Ginger. She felt positive he was pretending to be happy, but he couldn't be with a possible lawsuit facing him. Her heart ached for him.

Ginger didn't know what the future held for her or Vittorio. But more than ever she wanted to help him any way she could because she was madly in love with him.

By ten after one in the afternoon, he drove them to a spot near the Colombina Hotel. After tying up the boat, they ate the fish salad and rolls he'd bought them.

Then to Ginger's surprise Vittorio got up and pulled out a slalom ski stored in a panel on the side of the boat. He examined it carefully.

She got up and walked over to him. "What are you looking for?"

His blue gaze darted to her. "This is the ski Paola hit."

"I didn't know you kept it on board."

"I forgot all about it until Casimiro mentioned it last night. He wants to know where it came from. He'll put a private detective on it and ask the forensics lab to take a look at it."

"It would be hard to trace, Vittorio."

"That's true, but if he can find the owner, he could prove negligence for leaving it in the water, which proved to be a hazard. I remember seeing a ski boat like mine in the distance before I took Paola on her last run. But it might not have come from it."

"I agree. It could have been out in the water floating around for days. Why don't you get out the ski Paola was using and we'll compare them?"

"Good idea." He walked over to get it and placed the skis side by side. "The brands are different. I can tell the one she hit looks newer than ours."

"A good investigator could check all the water ski outlets around Venice and come up with some names of buyers."

"Maybe. But the boats in the lagoon come from a dozen Mediterranean countries. I'm not sure it would make a difference if the owner were found."

She looked up at Vittorio. "Wouldn't that person have to pay a fine?"

"Possibly, but not enough to get rid of his gambling debts."

"But the accident did affect her foot permanently."

More guilt stabbed him. "I'm so sorry you've been dragged into this, but please stop worrying. Casimiro still thinks this whole business won't be necessary, but he never leaves a stone unturned."

"I'm glad."

"*Grazie al cielo* you're on my side. Now I'm afraid it's time for you to take a water taxi to the hotel. It's not far from here. I'm sorry I can't carry your luggage for you."

With male dexterity, he picked them up to leave on the dock for her. "I'll call you as soon as I'm free and we'll make our plans. I can't wait to show you off tonight." He kissed her cheek before helping her out of the boat.

Ginger stared back at him. "Good luck today, Vittorio."

A minute later he'd untied the boat and disappeared up the Grand Canal. Vittorio had become her whole world. As she turned to hire a water taxi, two men impeded her progress.

"Smile for the camera, Signora Lawrence."

Ginger almost fainted because she realized the paparazzi had been following her and Vittorio since they'd left the villa. Paola's father was out for blood. Who knew how many pictures they'd taken?

Ginger grabbed her bags and got in the water taxi. "Take me to the airport." After sitting down, she phoned Vittorio. He answered on the third ring.

"*Bellissima?* What is it?"

"Two paparazzi have been following us since we left the villa. They walked up to me after you let me off and took pictures of me standing there."

"Don't worry about them. None of it matters."

"How can you say that? I'm sure they're following me right now. We're not deceiving anyone. It makes no sense for me to go to another hotel. I'm in a water taxi and headed for the airport. I can't stay here any longer and make your problems worse."

"Tell the man to stop at the palazzo!"

"That isn't the answer, Vittorio. I should have left for home days ago."

"Your home is here with me!"

"At the palazzo?"

"Where else? It's time my family got to know the woman I've fallen in love with. I *have*, you know."

Ginger almost dropped the phone. "You don't mean that," she half gasped.

"Because I haven't taken you to bed yet? You know the reason why."

"That's not it—we've only been aware of each other's existence for a matter of a few weeks. It's too soon!"

"My heart doesn't recognize time. I wanted all of you forever the first time I saw you. If you can deny that you didn't feel the same way, then it means my brother was wrong."

"What are you talking about?"

"This morning he told me you love me the way I love you."

She reeled. "He *said* that?"

"He's given us his blessing and plans to come to our wedding."

Ginger had started to tremble and couldn't stop. Vittorio wanted to marry her...

"Signora?" the driver called to her in a loud voice. She turned her head to look at him, surprised because they'd stopped in the middle of the Grand Canal. Beyond him Ginger saw Vittorio in his boat, waving his hands over his head, preventing them from moving forward. She almost went into cardiac arrest.

"The signor wishes you to get off the boat here. He says you can't leave. He is dying of love for you."

The man put a hand over his heart. His theatrics were hilarious.

By now a dozen different watercraft had slowed down and were watching to see what was going on. She felt her body grow hot with embarrassment. "Please take me over to that building." That's when she realized they were stopped in front of the palazzo.

He flashed her a broad smile. "*Si*, signora."

The man spoke in undecipherable Italian to Vittorio and took them over to the parking area at the base. She heard whistles. People started shouting and clapping. Vittorio followed and drew next to the taxi.

She feared her cheeks were a bright red. The two men talked some more. While Vittorio paid him some bills, she reached for her luggage and got out of the boat.

He swooped down and gripped her upper arms. "Now we've really put on a performance for Renaldo. I could not care less if the pictures are on the nightly news for weeks on end."

After giving her a kiss to die for in front of everyone watching, he picked up her bags and ushered her inside a recessed, colonnaded logia. From there they went into the spectacular entrance hall of the principal floor of the fabulous palace.

Vittorio put the suitcases down and pulled her into him. "Before we take another step, I'm waiting to hear your answer."

Both of them were out of breath. "Do you really need me to say it?"

"Don't be cruel to me, Ginger."

"Darling, the last thing I would ever want to do is hurt you. Of course I want to marry you! With every part of my being I want it. I've dreamed about being your wife until it's almost driven me mad. I was afraid I might never hear those words from you."

Vittorio's hot blue eyes fastened on her, causing her heart to leap. "That first night aboard ship when I saw you, I was just existing. When I met you, I was so aware of you, it was shocking. I thought I was dead inside, but meeting you caused sensations in me I couldn't deny, and I suddenly felt alive."

"So did I," Ginger confessed. "When I decided to come to Italy, it was to leave the pain behind. But until I met you, I felt the opportunity had been wasted on me. I was beyond feeling.

"When I think about it now, I shudder to realize that if it hadn't been for Magda Collier, I would never have ended up in Italy. That whole journey led me to you. I love you, Vittorio. I love you so much you can't imagine."

He clung to her. "We have to get married right away. Until we do, I want you to accept this." She watched him pull the signet ring off his finger and slide it on the ring finger of her left hand. "I know it's too big, but it tells everyone you're the love of my life and makes our engagement official."

"Vittorio," she whispered unsteadily. She smoothed her thumb over the garnet Della Scalla crest. "How can we plan anything when you have this lawsuit on your hands?"

"That's not going to stop us. I refuse to wait any longer to hold you in my arms all night long. Does your father know about me?"

"No, but I'm sure he suspects something has happened to me because I keep putting off going home.

I'll call him tonight. The last time we had a long conversation, he accused me of sounding excited. Little did he know I was on my way to the monastery, praying I'd find you with your brother. It was all I could think about."

He pressed his forehead against hers. "After the meeting with Casimiro, we'll call him and settle on a date. Speaking of my attorney, he's upstairs in the salon with my mother and Maria. Let's go up. I want everyone to meet my future wife."

Vittorio's future wife. What heaven those words conjured.

He put his arm around her shoulders and walked her through the palazzo. Its Renaissance style incorporated tapestries and ornaments that worked in harmony with pieces and paintings of history hiding in every nook and cranny. To think he'd grown up here...

The marble staircase led to another enclosed balcony of delicate design where Vittorio's family was seated on exquisite upholstered love seats and chairs. When they saw her with Vittorio, all three of them stood up. The silver-haired attorney was probably sixty years old.

Vittorio's arm slid to her waist. "Mamma? Maria? You've met Ginger already. Casimiro Melchiorri? May I introduce you to my fiancée, Ginger Lawrence, from Costa Mesa, California. Today she agreed to marry me."

Ginger heard a cry from his mother. Maria looked stunned.

"We plan to be married as soon as possible no matter the stage of the lawsuit. I can't live without her."

Casimiro smiled and shook her hand. "I understand

why. I'm very pleased to meet the future contessa. Congratulations to both of you."

"Thank you. I'm so thankful you're going to be Vittorio's attorney."

"It's my honor to represent the son of Mario Della Scalla. Our friendship goes back a long way."

Vittorio led Ginger over to one of the love seats and they sat down. She leaned forward. "Vittorio says you're the best, signor. I'm afraid he's going to need the very best."

Casimiro smiled. "Don't worry about the news Renaldo made sure got on TV from fifteen years ago, proclaiming Vittorio a teenage, negligent drunk. It doesn't wash. After we countersue Signor Coronna and subpoena the Della Scalla board to give testimony to do with the vote coercion, I'm afraid he's going to be the one in the news before long."

His glance flicked to Vittorio. "Were you able to pick up the warrants?"

"Yes. I asked the water ambulance office and the doctor's office to fax all the reports to both of us, Casimiro. You should have them now."

"Excellent. This problem will be wound up soon because he doesn't have a case. It's so sad. I know Paola is your best friend, Maria. I'm sorry this experience has happened to her."

"So am I. She's so embarrassed."

"It's a shame her father doesn't realize what he's doing. The loss of a daughter's love would be no small thing. It's my hope this can be settled out of court when Signor Coronna considers how much collateral damage could end up against him."

"We all want that," Vittorio murmured.

"What about the ski in question?"

"It's out in the boat. Ginger and I compared it with the one she was using. Our ski is an older model."

"I'll ask the private investigator to come by and pick up both of them. I'm not sure we'll need the information, but it won't hurt to look into it. Vittorio? I've taken Maria's deposition. Now let's go into your study so I can gather the names of the board members. I'll start taking their depositions over the next two days while I'm in Venice."

Vittorio got to his feet. "Mamma? I've asked Ginger to stay with us for the time being. If you'll show her to one of the rooms and ask Diana to bring up her luggage from the foyer, Casimiro and I will disappear for a little while."

He squeezed Ginger's hand that wore his ring. "I'll phone you as soon as we're through. Remember we have a date to go to dinner and dancing."

"I haven't forgotten."

As soon as the two men left the salon, his mother said, "Maria? Show Signora Lawrence to the Giacinta Suite."

Ginger got up from the couch. "Thank you very much." She followed Maria through several ornate hallways to a beautiful suite with a huge mural of hyacinths.

"The bathroom is through there. Diana will be up shortly." She turned to leave.

"Maria? Please don't go yet. I didn't know Vittorio was going to ask me to stay here. I realize it's a big shock, and I can tell your mother is upset. How can I make things better for both of you? I love your brother so much and want us to get along. It'll take time, of course, but if there's anything I can do…"

"You want the truth?" She stared directly at Ginger.

"Of course."

"My brother is one of the wealthiest men in Italy. It's hard for Mamma to see a young woman from another country, who's Paola's age and looks like you, to come along just as our father passed away and turn my brother's world upside down.

"Do you have any idea how many women have hoped to be in your shoes besides Paola? Educated women from fine Venetian families. Mamma feels like she's in a bad dream."

"Is that how you feel?"

"I don't know you, but I can see my brother is besotted with you."

"As I am with him. Tell me something. How old do you think I am?"

"Twenty-four."

"Actually, I'm twenty-seven, going on twenty-eight. Do you know what I do for a living?"

"No."

"I teach college students at Vanguard University about early-nineteenth-century romance writers and poets. I've been in Italy for the last five months doing research on Lord Byron. That's how I came to meet Vittorio and your brother Gaspare at the monastery."

Maria blinked. "You're a professor?"

"Not in the fullest sense of the word. I've also been married, but over two years ago I lost my husband to bone cancer before we could have children."

A pained look crossed over her face. "I had no idea."

"We were so happy. He was a wonderful man.

When he died, I wanted to die, too. But in time I knew I had to move on and came to Italy to help get over my pain.

"Once I met your brother, I fell in love again. It happened fast for both of us. So fast, in fact, we've been afraid to believe it. I adore him.

"As for his money, it means nothing to me. I have my own because, like you, I was born into a family where my father is one of the wealthiest men in California. Do you think any of this information could help your mother see me in a little different light? I hope so because I know how much you and your mother mean to Vittorio. One day I hope we can be friends."

Maria nodded. "I want that, too. I've never seen my brother so happy in my life." Her eyes filled with tears. "Forgive us for being so judgmental."

Ginger smiled. "I'm sure I would feel the same way if our positions were reversed, but my mother died when I was born and I didn't have siblings."

"Oh, no—" She wiped her eyes. "I'm sorry we've been rude to you. We'll do better." As she left the maid entered, bringing the suitcases.

Ginger thanked her and walked to the bathroom to take a shower. She put the signet ring on the sink, afraid to lose it. Later she'd twine a piece of tissue around the band to keep it on her finger.

She needed to get ready for her evening out with Vittorio. They had their future to talk over. She would have to rely on her simple black dress with the cap sleeves. While she waited, she phoned her father and woke him up again.

"Dad? It's a good thing you're lying down. I just

got engaged to the most fantastic man on earth and couldn't wait to tell you the news."

Ten minutes later she was still on the phone with him when her phone rang with Vittorio's caller ID.

"Dad? I've got to go. Vittorio and I will call you later. Love you so much."

She hung up and clicked on. "Hi! Is your meeting over?"

"Yes. I've just showered and will meet you in the foyer in twenty minutes. *A presto, bellissima.*"

CHAPTER ELEVEN

JUST AS VITTORIO was putting on his suit jacket, he heard a knock on the door of his suite. "*Chi è?*" he called out.

"It's Maria."

He knew his actions had caused an earthquake in their household. In fact the tension had been building since Paola's accident last year. Before then he could always count on his sister to seek him out and talk things over. But for the last eight months she'd stayed away, which was why this visit came as a surprise.

Vittorio walked through to the sitting room and opened the door.

"Can we talk for a minute?" she blurted.

"What's wrong?"

"Oh, Vittorio—forgive me!" She threw her arms around him. Mystified, he hugged her back while he waited for an explanation.

"I should never have gotten upset with you because you didn't love Paola. I had no right. After I took Ginger to the Giacinta Suite, she asked what she could do to make things better for me and Mamma. I said some cruel things, and she was so kind back. I can see why you love her."

Nothing could have pleased him more than to hear that admission. "I sprang this on you two because I was afraid she'd leave for California to get out of Renaldo's way. I couldn't let her go."

Maria let him go and wiped her eyes. "One of Mamma's concerns was that Ginger was marrying you for your money. She felt really ashamed when I told her Ginger has her own money. I learned her father is a very wealthy man."

What?

"We've been so judgmental. I just had to come and tell you that she has a sweetness about her. You deserve a woman like that."

"Do you know Gaspare told me the same thing about her? Thank you for telling me this. In time you'll learn to love her." Vittorio gave her a kiss on the forehead. "If you're going downstairs, I'll go with you. Tonight we're celebrating our engagement."

Maria went with him as far as the salon, where he kissed his mother and said good-night to Casimiro, their guest for the next few days.

When Vittorio went down to the foyer, his breath caught to find Ginger waiting for him. She looked stunning in anything, but the black dress was doubly provocative because of her black hair and gray eyes.

"You're so beautiful it hurts."

"It would probably embarrass you if I told what a gorgeous man you are. Every woman in Venice will be jealous of me tonight."

They left the palazzo for the boat. He helped her inside and drove them to the Hotel Carlton, where he'd reserved a table in the La Cupola restaurant. They were shown to their table and served a main course of lobster risotto, followed by six other courses and wine.

"Vittorio—if we eat any more, we won't be able to go dancing."

He examined each exquisite feature. "I want us to remember this night. For years I wondered if I'd ever meet the right woman for me. Then you came into my life. I'm still afraid this could be a dream."

Her eyes grew serious. "I'm never going to disappear on you. You have to believe that!"

"My heart almost failed me earlier today when you said you were headed for the airport."

A fetching smile appeared. "Well, you certainly fixed it so I didn't get away."

He reached for her hand. "After the ten o'clock news, the country will know exactly how I feel about you. I set the TV to record it. One day our children will enjoy watching their father pursue their mother."

"I love you, Vittorio. I can't wait to have your baby." He felt the throb in her voice.

"Do you love me enough to admit why you told Maria something earlier this evening you've never told me?" She had to know what he meant.

"When you're a child, you don't realize your family has money. I certainly didn't and never considered my father's wealth vital to my existence. To be honest, I felt privileged because I had such a wonderful father, not because I knew he had money.

"But when your mother came to the villa and intimated I was an opportunist, I had to look at everything differently."

"Mamma should never have spoken to you like that."

"Don't be upset with her. As I told your sister, if our situation were reversed, I'm sure I would have said the same thing. Your mother has loved you all these years and wants to protect you. I wish I'd known my mother. You're lucky she cares so much and fears you'll lose everything if you leave the company.

"I can understand that fear. The other day when you said you were going to resign, a part of me rejoiced because I knew that if you ended up in financial trouble, I had an inheritance that could help you start your own business and provide for your family if you had to. I'd do anything for you."

Vittorio was not only humbled, but dumbfounded. "What you've just said means more to me than you will ever know. But you don't need to worry. I've been making investments with my own earnings for years that will always take care of us."

"That doesn't surprise me. I just want to assure you that you can always count on me. We're in this together, whatever happens."

Vittorio shook his head. "All this time I've worried you were running out of money and had to get back to work. I would have paid your bill at the hotel if I'd thought you would let me."

"I know you would have. That's the kind of man you are. I've seen your generosity in so many ways."

"Ginger—" he squeezed her hand harder "—I know you're giving up your career in California to marry me."

"But I'll find another one here and learn Italian, too. If I could find a publisher for my books, who knows where that career could take me. But for now I'm excited to become your wife and hopefully a mother to the children we want to have. I'm entering into a new chapter of my life with you.

"I called Dad tonight and told him I hope he and Nora will spend a lot more time over here with us."

"That brings me to what I want to talk over with you. How do you feel about the villa?"

Ginger laughed quietly. "That's one of those questions you sometimes ask when you already know the answer. I have to live around water. When we went out on the sand that first day, I thought I'd walked into a piece of heaven and I never wanted to leave."

"That settles it. We're going to make it our home."

"Oh, Vittorio—is it possible?" Her eyes shone like stars in the candlelight. "The trouble is, I'm sure Maria feels the same way about it."

"Naturally she loves to go out there to water ski, but she's never loved it the way I have. The palazzo is her favorite place to be. When the time comes, she'll inherit it, which is as it should be."

Ginger leaned forward. "If the villa is our home, she and the rest of your family will always be welcome. When Maria wants to spend time there with a boyfriend or the man she expects to marry, you and I can take a trip and let her have the place to herself for as long as she wants."

Vittorio needed to get Ginger alone. "Before we leave, let's make plans for our wedding. The soonest we can be married is three weeks. My parents were married at the Santa Maria dei Miracoli church. How would you feel about being married there, too?"

"I'm sure it would please your mother. All I care about is getting married to you."

"Then we'll talk to the priest tomorrow. Are you ready to go dancing?"

"Much as I'd love it, let's go back to the boat first and call my father. I promised he'd get to speak to you before the night was out. He's been worried about me for a long, long time. Our joyful news has already added years to his life."

Ginger had no idea that her love had transformed Vittorio.

They left the hotel and went out to the boat. He drove them to the base of the palazzo, where they could be alone to talk with her father. Then he'd take them to a club.

After turning off the engine, he listened while she made the call. They both talked to Wally and Nora, two people he found totally accepting and congenial.

But as time went on, his old fear that she might disappear on him surfaced when Ginger told her father she'd fly home the day after tomorrow and stay for a week so her parents could give her a party. She also needed to go see her boss at the university and resign in person. Her office would have to be cleaned out. There was major packing to do.

The thought of her being gone that long turned Vittorio inside out. They agreed on five days. That was all.

Though she reasoned that it would give him time to concentrate fully as CEO and be on hand for any meetings with Casimiro, it sounded like a lifetime. He'd gotten used to being with her continually and actually dreaded their separation.

When they hung up and drove to the club where he'd taken her before, Vittorio clung to her, unable to make small talk. Each day apart would feel like a lifetime. If anything went wrong...

Ginger read his mind. At one point she stopped dancing and lifted her eyes to him. "Vittorio, if you'd rather I didn't go, I won't. Dad will understand. After all, they're flying over for the wedding. I can have a talk with my boss on the phone and explain the circumstances. Nora will go over to the university to get my things from the office."

"Don't say any more," he whispered against her mouth. "I'm being selfish. After having found you, I'm afraid to let you out of my sight. I won't be able to get a thing done while you're gone.

"If you must go—and I know your father is counting the minutes—then I insist you fly on the Della Scalla private jet. Our pilots are the best. When I tell them the future Signora Della Scalla is on board, they'll know to guard and protect you with their lives."

Ginger put her arms around his neck. "Don't you know the last thing I want to do is leave you? It's hard to believe Paola's father is still going ahead with the suit. *You're* the one who needs to be extra careful right now. If you don't hire some bodyguards, *I* will."

Her words saved him from a complete meltdown. "It's already been taken care of."

She hugged him.

"Nothing's going to happen to either of us!" Vittorio caught her around the shoulders and ushered her out of the disco. They walked out to the boat and got in. He was glad the palazzo was less than a kilometer away. The sooner they reached the protection beneath it, the better.

Three weeks later

Pictures were being taken as Vittorio rushed a glow-ing Ginger out of the palazzo to the boat under an early-evening July sky. Still wearing her wedding dress and veil, she threw her bouquet to Maria, who caught it. She had an idea Vittorio had arranged for the florist to decorate the boat with flowers. Talk about feeling like a cherished bride...

Vittorio, who looked magnificent in his wedding suit of light gray, helped her to be seated and started the engine. Everyone who'd come to the wedding re-ception waved and cheered as they emerged from the palazzo entrance along the Grand Canal.

To make it perfect, Abby and Raoul had come and stood with Zoe to wave them off. That day in Swit-zerland when the three girls had tried to decide what to do about the change in their vacation plans, Ginger could never have dreamed up this scenario.

Ginger's father and Nora, along with Cherry and Bob, stood next to Vittorio's mother. Gaspare and Maria stayed on her other side with their relatives. It was a real miracle that he'd been given the privilege of leaving the monastery to attend the wedding. She knew it had meant everything to Vittorio.

Only one thing robbed them of pure joy as they made their way to the villa. The trial had been set for a week from today. Renaldo had gone forward and served Vittorio, but Casimiro assured her they were ready for him.

Vittorio held her hand as they glided through the water toward the villa, which was now their home and the place where they were going to honeymoon. After the trial was over, they might go on a trip, but that didn't matter to her. Right now her heart was thumping so hard, she could hardly breathe.

Five days away from him had been too long. She was home now and would never leave him again, and tonight was her wedding night. She felt like she'd been waiting forever to lie in her husband's arms.

Ginger thought she'd been running a temperature from the moment she'd walked down the aisle of the famous marble church with her father. To see Vittorio standing there waiting for her at the altar and the way he'd engulfed her with his burning blue gaze, she'd had a fluttering sensation in her chest that wouldn't go away.

Before long they reached the villa, where everything had been prepared ahead of time. Vittorio tied up the boat and helped her to step out. When she saw his white smile, she knew what was coming. He swept her into his arms.

"*Mia sposa*, I hope you're ready to be loved into oblivion."

"I've been ready since the night I looked into your eyes. Thank heaven we don't have to wait a second longer."

Ginger knew where he was taking her. After crossing over the threshold, he carried her up the stairs as if she weighed nothing and took her to the bedroom she loved. "I've dreamed about being in this room with you since you first brought me to the villa."

After Vittorio put her down, Ginger removed her veil and put it on a chair. When she turned, he undid the buttons on her wedding dress and helped her step out of it. With a quick toss of his jacket and tie, he carried her over to the bed and followed her down on the mattress.

They were both out of breath. He looked into her eyes with such hunger, she shivered in ecstasy. *"Ti amo, mia amata.* Give me your mouth before I die of wanting."

Ginger was already there, devouring him the way she'd been afraid to do before they took their vows. Until tonight she'd worried about losing complete control. Though she'd known the wonder of intimacy in her first marriage, this was a new experience for her and Vittorio. She wanted to come to him as if it were her first time.

The wait had been agonizing, but the thrill of worshipping each other with their bodies had brought her rapture she'd never known before. They'd gone to bed at twilight making love like she'd never even imagined in her dreams.

Their bedroom was filled with sunlight before they stopped long enough to fall asleep in each other's arms. Two hours later Vittorio covered her mouth with his own and swept her away again. Her husband and lover thrilled her to the very depths of her being.

Later he left the room and came back with a tray of food. They ate on the bed. Soon he put the tray on the floor and Vittorio made unhurried love to her until she cried out from too much pleasure.

Afterward they lay side by side with his powerful legs trapping hers. The love in his eyes made her feel immortal. "Have you figured out which poem Byron wrote yet?"

How she loved this man. She'd had some time to

think about it and thought she knew. "Why don't you tell me, or better yet, recite it."

He had buried his face in her hair. "I couldn't, but it says she walks in beauty." Suddenly he lifted his head and stared down at her with those penetrating blue orbs.

"You're the most beautiful thing in my life. I'm not just talking about your face and figure. I'm talking about the person you are. He covered a lot of territory in that poem. But the last line convinces me he could have been writing about you. 'A heart whose love is innocent.'

"That's you. Sweetness and innocence. I don't know how I was so blessed to have a wife like you, but I swear I'll love you till the day I die and beyond.

"Don't ever stop loving me," he cried.

A phone call three mornings later brought Vittorio out of his entrancement long enough to answer it. Ginger lay in the crook of his arm and looked at him with some concern. They'd been in another world and weren't ready for anything to disturb them.

"Pronto?"

"Vittorio?" It was Casimiro. "Forgive the intrusion, but I wanted you to know that Renaldo Coronna has dropped the suit. The very generous, undeserved settlement you offered him from your own funds helped cover his gambling losses. He has agreed to resign from the board. I've told your family, and they are ecstatic."

Of course they would be.

"One more piece of good news. Without exception, every deposition taken from the board members revealed that they would have voted for you no matter Renaldo's agenda. None of them will accept your resignation. Your uncle will be very happy to keep running everything until you decide to go to work. Congratulations!

"Now go back to what you were doing and tell that gorgeous wife of yours all is well."

Vittorio's throat had almost closed up from emotion. "You have my undying gratitude. I'll never be able to repay you enough for taking the case on so fast. I understand now why my father considered you a cherished friend. *Grazie*, Casimiro. *Mille grazie*."

"It has been my pleasure, believe me."

"Vittorio?" Ginger cried after he hung up. "What's happened?"

He slid his hand to her flushed cheek. "It's over. Renaldo dropped the suit. The board still wants me to head the company."

"Oh, darling—" In the next breath she broke down sobbing. Quiet sobs that shook him and told him she'd gone through a world of suffering on his behalf. "My prayers have been answered."

"Mine, too, *bellissima*." Vittorio gathered her against him and kissed the moisture from her eyes and face. "Your faith helped me get through all this."

"That's because you're the most wonderful man who ever lived. Renaldo didn't deserve the money you offered him to get out of his troubles gracefully."

"My father would have done it."

"I'm sure of that. You're just like him. Kind and good and honest. My concern now is for Paola. We have to pray she'll meet a special guy who will make her happy again. She and Maria have been close for too long to let this destroy their friendship."

Vittorio nodded his dark, handsome head. "I'm thinking of introducing my private secretary to her. He's single and I like him."

Ginger shot up. "Rico is very attractive!"

"You never told me that."

She kissed his chin. "You need a shave."

"Don't change the subject."

"No man could compare to you, and you know it." She kissed his mouth. "What do you think if we had a party out here soon and Maria convinced her to come so she could meet him? I'll talk to her."

"We'll do it. But it might be weeks from now."

"Why?"

"Because I'm not willing to think about anything else except making love to my stunning wife. Come closer, *bellissima*. You want my baby? I want yours, and I'm willing to do whatever it takes, for as long as it takes to satisfy both our wishes."

He lowered his mouth over hers, ready to be swept away by her tender loving, today and forever.

* * * * *

To the men and women I worked with at
the 58th Special Operations Wing, formerly the
1550th Aircrew Training and Test Wing. So proud to
have been part of such a dedicated band of warriors!

With special thanks to my pals Joann Henderson
and author Krysta Scott, both of whom served
as watchdogs for the protection of children.
Thanks sooo much for the excellent advice
on child advocacy and adoption procedures.

Chapter One

The reek of stale peanut shells, spilled beer and cigarette smoke smacked Alexis in the face the moment she stepped inside the Cactus Café. Her nose wrinkled as she surveyed the patrons of the run-down bar on a corner of Albuquerque's Central Avenue. She should've guessed the tough, combat-seasoned men and women who'd worked for the legendary Colonel Mike Dolan, call sign Badger, would pick a dive like this for their annual drunk.

Except they didn't conduct a Badger Bash *every* year. Only when three or more of them happened to be on the same continent at the same time. And they didn't get drunk, she'd discovered the first and only other time she'd attended a Badger Bash. She'd been a guest then, along with a few other wives, boyfriends and significant others. The chance-met date of one of the participants, invited on the spur of the moment. That moment that now looked to make a serious change in the direction of her life.

They'd gotten just a little loose at that Bash. Laughing and snorting in their beer as they took turns adding to the absurdly ridiculous tales of Colonel Dolan, hard-ass squadron commander and the world's studliest Special Ops pilot.

Alexis had left that Bash convinced Dolan's subordinates had fabricated his whole larger-than-life persona. The colonel's adventures were too fantastic, his kill ratio too unbelievable, his success with the female half of the population *way* too improbable.

Then again, she'd left the gathering in the company of one of the Badger's protégées. Major Ben Kincaid. Also a Special Ops pilot. And a world-class stud. One long weekend with the major had pretty much made a believer out of Alex.

Now Kincaid was here. In Albuquerque. Just seeing him again after all this time knocked the breath back down Alex's throat. He was leaning against the bar, one boot hooked on the rail, his jeans and black knit polo shirt hugging his long, lean frame and a grin tipping a corner of his mouth. Ruthlessly, she banished the memory of that mouth moving over her. Moving over *every* part of her.

This was business.

A very desperate business.

Dragging in a determined breath, she stepped out of the shadows of the bar's entrance and let the door whoosh out the hot New Mexico night. As she wove her way through the Cactus Café's beer-stained tables, smoky haze bit into her lungs and the country-pop cross-over nasal whine blasting through the speakers assaulted her eardrums.

She didn't recognize the man talking to Kincaid. Another military type she guessed from the buzz-cut hair and easy slouch that somehow still managed to convey a careless self-confidence. She *did* recognize the woman with the two men, though. The blonde was another of Badger's protégées that Alex had met at the previous Bash. Susan Something. Alex couldn't recall her last name but she did remember that the woman owed her call sign Swish to the ponytail that teased her shoulder blades seductively. That was the version put out for public consumption, anyway. A grinning Kincaid had indicated there was another version, known only to the chosen few.

Swish caught sight of Alex first. A frown creased her forehead as she tried to fit the face to a name or place. She made the connection while Alex was still a few yards away. Arching a delicately penciled brow, she nudged Kincaid with an elbow. Either he was too involved in the other man's story or he mistook the poke for something more intimate. Smiling, he curled an arm around her shoulders and rubbed his palm up and down her arm.

The absentminded caress stopped Alex in her tracks. Damn! Had Love-'Em-and-Leave-'Em Kincaid changed his modus operandi? Her carefully constructed plan would disintegrate if the easy camaraderie Alex had observed between him and Swishy Susan two years ago had developed into something deeper. Something more permanent.

Then the blonde dug her elbow into Kincaid's ribs

again. Hard enough to get his attention this time. His beer sloshing, he winced and sent her a pained look.

"Hey!"

"We've got company," the blonde said. "Someone from your checkered past, if memory serves."

Swish tipped her chin. Kincaid followed her lead. Under other circumstances the blank look when he spotted Alex might have bruised her ego. Instead, it confirmed that the major was still the right man for her job.

Cutting past the last few tables, she joined the three of them at the bar. "Long time no see, Cowboy."

That was his call sign. Cowboy. Reportedly gained when he'd swooped low over some grazing longhorns and stampeded the whole herd across thirty miles of Texas panhandle. Much to the displeasure of several local ranchers, he'd confided to Alex.

"Long time," he agreed.

There was just enough of a question buried in his reply to confirm that he didn't have a clue who she was. Alex wasn't surprised. She'd changed considerably since Vegas. Her hair, her style of dressing, her life.

Still, they *had* spent two days and three extremely erotic nights together. She couldn't help feeling a little piqued. With a cynical smile, she held out her hand.

"Alexis Scott. Las Vegas. Two years ago."

She could see him make the connection. Those electric-blue eyes widened, made a quick trip south, zipped back up to her face.

"Alex! Damn. You're looking good."

She should be. She'd donned her best armor in preparation for this meeting. The subtly dramatic makeup. The snug short-sleeved black tank sparkling with turquoise and silver crystals along its low-cut scoop neckline. The slim black jeans with matching crystal trim on the pockets. The black boots with ice pick heels. She'd even coaxed some curl into her shoulder-length auburn hair.

"You're looking good, too" she had to admit as she mirrored his quick inventory. His dark hair was a little shorter than she remembered from Vegas. The white squint lines at the corners of his eyes were pretty much the same, though. So were the square chin, the strong neck and the muscled shoulders under his faded denim shirt.

"What are you doing in New Mexico?" he asked, jerking her back to the here and now.

"I moved here last year."

"With…" He cocked his head. "What was his name? The real estate tycoon?"

"Bryan, and no."

She'd started dating Bryan a month or so after her wild weekend with the hotshot special operations pilot. She and Bryan had progressed to the exclusive stage when Kincaid called her some four months later. He'd been in Iraq, he'd explained. Then she'd explained her situation at the time, at which point he'd cheerfully wished her and Bryan the best and disappeared from her life again.

Not that Alex had ever expected her weekend with the major to result in any kind of long-term relationship. Kincaid had been up-front with her about his single state. No ties, no obligations, not even a pet goldfish. Short-notice deployments flying heavily armed gunships into hot spots around the world didn't make for either stability or durability in relationships. Alex suspected there was more to his deliberately casual philosophy of life and love, but they hadn't spent enough time together for her to want to dig deeper.

But now…with so much on the line… Kincaid's here-today, gone-tomorrow philosophy formed an essential element of her desperate scheme. She itched to get him away from his friends and lay out her proposition but curbed her impatience while he introduced the other two.

"This is Susan Hall. She served as a comm officer under the Badger."

"We met at the Vegas bash," the blonde said with a friendly nod. "Good to see you again." Her gaze lingered on the sparkling turquoise and silver decorating Alex's top. "Love the bling."

"Thanks. This is one of my most popular designs."

"You designed that?"

"It's what I do for a living."

Swish looked as though she wanted to pursue that, but Kincaid hooked a thumb at the man beside him. "Blake Andrews. We call him Dingo for reasons that can't be explained in polite company. Careful what you say around him, by the way. He's a cop."

"Ex-cop," Dingo corrected. "I hung up my shield with my air force uniform."

His palm was callused, his handshake firm without the iron crunch some men thought necessary to demonstrate their virility. The pleasantries observed, Kincaid asked Alex if she'd like a beer.

"I would. Thanks. And could we talk? You and I? If your friends will excuse you for a few minutes."

"Sure. Why don't you grab that table?" He gestured to one just being vacated. "I'll bring your beer."

Ben raised his bottle to signal the bartender, then watched as the unexpected visitor from his past headed for the corner table. Now that she'd stirred the memories, they played out inside his head in vivid detail. She was slimmer than he remembered. And her hair was different. Longer, he thought. Shot with streaks of red and deep, dark gold. Those chocolate-brown eyes were the same, though, and that full, sensual mouth. All in all, Ben decided with a kick to his gut, the overall package was pretty damned outstanding.

Dingo shared his assessment. "You lucky bastard," he muttered as he followed her progress across the room.

Swish was more interested in the sparkles. "Find out where I can get one of those shirts."

Yeah, right, Ben thought wryly as the bartender handed him a dew-streaked Coors. Like he was going to talk T-shirts with a woman he could only hope wanted to take up where they'd left off in Vegas.

Maybe this time it would work. It hadn't last time. Truth was, he'd tried to reconnect with the auburn-haired hottie after their wild weekend. Just days after he'd returned from a four-month deployment to Iraq. Just his bad luck that she'd already hooked up with someone else. Some hotshot Realtor.

Ben was surprised by the regret that news had spurred. He'd thoroughly enjoyed their weekend together. And not just in the opulent suite at The Venetian he'd taken her to after deserting his pals at the Bash. Alexis Scott had kept him grinning with her lively recap of the joys and challenges of designing what passed for costumes at Vegas's risqué revues and surprised him with her savvy knowledge of video marketing techniques. He'd shaken off the regret soon enough, though. Another no-notice deployment, this one a humanitarian mission to earthquake-ravaged Haiti, had shoved that weekend out of his head.

Maybe, just maybe, she was thinking to rekindle old fires. Hoping fervently that was the reason for her unexpected reappearance in his life, he took a seat and passed her the beer.

"Thanks." She raised her bottle in a toast. "Here's to Vegas."

"To Vegas."

She tipped her head back and took a long swallow. Ben did the same, but the glitzy stuff on the low neck of her T-shirt did exactly what he figured it was supposed to. Damned if the sparkling crystals didn't catch his gaze. And hold it!

His, and every other male's within a twenty-foot radius. He saw the stares, caught the elbow jabs. No wonder Swish wanted to know where to buy one of these seemingly sedate but disturbingly provocative T-shirts. Just in time, Ben managed to drag his gaze from the seductive valley between her breasts.

Her head tipped forward, her brown eyes met his. "I suppose you're wondering why I tracked you down."

"I was kind of hoping it was my charm and suave good looks."

A quick smile flitted across her face. "That's part of it."

"What's the other part?"

"Parts," she corrected, her smile fading. "There are several."

She glanced down and picked at the label on her beer with a fingernail. When she looked up again, Ben had the impression she'd steeled herself for something that ranked up there on the fun meter right alongside a colonoscopy.

"There's a child. A little girl."

He didn't move. Didn't alter his politely curious expression. But his stomach contracted and his mind razored back to their nights together.

He'd used protection. A whole damned box of protection, if he remembered right. Yet the possibility that one of those little suckers hadn't worked had his knuckles going white on his beer bottle.

It wasn't that he didn't want kids. He did. Someday. Maybe. Hell, he was only thirty-two. Plenty of time yet.

Except now he had to face the possibility time might've run out. His spine going rigid, he waited for the hammer to fall.

"Well," she said, spearing through his whirling thoughts, "I guess she doesn't really qualify as a *little* girl. Maria's seven, and the sweetest, smartest, most loving…" She broke off, her brows snapping together. "Kincaid?"

"Huh?"

Her scowl deepened. "Am I boring you?"

"What? No."

"You looked like you were a thousand miles away."

"I heard every word. Maria's seven and sweet and smart and…" he couldn't suppress a huff of laughter "…not mine."

"Yours?" She jerked back in her chair. "Why on earth would you…? Oh!"

Her astounded expression morphed into one of unholy amusement. Then something that looked a whole lot like chagrin.

The amusement Ben could understand. The chagrin got him nervous all over again. Especially when she went back to peeling off strips of the wet label.

One corner of his brain could hear Charley Pride's "Kiss an Angel Good Mornin'" above the clink of glasses and buzz of conversation. Another corner registered the fact that Swish and Dingo were keeping him under close surveillance. But the main cortex, the cerebrum or cerebellum or whatever the hell part processed danger signals, was flashing a red alert.

"Back up a few steps," he instructed. "Tell me what seven-year-old Maria has to do with you and me and Vegas."

"I want to adopt her."

"And?"

She sucked in a deep breath. Manfully, Ben kept his eyes above the bling. Mostly.

"Ordinarily, that wouldn't be a problem. Most states, including this one, allow single-parent adoption. But in Maria's case, there are special circumstances that make it necessary for me to…ah…have a husband."

"Whoa!" He plunked his beer on the table. "I hope you're not thinking what I think you're thinking."

"As a matter of fact…" Those warm brown eyes cut through the cigarette haze to lock with his. "I came here to… I need to ask… Oh, hell. The thing is, I want you to marry me, Major."

Before he could recover enough to ask what the hell she was smoking, she tacked on a caveat.

"Temporarily."

She was crazy. Certifiably nuts. He could've kicked himself when curiosity made him ask.

"How temporary?"

"Six months. Or less, depending on…well…circumstances. And I promise there'll be no strings." She rushed on. "No obligations on your part, financial or otherwise. Just your signature on a marriage certificate before you take off again for parts unknown."

"Look, lady, these 'circumstances' you keep referring to make me think that what you're suggesting comes real close to fraud."

"It's not fraud! I've discussed this with my attorney. He's assured me what I'm doing is legal. And you don't have to declare me your spouse or dependent or whatever the military term is. I promise, I won't make any claim on you or the air force."

"Doesn't matter whether you make a claim or not. If we're married, we're married. That entitles you to whatever privileges come with the ring." He shoved back his chair. "Sorry, you'll have to find another—"

"I'll pay you."

"'Scuse me?"

"Five thousand when you sign the wedding certificate, another five when we divorce."

Okay, now he was pissed. Ben almost started to blister her with a few well-chosen words about what she could do with her money but the sudden flash of desperation in her eyes had him biting back the words.

"Please!" The table wobbled as she pushed to her feet and threw a quick glance around the noisy bar. "Can we go somewhere quieter? So I can explain these…these special circumstances? Five minutes," she pleaded. "Please. Give me just another five minutes."

If Ben had a lick of sense he would've wished her a happy life and rejoined his buddies. Now that his anger had cooled, though, he wanted to hear what the hell was behind her crazy proposal.

"My ride's outside. We can talk there."

She started for the exit while Ben detoured to tell his friends that he was stepping out for a bit.

"Riiight," Dingo drawled. "Have fun."

"And find out where I can get one of those shirts," Swish called after him.

The hot desert night hit with a wallop after the air-conditioned bar. Ben shrugged it off as he caught up with Alexis.

"I'm parked over here. Careful."

He took her elbow to steer her around a man-size pothole. A relic of the old Route 66 heyday, the Cactus Café had long passed its prime. Half the bulbs in the illuminated sign that gave the place its name had burned out. The rest shed only a flickering green glow over the pitted dirt lot.

He beeped the locks on his muscled-up Chevy Tahoe and opened the passenger door for her. She had a long step up from the running board but Ben resisted the temptation to provide any help with a palm under her rear. Once behind the wheel, he keyed the ignition and lowered all four windows to let out the trapped air.

"Okay," he commented as he settled against his seat, "the clock's ticking."

"My sister married a single dad with a young daughter. Janet—my sister—adored the girl. Then, last year, Janet was diagnosed with stage four ovarian cancer and I moved to Albuquerque to help take care of her. She died within six months of the initial diagnosis and I've had custody of her stepdaughter, Maria, since."

"Why did you get custody instead of the kid's father?"

"Because the scumbag walked out on Janet less than a week after she found out she had cancer. And he's now in prison for dealing drugs."

She kept her voice flat and the words succinct, with no hint of the anguish Ben knew she had to have gone through.

"I want to legally adopt Maria but her father won't agree to the adoption."

"Why not?"

"Spite. Pure and vicious and vengeful." Her lip curled. "Before he got busted for drugs, I went after him for child support. He got hauled into court several times. That pissed him off so much he would cut off his own nose to spite me."

"He sounds like a real winner."

"A real loser, you mean."

She stared out the open window for a few moments, presenting a profile that showed a taut, angry jaw. When she faced Ben again, he had to admire her rigid self-control.

"The court awarded me temporary custody. Since Maria and I aren't related by blood, though, the judge refused to revoke her father's parental rights and approve an adoption over his objections. Especially since I would be a single mom. Judge Hendricks," she said with a twist of her lips, "doesn't hold a high opinion of single, working women attempting to acquire a ready-made family."

"Which is where I come in," Ben drawled, enlightened.

"Right." Her eyes were dark pools in the flickering light. "I don't want a husband, but I *need* one. Temporarily."

"I guess I can see that. But why me, for God's sake? We barely know each other. Surely you have better candidates to pick from."

"No, you're perfect."

He gave a snort of laughter. "I must have performed better in Vegas than I remember."

The quip didn't raise an answering laugh, and her total lack of response told him she really meant this absurd proposition.

"I'll admit the sex was pretty good…" she said with a shrug.

"Thanks."

"Okay, extremely good. But I'm going to be up-front with you. Sex can't play in any deal we work out. Our marriage has to be in name only. I can't risk getting emotionally involved. Not with Maria to consider. And you don't want any entanglements. You made that clear in Vegas."

Damn! He must've come on like a complete jerk. At least he hadn't lied to her. Still, her blunt assertion that all he'd been interested in was getting her horizontal hit too close to the mark.

"Correct me if I'm wrong," he countered drily, "but sex was the only thing we had in common in Vegas. With that off the table, I'm having a little trouble seeing why you think I'm the perfect choice."

"Because you're military. That's a plus in this city. With such a large percentage of the population either working on or associated with the base, Albuquerque is nothing if not pro military. A husband in uniform has got to play in my favor with the judge."

She hunched sideways, her shoulder wedged against the door and her face dead serious in the dim light.

"As an added bonus, you're Special Ops. That means you're gone more than you're home. Your absence is a built-in excuse if the court orders an unscheduled home visit and finds no husband in residence."

"Convenient," he drawled.

"Yes, it is." She must have sensed she hadn't convinced him. Her voice took on an urgent note. "I won't make any demands on you, Kincaid, or tie you down. I promise! And you'll be helping a little girl who's lost almost her entire world."

Still Ben hesitated. The scheme edged too close to fraud in his mind. He was tossing possible legal ramifications around in his mind when she fumbled her phone out of the little purse slung over one shoulder.

"Here." She opened the phone and jabbed the photo icon. "This is Maria."

The lit screen displayed a dark-haired, dark-eyed girl with an impish smile and a doll cuddled up to her cheek.

"She's a great kid. And really smart. She downloads a new book from the library every week. And…" She broke off, her voice thickening. "She helps in my business. I use her to model my line of kids' clothing."

When she feathered a finger over the sparkly red heart on the girl's T-shirt, Ben caught the glimmer of tears in her eyes. She blinked them away and scrolled to another photo.

"This is my sister, after her loving husband lit into her about the mounting medical bills."

The face in this photo was older, painfully gaunt, and sporting a vicious black eye.

"That slime is capable of doing the same—or worse— to his daughter," Alex said, her voice low and vibrating. "Which is why *I'll* do whatever I have to, to keep him away from her."

She clicked the phone off, shoved it in her purse and locked her gaze on Ben's face. "So will you? Marry me?"

She'd played him. Ben knew it. She'd shown him those pictures, hoping they would kick his protective instincts into high gear. Counting on it!

No matter. The ends in this case appeared to justify the means.

"Yeah, I will."

She blew out a long breath. "Thank y—"

"On two conditions."

Her face closed in, turned wary. "Which are?"

"First, if you mention paying me again, the deal's off. No way I'm going to take money you'll probably need for the legal battles still ahead."

She didn't try to hide her relief. "I can live with that. Second?"

"If we're going to do this, we have to do it tomorrow."

"*Tomorrow!* Why?"

"Remember those pluses you just enumerated? Particularly the one about me being gone more than I'm home? My unit's heading across the pond. We're going wheels up at o-dark-thirty Monday morning."

"But tomorrow's Sunday! The country clerk's office won't be open to issue a license."

"Then I guess we'd better make a quick trip to the scene of the crime." He had to grin at her blank look. "Vegas, sweetheart. Vegas. I'll take care of the details. Just give me your address, phone number and email. I'll let you know what time I'll pick you up in the morning."

Alex exited the Cactus Café's dusty parking lot and drove home in a swirl of emotions. This was what she wanted. This was the scheme she'd paid her high-priced lawyer to help her devise. It didn't do a bit of good to remind herself that she'd resisted putting that scheme into play until she'd discovered this year's Badger Bash would take place at the Cactus Café.

She'd known for months that Major Ben Kincaid was stationed right here, in Albuquerque, at the vast, sprawling military installation dominating the south part of the city. Kirtland Air Force Base was home to a dozen or more military units, including the premier training squadron for Special Ops aircrews and pararescue personnel. It hadn't taken much sleuthing to confirm he was one of the instructors assigned to the 58th Special Operations Wing.

Alex hadn't acted on that knowledge, however, as much as she'd wanted to. Her life was complicated enough with her rapidly expanding business, taking care of Maria, and trying to ramrod an adoption through a confusing and complicated legal system.

Then Eddie Musgrove, damn his putrid soul, had appeared in court. In restraints and an orange prison jumpsuit, no less. Despite the fact that he was a deadbeat dad and convicted felon, he'd convinced the doddering, dyspeptic, *misogynistic* judge that a single working woman wasn't a suitable parent for his daughter. He'd also convinced the judge that the photo of his wife with that black eye was a result of a misunderstanding. He'd never laid another hand on her, or so much as touched his daughter in anger.

Furious and more than a little desperate, Alex had brainstormed the next course of action with her lawyer. After discussing and discarding several options, she and Paul Montoya had decided on the one—the only one!—that seemed doable.

Then she'd hit the computer. She was searching for a contact number for Major Benjamin Kincaid when she saw a flash about the Badger Bash. It was here this year. At the Cactus Café. Central Avenue. Starting tonight. And sure enough, Kincaid had been there. Her one-time lover and prospective groom.

She still couldn't quite believe he'd accepted her desperate proposal. Now all she had to do was go home and dig through her closet for something to wear to her wedding.

Chapter Two

"Why can't I go, too?"

Alex swallowed a sigh and gave Maria the same answer she had the previous four times. "Because this is a quick trip. I'll be home in time to pick you up at Dinah's before bedtime."

"But you *promised* to take me 'n' her to the BioPark today."

"I know, Kitten. We'll go next weekend. Cross my heart!"

Raising the scrubber she'd used to rinse the breakfast dishes, Alex air-sketched an X on her cream-colored tunic. Swarovski crystals danced along the tunic's hem and sweetheart neckline. Paired with palazzo pants in the same clingy fabric, it was as close as she'd been able to come to wedding white.

Maria remained as unimpressed by Alex's sartorial

efforts as by her heart crossing. Her lower lip jutting mutinously, the girl took a just-rinsed plate and jammed it into the dishwasher.

"I want to go," she said again. "I haven't seen Aunt Chelsea in a long time."

The "aunt" was an honorary title for Alex's former Vegas roommate and best friend. The two women had kept in touch since Alex jettisoned her life in Vegas to move to Albuquerque. Laughing, vibrant Chelsea visited whenever she could get away from her job performing in the chorus line at the Flamingo Hotel and Casino's flashy review.

"Chelsea was here last month," Alex reminded Maria. "This trip will just be me and Major Kincaid."

"I don't like him."

"How do you know? You haven't met him yet."

"But you're gonna marry him!"

"Yes, I am."

Alex had spent long hours last night trying to decide what to tell Maria about Ben Kincaid. After much agonizing, she'd decided to stick as close to the truth as possible.

As she'd explained over breakfast this morning, she and the major had met two years ago and had a wonderful time together before going their separate ways. Still clinging to the truth, she related that she'd lost touch with him until she saw a notice of his old squadron's reunion on Facebook. On a whim, she'd gone to meet him last night, and they realized they were in love and decided to get married.

Maria hadn't bought it. Still wasn't buying it. Cutting off the tap, Alex wiped her hands on a dish towel and sagged the girl's hands in hers.

"I told him all about you, Kitten. How you love to read. How you aced your spelling test last week. How you help me with my designs. Ben can't wait to meet you."

With a pout that had her lower lip jutting out ominously, Maria jerked her hands loose and crossed her arms over her thin chest. "He can wait all he wants. I don't want to meet *him*."

Alex bit back another sigh. Every website she'd pored through about seven-year-olds warned that this was a touchy transition period. They weren't yet adolescents, but they no longer needed constant supervision. Yet they still hovered between that budding independence and clinging to their trusted anchors. For Maria, that anchor was Alex.

Unfortunately, Alex couldn't risk explaining the real reason for her quickie Vegas wedding. The marriage had to look real. Feel real. Even to Maria.

Especially to Maria. Alex didn't doubt for a minute that the girl's scumbag dad would try to use her fake marriage to undermine Maria's tentative sense of security.

"You'll like Ben, Kitten. You will. He's…"

Sexy as hell? Beyond amazing between the sheets? Desperate, Alex glommed on to one of the few non-bedroom activities she and Ben had shared during their brief weekend together.

"He's a pizza freak. Just like you."

"Does he like the pineapple, green olives and barbecue chicken combo?"

"I don't know. But I bet he will if you get him to try it."

Maria's lower lip did its thing again. Elbows tight, black eyes stormy, the girl was a fifty-two-pound bundle of *not happy*.

As ferocious as it was, the scowl sent a wave of hot,

liquid emotion pulsing through Alex. God, she loved this stubborn little person! Surprising, really, since Maria seemed to exasperate her as often as she melted every corner of her heart. Where had this confusing, conflicting, swamping love come from? Not through any blood ties, certainly. And not just because of her promise to her dying sister.

Janet's death had left Alex riddled with guilt. It was several months before she could admit the truth. She'd loved her sister but hadn't really liked her.

Janet was two years older and their father's acknowledged favorite. Secure in that superior position, she'd ignored her younger sibling for most of their childhood. That changed in middle school, thanks to Alex's swan-like emergence from gawky prepubescence to curvy preteen. Suddenly, the little sister got all the attention, and the gap between the two had widened even more.

After high school, the Scott sisters had followed separate paths. For Janet, it was a stint as a backup singer with a band no one outside of the musicians themselves and a few of their close friends had ever heard of. She'd capped that with marriage to the drug-addicted bass guitarist, whose lack of talent was matched only by his absence of anything approaching a sense of responsibility to Janet and the child he'd fathered with his long-absent girlfriend.

Meanwhile Alex had parlayed a bachelor's degree in Fashion Design and Merchandising into an apprenticeship with one of Las Vegas's premier costumers. It didn't matter that most of the costumes she worked on consisted of rhinestone-studded G-strings and star-shaped pasties. She'd loved the vibrant, tawdry, behind-the-scenes action of casino showrooms. The fact that her roommate was a chorus girl in the Flamingo's glitzy troupe had only added to the fun.

Then, just a little over a year ago, Janet had called with the devastating news that she'd been diagnosed with stage four ovarian cancer. She'd also admitted that her scuz of a husband had deserted her and her stepdaughter. In what seemed like a heartbeat, Alex's life had veered in a different direction.

She'd never intended to assume guardianship of Maria after her sister's slow, agonizing death. That was a father's responsibility, after all. But by then Eddie Musgrove was in prison and there was no one else to take charge of his daughter.

Now Maria's life was taking another unexpected turn. One Alex knew the girl couldn't help but view as a threat to her shaky security. Aching for her, she tried again to soften the blow.

"Ben won't be around much, sweetie. Like I told you, he's in the air force and has to go where they send him. That's why we're getting married on such short notice. He's leaving early tomorrow morning. So you'll have to wait a few months before you even meet him."

By which time, God willing, the adoption would be finalized and Alex would be planning a divorce as quick and painless as the wedding.

"Is your backpack ready?" she asked Maria. "Dinah and her mom will be here to pick you up any…" The tinkle of the door chimes cut her off. "That's probably them now. Go get your backpack, Kitten."

The door chime rang again and Alex hurried down the tiled hall of their rented casita. The two-bedroom adobe unit was part of a new complex just a few blocks from Albuquerque's picturesque Old Town Plaza. The prime location meant a higher rent than Alex wanted to pay, but the complex was within walking distance of Maria's school and close to a warehouse where Alex rented operating space for her business.

She opened the door expecting Maria's cheerful, chubby, freckle-faced friend and her mom. Instead, she found her groom standing under the portico of woven piñon branches. Flustered, Alex ran a quick eye over his dark slacks and crisply ironed blue oxford shirt to the carryall he toted in one hand.

"Are you early or am I late?" she asked.

"I'm early, but I thought I'd better bring a few things over while I could."

"What things?"

He hefted the leather carryall. "You might want to have some evidence of a husband around the house. For those unannounced home visits."

"Oh," she said stupidly. "Right."

She stood aside so he could move out of the blinding morning sunlight into the shady cool of the entryway. Although her small bungalow looked like a square adobe box on the outside, Alex had unleashed her creative juices on the inside.

"Nice," Ben commented as he ran an appreciative eye over the sand-colored floor tile, the ochre walls and the antique wooden hall stand painted a bright turquoise. Alex had added a hand-painted border of colorful cactus blossoms around the mirror and replaced its plain brass hooks with whimsical coyotes wearing a variety of cowboy hats and sombreros. Maria's book bag hung from one howling coyote, Alex's purse and car keys from another.

She'd continued the Southwestern motif in the living

room framed by a wide arch and visible from the entry hall. The hues were muted desert tans and golds splashed with jeweled accents in mauve and turquoise and sunset orange. The combination kitchen-dining room was just as colorful. Ben murmured his appreciation of the decor as Alex led the way down the hall to her bedroom.

"I have no idea how long this deployment will last," he told her. "But I'm up for reassignment when I get back, so I moved out of my apartment a few days ago and put my stuff in storage. All I have here are a couple changes of clothes, some underwear, a pair of sweats and—"

"Is that *him*?"

The belligerent question flew at them from the doorway of Maria's bedroom. They turned to find her standing with feet planted and arms crossed.

"Yes," Alex answered with a determined smile, "this is Major Kincaid. Ben, this is my niece and soon-to-be daughter, Maria."

The "niece" was honorific since she and Maria shared no actual blood tie, but they both hoped to eliminate the "soon-to-be."

"Hi, Maria. Alex said you were smart and a whiz at spelling. She forgot to mention how pretty you are."

The ploy was only partially successful. The arms remained crossed but the lower lip retreated a little.

"I'm sorry we won't be able to spend any time together before I leave tomorrow," he told her, unknowingly echoing Alex's attempt to soften the impact of a stranger dropped suddenly into her life. "Maybe we could get to know each other a little by email. I'll send you pictures of my crew and the places we fly into and you can tell me about school and your friends. Would that be okay?"

"I guess," the girl said sulkily. "Except Alex only lets me on the computer when she can watch what sites I go to."

"That makes sense. There's some real scary stuff on the internet." He unzipped his carryall and fished out a tablet encased in hot pink. "That's why the iPad I brought you comes with strict parental controls. If it's okay with Alex, you could use this to keep me posted about what's happening here."

The sulk disappeared, and the girl's eyes went wide with excitement. "Oh, wow! My very own iPad! I've been wanting one." In almost the next heartbeat, she zinged from excited to dejected. "But Alex says I have to wait for my birthday to get one."

"When's that?"

"September 9."

"Hmm." He scraped a palm across his chin and pondered the dilemma for a few moments. "How about we consider it a wedding present instead? From me to you. That okay with you, Alex?"

She could have kissed him. In one smooth move he'd eased a little of Maria's uncertainties and given her the expensive gift she'd been angling for ever since her friend Dinah got one last Christmas.

"It's okay with me." She turned a warning glance on her ward. "But only after I put on a code restricting access to the app store."

"I already engaged it," Ben assured her. "I'll give you the passcode later. She's good to go."

"Can I play with it now? Please, Alex. *Please!*"

"I guess. Do you want Ben to show you how to work it?"

The seven-year-old gave her a look of utter disdain. "Dinah and I play on hers all the time."

"Okay, if you're sure you know what you're doing."

"Aleeeeex."

With that parting shot, she whirled, took her prize to her bed and belly flopped onto her Princess Elsa comforter.

"Pretty slick," Alex murmured as she escorted Ben to the master bedroom. "But how in the world did you find time to buy an iPad and download those applications?"

"I hit a twenty-four-hour Walmart. Then I had Swish and Dingo test fly the apps while I set us up for Vegas. They congratulated me on our upcoming nuptials, by the way, and sent you their heartfelt condolences."

"Did you tell them our arrangement is only temporary?"

"No. Did you tell Maria?"

"No." At his questioning look, she shrugged. "I said we'd reconnected last night after two years and rekindled a hot romance."

"Close enough." The lines at the corners of his eyes crinkled. "We *did* reconnect and the romance *was* pretty hot."

Dammit! That lopsided grin should come with a warning label.

"Give me a sec," she said, pulling herself together, "and I'll empty a drawer for you."

His neatly folded underwear didn't take up even a fourth of the drawer. Similarly folded socks, gym shorts and sweats barely filled the rest of the empty space. He arranged the three shirts he'd brought over knife-pressed slacks and squeezed the hangers into her jam-packed closet. His one pair of sneakers and one pair of boots looked lost amid her racks of slings and mules and wedges and jeweled flip-flops.

She caught him eyeing the colorful array and gave

an embarrassed laugh. "I can't help it. Shoes are my comfort food."

"Whatever works. I'm into *Game of Thrones* myself."

"The HBO show?"

"The books. But I'll admit I've watched the video of Cersei walking naked through the streets of King's Landing more than once."

"I don't know," she mused. "I kind of liked Daenerys Targaryen's hunky husband."

"How come I didn't discover that you're a *Game of Thrones* devotee during our weekend together? Wait. Scratch that. We were pretty much otherwise occupied, weren't we?"

"Pretty much," she agreed with a flutter just under her ribs.

She'd have to think about that jittery sensation. Later. After they got back from Vegas and Ben was on his way to wherever.

Right now she had all she could handle with her prospective groom propping a baseball bat in the corner of her bedroom and hooking a ball cap emblazoned with 2014 Badger Bash on a corner of her dresser mirror.

"A little extra touch," he explained. "In case you have to spin the tale of where we met."

"Good thinking." She eyed the almost empty carry-all. "What else is in there?"

"Just a few challenge coins."

"Okay, I'll bite. What's a challenge coin?"

"A sort of unit patch. Every squadron or wing has its own. Then we trade with other units. Like baseball cards from the '50s." He rooted around in the bag and produced a handful of disks decorated with various designs. "You have to carry a coin on you at all times or you might get stuck buying a round of drinks for the house if challenged."

When she moved in for a closer look, he shuffled a coin out of the small pile. The enameled surface showed a four-engine aircraft painted a dull gray. "This is my bird, the MC-130J Commando II."

Another featured a fierce-looking eagle on a field of blue with an olive branch clutched in one claw and thunder bolts in the other. The lettering around the seal widened Alex's eyes. "Is this from the president?"

"Yeah, we hauled POTUS for a couple classified missions."

Impressed, she fingered a colorful coin displaying an orange-and-blue-striped lizard surrounded by lettering in an unfamiliar script.

"Where's this one from?"

"A little island off the west coast of Africa nobody's ever heard of." Wry amusement flickered across his face. "That was one of the hairiest approaches I ever made. A short, unimproved dirt airstrip that ended in a fifteen-hundred-foot drop to the ocean. I'd just as soon not fly in there again anytime soon, even if the locals did brew up one helluva brand of fermented guava juice."

And Alex thought her brief stint as a Vegas costume designer had been exciting! She'd rubbed elbows with a few stars, none of them A-listers but still glamorous in their own way. She'd never hauled a president around, though, or landed on a remote African island.

But suddenly, inexplicably, she couldn't wait to get back to Sin City. She'd only be there a few hours. Just long enough for them to pick up a license and say "I do." Yet for those few hours in that fairy-tale land of fake pyramids and Italian castles, she could be her old self again.

Impatiently, she checked her watch. Their flight would depart in a little over two hours. Plenty of time at an airport that didn't see anything even remotely resembling the crowds at LAX or JFK. Still, they needed to be sure to make both the outbound *and* the return flight later this evening so Ben could report for his deployment processing early tomorrow morning.

Worried that Dinah and her mom had been delayed by the orange road-construction cones that sprouted all over the city like mushrooms, Alex slid a hand in the pocket of her slacks to retrieve her phone. Thankfully, the Madisons pulled in to the drive just as she was keying their number.

"Sorry we're a little late," Pat Madison huffed when Alex opened the door to her and her daughter. "Rio Grande Boulevard's down to one lane north of Mountain Road. Some kind of accident."

"No problem. Thanks for keeping Maria today. I'll pick her up around eight thirty this evening, if that's not too late."

"That's fine."

"Dinah! Look what I got."

Maria skipped out of her room hefting her iPad, and Dinah cooed in delight.

"Cool! Now we can play Crazy Farm together. But you said you had to wait for your birthday before you got one."

"Ben brought it for me. He's…uh…" She swiveled to face the man who emerged from the master bedroom. Her lips pursed as she tried to decipher their connection. "When you 'n' Alex get married, will you be my uncle?"

"I guess so."

"Even if she's not really my aunt?"

"Well…"

"What about when she adopts me? She'll be my mom but you can't be my dad 'cause I already have one."

"How about we figure all that stuff out as we go?"

Dinah's mother followed the exchange with considerable interest. She knew about Maria's deadbeat dad. A single mom herself, she'd been a fierce advocate and trusted advisor in Alex's adoption campaign. Still, she'd expressed both surprise and concern when Alex called and explained why she needed her friend to keep Maria for the day.

Pat's concern seemed to lessen appreciably at meeting Ben. She took his hand in a no-nonsense grip and ran a frankly approving glance over his tall, lean form.

"So you're the phantom major from Alex's past. I'll admit I was a little skeptical when she called last night but what the hay. The woman's lived like a menopausal nun ever since she moved back to Albuquerque. If she's going to discard her habit, it might as well be for someone who looks like he could make it worth—"

"Pat!" Hastily, Alex cut her off. "We have to catch a plane."

"Okay, okay. C'mon, girls. Let's go."

Mere moments later Ben shoved the key in the ignition of his midnight-black Tahoe, pulled out of the drive and aimed for the airport. As he wheeled through the light Sunday morning traffic, his gaze cut to his prospective bride.

Alex hadn't spoken more than a dozen words since she'd kissed Maria and hustled her out the door. He wouldn't be surprised if she was having serious doubts about this shotgun wedding. God knew, he was. But he waited until he'd joined the traffic heading south on I-25 to comment on her obvious nervousness.

"There's still time to back out."

"I know."

She didn't look at him, just stared out the windshield as they cruised past the towers of downtown Albuquerque.

"It's your call, Alex. You don't have to do this."

That shook her out of her funk. She angled to face him and pulled on a smile. "Yes, I do. And in case I forget to tell you later, I'm more grateful than I can say. I owe you, Cowboy."

For some reason, that irritated the heck out of Ben. He didn't want her thanks any more than he wanted her to owe him. The fact that he didn't know what exactly he *did* want from her irritated him even more.

Oh, hell. Who was he kidding? He knew precisely what he wanted. The memory of this woman naked and languorous and stretched out in bed had kept him awake and aching for most of last night.

The plain truth was that he wanted her naked again. Sated and smiling and sleepy amid a tangle of sheets. Preferably in a luxurious suite similar to the one he'd taken her to their last time in Vegas. Instead, he was going to zip down to city hall, fork over fifty bucks for a marriage license, participate in a hurried ceremony and hustle his new wife aboard a flight back to Albuquerque almost before the ink had dried on their marriage certificate. Not exactly the wedding of any woman's dreams, even if she insisted that's exactly what she wanted.

* * *

Give the time change, they landed at McCarran Airport a mere thirty minutes after their Albuquerque take-off time. To Alex's surprise, a uniformed driver was waiting when they walked out into the arrivals area. The chauffeur escorted them to a stretch limo half a football field long. Alex folded herself into the decadently luxurious back seat and hiked a brow when she saw the label on the champagne bottle nested in a silver ice bucket.

"Veuve Clicquot?"

"You only get married for the first time once."

"True."

"Too bad I don't have my dress uniform and sword," he said as he peeled off the foil and unscrewed the wire cage. "Badger learned the fine art of sabering champagne while serving a stint at the US Embassy in Russia. He taught a few of us the trick during some downtime on a rotation to a former French colony that shall remain nameless."

"He was real, this colonel of yours?"

"Oh, yeah." Ben got the cork out smoothly despite the lack of a saber and filled two crystal flutes. "Here's to that first time."

It was as good a toast as any, Alex thought, given the circumstances. With a nod, she tipped her glass to his.

The familiar landscape rolled by outside the limo's window as the driver took I-15 toward downtown and the Clark County courthouse. To the right were the improbable castles and pyramids and glass towers of the Strip. To the left, the Spring Mountains rose in majestic splendor. Alex had lived here almost four years and still thought of it as home.

"By the way," she told Ben, "I called the woman I

used to room with here in Vegas. She's a dancer at the Flamingo and has a matinee show but said she could slip away long enough to meet us at the Bellagio and act as a witness."

"I called a pal, too. He's stationed at Nellis and agreed to do the same."

Alex took another sip of the champagne, hoping that the presence of two friends instead of strangers would make the quickie wedding seem a little more real.

As smooth as the champagne was, she confined herself to those two sips during the drive downtown. Once they'd obtained the marriage license, though, her nerves revved up and she gulped down what was left in her glass.

Ben's choice of the wedding venue had surprised her. Given the short notice, she'd expected a no-frills, hurry-up-and-say-I-do ceremony at one of Vegas's tacky little wedding chapels. She certainly hadn't expected the Bellagio, but given a choice it would've been among her top three or four picks.

The Bellagio's famed dancing fountains were delighting crowds of tourists when they pulled up at the main entrance, where an event planner in an Armani pantsuit was waiting with clipboard in hand and a warm smile on her face.

"We're ready for you, Ms. Scott, Major Kincaid. This way, please."

The planner led them through a lobby festooned with fabulous glass chandeliers to a private terrace overlooking the lagoon. The fountains were just finishing a lavishly choreographed sequence to "Time To Say Goodbye" sung by Sarah Brightman and Andrea Bocelli.

"Lex!"

The high-pitched squeal that pierced the music and splash of cascading water came from Alex's former roommate. A statuesque five foot ten, brimming with energy and surgically enhanced everywhere it counted, Chelsea had tossed a light wrap over a costume that consisted of spangled flesh-colored stockings, a rhinestone-studded G-string and a pearl-encrusted bra. A sparkly cap concealed her glossy black hair and buckled under her chin. The ostrich feathers topping the cap bobbed as she rushed across the terrace to engulf Alex in a rib-cracking hug.

"I still can't believe you talked someone into agreeing to your crazy scheme," she exclaimed when they disengaged.

"I can hardly believe it, either."

"You sure you want to go through with it?"

"I've run out of options."

"Mmm. How's Maria?"

"Fine. She sends her love. And her congratulations on moving up to second lead. You deserve it."

"I think so, too. I've got the best strut in town, even if I do say so myself." Her inch-long fake eyelashes fluttered as she aimed them at Ben. "So this is the sex machine you spent that wild weekend with?"

As best Alex could recall, she hadn't used quite that term to describe Ben. She had to admit it wasn't too far off the mark, though.

"Chels, this is Major Ben Kincaid. Ben, Chelsea Howard."

Although Ben topped Alex by a good five or six inches, he stood eye to eye with the long-legged dancer. He held out his hand but, before Chelsea could take it, another arrival rushed out on the terrace.

"Sorry, Cowboy. Damned traffic was backed up for a… Well, *hel-lo.*"

The new arrival's eyes locked instantly on Chelsea. His sand-colored flight suit dotted with subdued military patches told Alex this had to be Ben's pal from Nellis Air Force Base. Ben confirmed it when he pried his friend's attention away from the dancer long enough to make the introductions.

"Brace yourself, Alex. This sorry excuse for a combat systems officer is Captain Jerry Floyd, call sign Pink… for obvious reasons."

"Pink Floyd. Got it."

"And you're the woman who finally caused Cowboy to crash and burn." He pumped Alex's hand gleefully. "The news that he's going down in flames flashed around the internet with the speed of light this morning. I had to promise to post a picture of the two of you as soon as the deed is done. No one's gonna believe it otherwise."

"Speaking of doing the deed," Chelsea said, "I hate to hurry you, but I have to get back to the Flamingo."

"No problem," Ben replied easily. "We're ready, aren't we, Alex?"

As ready as she'd ever be. Still, her throat went dry when the minister launched into the time-honored, "We're gathered together to witness the joining of this man and this woman…"

She had another uncomfortable moment when the minister asked for the rings. They hadn't had time to pick them out but, thankfully, Ben had ordered plain gold bands as part of the wedding "package."

"You'll have to have it sized," he murmured as he slipped it over her knuckle.

Mere seconds later the by-the-hour minister pronounced them husband and wife. Beaming, he gave the new groom the go-ahead. "You may kiss your bride."

Prepared for this part of the ritual, Alex tipped her face for Ben's kiss. He was good at this, she remembered from their weekend together. What she hadn't remembered was *how* good.

His mouth brushed hers lightly. Then again. Slowly. Deliberately. She breathed in the warm scent of skin. Felt a sandpapery prickle where his chin scraped hers. Then he curled his arm around her waist, drew her in close and really got into it. When he raised his head and smiled down at her, her heart was jackhammering inside her chest.

"Hello, wife."

She gulped. "Hello, husband."

He looked like he was about to say something else but the event planner intervened with an apologetic smile. "I'm sorry, Major, but we've got another wedding scheduled on the terrace in fifteen minutes. Shall we move to the railing and take some pictures?"

Chelsea threw off her wrap and struck her best showgirl pose. Pink went to parade rest beside Ben. And, as if on cue, the fountains spurted and began dancing to Elvis Presley's rousing rendition of "Viva Las Vegas." Alex had to grin at the tableau they presented as the photographer did his thing.

The wedding planner was good. And quick! She accessed a nearby printer and slid copies of the best photo into silver-tinted souvenir frames, then gave one to Alex, Chelsea and Pink while the photographer texted the original JPEGs to their phones.

"You sure you guys can't stay over for a few days?"

Chelsea asked Alex as she covered her showgirl splendor with her wrap again. "I could get you an employee discount on the bridal suite at the Flamingo."

Alex was tempted. So tempted. Her mouth still tingled from Ben's kiss and memories of their nights together were crowding front and center in her mind.

"We'd love to but…"

"Yeah, you told me. Hubby's unit is deploying early tomorrow morning. Not much of a honeymoon, kid. Guess you'll have to make up for lost time when he gets home."

"Not likely," Alex murmured, "seeing as we'll probably be divorced by then."

"Ya never know," the showgirl murmured with a sideways glance at Ben. "Ya just never know."

Chapter Three

Ben had considered several options to kill the four hours between the wedding and the flight back to Albuquerque. His first choice was a room right there at the Bellagio. With a little luck and a few smooth moves, he might've been able to convince Alex to forget her no-sex condition.

Although…

His gut told him she was right to keep their pseudo-marriage platonic. By this time tomorrow he'd be sprawled in the back end of a C-17 with ten other aircrews being ferried across the pond as replacements for a squadron that had flown more than twice its share of combat missions. By the time he rotated stateside again, his brief stint as a married man would most likely be a distant memory. Going horizontal with his sexy bride might generate some happy memories to take with him.

Unfortunately, a few hours between the sheets would also complicate an already weird situation.

His second choice to fill the four hours was to take Alex out to Nellis and give her an up close glimpse of his world. But that would generate too many questions about his supposed marriage if Pink or any of his pals got wind of it. The news that Cowboy was playing tour guide to his new wife instead of heating up a honeymoon suite would hit every Special Ops news feed around the globe.

His third and only viable option was to treat his bride to a lavish wedding feast before they headed to the airport. He pitched the idea when they were once again ensconced in the limo.

"I don't know about you but I need more than airline peanuts to sustain me until we get back to Albuquerque. What say we celebrate our nuptials with a late lunch–early dinner at one of Vegas's many eateries?"

"That sounds wonderful!"

The barely disguised relief in her response told Ben she'd been worrying over ways to fill their postwedding hours, too.

"Do you have a place in mind?"

Nobly, he left the choice to her. "Your town, your call."

"Well…" she said with a quick grin.

Damn! Why hadn't he remembered how her eyes gleamed with flickers of gold when she smiled. Probably because they hadn't had much to twinkle about since they'd reconnected.

"There is one place," she told him. "But it doesn't exactly qualify as elegant."

"Your town," he repeated, thoroughly intrigued by those bright eyes.

* * *

Okay, Ben thought some minutes later, he might have made a serious error in judgment by turning the choice of eating establishments over to his bride.

He got his first clue when she leaned forward, tapped the window separating them from the chauffeur, and directed him to Pancho's Cantina on East Hacienda Boulevard. The second was when they pulled in to a dirt parking lot and Ben surveyed a structure that looked like it had started life as a garage. Rusted sedans and a burned-out bus sat off to one side of the establishment. Dented pickups with gun racks decorating their rear windows crowded the front entrance.

"This is your favorite place to eat in Vegas?" Ben asked. "A city with as many four- and five-star restaurants as Paris or London?"

"Pancho's green chili and sour cream enchiladas will melt your soul," she asserted confidently before scooting forward to rap on the window divider again. "Have lunch with us, Ernie. You'll be our special guest."

The chauffeur's glance cut to the rearview mirror. Ben endorsed the invitation with a nod. Why not?

Ten minutes later the three of them were seated in a booth and scarfing down what could only be described as fifty-megaton salsa. Ernie, they discovered, was actually Ernesto Constanza and a transplant to Vegas from south Philadelphia. Ben listened while he and Alex exchanged increasingly humorous tales of living and working in Sin City. Ernesto's anecdotes edged closer to the mob than Alex's, although Ben hiked a brow at the instances she sketched of strong-arm tactics by the unions.

When Ernie excused himself to hit the men's room,

Ben had to ask, "Did Chelsea really fork over part of her paycheck for a year to get her first break in Vegas?"

"It was either that or sleep with the slug who was doing the hiring."

"What about you? Did they lean on you, too?"

She shook her head. "I was lucky enough to be hired right out of college by one of the really, really great guys in the costume business. Don kept our union steward in line. He was also openly, proudly gay. The only threat to my somewhat dubious virtue came from the aircrews who converged on Nellis for Red Flag."

No surprise there. Red Flag was a massive combat training exercise that brought a host of air, space and cyber forces of the US and its allies to the Nevada Test and Training Range. The range's fifteen thousand square miles of desert provided a target-rich environment, realistic threat systems and an enemy force that couldn't be replicated anywhere else in the world. Ben and his crews had dodged more simulated surface-to-air and air-to-air missiles in the skies above Nevada than he wanted to count.

"I managed to resist the Red Flag crews." With a rueful smile, Alex leaned forward and propped her elbows on the table. "Can't say the same for a certain Badger Basher."

God! Did she have any idea how seductive she looked right now? The sparkles on her heart-shaped neckline pulled Ben's gaze like airfield approach lights. He tried, he honestly tried, not to stare at the swell of creamy flesh above those sparkles but he was sweating by the time the waitress dumped three platters the size of B-52s on the table.

Pancho's house special didn't do much to douse the heat in his belly but it did fill him up enough to pass on the airline's peanuts during the short flight back to Albuquerque. The sun was just beginning to sink toward the volcanic peaks across the Rio Grande when they exited the terminal. Streaks of red and gold and flaming orange tinted the sky as they claimed Ben's SUV and drove to Pat and Dinah's house to pick up Maria.

"So?" Pat asked when she answered the door and ushered Alex inside. "How was Vegas?"

"Still bright and glitzy and completely unreal."

"Your friend Chelsea make it to the ceremony?"

"She did. So did Ben's best man. They were both in uniform. Mostly."

Keying her phone, she brought up the souvenir wedding photo that the wedding planner had texted to her and Ben's phones.

"Darn! No Elvis?"

"No, thank goodness. Not that anyone would notice with Chelsea spilling out of her halter."

"True."

Alex tucked her phone back in her bag. "How were the girls?"

"Fine. They wore themselves out and are both zonked out on the sofa." She slanted Alex a quick glance. "Sure you don't want to just leave her here tonight? This being your honeymoon and all?"

"They have school tomorrow. It's enough of a battle to get Maria up and out the door at our own house. You'd need a bulldozer to do it here."

"Your call. You get her, I'll carry her backpack."

Alex had to stifle a grunt when she lifted the fifty-plus pounds of sleeping child. Maria woke only long enough to whine petulantly at being disturbed before wrapping her arms around Alex's neck.

When the two women appeared by the car, Ben popped out of the driver's seat and opened the rear door. Maria had outgrown her booster seat and five-point harness months ago but she was too sleepy to just buckle in and leave all slumped over.

"I'll ride in the back with her," Alex told him.

Unfortunately, she had Maria's head pointed the wrong way and couldn't slide her into the seat. She tried angling around. That didn't work, either.

"Here, let me."

He transferred the sleeping girl from Alex's arms into his. Maria gave another bad-tempered whine, then rolled into his chest and burrowed in. Ben looked so startled at having the seven-year-old's nose stuck in his chest that Pat laughed and Alex had to smother a smile.

"She's always cranky when she's half-asleep," she apologized. "I'll slide in first and you can hand her to me."

They reversed the process after the short drive to the casita. Ben cut the ignition, climbed out and opened the passenger door to gather the still-sleeping child in his arms. Maria didn't whine this time. Just drew up her knees, mumbled something incoherent and cuddled up against him again.

Alex slid out and refused to acknowledge the pain that lanced into her. Why couldn't Maria's father have cradled her like this? Held her just *once* and showed some love?

In Janet's last, agonizing months she'd admitted that her absent husband had resented Maria's claim on her time and attention. Eddie had never played with the girl. Never showed her any affection. And in one of his drug-induced highs, he'd claimed that his former girlfriend had slept with half the band before she dumped the kid on him and took off for parts unknown. Any of them might be the kid's father. Alex had settled that with a court-mandated DNA test when she'd gone after the bastard for child support.

Except, she acknowledged grimly as she unlocked the casita's front door, her determination to get the deadbeat dad to own up to his responsibilities had totally backfired. The incontrovertible proof that Eddie was, in fact, Maria's father had come less than a week before his arrest on drug charges. Now the asshat was in prison, still not contributing to his daughter's welfare and getting back at Alex by blocking every one of her attempts to adopt his daughter.

Her sham marriage to Kincaid had to tip the scales, she thought furiously. It *had* to.

Her jaw tight, she led the way to Maria's room and yanked down the bed comforter. Ben hooked a brow at the suppressed violence but eased the girl into bed and murmured that he'd wait in the kitchen while Alex got her undressed and settled for the night.

Alex had sternly banished all thoughts of her sister's ex by the time she followed the scent of fresh brewed coffee to the kitchen. Ben was leaning a hip against the counter with a steaming mug in one hand.

"Helped myself," he said, hiking the mug. "Hope you don't mind."

"No, of course not. I'll have some, too."

Yikes! The first sip reminded her of their weekend together, when he took his coffee strong enough to grow hair on his chest.

Not that Major Ben Kincaid would final in any of the

hairy chest contests conducted with some frequency in Vegas's less reputable lounges. Chelsea had dragged Alex to one but the fur-covered contestants had totally turned her off. Ben, she now remembered, sported a light scatter of silky black that dusted his pecs, arrowed down his chest to his belly and…

No! She'd better stop right there! She'd laid out the conditions for their fake marriage up front. No point in renegotiating them at this point. Not when he was taking off for parts unknown in a few hours. Which reminded her…

"You mentioned that you moved out of your apartment and put your things in storage. Where were you going to stay tonight?"

"I've got a room at the Transient Lodging Facility at Kirtland. But…" He glanced at his watch and shrugged. "I have to be at the Base Ops with my crew at 0400. I'll probably just hit the TLF to change into my uniform, then hang in the crew lounge until takeoff."

"You're not going to fly across country with no sleep!"

"Not hardly." He laughed. "Remind me to explain air force regs governing mandatory crew rest to you sometime."

The mutual realization that he wouldn't be around to explain crew rest…or anything else…hung in the air until he broke the awkward silence.

"My crew is one of ten being ferried across the Atlantic in the back end of a C-17. The transport crew will do the flying. The rest of us will spend the whole flight sawing z's."

"Can you tell me where you're going?"

"No. Sorry."

The silence stretched a little longer this time. Alex took another cautious sip of coffee and was hit by the unsettling realization that the kitchen she'd so lovingly decorated was just the right size for her and Maria. She'd painted the walls a sunny yellow herself and spent hours haunting Old Town's bazaar for the terra-cotta sun faces arranged above the cooktop. Ben, however, seemed to shrink the kitchen's proportions by at least a third.

It wasn't his height, she had to concede, or those broad shoulders. It had to be that Special Ops confidence. The quiet air of authority he exuded even with his back in a lazy curve and his hips propped against her kitchen counter. Somehow, some way, he owned the room.

"Why don't you hang here for a while?" she suggested.

He looked interested. *Very* interested.

Reluctantly, Alex popped his bubble. "We could go into the living room, put up our feet and talk."

"Right. Talk."

"I might need to know more about my…uh…husband than his name, rank and serial number."

Dammit! She'd better learn not to stumble over the *H* word. And, she realized as she led the way into the living room, she actually had no clue what his serial number was.

"It's the same as my Social Security number," he replied in answer to her embarrassed question. "I'll take a photo of the SS card for you. Also my military ID, which has a different number. You might need both."

He laid them on the coffee table, clicked a quick photo and texted it to Alex's cell phone. The JPEG nestled next to their wedding certificate and the picture with Chelsea and Pink in her phone's photo album.

She bit her lip as she studied Ben's face on his military ID card. She had absolutely no intention of making any spousal claim on him. All she wanted—all she needed—was his signature on a marriage license. She wasn't about to risk being accused of fraud by the air force. Or by the state of New Mexico, although she skated closer to the line with the state than she did with the military.

The thought caused a little flutter in her stomach. Resolutely, she banished it. Maria was worth the risk. A thousand times over.

Which brought her back to name, rank and serial number. If she was going to sway the Neanderthal judge who'd sustained Eddie's objection to the adoption because of Alex's single status, she needed to know more about her groom. Kicking off her shoes, she sank back against the overstuffed sofa cushions and tucked her feet under her.

"I know this sounds really manipulative... Okay, it *is* manipulative. But it would help if you tell me a little about yourself. Just in case I need to provide some details about my absent spouse."

Ben stretched out in the saggy armchair opposite her. "What do you want to know?"

She shrugged. "Your favorite ice cream. Your shirt size. Your mom's and dad's first names. Where you graduated from high school."

"Plain vanilla. Fifteen-and-a-half neck, thirty-three sleeve. Alice and Ben Senior. Although," he added sardonically, "the 'senior' part's a little iffy. My mother was fairly sure the trucker she lived with for a few months fathered me, but they parted ways long before I was born. Never saw him, never wanted to. Mom took off when I was about eight or nine. It was pretty much a series of foster homes after that."

Uh-oh! The casual way he'd tossed that out didn't pass the smell test. With a quick kick to her gut, Alex guessed he'd just shared the real reason he'd agreed to her outrageous proposal. Apparently, his childhood had been as rootless and haphazard as Maria's. His next comments confirmed her guess.

"As for high school, I dropped out after my junior year. The oil fields were hiring," he related with a careless shrug. "I'd had enough of foster homes and didn't see the need for a diploma, so I lit out on my own. The air force recruiter who had me in his sights didn't see it the same way."

"He talked you into going back to school?"

"Not hardly. Staff Sergeant Rakowski wasn't taking any chances. The man rode me like a half-broke mule until I got my GED. And he was there, looking as smug as all hell, when I headed off to basic training."

Fascinated, Alex encouraged him to continue. "And?"

"From basic I went to aircraft maintenance school. I was actually a pretty good wrench bender, but the air force provided one hundred percent tuition and fees for college. So I filled my off-time working on a bachelor's degree. After that I applied for Officer Training School. Then flight school. Then Special Ops."

He shook his head, looking almost as amazed as Alex was impressed. She didn't know very many men or women who'd made the leap from high school dropout to command of an aircrew and a multimillion-dollar aircraft.

"The transformation didn't stop there," she guessed.

"No," he admitted with a laugh that was 1 percent embarrassed and a 99 percent self-deprecating. "Eight years of flying into every godforsaken corner of the world earned me a good number of 'applied science' graduate credits. I added another twenty hours of course work and walked away with a master's in International Affairs. Sergeant Rakowski had retired by then, but he was right there again when I was awarded that piece of parchment."

"Sounds like he was a pretty good stand-in for your absent dad."

"He was," Ben said easily. "Just like the military's been a stand-in for my otherwise nonexistent family."

Alex shifted, fighting off a twinge of guilt. He didn't make any reference to the fact that he'd just acquired another family. It was too temporary, too ephemeral to factor into his personal history. The realization hit even as she was thinking how her perspective of this man had changed so drastically. Ben Kincaid's past had been the furthest thing from her mind when they'd met two years ago. All she'd seen then were those bedroom blue eyes, that sexy smile and the impressive shoulders he sported under his flight suit.

Now the memory of her purely visceral reaction made her squirm. The truth was that the man she'd hooked up with in Vegas bore little resemblance to the man she'd married a few hours ago. Oh, the eyes and the smile were the same. And she was having to fight increasingly erotic fantasies that involved peeling off his shirt and sliding her palms over those sleek, muscled shoulders.

The fact that Maria was asleep just a few yards away pretty well axed those fantasies. Not to mention the preconditions to this…arrangement…they'd entered into. Still, as he made a quick trip to the kitchen to refresh his coffee, Alex couldn't help thinking there were so many more dimensions to Ben Kincaid than she'd guessed.

"What about you?" he asked when he returned. "Favorite ice cream, dress size, Mom's and Dad's first names?"

"Rum raisin, I'm not saying, Helen and Tom."

"Your folks weren't around to help when your sister got sick?"

"They tried, but they live in a retirement community in Florida and aren't in very good health themselves. To make matters worse, Janet's scuz bucket husband pretty well sucked them dry of their savings with heartrending tales of her medical expenses. None of which he paid, of course. The money went to drugs, right up to the day he got busted."

"So you moved to Albuquerque and have assumed sole responsibility for the scuz bucket's daughter."

"Maria had lost both her stepmom and her dad. I couldn't take her away from her friends and school, too. And it turned out my talents were pretty portable. I'm doing way better as an entrepreneur than I did as an apprentice."

"That right?"

"If it wasn't so late, I'd show you my production facility. It's only rented warehouse space," she admitted with a laugh. "Nothing high-tech. But my eight employees and I are filling upward of a thousand orders a month. Mostly T-shirts and tank tops but once in a while I get ambitious and match tops to bottoms."

His gaze roamed over her outfit and lingered on the scoop neckline. "Are all your designs as sparkly as the one you're wearing?"

"Yep." Alex couldn't help basking a little in his obvious approval. "I'm the queen of bling. Literally. My trademark is my initials stitched inside a silver crown."

"Swish wants to know where to place an order."

"I'll give you a card with the URL for my website before you leave."

"Better give me a handful. I'll pass 'em out to the guys. They're always trying to figure out what to order their wives or girlfriends for birthdays or Christmas."

"Won't that be a little hard to explain?"

"What? The cards or the silver crown?"

"All of it. The cards…" she tipped her chin toward the hand holding his coffee mug "…the ring, the wife."

"I can guarantee that Swish and Dingo and Pink have already spread the word," he said drily. "The fact that I've traded in my carefree bachelor existence for a hottie with red hair, chocolate-brown eyes and a little girl will be old news by now."

Alex suspected he wouldn't get off that easy but didn't press the matter. Snuggling deeper in the sofa cushions, she asked him to tell her what he could about his unit and the kinds of missions they flew.

He could only touch briefly on their military operations but went into some detail on the humanitarian missions he'd participated in. They varied widely, from flying in rescue teams after the earthquake in Nepal to air-dropping food and medical supplies to hikers stranded high in the Rockies. Fascinated, Alex didn't realize how much time had slipped by until he checked his watch.

"I'd better go. I need to swing by the Transient Lodging Facility and change into my uniform before I check in at Base Ops."

"Oh. Okay."

She uncurled and pushed off the sofa. Not for the first time, the enormity of what she'd asked him to do hit her square in the chest. "I don't know any other way to say this, Ben, except…thank you."

"You're welcome. Let me know how it goes with the adoption."

"I will. And you stay safe."

"Do my best."

They kept the kiss easy. A friendly goodbye that left Alex awake and aching long after he'd driven off and she'd crawled into bed.

The call came in the early hours of the morning, just after 6 a.m. Dragged from a deep sleep, she fumbled for the cell phone on the nightstand and squinted groggily at the number flashing on caller ID. She didn't recognize it and smothered a curse that some idiot telemarketer or political hack would send out robo calls this early.

She started to slam the phone back down but saw that the caller had left a voice mail. She punched the icon to listen to the recording. The brief message brought her jerking straight up.

"Ms. Kincaid, this is Sergeant Johnson. I'm a med tech at the 377th Medical Group at Kirtland. There's been an accident. We're notifying you as Major Kincaid's next of kin."

Chapter Four

There's been an accident.

The words thundered in Alex's head as she scrambled upright and hit dial. The phone rang five, then seven, then eight times with no response. Swearing, she killed the call and tried again. More unanswered rings brought her out of bed and racing to the living room to turn on the TV. Horrific visions of a crashed plane engulfed in flames filled her frantic mind as she stabbed the remote, searching for breaking news. All she found on the local channels were early morning traffic and weather reports.

She got on the phone again and Googled the 377th Medical Group. When she dialed the group's main number, a recording informed her that the clinic was currently closed but was a "joint venture" with the VA hospital and after-hours queries would be forwarded to the VA's main switchboard.

"I received a call from the air force." She got it out in a rush when the switchboard operator answered. "My husband's been hurt."

She didn't stumble over her married status this time and was too frightened to notice.

"I'll put you through to the ER."

Yes, the tech who answered confirmed, Major Benjamin Kincaid had been brought into the ER two hours ago. No, he couldn't release details of the major's condition over the phone except to say he was currently in surgery.

"Oh, God!"

Trying not to panic, she hit the speed dial number for Pat Madison. An early riser, Pat was already up and quickly agreed that Alex could drop Maria off as soon as she could drag her out of bed. Alex threw on some jeans and a tank and shoved her feet into flip-flops before hitting the light switch in Maria's room.

"Hey, Kitten. Wake up."

"Nooo." Maria flopped onto her belly and buried her face in the pillow.

"You need to get up. Now!"

Ruthlessly, Alex hustled the whining seven-year-old out of bed. She had the cranky child in her school uniform and out the door in less than twenty minutes. Pat Madison promised to feed both girls breakfast and asked Alex to call with an update as soon as she knew anything.

The morning rush hour hadn't yet swelled to its peak, thank God. Even with the ever-present orange traffic cones, Alex was able to cut across on Lomas, then zip down San Pedro with minimal stops. The sand-colored, multistory complex housing the VA Medical Center backed up to Kirtland but wasn't actually part of the military installation, so Alex didn't have to worry about getting through base security. She vaguely recalled reading something about how the military and veterans population mutually benefited from this shared, state-of-the-art facility but economic efficiency was the last thing on her mind as she parked and rushed through the main entrance.

The pink-coated volunteer at the central desk checked the computer and confirmed that Major Kincaid was out of surgery and in recovery. Following her directions, Alex hurried down three different corridors. She was breathless and fearing the worst when she buzzed for entry into the surgical recovery unit and checked in at the nurses' station.

"You can go on back, Ms. Kincaid. Your husband's in unit four."

She nodded to the semicircle of glass-and-curtained cubicles behind her. The curtain was drawn on number four. Once again fearing the worst, Alex steeled herself to rap lightly on the glass.

"Yo."

Encouraged by the hearty tone, she edged the curtain aside. Relief swept through her when she saw Ben sitting on the side of a bed with a hospital gown hiked up around his hips and his left foot and leg encased in an orange cast.

"Alex?" Surprise chased across his face. "What're you doing here?"

"Sergeant Somebody called me. He said you were in an accident and he had to notify your next of kin."

"Oh, for…!" Ben shook his head. "That must've been Sergeant Johnson. He conducted our final medical out-brief and heard the guys giving me guff about our abbreviated honeymoon. Since he accompanied me to the hospital, I'm guessing he went through my wallet while I was in surgery and found the card with your name and number on it."

"Why were you in surgery? What happened?"

"Stupid accident. A couple of us were helping the loadmaster on-load our pallets of gear when a tie-down snapped. Damned pallet rolled back, right over my foot."

"Oh, no!"

"My boot protected me from the worst of it, but I crunched some bones bad enough that they had to put in a couple screws. I'm waiting for the doc now to tell me how long I'll be in a cast."

The surgeon appeared almost as if on cue. Accompanying him was another physician, this one wearing an air force flight suit. Both men looked a question at Alex, then nodded when Ben introduced his wife.

"The pallet did a number on your husband's fourth and fifth metatarsals," the surgeon explained. "They fractured right where the long bones join the base of the foot. The good news is the pins I inserted should help them fuse cleanly. The bad news is they're at the outer edge of a lower extremity and thus get a reduced blood supply, so they take longer to heal than other fractures."

"How long?" Ben wanted to know.

"You won't be able to put any weight on that foot for five to six weeks. If things look good at that point, you should graduate to a walking boot, with a return to full activity in three to four months."

"Three or four months! You're kidding!"

"Wish I was."

"C'mon, Doc. I've hurt worse than this from a flu shot."

"You might think differently when the anesthesia

wears off completely," the surgeon drawled. "I'll pre-scribe some pain pills to get you through the next few days. Also a pair of crutches. You're going to need them. Then I'll see you back here in a week to check the incision and change your cast."

Thoroughly disgusted, Ben turned to the doc in the flight suit. "Sounds like I'll be DNIF for a while."

"Sounds like. I'll put you on bed rest for forty-eight hours, limited duty after that."

Alex was still trying to figure out what DNIF and limited duty meant when the surgeon addressed her again. "A nurse will provide you with post-op instructions, Ms. Kincaid, then we'll send someone in to help your husband get dressed."

Taken by surprise, she blinked. "You're letting him go home?"

Which would've been a good thing, she thought with a gulp, except he didn't have a home to go to. He'd moved out of his apartment. Put his things in storage. Hadn't expected to return to New Mexico.

"He'll be fine," the surgeon assured her, "as long as you make sure he follows the instructions."

"Good luck with that," the flight doc added drily.

When the curtain swished shut behind them, Ben apologized. "Sorry they pulled you out of bed for this."

"It's okay. Although I have to admit the call shook me up. All the recording said was that there'd been an accident." She couldn't restrain a little shiver. "I didn't know if you were alive or dead."

"Here's your first lesson in military protocol. If I punch out, you won't get a call. You'll get an officer in dress uniform ringing your doorbell, usually accompanied by a chaplain."

"Thanks for the tip. If you don't mind, though, that's one visit I'd just as soon not experience."

Especially after the awful fears that had raced through her during the drive to the hospital. Not least of which was the grim possibility that she might be a widow before she'd really been a wife. That still churned a sick feeling in her stomach.

A nurse in surgical scrubs rattled the curtain back at that point. "I hear you're ready to hit the road, Major. I'll run through the discharge instructions, then we'll get you on your way."

Alex wasn't sure when she decided to take care of Ben during his post-op period. Probably halfway between the "no driving or consumption of alcohol or nonprescription meds for twenty-four hours" and "no making important decisions or signing any legal papers for the next thirty-six."

Whenever it hit, the idea was set in stone by the time the nurse finished reading the instructions and handed them to Alex to sign as the "responsible party." She signed where indicated and didn't realize she'd scrawled her unmarried name until she was almost done. Hiding a grimace, she was prepared to explain that she'd decided to keep her maiden name for business reasons, but the nurse merely tore off a copy of the form and passed it to her with the prescription for pain meds that the surgeon had ordered.

"And since you can't get your flight suit on over that cast," she told Ben, "we're chasing down a set of scrubs that will fit you. Hang loose a few more moments."

When she left, Ben sent Alex a wry look. "This turned out to be a helluva wedding night. Mind giving me a lift to Transient Lodging Facility?"

"You're not going to the TLF. You're coming home with me."

"Thanks, but I'm fine, Alex. I'll just rack out at—"

"You heard the instructions. No making important decisions for thirty-six hours. So I'm making this one for you."

"You've got enough on your plate taking care of Maria. You don't need to play nursemaid to me."

"I helped take care of my sister, remember? She said I didn't totally suck at playing nurse. So be a good major and follow orders."

"What about Maria? I thought we agreed to minimize the contact between her and me?"

She was still fumbling for an answer to that when a med tech almost as tall as Ben and every bit as muscular rolled in a wheelchair. A set of blue scrubs were folded neatly on the seat.

"Here you go, Major. I cut the pants off at the knees so they'll go over the cast. Let's get you into them and outta here."

"I can manage," the patient protested.

The tech ignored him, bent at the waist and held out the pants. "Right leg first. Now the left. Okay, ease off the bed. But don't put any weight on that left foot, sir! Lean on your wife."

The hospital gown parted just enough to give Alex a bird's-eye view of two really primo buns before she moved in and tucked a shoulder under Ben's arm. He accepted her help and balanced on his good foot while the tech eased the cutoff pants up over his hips. Once the drawstring was tied, Ben shrugged out of the hospital gown and reached for the V-necked top the tech handed him.

Alex's view this time was of a hard, flat stomach and tanned skin stretched taut over ribs. She kept a steadying arm around his waist as he thrust his arms through the sleeves and pulled the top on over his head. His waist seemed leaner than she remembered from their weekend together but the muscles on his arms and upper chest looked just as strong and sleek. It took some effort but she banished the memory of those arms locked around her and helped Ben pivot on his good foot so he could drop into the wheelchair the tech had ready for him.

"Hospital Supply will issue a set of crutches, Major. We can pick 'em up on the way out, then fill your prescription at the pharmacy. Ms. Kincaid, you want to drive your car around to the ER entrance? We'll meet you there in about fifteen minutes."

The morning rush hour was on its second round by the time they left the hospital and headed up San Pedro. The twenty thousand or so military and civilians who worked at Kirtland had pretty much flooded through the base's multiple gates. Now it was mostly office workers and retailers preparing to open shops who crowded the city streets.

Ben didn't say much during the short drive. His foot was hurting like hell, for one thing. For another, he hated that he'd miss the deployment. Special Operations Command would have to tap another pilot on short notice to fill his slot, and it was just that kind of sudden disruption of plans and home life that wreaked havoc on so many military marriages.

Then there was the matter of camping out at Alex's place for a few days. Disrupting *her* plans and home life. That hadn't been part of their bargain.

"I'm not sure this is a good idea," he said as she turned off San Pedro onto Lomas.

"What isn't a good idea? You having someone to check on you for the next forty-eight hours or me doing the checking?"

"Both of the above. Maria has to be nervous about our quickie marriage."

"She is," Alex admitted.

"I was supposed to be gone. Not part of her life long enough for her to form any sort of attachment."

"So we just have to make sure she doesn't form an attachment. I'll tell her you're sick. That she needs to stay out of your way and let you rest."

"I broke some bones, Alex. I didn't contract typhus or yellow fever."

"She doesn't have to know the details."

It was what he'd agreed to. Minimal contact. In and right out of their lives again. Yet the continuing deception was starting to rub Ben the wrong way. Bad enough that he and Alex had based their marriage on a lie. Now they had to add another layer of deceit. His jaw set, he finished the short ride in silence.

The awkward transfer from her car to her bedroom didn't improve his mood. He'd broken bones before. An arm as a kid, when he fell out of a tree. Two ribs during high altitude egress refresher training a couple years ago. He'd also compressed some disks at the base of his spine during a hard landing and narrowly missed losing an eye when the cockpit of his aircraft took rounds during a low, slow approach. You didn't spend twelve years in Special Ops without sustaining the occasional bodily injury. This was his first time on crutches, though.

He understood the physics. They were simple enough.

Each of the two struts supported half his weight. When angled forward at least twenty-five to thirty degrees, they distributed that weight and exerted enough friction force to keep the tips from slipping. Understanding the physics didn't necessarily equate to putting them smoothly into practice.

Navigating the terra-cotta tiled walkway from the drive to the front door required fierce concentration. The small step up to the front stoop almost landed him flat on his face. As a consequence, he was somewhat less than grateful when Alex guided him into the entry hall.

"You should probably lie down."

"I'm okay."

"You sure? You were up most of the night. And you still have anesthesia swimming in your system."

"I don't need to lie down."

"Ben, be reasonable," she said in the overly patient tone she probably employed with Maria. "The discharge instructions say you need to rest today."

"All right! I'll stretch out on the sofa."

She steered him into the living room and settled him on the couch with cushions under his head and his injured leg. The crutches she propped close at hand. A few adjustments tilted the wooden shutters at the right angle to block the bright morning light.

"I'll get some water so you can take the pills the doc prescribed."

"I don't need the pills."

Planting both fists on her hips, she studied him with an air of exaggerated patience. "Something tells me you don't like being laid up."

"You're right, I don't."

"Tough. Get used to it, Major. For the next few days, anyway."

Ben's scowl followed her as she disappeared into the kitchen. Yeah, okay. He could handle a few days. The nights were another story. What was he supposed to do? Just zone out here on the sofa while his bride curled up in bed just a few yards away?

"Hell," he muttered. "Just the way every man wants to spend his honeymoon."

That was his last cogent thought for a solid six hours.

The sun was slanting through the shutters at a sharp angle when he blinked awake and focused his blurry vision on a small round face. He recognized the dark hair and eyes but it took a moment to connect the patch on her white blouse with a school uniform.

"Hi, Maria. You just get home?"

"Uh-huh. Alex says you're sick 'n' I'm not supposed to bother you."

"Where is she?"

"Outside talking to Dinah's mom. Are you going to stay at our house now?"

"For a couple days."

"On the couch?"

"Maybe."

Her scowl clued him in to the idea that wasn't the right answer. Her next words confirmed it.

"Alex always lets me watch PBS after school. There's a program on today about whales. I want to watch it."

"Okay, no problem."

He reached for the crutches propped against the arm of the sofa. The truth was he needed to hit the head in the worst way. The hacked-off legs of his scrub pants required some careful maneuvering but he managed to lever himself up without exposing any moving parts.

"The TV's all yours, kid."

Ben was no stranger to high stress environments. Employing his MC-130's terrain-following and terrain-avoidance radars to infiltrate a hostile area of operations at 250 feet in adverse weather conditions required a cool head and a firm hand on the throttles. But damned if keeping his injured foot off the floor while thumping down the hall to the bathroom didn't require almost as much concentration.

His inability to master the crutches frustrated him. That, and the distinct possibility his injury would keep him off flying status for as long as three or four months. Still, he shouldn't take his frustration out on Alex. Not when all she did was follow him into the bedroom and remind him that the discharge instructions didn't include a shower.

"You can't risk getting the cast wet. And I should check the foot for redness or swelling now that you're up."

"You ever hear of SERE?"

"Not that I recall."

"It stands for Survival, Evasion, Resistance and Escape. Fifteen days of unmitigated hell designed to give crews the skills to survive in any environment if their aircraft goes down. We learn everything from constructing shelters to surviving on grasshoppers to burrowing into snowbanks to basic surgical techniques."

"And your point is?"

"I helped design the current curriculum, dammit. I know how to assess a wound for signs of infection."

"Well, ex*cuse* me."

Her indignation blunted some of his ire. "Sorry. I guess I'm just not used to feeling helpless."

"Could've fooled me."

"Again, I'm sorry. Look, why don't I make it up to you by buying dinner? Delivery," he amended quickly, thinking of their earlier conversation. "You order and I'll eat here in the bedroom to refrain from contaminating Maria."

The sarcasm was unintended but raised a flush on her cheeks.

"Just make my portion man-size," Ben said to get past the awkward moment. "I'm starving."

"What do you want?"

"Whatever. You decide while I hit the head."

She bit her lip, studying the bathroom door as it closed behind him, then let her glance drift to the wedding photo in its souvenir cardboard frame. She'd found a little artist's easel to display it on and positioned it on the nightstand. Another prop, like the baseball bat in the corner, the ball cap and the underwear in the dresser drawer.

Good Lord! Was it just yesterday morning that she'd cleared the drawer and some closet space for him? A day and a half since she'd zipped down to Vegas, married a man she knew only in the Biblical sense and introduced her fake husband into Maria's orbit? Short hours ago she'd assumed the role of "responsible party" for said husband?

A little stunned at how complicated her life had become in such a short, whirlwind stretch of hours, Alex retrieved an extra pillow and pillowcase from the linen closet in the hall. Ben would need it to prop his foot on tonight. Luckily, she'd changed the sheets on her bed while he was zoned out earlier that afternoon. Despite his tough, macho act, he was *not* spending the night on the sofa. It was okay for a nap but she wasn't about to have him tossing and turning and possibly jamming his injured foot against the sofa arm as the last of the anesthesia wore off and pain kicked in.

Speaking of which…

She was waiting with his pain meds when he clumped awkwardly out of the bathroom. Not surprisingly, he nixed the meds again. She swallowed a sigh but knew better than to argue this time.

He did, however, accept the offer of a thriller she'd finished a few days ago and had yet to return to the library. He also asked her to retrieve his cell phone from the bag with his belongings that they'd brought home from the hospital. A quick glance showed he had more than a dozen voice mails.

"I need to return a few of these calls." He nodded toward the alcove containing a pine plank workstation that served Alex as combination desk and artist's table. "Mind if I use your desk?"

"Of course not. Let me clear some space."

She shuffled together a half-dozen sketches and stacked several catalogs atop the files with invoices she hadn't input into her computer yet. She left a pad out in case he needed to make notes and made sure the armadillo pencil holder Maria had given her for her birthday was close at hand.

"I can boot up the computer if you need to access your email," she offered as he clumped over to the desk.

"I'll check them on my phone. But you could give me the password for your network, if you don't mind."

She waited until he was online. "Do you need anything else?"

"No, this is good. Why don't you go order supper? I'm—"

"Starving. I know." She did a quick mental review of the restaurants in the local area that offered delivery service. "How does Chinese sound?"

"Great. Especially if they have Szechuan beef on the menu."

"If they don't, what's your backup?"

"Lemon garlic shrimp."

The weirdness of their situation hit her yet again. She'd spent one wild weekend and one nowhere-near-as-wild day with this man. Yet here they were, talking Szechuan beef and garlic shrimp as if the choice of dinner entrées was the most important item on their agenda. Swallowing a small bubble of something that could've been either hysterical laughter or sheer disbelief, she left him sitting at her desk, checking his email.

It was best this way, she reiterated to herself as she called in the order. Minimizing contact between Ben and Maria for the next few days would be difficult but necessary to ease the separation when it came. Still, she felt like a total fraud when she informed the girl that Ben was hurting and would take his dinner on a tray in the bedroom.

Maria frowned but seemed to accept his absence from the dinner table. She even ate some of the green beans with cashews that Alex piled on her plate alongside the brown rice and pineapple pork. She dug in her heels, however, when Alex nixed her offer to let Ben share her fried ice cream.

"He ordered a banana spring roll for dessert."

"They're so small! And he's so big."

Alex couldn't argue with that.

"Ben gave me an iPad," Marie reminded her. "You always tell me that when someone gives me something, I should be polite 'n' find a way to say thank you."

"That's true. But…"

The girl's lower lip made an ominous appearance. "I want him to have my ice cream."

"Okay, okay. I'll take it to him."

"I'll take it. That way he'll know it comes from me."

"Maria…"

Alex might as well have been talking to herself. The seven-year-old had already jumped out of her chair, grabbed her plate and scooted toward the hall.

Chapter Five

An authoritative rap on the bedroom door diverted Ben's attention from the response he was drafting to an email from Swish asking a) how his foot was doing and b) how he was taking to married life. The first question was a helluva lot easier to answer than the second.

"It's open," he called out, expecting Alex.

Instead, a dark-haired sprite pushed into the room carrying a bright yellow bowl. "I brought you some fried ice cream. It's my *favorite* dessert," she informed him. "But I want you to have it 'cause you bought me an iPad."

Ben accepted the magnanimous offer with appropriate gravity but couldn't fail to note her air of noble sacrifice. "This is a big serving," he commented when she passed him the dessert. "Too much for me. Why don't you get another bowl and we'll share?"

Accepting with an eager nod, she left the door open

behind her. As a result, Ben caught most of her brief exchange with Alex, the most emphatic part of which was a clear, distinct "...and don't bother him!"

When the girl returned with a bowl and spoon, her expression had given way to one of wounded dignity. "Alex says I'm not supposed to bother you. Am I?"

Pinned by those dark eyes and that demand for a straight answer, Ben struggled with what was looking like an unworkable strategy of isolation and containment for a few moments before answering truthfully. "Nope, you're not bothering me."

"That's what I told her." Claiming half of the ice cream, Maria settled cross-legged at the foot of the bed. "Dinah's got Baby Dragons II on her iPad. Can I get it on mine?"

"We'll have to ask Alex."

Ben enjoyed the ice cream interlude more than he would've expected. Although some of the foster parents who'd taken him in had other kids, the survival instincts he'd developed early had made him pretty much a loner. Since striking out on his own, his exposure to young children was limited to brief interactions with the offspring of his squadron mates and even briefer operational contacts with children battered by war or nature's fury.

According to Alex, Maria's childhood so far had been almost as unsettled as Ben's had been. Yet he couldn't see any signs that it had made her sullen or introverted or distrustful. She was most definitely her own person, he discovered as her conversation jumped with dizzying speed from baby dragons to the latest Disney movie to the book she'd downloaded from the library.

"It's called *Anne of Green Gables*. Alex says it's a classic. That means it's really old. Have you read it?"

"'Fraid not."

"I just started but it's really good so far." Her lips pursed around her spoon, wiping it clean. "If you want, I can send it to your iPhone so you can read it, too. Then we can talk about it."

Ben refused to think of the ribbing he'd take if he got caught with a kid's classic on his iPhone. "Sure, send away."

"'Kay." She hopped off the bed. "I'll do it now. You can start reading it tonight."

Why not? Ben thought sardonically. It wasn't like he was going to be otherwise occupied.

Despite the tantalizing prospect of a children's classic, Ben opted for the paperback thriller Alex had dug up for him and stretched out on the bed. As master bedrooms went, this one was fairly small, with barely enough room for the bed, dresser, two nightstands and the desk tucked into an alcove that looked out on the enclosed back patio. Yet Alex's personal flair showed in the soft turquoise walls, the pierced tin mirror above the dresser, the burlap curtains and the headboard constructed of peeling birch logs.

With the door to the room still cracked open a few inches, Ben could hear Alex preparing Maria for bed in the next room. He picked up bits of their chatter about school tomorrow and a long debate on Maria's part over whether to wear her Cinderella or Princess Elsa pj's. That thorny issue resolved, Ben heard a faint gush of water and what sounded like a habitual admonishment.

"Up and down, Kitten. Brush up and down."

Ben had to marvel at Alex's patience. He knew she'd turned twenty-five last month. He'd made a note of her birthday when they'd filled out the forms for the marriage license in Vegas. That meant she'd barely graduated from college and begun her career in costume design when they'd met in Vegas two years ago. Yet she'd put her life on hold to move to Albuquerque and take care of her sister, then jettisoned it completely to assume temporary custody of her sister's stepdaughter. A little over a year later she'd married a near stranger to try and make that custody permanent.

Now, he discovered, as Maria's high treble floated from the other room, she intended to sacrifice her bedroom to the cause.

"Why'd you put blankets and your jammies on the other bed in my room?" the girl wanted to know.

"I'm bunking with you tonight."

"I thought married people were s'posed to sleep in the same bed."

"They usually do. But I don't want to risk kicking Ben's injured foot in my sleep."

"It's got a cast on it."

Out of the mouths of babes, he thought wryly.

"Davy Jenkins had a cast on his arm," the girl continued. "You could thump it 'n' write on it 'n' everything."

"I know, but Ben just got his this morning. He's not used to it yet so we have to be careful. Say your prayers now."

"I should write on Ben's cast. Or draw some daisies."

"I don't think he's the daisy type. Say your prayers."

"Stars, then. Or butterflies! He'd like butterflies!"

"Prayers, Kitten."

* * *

Ben wasn't surprised when Alex knocked on the partially open door a few moments later. "C'mon in."

She slipped in, closed the door behind her and grimaced. "I assume you heard the bit about cast decorations."

"I did. Thanks for putting the kibosh on daisies. You can't imagine the ration of grief I'd get if I waltzed into the squadron sporting a spring bouquet."

"You're not home free," she warned. "Although I will say Maria's actually pretty good at butterflies. She'll probably want to glue some sparkly crystals on their wings, though."

"Oh, Lord. Maybe I can talk her into doing a Spider-Man design instead."

"Or none at all," she said pointedly.

The message was about as subtle as a 20 mm cannon.

"Got it. You want me to keep her at arm's length."

"I do. It'll help close the hole when you disappear from her life."

"The way her father did."

"Exactly."

She was right. Ben knew she was right. Still, being lumped in with a deadbeat, drug-dealing dad stuck in his craw. Swinging his legs to the side of his bed, he grabbed the crutches.

"I heard the part about you sleeping on the other bed in Maria's room, too. I caught a glimpse of it earlier. It's kid-size."

"Doesn't matter."

"Sure it does. I'll take the couch and you can have your bed."

"No way. You're the patient. I'm the 'responsible party,' at least according to the air force. So I'm calling the shots for the next few days, Cowboy."

"Guess again, sweetheart."

Her hands went to her hips again. Ben figured they'd end up there a lot before she was shed of him in a day or two. Then his glance flicked from those slender, seductive hips to the breasts so deliciously outlined by her tank top, to her set jaw and tired eyes.

Crap! She hadn't slept much more than he had in the past twenty-four hours. She had to be totally wiped... and in no condition to camp out on a sofa.

"Sorry," he said, disgusted with himself for adding to her stress. "I don't mean to come on like such a Neanderthal. It's just...well..."

"Are you hurting?"

"Some," he lied.

More than some. Ben had been kicking himself six ways to Sunday for almost an hour for refusing to take the pain pills. "As much as I hate to admit it, I need those meds the doc prescribed."

"Why didn't you say so!"

She hurried across the bedroom and snatched the plastic bottle off the dresser. After wrestling with the childproof cap, she dumped two pills into his palm, disappeared into the bathroom and returned with a tumbler of water. As reluctant as Ben was to dull his senses with opiates, he tossed back the pills and eased his legs onto the mattress.

"It'll take a while for the wonder drugs to work their magic." He patted the covers beside him. "Keep me company until they do."

When she hesitated, he grinned. "What? Remembering the last time we were in bed together?"

"And you aren't?"

"Oh, yeah. That weekend's been on my mind more than you can imagine the past few days. But we're both fully clothed and I just popped some pills. You're safe."

Tonight, anyway. Ben wouldn't make any guarantees about the days or nights to come.

"Tell me about your business," he prompted, patting the comforter again. "How'd you get started and build up so fast to those thousand-plus orders?"

Alex hesitated. Her head told her stretching out next to him was a mistake. She couldn't seem to quell the ridiculous flutters his proximity caused. Or the erotic memories it generated!

Yet every instinct she possessed said she could trust Ben to hold to his word. Strange, really, given how little time they'd actually spent together. But trust him she did. At least enough to kick off her flip-flops, ease onto the bed and stuff a pillow behind her back.

"It didn't feel as though the business grew very fast during that first, scary year," she admitted with a grimace. "Maria and I lived on my sister's small insurance policy and my pitiful savings for almost that entire year. I used the time to experiment with designs and search for wholesalers selling supplies I could afford. At one point I took a job flipping hamburgers while Maria was in school and set up a miniproduction line in the living room at night."

"You didn't think about quitting?"

"Every day. I even set a drop-dead date. If Alexis Scott Designs hadn't broken even by that date, I would've packed it in."

"What got you past the deadline?"

"Not what," she corrected with a smile, "who. Chelsea strong-armed every gal in the Flamingo chorus line into buying at least one of my T-shirts. The guys, too. Then she sent them out with strict instructions to strong-arm *their* friends. I had to hire my first employee to fill all those orders."

"The first of how many?"

"I've got six full-time now, two part-time."

She wiggled her back against the pillow to get more comfortable. The birch-pole headboard was unique and beautifully Southwestern but not exactly the most comfortable for propping her shoulders against.

"Here, scoot closer."

Uh-oh. Another mistake. She knew it even before she inched sideways. She held herself stiff but had to admit the arm Ben slipped around her shoulders added considerably to her comfort. The blue scrub shirt just inches from her nose carried the faint scent of hospital starch and warm male. She was taking a surreptitious sniff when a question rumbled up from the chest so close to her own.

"Where do you get the ideas for your designs?"

"Anywhere and everywhere." Despite the warning sirens going off inside her head, she relaxed against him. "Most of the time, though, I tend to stick to colors found in natural combinations. Turquoise and silver. The black, brown and gold in tiger's eye. The pearlescent and pink of opals. Then I arrange the beads and crystals in a way that tells a story, at least to me."

"Yeah?"

"The first shirt I made for Maria had a kitten on the front. I did the fur in silver and gray beads and gave it a little pink nose. She wouldn't take it off for a week. That's how she got her nickname."

"Mmm."

The rumble was deeper this time. More drawn out. Cautiously, Alex angled her head and saw his eyes had closed. She bit back a smile as her gaze tracked down from the dark lashes curved against his cheeks to his nose to his lips. They were parted just enough to let his breath rustle in, then out, with each rise and fall of his chest.

She was still conducting her leisurely inventory when the rustle gained volume. Within moments it was perilously close to a snore. Alex debated whether it would wake him if she eased off the bed. Probably. Best to let him sink a little deeper first. She'd just nestle her cheek on his shoulder and rest for a few more minutes...

"Wake up!"

The petulant demand was accompanied by a sharp poke in Alex's arm.

"Huh?"

"You hafta walk me to school."

Blinking owlishly, Alex pushed up on one elbow. Or tried to. The heavy weight draped around her waist pretty much anchored her in place. Squinting, she brought Maria's scowling face into focus.

"What time is it?"

"Late. I already ate my cereal 'n' banana."

She'd dressed herself, too. In the same white blouse and navy blue plaid skirt she'd worn yesterday. Alex frowned at the wrinkles in the blouse but a quick glance at the digital clock on the nightstand nixed all thought of ironing.

"Yikes! It's almost eight fifteen. We have to get going!"

The girl's scowl stayed in place while Alex detached the dead weight from around her waist and tossed aside the covers that had somehow wrapped around her during the night.

"You said you weren't going to sleep in the same bed with Ben," Maria reminded Alex as she shoved her feet into the flip-flops she'd discarded last night.

"I wasn't. I didn't. I mean, we didn't sleep…"

Okay, she'd better not go there.

"Ben's foot was hurting," she said instead, "so I gave him his medicine and was waiting to make sure it did the trick when we both just fell asleep."

She tugged down the T-shirt that had twisted around her midriff and made a beeline for the bathroom.

"Two minutes, Kitten. Two minutes, then we'll head for school."

The three-block walk through the soft May morning wiped the cobwebs from Alex's mind. At the tall, old-fashioned wooden gates of the San Felipe School, she gave Maria a quick kiss and nodded to the volunteer who made sure only students and authorized adults entered the campus.

Then she watched while her charge joined the stream of kids in blue-and-white uniforms hurrying to their classes. The school formed part of a compound that included a convent, a rectory and the church started by Father Manuel Moreno in 1705. Dominating the north side of Old Town Plaza, the historic mission church featured twin towers and five-foot-thick adobe walls.

Jesuit priests had taught boys at the school for more

than a hundred years. The Sisters of Charity had done the same for girls. Although most teachers were laypersons now, they still held to their predecessors' teaching methods. Thank goodness they offered greatly reduced tuition to needy and exceptional students. Maria had qualified on both counts, and loved the strict order and discipline. Even the uniforms. Probably because she'd lived through so much uncertainty and disruption elsewhere in her young life.

And now, Alex thought with a sigh, she'd added yet another element of uncertainty in the shape of a here-today, gone-tomorrow air force pilot. The thought made her cringe and send decidedly unfriendly thoughts zinging through space to the judge who'd driven her to drastic action.

She needed to call her lawyer, she reminded herself as she started to walk home. Inform him…and the court… that her marital status had changed. She'd also better prepare for a court-directed home visit by the hearing officer assigned to Maria's case. Judge Hendricks might be stuck in the last century, but he wasn't completely senile. He might well suspect the quickie marriage was a sham and could demand hard evidence to prove otherwise.

The realization stopped Alex in her tracks. If the judge found out Ben hadn't deployed with his unit… that he'd been injured and had subsequently moved into the Transient Lodging Facility on base because his loving wife couldn't be bothered to care of him long-term…

Hell, hell, *hell!*

Suddenly overwhelmed by the web of deceit she'd spun, Alex dropped onto one of the decorative iron benches ringing the plaza. The plan had seemed so quick and simple when she'd devised it less than a week ago.

Now it loomed in her mind like a potential disaster of epic proportions.

Visions of being hauled in front of the judge and charged with contempt of court or intent to defraud or whatever the old fart decided to throw at her cut through her mind like a jagged knife. What would happen to Maria then? To Ben, who'd participated in the sham marriage?

Half a heartbeat away from a full-blown panic attack, she wrapped her arms around her middle and bent over at the waist. Oh, God! What she wouldn't give right now to tuck her tail between her legs and scurry back to Vegas. To be single and unattached and stupid again. No responsibilities except getting to work on time. No invoices waiting to be paid or orders to fill or employees depending on her for their next paycheck. No seven-year-old demanding her constant attention or court proceedings hanging over...

"Alexis?"

The hesitant query barely penetrated her incipient panic.

"Alexis, are you all right?"

Gulping in a ragged breath, she unbent. The mother of one of Maria's classmates stood beside the bench. Alex couldn't remember the woman's name. Or her son's. Only that the kid had a wide gap between his front teeth and had nursed a sort of crush on Maria for a whole week, or so she'd claimed.

"Are you ill? Do you need help?"

"No. No, thank you. I just...skipped breakfast and felt a little faint for a moment. I'm fine now."

"Are you sure? You don't look fine."

"I am. Honestly." Alex pushed to her feet and forced a smile. "Thanks for stopping to ask, though."

"My car's right around the corner. I'll drive you home."

"I just live a few blocks from here. The walk will clear my head."

"I wish you'd let me drive you."

"I'm okay. Really. But again, thank you."

The short walk actually did clear her head. So much that she realized she only had one choice. She and Ben should end their sham marriage now, before either of them got in any deeper.

Or…

Or…

They could make it real.

The thought crept up on her slowly, hesitantly. Like a stray puppy not sure of its welcome. A long-term commitment had in no way, shape or form figured in her plans. God knew she had enough on her plate to deal with. Yet the possibility burrowed its way in her head and, annoyingly, took on a life of its own.

Her overriding instinct was to reject it out of hand. She and Ben barely knew each other. Their lives were too different, too divergent. But…

Despite her instincts, the positives began to elbow out the negatives. Why *not* make it real? Neither of them could deny they were attracted to each other. And they'd certainly proved their sexual compatibility during that wild weekend. Plenty of couples would jump into marriage on that basis alone.

More important in her mind was that Ben sympathized with her determination to gain custody of Maria.

88

He wouldn't have agreed to her proposal otherwise. So what if neither of them was driven by that indefinable, ambiguous notion of *L-O-V-E*? Alex didn't need stars in her eyes or the fairy-tale promise of happily-ever-after. She needed—wanted!—the kind of safe, solid, nonturbulent relationship her every instinct said Major Ben Kincaid would provide. So she would ask him, she decided as she marched up the walk to her casita.

To marry her.

For real.

That was the plan, anyway. Right up until she let herself into the house, headed down the hall to her bedroom and found him encasing his left leg from toe to knee in Saran Wrap. Half amused, half exasperated, Alex tossed her house keys on the dresser.

"I hope you're not planning what I think you are."

He sent her a quick glance over his shoulder. "If you think I'm planning to hit the shower, I am."

"That's crazy. Look, there's a drugstore a few blocks away. I'm sure they sell some sort of waterproof sleeve to go over casts."

"I'll pick one up later. In the meantime..." The plastic whooshed as he tugged it from the roll and continued wrapping. "Remember that SERE training I told you about? If we didn't learn anything else during those weeks in hell, we learned how to improvise. You wouldn't believe what you can do with a standard issue poncho and some duct tape. This'll work just as well."

"But..."

"Sorry, Alex. Last time I showered and shaved was right before I picked you up for the flight to Vegas. I need to sluice off."

He gave the plastic a final wrap, tore off the end and tucked it in, then straightened and tossed the roll aside.

"Good thing I left some of my stuff here. Mind getting those blue jersey sweatpants and shirt out of the drawer for me?"

Since he was already peeling off the V-necked scrub top, Alex yielded to the inevitable. He was up on his good foot, the crutches in place and the scrub pants riding low on his hips when she returned with the requested items.

"I'll take a shower when you're done," she said, trying not to fixate on the wide expanse of bare chest filling her vision. "I feel pretty gritty, too, after sleeping in these clothes last night."

"Or..." he waggled his brows "...we could conserve water and take one together."

He'd tossed out the suggestion as a joke. Mostly. But once it was there, hanging between them, it generated a sudden charge.

The amused glint faded from his eyes and his voice took on a husky edge. "Seems like I recall us getting naked and wet before."

They had. At least twice in the shower and once in the hot tub that came with their suite. The memory of those erotic encounters made Alex's pulse skip almost as much as the knuckle he brushed down her cheek.

"I know we agreed that sex wouldn't be part of the deal," he murmured, holding her eyes with his, "but I'm willing to renegotiate the terms of our agreement if you are."

Alex caught her breath. Just moments ago she'd decided to offer him a choice to opt out of their marriage or dive all the way in. He'd just opened the door for her.

"You sure you want to complicate things between us even more than they already are?" she asked.

"Why not?"

His knuckle made another pass. Slowly. Deliberately. Then his hand slid to her nape. The palm was rough against her skin, the eyes holding hers deep blue and steady.

"The way I see it, we've already jumped aboard a moving train. Might as well see where it takes us."

"It could take us on a rocky ride."

"It could."

"Just to be clear, I'm talking long term here, Cowboy. You. Me. Maria."

That gave him pause. Hesitation flickered across his face. "I don't know how good I'll be at long term. Haven't had any practice at it."

"I'm willing to take my chances if you are."

His gaze was serious now, his hand still on her nape. "What about the hearts and flowers, Alex? The romance and passion? Isn't that what every woman looks for in a marriage?"

"Somehow I don't think passion will be a problem," she responded drily. "As for romance…?" Shrugging, she surrendered the last of her girlish dreams. "I suspect it's probably way overrated. But you can still back out, Ben. Now's the time to cut your losses and run. The odds are against us here."

He responded the way she suspected he always would to a challenge. His grin slipped out and all trace of hesitation left his face.

"Hell, Alex, life's pretty much one big crapshoot. Now, about that passion…"

Chapter Six

This wasn't the first time they'd locked lips since their explosive weekend in Vegas. Just a few days ago they'd sealed their wedding vows with a kiss. They'd shared another before he'd left for his aborted deployment.

Neither of those two experiences came anywhere close to the intensity of this one, however. Alex couldn't imagine how Ben maintained his balance with one foot off the floor and the crutches jammed under his arms, but he did. So well, in fact, that her chest was crushed against his and their hips were locked in a hard, intimate embrace.

The feel of him, the taste of him, started a slow smoldering in her blood. The heat gathered steam and flowed through her veins, searing the surface of her skin. She wrapped her arms around his waist, supporting him, supporting herself, while the flame burned hot and bright in her belly.

Alex couldn't remember the last time she'd felt this sudden, raging need. Not in the past two years, certainly. Taking care of Janet in her last weeks, assuming responsibility for Maria, starting a business and battling Janet's jerk of an ex for child support and custody... Those events had crowded one on top of the other and left her exhausted both physically and emotionally. Hooking up with some stud to relieve her tension had never even entered her mind.

Until now. Now all she could think of, all she wanted, was her hands on Ben and his on her. But first...

She broke the kiss and pulled in a shuddering breath. "You can't stay perched on one foot indefinitely. If we're going to do this, we need to get in the shower, then get horizontal."

"I vote we skip the shower," he said, his blue eyes stormy, "and go straight to horizontal."

Her heart was fluttering in her throat but she managed a laugh. "And waste all that Saran Wrap?"

Besides which, she really did feel gritty and was probably more than a little aromatic.

Thankfully, the shower was a roomy walk-in crafted with glass blocks and a tiled bench at the back that Alex found perfect for shaving her legs. It would work just as well for Ben.

"Drop your drawers, Cowboy, and take a seat."

He tried, but the drawstring on the shortened scrub pants had knotted and resisted his best efforts to get it loose. Alex watched him fuss with it for a few moments, then nudged his hands aside.

"Here, let me."

When she picked at the knot, her fingers brushed his stomach. He sucked in a quick breath and hollowed his belly. They were both rethinking the whole idea of a shower by the time the knot finally worked loose.

Then the scrub pants dropped and it was Alex's turn to suck air. Lord, he was buff! And ready! His sex jutted from the dark hair of his groin and had Alex rushing to get them both scrubbed down.

"Sit there."

Once he was positioned on the bench, she set the crutches outside the walk-in and shed her clothes with brisk efficiency. Feeling the pinprick of his admiring gaze on every inch of her body, she angled the showerhead away from him and turned on the taps. His eyes gleamed with appreciation as she soaped down…and narrowed in disappointment when she angled the showerhead so the water would reach his right side but not drench his left, then handed him the washcloth and soap.

"Aren't you going to do the honors?"

"You broke your foot, not your hand."

"Spoilsport."

"Think so?"

She leaned down and kissed him. Hard. "Do your thing, Cowboy, and I'll do mine."

Her "thing" consisted of knotting a towel sarong-like around her middle, lightly dusting with bath powder and dragging a brush through her tangled hair.

When Ben signaled that he was done, she turned off the taps but made him wait until the excess water swirled down the drain. Still not trusting the slick tiles, she grabbed another towel and spread it over the wet surface. Only then did she hand Ben the crutches.

She was right beside him when he exited the steamed-up glass blocks, ready to steady him if he teetered. He made it out safely, thank goodness, and she toweled him dry. The feel of him, the sculpted symmetry of those sleek muscles, kicked her pulse into overdrive again. Her breath was coming fast and shallow as she worked her way down, then up.

The movement of her hands over his body stirred him, too. The evidence rose right before her eyes. Before she finished blotting away the dampness, his sex was rampant again. But as obviously eager as he was, he took a moment to scrape a palm across his cheeks and chin.

"Do you have a razor handy? My shaving kit's with my gear, waiting for me at Base Ops."

"I've got one," Alex told him. "But I use it to shave my legs and the blade passed dull a week ago."

He winced and declined the offer. "We'll just have to work around the whiskers."

They would also, he advised ruefully, have to work around the fact that his emergency supply of condoms was in his shaving kit. "Unless you keep a stash handy," he said hopefully.

"Nope. Haven't had any reason to," she admitted with a wry grimace.

"Not a problem. If we didn't learn anything else in SERE training, we learned how to—"

"Improvise," she finished for him.

"Right." Stretching out on the bed, he swung his legs onto the mattress and patted his middle. "Climb aboard and let me demonstrate."

What woman could refuse such a romantic invitation? Laughing, Alex dropped the towel and straddled his waist. He obviously enjoyed the view she presented.

His gaze traced a lazy path from her breasts to her belly and back again. His hands followed the same route.

Lazy soon amped up to tight and hungry. His hands stroked her breasts and his busy fingers teased her nipples into stiff, aching points. A very persistent erection poked at her behind. Then he cupped her bottom, inched her forward and brought her within reach of his tongue. At which point he proceeded to rock her world.

Alex could only blame what happened next on the aforementioned dry spell. The orgasm hit with no warning. There was no buildup. No slow, delicious spiral of heat. Just a monster wave of sensation that slammed down on her, clenching her thighs, bowing her spine. She didn't try to fight it. Couldn't, even if she'd wanted to. Arching her head back, she rode the wild waves.

When the swirling finally subsided, she was so limp that she just fell sideways onto the mattress. Cradled against him, it was some time before she realized they weren't done. Or he wasn't, anyway.

He spun it out this time. Explored her slowly, almost methodically. Every touch, every taste seemed to leave its own special brand. When he had her strung tight again, she rolled onto her side and flashed him a wicked grin.

"Okay, Cowboy. My turn to improvise."

Ben barely had time to process her husky promise before her mouth closed around him and every ounce of blood in his head shot south.

Ben's eyes were closed when she pried hers open some moments later. Crossing her hands on his chest, she propped her chin on them.

"Wow," he grunted, his lids still shut.

"Wow," she echoed. "Was it this good two years ago? In Vegas?"

He opened one eye and squinted at her. "I can't remember my name right now, never mind what happened two years ago."

"I didn't hurt your foot, did I?"

"Oh, babe. My foot's never had it so good. Neither has the rest of me."

Alex threw a casual glance at the clock and gave a gasp of dismay. "Oh, Lord! It's almost ten. I should've been at the warehouse an hour ago. Thankfully, one of the women who works for me has a key. She'll have let the others in. But I'd better get it in gear. What about you?" she asked as she pushed off his chest. "What's on your agenda for the rest of the day?"

"I should check in at the squadron. Then pick up my gear bag and my car and get some things out of storage." He propped himself up on one elbow. "If you're serious about extending the terms of our agreement, that is."

"If I wasn't before, I am now." She traced her forefinger along his whiskery chin. "Think we can make this work for us, Fly Boy?"

"We've got as good a chance as anyone."

She wondered. Not every bride came with a seven-year-old who might or might not become a permanent fixture in her groom's life, depending on a cantankerous old judge. And not every groom's career zinged him from one side of the globe to the other with little or no warning. The flight surgeon said he'd be off flying status for three to four months. After that…

The question of how long he'd remain in Albuquerque added another wrinkle to her carefully laid out plan, one she hadn't contemplated before. The judge had granted

Alex only temporary custody. He'd never let her take Maria out of state, much less out of the country. Not until the adoption went through, anyway.

Feeling the weight of all the uncertainties hanging over her, she edged off the bed and gathered the damp towels. "Give me an hour. I'll check in at the shop, then drive you to the base."

"That works, if you can spare the time. If not, I can Uber in."

"I'll take you."

True to her word, Alex was back within an hour. Since she would most likely be meeting some of Ben's coworkers, she debated changing her jeans and amber-colored tank for something a little dressier. The golden-eyed dragon with the glittering scales that spilled over one shoulder of the tank was a favorite design, though, so she decided to go with it.

Ben had cut the elastic cuff off the left leg of his jersey workout pants so they fit over his cast. The matching dark blue shirt sported a stamped patch on one shoulder. A closer inspection showed a female huntress driving a chariot though rolling clouds, her bow in hand. The lettering below read 58th Special Operations Wing. The lettering wasn't really necessary, Alex thought. The torso displayed to perfection by that all stretchy blue jersey could only belong to someone assigned to Special Ops.

Mere moments later, they were in her car and on their way. Alex had driven past sprawling Kirtland Air Force Base many times but this was her first foray inside the base perimeter. After Ben flashed his ID at the guard, she followed his directions past nondescript tan-colored buildings accented with equally blah chocolate-brown trim. The base shared its almost three-mile-long runway with the Albuquerque airport and was, she now learned, divided into two distinct areas.

She'd read enough coverage in the local papers to understand the east half of the base was home to Sandia National Laboratories. She also knew the lab had the scary mission of ensuring the US nuclear arsenal was safe, secure and reliable, and could fully support the nation's deterrence policy. Ben added to her scanty knowledge by informing her that Sandia Labs acted as the engineering arm of the US nuclear weapons network.

"Is it true they stockpile nukes in those mountains?" she asked with a nod toward the jagged ridge to the east.

"Where'd you hear that?"

The sharp retort swung her head in his direction. "I don't know. I probably read it in the papers."

"I don't think so."

"Or heard it somewhere."

His face was a cool mask. Obviously, this was not a topic for general discussion.

"Okay," she said. "Message received."

A two-lane road took them to the west side of the base. Bordered on both sides by high desert sand and scrub, it skirted the end of the runway. Once they reached another cluster of buildings, Ben pointed out those belonging to the Air Force Space Vehicles Directorate.

The directorate, he explained, was charged with exploring the military frontiers of space. A couple of turns took them to the hangars, aircraft and operations facilities of the 58th Special Operations Wing.

Alex had picked up a little about the 58th's mission while researching this year's Badger Bash. She knew the wing was the primary training facility for all Air

Force Search and Rescue and Special Ops aircrews. She also knew it had a long and distinguished history dating back to World War II. Ben provided more colorful detail.

"Those are MC-130Js," he told her as they cruised past a flight line dotted with squat, four-engine aircraft. "They've been around since the '70s," he added, "but with all her new avionics and engine upgrades, that babe can take off and set down on a dime."

She suspected he might be exaggerating just a bit. "Is that what you fly?"

"Primarily, although I'm also qualified on the H and W models."

She eyed the planes. She knew nothing about military transports but these looked bulldog tough.

"So, like, what do you do specifically?"

"Specifically, my crew and I fly Special Ops teams into target or hostile zones, then get them out again. We also keep them supplied with beans and bullets while they're on the ground. Other 58th crews conduct psyops, and do helicopter and vertical lift air refueling."

"Oookay," she said, trying to understand the full scope those activities.

"Our crews have logged thousands of hours flying humanitarian missions, like the ones I told you about."

"I can't imagine how you managed to air-drop food and medical supplies in Nepal. I saw the pictures of all the devastation on TV. Hitting the drop zones there must have been tough."

"It was but, with our dual ring-laser gyroscopes and integrated GPS, we've got almost pinpoint accuracy, day or night."

Alex was impressed and said so.

"Play your cards right," he told her, "and I'll wrangle you a ride on one of our spousal orientation flights."

Feeling more than a little overwhelmed by all she was learning about the man and the organization she'd married into, Alex stored up a cache of vivid impressions. The big, bustling base. The aircraft bristling with antennae and armaments. The sense of energy and purpose that hung over all.

Ben gestured to a building bracketed between two large hangars. "That's Base Ops. I need to stop there and retrieve my gear."

Alex wasn't sure whether she would be allowed inside but Ben flashed his ID again and got her access to the passenger lounge. Several of the uniformed personnel on duty sympathized with his cast and crutches and expressed the hope that he'd be back in the cockpit soon.

Ben thanked them and introduced Alex. The predominant reaction was openmouthed surprise, followed by hasty congratulations. Then a broad-shouldered sergeant volunteered to retrieve the personal items taken off the plane after Ben's accident.

"Hang loose, sir. I'll get your gear."

He disappeared into a controlled area and returned with two large bags, several smaller ones and a bulging backpack. At Alex's surprised look, Ben explained the assortment.

"Since we were doing an initial crew swap-out, we had to carry most of what we'd need."

"If you say so," she said, surveying the collection dubiously.

"The duffel contains my personal items," Ben explained. "Spare uniforms, extra pair of boots, assorted jeans and T-shirts, workout clothes and so on. The A bag contains our protective gear. Helmet, web belt, body armor, sleeping bag, canteen kit, mess kit. There's a B bag for cold weather gear, but we weren't hauling that for this mission." He toed a lumpy, zippered sack. "This is our D bag, with special chemical warfare protective equipment for flight crews."

The sheer volume of the equipment he had to carry with him on deployment was astounding…and more than a little scary. That pile of gear also told her she had a *lot* to learn about being a military wife.

"What about the backpack?" she asked to cover the feeling that her world had taken a sudden, unexpected tilt.

"My laptop, extra socks, MREs, flashlight, insect repellant, a couple of paperbacks, my shaving kit with its emergency stash of…uh…M&M'S."

Among other things, Alex recalled. She glanced up, caught the wicked gleam in Ben's eyes, and suspected they'd put those "M&M'S" to good use later tonight. Stupidly excited at the thought, she snagged the backpack. The sergeant hefted the A and D bags. When he reached for the duffel, though, Ben preempted him.

"I've got it."

"You sure?"

"I'm sure."

Alex and the sergeant exchanged glances when Ben grabbed the handles of the duffel bag and let the weight rest against the side of his crutch. Neither of them said anything, though, as they followed him out to the car.

Alex got behind the wheel again, reflecting on Ben's spurt of stubborn independence. Between that and the earlier incident with the Saran Wrap, she was fast getting the impression that her husband had no intention of pandering to his broken foot.

* * *

He confirmed that impression at their next stop. The 58th Operations Group was housed in a low one-story building only a few blocks from Base Ops. As Ben thumped down the hall, military and civilians poured out of open offices to say hello and commiserate on his injury. Again, he took time to introduce his wife. Again, Alex was treated to expressions that ran the gamut from surprise (mostly male) to delight (mostly older female) to barely disguised disappointment (almost every female under fifty.) By the time they reached his boss's office, she'd solidified another distinct impression. The Special Ops community was tight. Very tight.

When they were shown into the director of operations' office, it was Alex's turn to blink in surprise. Lieutenant Colonel Amiée Rochambeaux defied the Special Ops stereotype. The petite brunette sported a molasses-and-magnolias complexion, a Cajun drawl, shiny silver pilot's wings, and a rack of ribbons that climbed up almost the entire left side of her uniform blouse.

With a quick glance at Ben's neon orange cast, she rose and came around her desk. "I heard you took a hit, Cowboy. In more ways than one," she added as she turned both a smile and a frankly assessing gaze on the woman beside him.

"This is Alexis," he said by way of introduction. "My wife."

The brunette thrust out a hand. "Good to meet you. And good luck housebreaking this oversize hound dog. Please, have a seat."

She gestured to a small conference table and joined them there.

"I got the flight surgeon's report, Cowboy. He indi-

cates you'll be DNIF for three to four months. Sorry."
She interpreted for Alex, "That's 'Duties Not Involving Flying.'"

Alex nodded. After Ben's reaction to the acronym
yesterday morning, she'd more or less figured out the
meaning by herself.

"The Personnel Center was making noises about
sending you to the 1st Special Operations Wing at Hurlburt after your deployment," the colonel said, addressing
Ben again. "There may be a deputy Director of Operations position opening up."

Alex's stomach tightened. Ben had told her he was
up for reassignment when he returned from wherever
he was supposed to have been going. She had no clue
where Hurlburt was but a move now, before the custody
hearing, would add another five or six layers to their already complicated situation.

To her relief, he'd obviously been thinking along the
same lines. "I talked to the Personnel Center this morning," he told his boss. "Nothing's firm yet on Jernigan.
They suggest I hunker down here until I'm back on flight
status and see what opens up for a follow-on assign-
ment in the meantime. I agreed, since that works best
for Alex and me. If you don't mind me returning to the
fold, that is."

"Actually," the colonel drawled, "the boss already
informed me that he wants you to take over as acting
chief of Simulator Operations. Think you can do that
with one leg in a cast?"

"One leg and both arms."

Rochambeaux permitted herself a wry smile. "That's
what I told him. You start tomorrow." She rose and gave
Alex a look of exaggerated sympathy. "'Fraid you'll be

stuck with this gorilla clumping around the house for the foreseeable future."

"It'll be tough, but I think I'll survive."

"I'm sure you will. Just out of curiosity, where did you two meet?"

"In Vegas, two years ago."

"Ahh! The Badger Bash, right?"

"That's right."

"I missed that one. Missed this one, too, dammit. I tried to get back from DC in time but no luck. Next year for sure."

While the women waited for Ben to get his crutches in position, the colonel eyed the dragon curling over the shoulder of Alex's amber-colored tank. "Great shirt. Did you get it around here?"

"Actually, I made it."

"No kidding?"

"I design and manufacture jeweled tanks, Ts and jackets for a living. I sell mostly to retail outlets, but I have some products available for individual order on my website if you're interested."

"Definitely." The colonel leaned in for a closer look, then tipped her chin toward the patch on Ben's shirt. "Could you do something like that?"

"Sure."

Alex doubted a Diana the Huntress decked out in gold crystals would appeal to the macho, he-man types in the 58th but she could certainly produce one for this petite and very feminine colonel. Or more than one, she amended when Rochambeaux suggested a T-shirt or tank with the squadron logo would be a hit with the wives and other women assigned to the unit.

"I'll work up a prototype," Alex promised.

* * *

Their next planned stop was the storage facility where Ben had left his car and personal belongings. His stomach was rumbling, though, so he suggested a pit stop first.

"Sounds good," Alex agreed, feeling a little empty herself. Nothing like steamy morning sex to work up an appetite. "Any place special you'd like to go?"

"How about the K&I Diner? It's close and quick."

Alex had to smile. The diner held a well-deserved reputation among military and civilians on this side of town for gargantuan servings of their house specialty.

"Think you can handle a Travis?" she teased Ben.

"A half Travis maybe, but I was thinking more along the lines of posole and green chili chicken enchiladas."

She exited the base at the Gibson Gate, cruised past the airport and turned south on Broadway. A few miles later she made a quick U-turn and pulled into K&I's jammed parking lot. The popular eatery had begun life as a truck stop but its signature dish of crisp french fries mounded over enchiladas and drenched in chili sauce had gained a huge following. The decor was still no-frills, though, and the service just as efficient.

The server manning the door took one look at Ben's crutches and waved him to the head of the line. He shook his head. "I can wait."

The others waiting for tables weren't having it. They urged him forward, which left him with the choice of appearing ungracious or following the server to a just-emptied table near the entrance.

"Do you think other women and wives in your squadron would really be interested in a specially designed

58th Wing tank?" Alex asked when they'd put in their order.

"I do." He took a slow, appreciative survey of her amber-colored top. "Especially if they thought they would look as good as you do in it."

She couldn't help preening but his next comment sharply refocused her thoughts.

"Why limit your outreach to the 58th, though? Special Ops is a monster community. The air force even bigger. Why not tap into the overall military market?"

"I haven't actually checked into it but I've always heard doing business with the government is a bureaucratic nightmare."

"It can be, I guess, unless you have help navigating the maze. I could make a few calls if you want. Find out how to get your products into the military exchanges on base."

The prospect of breaking into that huge market was both daunting and ferociously exciting.

"Let me think about it," Alex said, her head filled with numbers.

Chapter Seven

After lunch they drove to the storage facility where Ben had left his Tahoe and household goods. At his direction, Alex retrieved two sealed cartons of clothes and uniform items from a small storage unit and loaded them into his midnight-black SUV. The boxes didn't take up even a third of the cargo area.

"Is that all you need?" she asked.

"I lit out for the oil fields with just the clothes on my back," he replied, shrugging. "I'm used to traveling light."

She glanced back at the now almost empty storage unit. All that remained were a pair of snow skis propped in a corner, a half-disassembled universal gym, a box marked "electronics" and another marked "kitchen & bedroom."

"Doesn't seem worth it to pay rent on a storage unit

for just those few items," she commented. "Why don't we have them moved to my shop? I've got plenty of room. We could set up your gym there, too, if you want to work out."

He hesitated. It was just a guess, but Alex wondered if he was reluctant to cut his last link to his carefree bachelor days.

"Sounds like a plan," he said after a moment. "I'll get a couple of guys from the squadron to help move the stuff."

He followed her home. Alex kept checking her rear-view mirror but Ben didn't appear to have any difficulty operating the Tahoe with his uninjured right foot. They reached the casita without incident and hauled his gear bags and the two cartons into the house.

Adding his additional clothing and uniforms to those he'd previously left at the house required some serious closet scrunching. The multiple gear bags they simply stacked in a corner. That done, Alex checked her watch. The idea that she might tap into the military market was still swirling around in her head.

"I've got a couple hours before I need to walk Maria home from school. If you're not too wiped, I could show you my workplace."

"I'm fine. Let's go."

The warehouse that housed AS Designs was just a short distance away. But despite Ben's assurance that he could handle the walk, Alex insisted they drive over. Her shop was located in a long, low commercial facility. Semis were backed up to several loading docks. Panel trucks sporting logos advertising everything from furniture upholstery to pool cleaning services occupied the parking spaces in between. AS Designs occupied the end unit.

Ben wasn't sure what he was expecting when he followed Alex through the door of her shop. Stacks of cardboard cartons spilling multicolored T-shirts and denim jackets, maybe. The clack of machines stamping designs on fabric, punctuated by the chatter of women hunched over workstations, up to their elbows in rhinestones. Instead, he found himself in a brightly lit open space with a long table bisecting the front half of the work area. Giant blue plastic storage bins with neat labels showing pictures of their contents lined one wall. The opposite wall displayed artistically arranged samples of finished products in a rainbow of colors and sizes.

Five women sat at the table. Three had black hair and dark eyes that suggested either Hispanic or Native American heritage. The fourth was a twentysomething Goth, complete with a chalk-white complexion, kohl-rimmed eyes and more facial piercings than Ben wanted to count. The fifth was bottle blonde, blue eyed and so heavily pregnant she could barely pull her ergonomic chair up to the table.

The table, Ben saw, had inserts which tilted like a drafting board so each woman could work at her own, comfortable angle. Each worker also had a circular lazy Susan within easy reach. On it was a round container divided into pie-shaped sections filled with crystals and other doodads. The women worked from a stack of neatly folded garments, applying beads and crystals in colorful appliqués. Their completed items went into more plastic bins. Red ones this time. The overall impression was one of ruthless efficiency.

The five women ceased all activity the moment Alex and Ben appeared. She must have broken the news of her marriage when she'd come in earlier that morning because five pairs of eyes raked Ben from head to the socked toes sticking out of his cast.

"*Hola*, Alex," one of the woman said. "*¿Es este tu esposo?*"

"*Sí.*"

She waggled her brows. "*Es un trozo.*"

Ben's Spanish was limited but he figured from the grins—and the quick wash of pink in Alex's cheeks—that he'd just been complimented. Nobly, he refrained from returning the grins while his wife made a general introduction.

"Everyone, this is Ben."

He thunked his way down the length of the table, shaking hands with the three women on the near side and reaching across to the two on the other side. Alex then introduced him to a sixth woman stationed in the rear half of warehouse space. That was partitioned into several separate areas. One had an unpainted metal rolling door and was obviously used for receiving and shipping. A small glassed-in cubbyhole functioned as an office. The third and largest area, Alex explained with a touch of pride, was where they did their imprinting.

"Most large T-shirt companies use screen printing. They create a stencil of the basic design, then apply layers of different colored ink to re-create it on the product. That produces a vibrant imprint but requires time and significant material costs."

Ben glanced around the squeaky clean imprint area. There was no odor of ink, no color-filled pans or rollers. Instead, two sturdy worktables supported oversize printers with wide feeder trays.

"Luckily," Alex continued, "I got into this business just as digital printing was coming into its own. Basically, I do the designs on my computer, either here or at home. Then I upload them to one of these laser printers, which transfers the design directly onto the fabric. The color's not as dramatic as in screen printing but what we lack in vibrancy we make up in precise detail."

"And sparkles," the woman at the printer added with a wide smile.

"And sparkles," her boss confirmed. "Why don't you show Ben how it works, Terri?"

"It's pretty simple," the pudgy, sandy-haired operator said as she positioned a silver-hued T-shirt on a flat tray. After smoothing out anything that even remotely resembled a wrinkle, she slid the tray into the printer and pressed a button. A few seconds later the tray popped out again. The silver T-shirt now sported the head, flowing mane and spiraled horn of a unicorn outlined in shades of gray and glistening black.

When the operator held the shirt up for Ben's inspection, Alex couldn't resist bragging. "Terri's our best printer. She averages close to ninety imprints an hour."

"But you still hold the record," the older woman commented. Her smile took on a mischievous tilt as she turned back to Ben. "A few months ago Alex did a hundred and twenty-three in one hour. We've been telling her for ages that she needs another outlet for all her bottled up energy. I'm glad she finally found one."

"Me, too," Ben agreed solemnly.

Terri snorted, the other women laughed and Alex hastily intervened. "From here, the printed products go to a workstation. Caroline's working the unicorn order."

Despite the young Goth's mascara-caked lashes and multiple facial piercings, she worked with the delicate touch of an Italian Renaissance master. Her nimble fingers wielded a pair of tweezers and an applicator of what looked like an industrial brand of superglue with astonishing speed and dexterity. Plucking strings of crystals in descending circumferences from the lazy Susan, she highlighted a few strands of the mane, then spiraled up the horn before adding a pair of piercing crystal eyes. The result was minimal, mystical and startlingly dramatic. She then attached a label that read "Embellished by Caroline," folded the shirt, and added it to those nested in the red box on her right side.

"Every one of our products is hand-worked," Alex related. "I stress that in our advertising to justify our prices."

"Who do you sell to?"

"We still take small personal orders via our website. Most of our current production, though, goes to boutiques and online retailers."

Ben tipped her a considering look. "Think you can continue the personal touch if you double or triple your sales?"

She glanced around her shop, and her rueful expression summarized the eternal struggle between the artist and the entrepreneur. "I'll have to cross that bridge when and if I come to it."

Guessing she had some serious work to catch up on after their trip to Vegas and taking care of him for the past few days, Ben tried to convince her that he wanted some exercise and would walk back to the casita.

"I do need to get a few things done," Alex admitted, "but you aren't walking anywhere. Take my car. And the house keys," she added belatedly as she passed him the key ring. "I'll get another set made tomorrow."

"I can take care of that," Ben offered, pocketing the keys. "I can also pick Maria up from school if you want."

Alex hesitated. She hadn't yet decided the best way to let Maria know that Ben would be a more or less permanent fixture in their lives. Maybe having him meet her at San Felipe's would kick-start that process.

"I'll call the school and let them know you'll be picking her up. You'll have to park in the square and go to the adobe gate at the entrance to the school yard to show your ID."

"Not a problem. We'll see you at home."

Alex chewed on her lower lip as she watched him crutch his way to the door. Now that her postcoital glow had faded, she could only pray they'd made the right decision by transitioning from what had been intended as a quickie marriage and divorce to a longer-term commitment. Which reminded her...

"Excuse me a moment," she told her employees, all of whom were obviously eager to share their impressions of their boss's new husband. "I need to make a call."

She retreated to her cubbyhole of an office and hit the speed dial for Paul Montoya. The attorney specialized in family law and had come highly recommended. Thankfully, he charged for his services on a sliding scale that allowed him to take on clients who might otherwise have to rely on court-appointed pro bono attorneys. Alex could afford him. Barely.

She expected to be asked to leave a message and was surprised when she got put through. Montoya's gruff greeting put her on instant alert.

"Hey, Alex, I was just going to call you."

A dozen different reasons for him to contact her

flashed through her mind. Not least of which was that the judge had ruled against her petition for adoption.

"Why?" she asked, her heart hammering. "What's happening."

"Maria's father is scheduled for a parole hearing next month."

"You're *kidding*!" Surprise dropped her jaw. "The bastard's served less than half his sentence."

"Yeah, I know. And *you* know the problem. New Mexico prisons are understaffed and overcrowded. Our legislature's trying to pass an emergency funding measure to increase recruitment of corrections officers. Until that goes through and additional guards get hired and trained, the state has to rotate out its prison population."

Rotate out. Alex's lip curled. What a disgusting euphemism for putting creeps like Eddie Musgrove back on the street.

"How does the parole hearing affect the custody hearing with Judge Hendricks?" she asked urgently.

"Best guess, Hendricks will delay the hearing until Maria's dad can be present."

"Damn!"

"I know that's not what you want to hear. But it'll work to our advantage if Musgrove is present and we can get him to admit he's opposed the adoption out of spite."

"*If* we can get him to admit it."

Remembering the pain that sleaze had caused both Janet and Maria made anger boil in Alex's chest. The sensation was so fierce and hot that she almost forgot the original reason for her call. It didn't hit until Montoya promised to get back to her as soon as he knew the results of the parole hearing.

"Wait! I have news, too."

"What's that?"

"I'm married."

A flat silence followed the announcement. After that came a low whistle. "I didn't think you'd really go through with that crazy scheme."

"You didn't think it was so crazy when I discussed it with you."

In the best lawyerly tradition, Montoya dodged the bullet. "Fax me a copy of the marriage certificate ASAP."

"Okay."

"And give me some detail to take to Judge Hendricks."

"Like what?"

"Names, dates, places. Anything that'll make this sound legit."

"His name is Benjamin Kincaid. He's an air force major assigned to Kirtland." The well-rehearsed patter rolled out easily. "We met two years ago in Vegas and reconnected this past weekend."

"Uh-huh." Montoya dripped sarcasm like a leaky oil pan. "And the flames just spontaneously reignited."

"Pretty much."

"You do realize how convenient this sounds."

"I do." Alex gripped the phone. "Believe me, I do."

"Well, let's hope the judge buys it. Fax me that certificate," he instructed again, "and I'll get back to you."

When Alex said good-night to her crew, locked the shop behind her and walked the few blocks through the hot May night to her home, she was still chewing over Montoya's unwelcome news. She spent most of the short walk to the casita debating whether to tell Maria that her dad might be out of prison and on the streets again in the near future.

As if the prospect of Ben infiltrating the girl's world on a somewhat permanent basis wasn't unsettling enough! How much more could the ground shift under a seven-year-old's feet before it opened up and swallowed her? The question bit at Alex so viciously that by the time she rang her front doorbell, her stomach was in knots.

The excited little girl who answered the bell looked so different from her mental image that Alex blinked.

"Why are you so late?" Maria wanted to know. "Ben 'n' me made dinner."

"Ben and I."

"Ben 'n' I. It's all ready. I wanted to call you but he said we had to wait."

"Sorry," Alex murmured, still trying to adjust to the novelty of a prepared dinner. "I got busy at work. What are we having?"

"Mac 'n' cheese." Maria skipped down the tiled hall, her excitement still bubbling. "With black beans 'n' chicken 'n' some green stuff in it. Broccoli or peppers or something. Ben cut those up while I heated the water for the noodles. 'N' I didn't let it boil over or anything."

"Wow! I'm very impressed."

Even more impressed when she saw the table was set and a bottle of Chilean red was breathing on the counter.

Ben pivoted away from the stove on his good foot to greet her. "Maria's got the makings of a great little chef."

"News to me," Alex commented, aiming for the wine.

She could really use a glass. The possibility that Eddie Musgrove might be paroled was bad enough. Even worse was the possibility Judge Hendricks might delay final adoption proceedings pending the parole hearing. She tried to get her mind off both and enjoy a dinner punctuated by Maria's lively chatter about school and the new game she wanted to download to her pretty pink iPad. Alex's somewhat absentminded approval sent Maria scurrying to her room right after dessert to retrieve her iPad. She came racing back with the device in hand and an impatient request for Alex to screen the game.

"It's Baby Dragons II."

She shifted from foot to foot while Alex checked the parental guidelines and scrolled through the reviews.

"Dinah's got it," Maria grumbled. "Her mom's already checked it out."

Alex replied with the universally noncommittal, "Mmm."

More antsy than ever, Maria crowded close while Alex downloaded the app and tested both Dragon Flight Training and River Raft with Your Dragon. Wisely, Alex disabled the in-app purchase feature before surrendering the iPad.

"Yes!"

Racing for the living room, Maria hopped onto the sofa and was instantly immersed in baby dragons. Alex didn't bother to remind her that clearing the table was one of her chores. Especially when Ben poured a little more wine, sprawled back in his chair and voiced a quiet question.

"Did something happen after I left you at work? You seem distracted."

She glanced over at him, surprised. They'd been married only a few days and he was already reading her moods? She threw a quick look in Maria's direction to make sure she was totally absorbed.

"I called my lawyer after you left," she told Ben quietly. "To let him know about us."

"And?"

"And he informed me that Maria's father is scheduled to meet the parole board next month."

"Uh-oh."

"Uh-oh is right." She shot the girl another quick look. "My lawyer thinks the family court judge may delay the final adoption hearing so the jerk has a chance to make his case in court. I'm more worried he may show up here."

Ben didn't alter his slouch but Alex couldn't miss the way his eyes suddenly narrowed. "Tell me again what he's in for."

"Drugs, mostly. Selling and transporting. It didn't help his case, though, when he tried to resist arrest."

"He also blackened your sister's eye, if I recall correctly."

She'd forgotten that she'd showed him that picture of Janet. She'd done it for effect but the inescapable truth now made her squirm.

"According to Janet, that was the only time he got violent with her. And she swore to her last breath that Eddie loves his daughter in his own careless way…"

Her voice trailed off, conveying anything but certainty. Ben had no doubts, however. He'd spent too much time in and out of foster homes to trust a "careless" parent. Especially one caught up in drugs. Keeping his thoughts to himself, he made a seemingly casual observation.

"Then it's a good thing I'm going to be around awhile. Between us, we should be able to keep Maria safe."

He had no trouble interpreting the emotions that

flooded her warm brown eyes. Relief, first. Gratitude, next. Her smile conveyed both as she reached a hand across the table to grip his.

"I know I've thanked you for agreeing to marry me. At least, I think I have. If not, I do. From the absolute rock bottom of my heart."

Okay. All right. Ben was rational enough to know that the annoyance her fervent comment generated was completely irrational. Yet the stone-cold fact was he didn't want her gratitude. Or a marriage made "real" by lust and by circumstance.

What he wanted…

What he expected…

Hell! This woman had tied him in so many knots over the past few days that he wasn't sure exactly *what* he wanted to come out of their crazy agreement.

"You did thank me," he returned curtly. "Several times."

She drew back, blinking at the clipped response, and Ben cursed under his breath. *Smooth, Kincaid. Really smooth.* Shoving away from the table, he pushed to his feet.

"Let's get the kitchen cleaned up. Then I'll give Maria a run for her dragon money."

"You cooked," Alex responded with more than a hint of frost. "I'll clean."

Smothering another silent curse, Ben jammed the crutches under his arms and rounded his end of the table. When he intercepted her halfway to the sink, she stopped, plates gripped in both hands, and tipped him a cool look.

"Sorry," he said. "That came out wrong. What I meant to say… What I *should* have said is that no thanks are necessary. We both went into this with our eyes open."

"True, but—"

"No buts. I'm a big boy. I know what I'm doing."

Most of the time. This, he decided as he looked down into her worried eyes and pouty lips, wasn't one of them. With an urge so sudden and sharp it almost unbalanced him, he wanted to swoop down. Plunder that ripe mouth. Kiss the worry from her eyes.

The need to taste her rose in swift, sharp spikes. He had to curl his fists around the crutches' hand supports to keep from grabbing her, dirty dishes and all, and backing her against the sturdy kitchen table. The only thing that restrained him was the fact that they now shared a bed…and had the whole night to enjoy it.

The thought sent him whirling on his good foot and aiming for the living room. Maria looked up at his noisy entrance, her small hands poised over the iPad. Her smile was quick and tentative and tugged at his heart. With a silent, savage vow that no asshat drug dealer was going to hurt her as long as he was around, Ben clumped over to the sofa.

"Okay, kid, let's see how good you are at this dragon stuff."

Chapter Eight

Alex couldn't believe how quickly each member of her little family acclimated to each other over the next few days. Part of that was due to the fact that, despite his injury, Ben worked long hours, with an occasional night shift thrown in. They were nearing the end of a crew training cycle, he explained. Civilian contractors actually operated the sims and programmed the results, but military special operators with actual combat experience oversaw the operation. A key aspect of his new job was to maximize simulator time with around-the-clock shifts.

Between those training sessions, Ben made the required follow-up visit with his surgeon. Alex insisted on accompanying him to make sure she understood how the healing process was going. Thankfully, X-rays showed the bones had already begun to fuse and the doc shortened his prognostication that his patient would be on crutches from six weeks to five. Relieved and determined, Ben shortened that to fit his own timetable. Alex tried to suggest he was risking a permanent injury but he assured her that he wasn't going to go all stupid.

At work, Alex had ramped up her schedule, as well. She got a big new order for French-themed T-shirts from the Paris Hotel and Casino in Vegas, courtesy of her old boss's connections with the owner. One hundred and twenty S-M-L-XL Ts in three different colors and designs. Thankfully, Dinah's mom was only too happy to earn extra cash babysitting during the extra hours Alex put in at her shop.

Even when she and Ben came home whipped, however, they seemed to magically revive when they tumbled into bed together. Some nights were fast and wild and ignited a smoldering fire in Alex's blood. Others, Ben's oh-so-skilled hands and clever mouth had her drifting a tide of exquisite sensation as soft and enveloping as a cloud.

The evenings neither she nor Ben had to work, though, they devoted to Maria. To Alex's relief, the girl adjusted to Ben's presence in their lives with surprising ease. Probably because he went all out to engage her interest and affection.

His first real success was a visit to the Albuquerque BioPark on a bright, sunny Saturday afternoon. Just him and Maria flying solo. Located along the Rio Grande near the heart of the city, the park environs included a zoo, an aquarium, botanical gardens and Tingley Beach with its ponds, walking trails, bike paths and pedal boat rentals. Alex had sent them off with explicit instructions to Maria not to let Ben overdo it on his crutches and similar orders to Ben not to let Maria wheedle too many ice-cream cones out of him. They returned four hours later with noses tipped red by the bright May sun and dozens of digital photos on Ben's iPhone.

Alex was curled up on the sofa, a sketch pad in hand, when they got home. Maria plunked down beside her and proceeded to provide a running commentary of the photos while Ben leaned over the back of the sofa. Alex could smell the sun caught in his shirt, almost feel the heat from his body as he leaned closer. Distracted and more than a little disconcerted by the tingles his close proximity roused, she forced herself to focus on the photos.

It wasn't hard to pick out the ones Maria had taken. Most were off center and not quite in focus. A couple were surprisingly good, though. One in particular snared Alex's gaze. It was obviously a selfie. Maria's face nested cheek to cheek with Ben's. Their chins were tipped, their lips stretched into wide grins and their eyes filled with laughter.

"What was so funny?" Alex wanted to know.

"Me," Ben admitted wryly. "I was trying to balance on my good leg, hold Maria with one arm and shoot the selfie with the other. We both almost went butt-first into a prickly pear."

Alex didn't quite see the hilarity in that. "I'm glad you didn't. I don't relish the thought of tweezing cactus needles out of your behinds, as cute as they both are."

That made Maria giggle and Ben smother a snort. Thankfully, he didn't remind Alex that she'd delivered a somewhat more descriptive assessment of his posterior only this morning. At the time, he'd been lying on his belly while she straddled his thighs and massaged all accessible areas. The contrasts had fascinated the artist in her. The tanned skin of his shoulders and back. The crinkly hair at the base of his spine. The taut, white buttocks above those muscular thighs. And then he'd rolled over and treated her to another palette of...

"Ben thinks we should get a kitten."

Jerked from her erotic memories, Alex blinked. "What?"

"We should get a kitten," Maria repeated. "'Cause, you know, that's what you call me."

Alex shot a reproachful glance over her shoulder before replying. "We talked about this before. You're in school and I'm working. It's not good for a kitty to be alone all day."

"School gets out in two weeks. I could stay home and play with it."

"You'll be at day camp."

"I don't want to go to day camp. It's stupid and boring. I want a kitten."

"Maria..."

"You promised. You did, Alex."

"I said we'd consider it when you're a little older and can take care of a pet."

"I can take care of it now. I'll put milk in its bowl 'n' scoop up its poop 'n' comb its whiskers. Besides," she added with a pout, "you 'n' Ben get to play together. All that kissing 'n' stuff. I should have someone to play with, too."

"She's got a point," Ben murmured.

Not sure she liked being ganged up on, Alex beat a strategic retreat. "Let's talk about it again when school's out."

And there it was. The ominous lip jut. Accompanied by beetled brows and crossed arms. "I want a kitty now."

"We'll talk about it when school's out."

"That's two whole weeks away. I—"

"Don't be a pog, kid."

Maria turned her scowl on Ben. "What's a pogue?"

"Pog. *P-o-g*. Originally, it referred to 'people other than grunts.'"

The arms dropped and curiosity replaced the pout. "What's a grunt?"

"Someone in the infantry. A ground pounder. Nowadays it pretty much means anyone who's a sorry excuse for a soldier."

"I'm not gonna be a soldier. I'm gonna fly airplanes, like you do. C-one… C-one…"

"C-one-thirties."

"Right." Her nose wrinkled. "Not those sissy fighter jets."

"That's my girl."

Alex listened to the exchange with growing surprise. Not at Maria's newest career choice. Last week she'd wanted to be a doctor. The week before, a nun like Sister Mary Catherine at school. What had Alex's heart pinging was the way Ben had turned her sulk into a beaming delight with a simple smile of approval.

"Why don't you pull up pictures of the 130 on your iPad and I'll show you all the moving parts?" he suggested.

"'Kay."

When Maria hopped off the sofa and shot out of the room, Ben took her place. He sank into the cushions, propped his crutches against the coffee table and hooked an arm over the sofa back. His fingertips burrowed under Alex's hair and stroked her nape. The touch was light, casual and electric.

"Sorry about the kitten," he said ruefully. "I should've guessed it was still up for debate when Maria assured me you'd sort of, pretty much, mostly agreed to one."

"I sort of, pretty much, mostly did. Sometime in the future."

"Looks like the future may arrive sooner than expected."

"Looks like," she agreed as the pads of his fingers teased the fine hair on her nape. Each one seemed to stand up and quiver in ecstasy.

He leaned closer, almost tipping her into his lap, to peer at her sketch pad. "You're working on a jazzed-up version of the 58th Special Ops patch?"

"I am."

She'd downloaded a JPEG of the trapezoidal patch with its depiction of Diana the Huntress in full warrior mode. After printing it onto paper, she'd tried different colored glitter pens to pop the colors.

"I thought I'd use gold crystals to highlight the edge of the patch. Then a paler gold for her armor and silver for her bow and arrows. The stags harnessed to her chariot I'll do in amber, the chariot itself with just a touch of pearlescent. What do you think?"

"I think it's sierra hotel. Shit hot," he translated at her blank look.

Obviously, both Alex *and* Maria needed a tutorial in military slang. Tucking *sierra hotel* away for future reference, Alex studied her sketch.

"You really like it?"

"I do. I wouldn't want all those sparkles on my uniform during a night approach using NVGs. Night vision goggles," he interpreted again. "But I'm betting every female in the squadron will want this version of the patch on a ball cap or T-shirt."

She bit her lip, alternating between pleasure at his approval of her design and shivery delight at his touch. She had to stop, take a breath and remind herself that Maria would bounce back into the living room at any moment.

In almost the next breath, she caught herself wondering if she could arrange a sleepover for Maria at her friend Dinah's house. Just for tonight. And maybe convince Dinah's mom to take her to church with them tomorrow. Then Alex and Ben could "play" all night. Sleep late in the morning. Laze over coffee and a bagel. Hit the sheets again.

Guilt washed over her. She couldn't believe she was actually considering dumping Maria on the Madisons just to wrangle an extra few hours in the sack with Ben. Disgusted with herself, she added a final stroke or two to her sketch.

"I'll transfer this to my computer and make up a sample T-shirt. If it doesn't violate some rule or regulation, maybe you can take it into the squadron and conduct some market research."

"I have a better idea. Why don't you make up a sample T-shirt and wear it to the Memorial Day picnic? Better yet, make two. One for you and one for Maria."

She angled around and found herself cradled in the V of his arm. "What Memorial Day picnic?"

"The one sponsored by the 58th prior to the air show. It's more or less a mandatory commander's call for anyone not deployed or otherwise out of town. The old man believes in wholesome family outings."

"Unlike the annual Badger Bash," Alex said drily.

"*Extremely* unlike the Badger Bash. I usually try to

avoid these picnics like a bad case of the cl—" He caught himself and grimaced. "Let's just say grilling hot dogs and making balloon hats don't figure real high on my list of fun things to do. Or haven't up to now."

The guilt rolled in again. "You don't have to do either for us, Ben. Maria and I will get along fine without hot dogs or balloon hats."

"Oh, no you don't!" He tightened his arm and gave her shoulders a squeeze. The pressure tipped her just enough to topple against his chest. "No way you're bailing on me, woman. If I have to go, you have to go."

She grinned and was about to confess that she had a secret weakness for hot dogs when a loud huff sounded behind her. A glance over her shoulder showed Maria with her iPad tucked under her arm and a thoroughly indignant expression on her face.

"That's what I mean," the girl accused. "You get to play with Ben. I should have someone to play with, too."

Alex knew when she'd been outmaneuvered. Sighing, she acknowledged defeat. "Okay, okay. We'll get a kitten."

With a happy screech, the seven-year-old launched herself at the sofa.

"Be careful of Ben's foot!"

Alex's warning came too late. Maria landed in a joyous bundle. Ben grunted and quickly hiked her off his bad leg. Then the three of them collapsed in a tangle of arms and legs.

After her unconditional surrender, Alex knew she couldn't hold out long against Maria's pitiful, soulful, doe-eyed demands to know *when* they could bring home a kitty. Once again yielding to the inevitable, she agreed to sooner rather than later.

The following afternoon the three of them made a visit to the only animal shelter in Albuquerque open on Sundays. Less than an hour later, Alex, Ben, Maria and a pink-nosed, gray-and-white bit of fluff found abandoned by the side of the road some days ago left the shelter. The kitten had been dewormed and given its shots but was skin and bones under her fur and cringed at every loud noise. She dug her sharp little claws into Maria's T-shirt and wouldn't let go even during a stop at a pet store to stock up on kitty necessities.

A hundred and fifteen dollars later, Alex stashed a bed, a climbing tower, a litter tray, a sack of kitty litter, and an assortment of toys, canned food and treats in the back of Ben's SUV. He'd insisted on picking up the tab as payment for his part in precipitating the cat crisis. He'd also engaged Maria in a lengthy discussions over a name for her new friend. So when they left the store, Sox—a personalized, shortened version of Special Operations Command—was wearing a pink collar with a heart-shaped tag that gave her name and a phone number to call if found.

Having spent that Sunday morning researching how to introduce a cat into a home with young children, Alex wrangled Maria's reluctant agreement that Sox would spend the first few nights in the quiet of the laundry room with her bed, climbing tower, scratching post and other toys. They'd also make sure she had accessible food and water. Once the kitten acclimated, that could change.

Alex had also drawn up a list of tasks for Maria that

included changing the water in her bowl daily and emptying the litter tray when necessary. At Ben's suggestion, she had Maria plaster sticky notes on the front, back and patio doors to remind them all to not let the kitten slip out and get lost.

Even with all the research, Alex wasn't prepared for the instant impact the tiny bundle of fur had on both her heart and her home. To her surprise and Maria's delight, Sox transitioned with astounding rapidity from timid and frightened to curious and playful. All it took was a tentative exploration of her new environment, a hearty meal and a feather ball on a string.

Maria's infectious giggles as the kitten chased and swatted at the ball put a happy glow in Alex's heart. And later, after she finally got the excited girl down for the night, the sight of Ben dozing on the sofa with a sleeping kitten curled up on his chest stopped Alex in her tracks. She stood at the entrance to the living room, one hand on the curve of the arch, and felt the floor beneath her make a seismic shift.

Oh, God! She could fall in love with this man. Hell. Why kid herself? She was already more than halfway there. Liking him and lusting for him and being so, so grateful for all he'd done for her and Maria were all balled up together inside her now. And as the old cliché always pointed out, the sum was so much greater than the individual parts.

Not exactly sure what to do about the tight wad of emotion squeezing her chest, Alex stood where she was a few moments longer. Then she eased down beside Ben, propped her feet next to his on the coffee table and let herself simply enjoy his warmth and the soft little rumbles emanating from the kitten.

* * *

Alex must have dozed off, too, because the chime of her cell phone startled her as much as it did Ben and Sox. She jerked upright and fumbled for the phone she'd left on the coffee table while Ben winced and gently extricated sharp little claws from the front of his knit polo shirt. Wide-awake now, Alex gave the caller ID a quick glance.

"It's Chelsea," she told Ben as she stabbed the talk button and put the phone to her ear. "Yo, girl. What's happening?"

"New hair, new shoes and a new show," her former roommate replied gleefully.

"Where? When? Tell me all," Alex demanded, thrilled for her friend.

"The hair this morning. Turquoise and silver streaks. Very chic, if I do say so myself. The shoes this afternoon. Ankle-strap sandals with four-inch heels in screaming red. The show's at Bellagio. I'm going to be performing in the freakin' Cirque du Soleil."

"Oh, Chels! That's fantastic!"

"I know. I'm *très* jazzed."

"You should be. You've worked… Hey, wait! Isn't the show at the Bellagio aquatic? With synchronized swimmers and high dives and dolphins or something?"

"Yeah. So?"

"So you don't know how to swim."

"I do, too."

"Chelsea! You almost drowned in the kiddie pool at our apartment building."

"Only because I tripped and fell in face-first. Besides," she said airily, "every cast member has to go through compulsory training in water aerobics before joining the show. If I survive that, I'm in."

"Good luck."

"Thanks. It doesn't start until next week, though. So I thought I'd zip up for a quick visit."

"Come ahead. We'd love to have you."

"'We,' huh? Sounds like you and Major Hottie are getting cozy there."

Even more than she knew, but with Ben listening to the one-sided exchange Alex didn't think this was the time to explain that they'd decided to give their fake marriage a shot at becoming real.

"How's Maria handling having a man around the house?" Chelsea wanted to know.

"Very well, actually."

"How about you?"

She thought about the previous night, and Ben's body all slick with sweat under hers. "Also very well."

"Hmm." Her friend thought about that for a moment. "I don't want to intrude on you newlyweds but I'd really like to see the kid. So why don't I boogie on up and stay with her while you and hubster go off somewhere for a belated honeymoon?"

When Alex hesitated, Chelsea picked right up on the brief pause.

"Don't tell me the bloom has already worn off the marriage license," she hooted. "You guys have been married, what? Two weeks?"

"Three."

"Have you had any alone time? Except in the sack, that is?"

"Not much."

"That's what I thought. You need to get your man

off and all to yourself. So here's what's gonna happen," she said in a brisk, authoritative tone. "I'll fly up for the Friday afternoon. You and Hot Cheeks can check in to some ritzy resort or hotel in Santa Fe. And neither of you will pack anything except a toothbrush and a smile."

"His work's been crazy, Chels. Mine, too. I'm not sure either of us can just pack up and take off for a weekend."

That got Ben's attention. He eased out of his slouch, careful to cradle the kitten as he did, and shot her a quizzical look.

"Talk to him and get back to me," Chelsea ordered.

"Anyone ever tell you that you're a bossy bitch?"

"You have, numerous times. Call me back."

When Alex hung up and angled toward Ben, she could see he'd obviously absorbed the salient points of the conversation.

"This coming weekend?" he echoed. "I think I can swing it if you can. Right now the schedule calls for us to get the last check ride done by Friday noon."

Alex could probably swing it, too. She and her team had worked like lumberjacks on steroids to fill the Paris Casino order. Still, she hesitated to push Ben, especially with his leg still in a cast.

"Seriously, we don't have to do this."

"Seriously, I think we do."

The blunt response took her aback. Surprised and a little hurt, she tipped her chin. "Why? I thought we've done pretty well given our unconventional start."

"We have. Extremely well. Doesn't mean I wouldn't jump at the chance to get you all to myself for an entire weekend." Easing his feet off the coffee table, he transferred a stretching, yawning Sox onto the cushion. "And don't interpret that to mean I want to get away from

Maria. I'm more in awe of her than I ever imagined I would be of a seven-year-old. She's smart and fun and totally fearless."

"Not totally," Alex countered softly, remembering the times the little girl had sobbed in her arms after Janet died.

"Okay, maybe not totally. But she's got it together enough to spend a weekend with her aunt Chelsea while you and I go someplace we don't have to keep the noise level to a minimum."

"Noise? You're worried about making noise?"

"Not me, sweetheart. You." Grinning, he reached out, cupped a hand around her nape and tugged her closer. "Those little grunts you make? Just before you climax? They're really screams fighting to come out."

"I do *not* grunt. Or scream."

"Oh, yeah, babe. You do." His mouth brushed hers. "I'm thinking we need to reserve an end unit. Or a separate unit altogether. I've got a real itch to hear you let go."

Alex didn't need any further incentive. When Ben called the next morning to confirm that he'd be able to get away by noon on Friday barring any unforeseen crises, she advised her employees that they would be shutting down for the weekend a few hours early and was on the phone to Chelsea mere moments later.

"If you're still good for a visit this weekend, Ben and I will take you up on the offer of a minihoneymoon."

"I'm still good."

"Any chance you can fly up Friday morning?"

"As a matter of fact, I can. My boss at Flamingo hired another dancer, like, three hours after I gave notice. Right now I'm mostly just training her and otherwise killing time."

"Great. I'll go online as soon as we disconnect and get your plane ticket."

"You don't need to buy my ticket. I volunteered for this gig, remember?"

"Do *not* argue. It's a done deal."

She yielded gracefully, then wanted to know, "Have you and Ben decided where you're going?"

"Someplace with solid soundproofing."

Chelsea's laughter bubbled through the phone. "Sounds like a plan to me."

Chapter Nine

Alex picked Chelsea up at the airport just after 10 a.m. on Friday morning. Her former roommate wasn't hard to spot among the throng streaming out of the controlled concourse. She measured five-ten in her stocking feet. Add her brand-new four-inch, ankle-strap sandals in screaming red and she towered over most of the other passengers.

Then there were the pushed-up, pushed-out breasts displayed to perfection by one of Alex's designs, complemented by the turquoise and silver streaks in her otherwise glossy black hair. Practically every head in the waiting area swiveled as she swept in.

"I love it," Alex declared after they'd exchanged fierce hugs and she got an up close look at her former roomie's hair. "You matched the colors in the T-shirt perfectly. You're a walking advert, Chels."

"I live to serve."

Hooking her arm through Alex's, Chelsea moderated her long-legged stride so the two friends could cruise through the terminal hip to hip. She then filled the drive to the casita with a lively commentary on her new gig, all the while dismissing Alex's concerns about her aquatic abilities. Ben hadn't made it home yet when they arrived but Sox provided an enthusiastic welcome.

"Whoa! What's this?" Dropping her weekender in the tiled hallway, Chelsea scooped up the kitten and aimed a quick glance at Alex. "I thought you intended to hold firm against Maria's pleas until the adoption went through?"

"I got outvoted."

"Interesting." Chelsea nuzzled the gray-and-white puff. "Any other changes I should know about?"

"Well…"

"What? Oh, Christ, Lex! You're not pregnant, are you?"

"We've been married just over three weeks, Chels. Hardly time to start reproducing. Besides, we're being careful."

"Yeah, sure. That's what they all say. So what other changes *are* you making?"

Alex stalled long enough to pour them both tall glasses of iced tea. They settled at the kitchen table, the kitten now nested comfortably between Chelsea's breasts.

"You remember how my plan called for a no-fuss, no-frills divorce a suitable time after the adoption went through?"

"Like I could forget?"

"Ben and I have decided to, uh, delay the divorce."

"Delay? For how long?"

"Indefinitely."

Her friend's brows soared. "Well, well, well. Didn't I predict something like this at the wedding?"

"Did you?"

"Yes, sweetcakes, I did. So what's the story? Is there something going on here I should know about?"

Alex smudged her finger along the rim of her glass. "It's complicated."

"What in your life isn't?" Chelsea huffed. "C'mon, Lex, spill it. What's the problem?"

"Oh, Chels, I feel as though I'm riding a roller coaster and can't get off. The wedding, Ben's accident, his moving in here, Maria's dad up for parole, the judge making—"

"Whoa! Back up! The Slime is eligible for parole?"

Chelsea's exclamation startled the drowsy kitten. Sox blinked awake and dug her claws into the warm, tender flesh of her nest.

"Ow!" Wincing, Chelsea extricated the sharp little barbs and repositioned the fur puffball. "When is this supposed to happen?"

"Within the next couple of weeks. And now the judge is making noises that he might delay the adoption hearing pending the decision of the parole board."

"Damn! That sucks."

"Big-time," Alex agreed. "My lawyer's fighting any further delay. He's also advised the court of my new marital status. We're not sure now, though, that the fact I'm married will make that much of a difference."

"Why the hell not?"

"This particular judge has a record of ruling in favor of natural over adoptive parents. If Eddie Musgrove gets out, lands a job, finds a decent apartment and continues to object to giving up his parental rights, my chances are iffy at best."

"But Maria doesn't even *know* El Slime. She's seen him, what, all of four or five times since your sister died?"

"Three."

The ugliness of those three visits could still raise a bad taste in Alex's mouth. On each occasion Eddie had shown only minimal interest in his daughter. His primary motivation the first two times was to get Alex to stop hounding him for child support. The final visit involved a desperate demand for cash to pay off the distributor who'd threatened to break a few bones if Eddie didn't deliver on what he owed.

Alex hadn't shared the sordid details of those visits with Maria. The girl was too young, too vulnerable. She didn't need any more trauma or turbulence. Now, though, Alex couldn't help wondering if she'd made a mistake shielding Eddie Musgrove's daughter from her father's real persona.

He'd been a mediocre guitarist at best. A skinny, ponytailed wannabe who wouldn't have hit the big leagues in a dozen lifetimes. Yet the bastard could ooze charm when he wanted to. Enough to dazzle the groupie who'd given birth to his daughter before she dumped the kid on Eddie and took off for parts unknown. Enough to convince Alex's sister that he really meant all those lies he spewed. He might ooze that same slick charm with the judge, too. The possibility made Alex feel physically ill.

"Maria loves you," Chelsea said, breaking into her grim thoughts. "Every bit as much as you love her. No way she'll want to go with a father she barely knows. Won't her wishes count with the judge?"

"God, I hope so."

Chelsea reached across the table. Her fingers were wet and cold from the condensation on her glass but the grip on Alex's forearm was tight and comforting. She and Alex might have totally different personalities. Their approach to life and love diverged at several critical points. Yet there was no one Alex trusted more.

Except maybe Ben. The realization sliced through her chaotic thoughts and brought a fresh wave of guilt.

"Then there's the fact that I've sucked Ben into a legal morass," she continued glumly. "If there's any hint our marriage isn't real... If the judge or the hearing officer or whoever comes out to interview us suspects I jockeyed him into marriage just to get custody of Maria..."

"But you said the two of you have decided to put all talk of divorce on hold," Chelsea said, obviously trying to make sense of the confusing situation. "Doesn't that mean you want to make a go of your marriage?"

Alex nodded, but the expression on her face had Chelsea cocking her head.

"Again I ask, what's the problem? You jumped at my offer to hang here with Maria so you and hubs could rack up some *us* time. Sounds like a genuine attempt at making it work to me."

"It is. And we're both grateful to you. It's just..."

"Yes?"

Alex smudged the rim of her glass again. "The more I get to know Ben, the guiltier I feel about fast-talking him into marriage. He's a great guy, Chels. Smart, dedicated to the service, supermacho yet—and he'd *never* admit to this—surprisingly sensitive. He's also amazingly patient with Maria." A smile tugged at her heart. "She's already decided she's going to be a pilot, just like Ben."

"Uh-oh."

Chelsea transferred the kitten from the valley between her breasts to her lap and sat up. Sox protested the displacement with a little mewl and a show of claws but curled right up again.

"I begin to see the problem," the dancer announced. "You're in love with the major, and he's in like with you and the kid."

"Yes. No. I mean, I'm not quite there but I'm close. Too damned close to want to hold him in a one-sided relationship. He deserves more."

"Maybe this is enough for him. You. Maria. A kitty and a home to come back to after his military missions."

"He gives that impression but…" She bit her lip. "I'm not sure it's enough for me. I told Ben I didn't need hearts and flowers, but I guess I'm still stupid enough to want them."

"Christ, roomie! Only you could get this whole thing ass backward. What's that stupid saying? First comes love, then comes marriage, then comes—"

"Some twit with a baby carriage," Alex finished drily.

"Right. You've got the kid. You've got the wedding ring. You've also got a man who's jumped through hoops for you. So you need to take him up to Santa Fe or wherever you're going for the weekend and make love to him until his brain slides sideways and every muscle in his body weeps. I guarantee you'll both come home awash in hearts and flowers."

Alex had to laugh. "Trust you to reduce things to bare-knuckle basics."

"More like bare-assed basics." She scooped Sox up and pushed away from the table. "Now show me what you feed this little critter, then go get packed."

"I'm already packed, and feeding him is Maria's job. Also cleaning the litter box, although she may need a little assistance with that."

"No prob."

Alex had just finished giving Chelsea a rundown of the kitty's routine when Ben got home. He was in uniform when he joined them in the kitchen. Surprised, she saw he'd traded his crutches and cast for a black orthopedic boot and cane.

"What's this?"

"Saw the doc this morning and he says I've got exceptionally strong bones, so the cast came off." He stumped across the tiles to drop a kiss on Chelsea's cheek. "Good to see you again."

"Ditto."

"Thanks for volunteering to Maria-sit this weekend."

"My pleasure. And," she added with a sly smile, "hopefully yours."

Ben responded with a grin and a quick nod to Alex. "Give me ten minutes and we're on our way."

He was true to his word. Showered, changed and toting a leather carryall, he insisted on carrying Alex's weekender, too.

"Remember," Chelsea murmured as Alex headed out the door. "Brain sideways, muscles weeping."

Tantalizing visions of just how she'd bring Ben to that extreme condition occupied Alex's thoughts for the better part of the hour-long drive to Santa Fe. She'd made the trip many times since moving from Vegas to Albuquerque, usually to check the silver-and-turquoise jewelry crafted by Native Americans and sold in every shape and size and price range to the hoards of international visitors who crowded the plaza. As a result, she wasn't particularly interested in the passing scenery that included a sweep down to the Rio Grande on the left and the Sandia Mountains standing stark against the sky on the right. Nor did she anticipate that Ben would want to play tourist once they arrived.

He didn't, but he surprised her with a request just as they hit the outskirts of the city. "Mind if we make a short stop to visit a buddy of mine?"

"No, of course not. Who is it?"

"Guy I was stationed with at Kadena. We flew a bunch of missions together and pretty much kept the economy of Okinawa afloat when off duty."

"Barhopping?"

"Karate," he replied, grinning. "Okinawa is actually the birthplace of karate. The schools there teach different styles than those taught in traditional Japanese schools."

Alex would have to take his word for that. She'd taken a few self-defense classes but they mostly involved knees to the groin and the heel of the hand to the nose.

"Joe was a 5th-dan black belt," Ben said as he flipped on the turn signal and took the exit for the Santa Fe bypass. "That's more or less equivalent to holding a master's degree in martial arts."

The city outskirts began to appear, the flat-topped adobe structures looking small and humble compared to the distant Sangre de Cristo Mountains. Snow glistened on the highest peaks, and the air was noticeably clearer. Sharper. More translucent. Santa Fe was two thousand feet higher in elevation than Albuquerque, which itself sat a mile above sea level.

"Joe was determined to get me to at least the high

school level of karate," Ben continued, "but we shipped
out before I passed muster."

"Shipped out to where?"

"Can't say, except to tell you it was hot as hell and
twice as nasty."

He flipped on the turn signal again and moved into
the left lane, following the sign directing them to downtown and museums. As soon as they crossed the over-
pass, Ben took a left onto Guadalupe Street, then another
quick left. And there, directly ahead of them, was the
entrance to the Santa Fe National Cemetery.

Alex gave Ben a startled glance as he drove through
the gates.

"Joe's aircraft took a hit from a SAM—a surface-to-
air missile—our last mission in that hellhole," he explained. "The plane exploded midair. We lost the entire
crew."

"I'm so sorry."

"Me, too. Joe was one of the good guys."

He steered the Tahoe down a wide asphalt drive toward a towering flagpole. On either side of the drive,
curving lines of tombstones wove through shady pines
and fragrant piñon trees. The markers were all uniformly
white and elegantly simple.

Except one. Ben slowed so Alex could take in a
rough-carved sandstone monument that showed a re-
clining soldier wearing boots and a cartridge belt, his
back slumped against a tree trunk.

"That's Private Dennis O'Leary," Ben told her. "According to legend, he was a miserably unhappy loner
who didn't fit in with his fellow troopers at Fort Wingate,
here in New Mexico. He went AWOL for several weeks
and was sentenced to a stretch in the guardhouse when

he returned. After his release, he waited until April 1, then shot himself."

"Oh, no."

"The story doesn't end there." Keeping his foot on the brake, Ben hooked an arm over the steering wheel and gazed past Alex at the reddish-brown monument. "O'Leary left a note instructing his bunk mates to take a wagon to a certain location in the mountains to retrieve a 'memento' he'd left there. When they got there, they found this tombstone. Can you read the inscription?"

Alex lowered the window and squinted at the sandstone scroll propped against the tree trunk. "I can't quite make out the words."

"'Dennis O'Leary,'" Ben recited for her. "'Private, Company 1, 23 Infantry, died April 1, 1901, age twenty-three years and nine months.'"

"He carved his own tombstone?"

"With the date of his death."

"Now, that is even more sad."

"He was interred at Fort Wingate, but when that fort shut down all the graves there were moved here."

Ben's gaze moved to the rows of white tombstones that flowed down the grassy slope behind Private O'Leary. Once again the Sangre de Cristos formed a dramatic backdrop, with cottony clouds drifting among their peaks.

"Joe was Native American," he told Alex quietly. "From the Cochiti Pueblo. A number of his relatives are buried here, including several who served as Navajo Code Talkers in World War II. Joe always said he was looking forward to joining them someday and hearing their war stories. His someday came a little sooner than anticipated."

Alex wasn't sure what to say so she kept still until Ben's mouth kicked up in a small grin.

"The Badger orchestrated the memorial service here at the cemetery. It was quite a send-off. Probably made a few of those code talkers wonder what the hell their relative had done to warrant that kind of demonstration."

Releasing the brake, he followed a winding road to a section of the cemetery shaded by pines. He pulled over, put the Tahoe in Park and killed the ignition. When he got out and rounded the hood to lean against the front fender, Alex joined him.

"That's Joe," he said, nodding to a tombstone just a few feet from the road. The marble was noticeably whiter than many of the older markers, but the inscription was as simple and moving as those on those around it. Just his name, rank, branch of service, birthday and the day he died.

"I swing by here every trip to Santa Fe," Ben commented, loose and relaxed against the fender. "It's so peaceful, and the memories are good."

For him, maybe. Staring at Joe Wilson's marker brought back those awful moments after the early morning call saying Ben had been involved in an accident. Alex had barely known him then, yet the panic had been so real, so sharp.

Gulping, she couldn't even begin to imagine how she would react if she got that same call now. Didn't *want* to imagine it. Suddenly cold despite the bright sun and warm May breeze rustling through the trees, she crossed her arms and rubbed away the goose bumps.

Ben finished his silent communion with his buddy a

moment later and pushed off the fender. "I'm starving. How about we check in to the hotel and grab some lunch?"

Since Alex had left the choice of a hotel for their getaway weekend to Ben, he'd decided to make up for not being able to stay at a plush Vegas honeymoon suite. A few queries at the squadron and some serious sleuthing via the net narrowed the choices to two five-star hotels. One was part of a high-priced chain. The other was an even higher priced boutique hotel a block off the plaza. Since the only room available was their ultraluxurious Governor's Suite, Ben had ignored the four-figure tab for the weekend and gone first class.

The hotel more than lived up to its five-star rating. Done in sand-colored adobe, it was single story and constructed Territorial-style around an enclosed courtyard, with the three rooms of the Governor's Suite comprising the entire south wing. The suite boasted dark-beamed ceilings supported by intricately carved corbels and kivas in both the living room and bedroom. Neither fireplace was likely to get much daytime use with the temperature hovering at a balmy seventy-three, but the nights at this elevation could still carry a chill. The bed, they discovered, was king-size, canopied and also elaborately carved. The Jacuzzi tub could fit both him and Alex with room to spare.

Sudden, intense heat speared into him as his gaze cut from the bed to the tub and back again. Thank God he'd persuaded the surgeon to cut off the cast and let him switch to a removable boot. He was ready—more than ready!—to make love to his wife without having to sling around that damned fiberglass tube. He was calculating how fast he could get Alex through lunch and

out of her clothes when she unknowingly gave a boost
to his fast-developing plans.

"Oooh, Ben, come look! We have our own private patio."

Her face was a study in delight as she led him through
a set of French doors into a walled patio complete with
a bubbling fountain, an outdoor kiva, a wrought iron
table and chairs, and two oversize loungers positioned
in the corner of the patio not shaded by a pergola sporting strings of red chili ristras. What looked to Ben like
every species of flower in the book filled strategically
placed clay pots. He recognized the pink geraniums and
the bright-eyed daisies, but the purple spiky things and
the brilliant orange blossoms on the vine climbing up
and over the walls were beyond his level of botanical
expertise. The hot tub tucked in a secluded corner of the
patio earned his instant approval, though.

"This is so gorgeous," Alex exclaimed as she dipped
her fingers in the fountain. "Instead of going out to lunch,
let's just order from the room service and eat here."

"Fine by me."

More than fine, in fact. Ben made quick work of re-
trieving the heavily embossed menu from the desk in
the sitting room and nailing down Alex's choice of tor-
tilla soup and a chipotle chicken wrap. He added beer-
braised elk tacos for himself and a bottle of white pinot
noir. He was no connoisseur but Swish had introduced
him to white pinot during an overnight in Oregon. Even
his grossly uneducated palette could pick out the hints
of apple, pear and ginger in the pale gold wine.

"Thirty minutes," he reported back to Alex.

"Great!" She swung around and started back into the
suite. "Just enough time to unpack and—"

"Unpacking can wait." Ben caught her elbow and

tugged her toward him. "Let's start with our own brand of appetizer."

She came into his arms, her brown eyes filled with laughter. "You sure we can stop once we start?"

"No, but I'm willing to take the chance."

Twenty seconds after her mouth opened under his, Ben realized stopping was *not* an option. Nor was taking it slow, which had been his intention right up until she shimmied out of her jeans and glitzy tank top.

Twenty seconds after that, he had her stretched out on one of the loungers. With another fervent prayer of thanks to the doc for agreeing to deep-six the cast, he tore at the boot's Velcro straps, kicked out of it and joined her on the lounger.

The prelunch quickie left Alex boneless with pleasure. The longer, far more languorous session that followed lunch and a leisurely soak in the hot tub had her thinking that this marriage business was pretty damned sweet.

Chapter Ten

The next day dawned bright and warm. Afterward, Alex would always think of that lazy Santa Fe Saturday morning as the last stretch of calm before the tsunami hit.

It began with her waking up in Ben's arms, which was *not* a bad way to start any day. She hummed deep in her throat as he rolled her onto her back and nuzzled her neck.

"You sound like Sox," he said, his voice husky in her ear as he fit his body against hers.

She loved the feel of him. The way he filled her. Stretched her. Used his mouth and his hands and his hips to propel her from sleepy to greedy to liquid with pleasure. When her climax hit, she arched her back and locked her calves on his, straining against him, pulling him deeper, fusing her body with his.

Afterward, she sprawled amid the tangled sheets and

wallowed in the last, tingling sensations while he pulled on his briefs and made coffee in the suite's minikitchen.

"Here you go. Two creams, no sugar, right?"

"Right." Wiggling upright, she took a grateful sip. "How come I'm all drained and limp and you're charging around like the Energizer Bunny?"

"Conditioning, sweetheart. Years of rigorous conditioning."

"You got a lot of this particular form of exercise, did you?"

"Maybe not *this* particular form." He laughed, dropping a kiss on her nose. "But you have to admit it's a great way to get the blood pumping."

She couldn't argue with that so she merely grunted and buried her nose in the mug.

Still bristling with energy, he headed for the bathroom. "I'll hit the shower while you get undrained and decide what you want to do about breakfast."

What she wanted, she decided when they were both dressed and enjoying a second cup of coffee on the patio, was quiche and a croissant at her favorite French bistro.

"Sounds good to me," Ben agreed.

They exited their suite into midmorning sunshine heavy with the fragrance of the honeysuckle and bougainvillea that spilled over the walls of their hotel. Alex shortened her stride to accommodate Ben's cane and uneven pace in the boot. Still, it took them only a few short moments to join the tourists thronging the long portico of the Palace of the Governors.

The shaded terrace was a prime locale for Native Americans to display their handicrafts on colorful blankets. Turquoise-studded silver jewelry sparkled in the sun. Hand-thrown pottery bowls and vases displayed distinctive designs from the various pueblos, as did the intricately woven baskets. Feathers and beads decorated hand-carved kachina dolls that ranged from just a few inches to several feet in height. One in particular stopped Alex in her tracks.

It was an Eagle Dancer, his feathered arms outspread. Turquoise beads decorated his leather clothing, and his head was a beaked mask. One foot was lifted and the body was tilted at an angle that instantly evoked the drumbeat of the dance. It was only about ten inches tall, but the delicate balance and exquisite carving thrilled the artist in Alex's soul.

"How beautiful!" She lifted her admiring gaze from the kachina to the elderly gentleman hunkered down on a red plastic crate behind his wares. "Did you carve this?"

He curved his lips in a smile that almost got lost in the mass of wrinkles crinkling his weathered skin. "I did. You know the Eagle Dancer? He's the ruler of the skies, a messenger to the heavens."

"The ruler of the skies," Alex echoed softly, lifting the piece to run a careful fingertip over the beadwork.

"Kachinas are our link to the spirit world," the old man said. "Each year they come down to earth and dance to bring life and renewal. When they return to the sky after the planting, they carry our prayers that the circle of life will continue."

An image of row upon row of white markers filled her mind. Her heart thumping, she made an instant decision. "I'll take it."

The seller's cataract-clouded black eyes widened. "Don't you want to know the price?"

"Alex," Ben murmured from just behind her, "maybe you should let me do the bargaining."

"No." She aimed a brilliant smile at the artist. "I know excellent work when I see it. I trust you to price it appropriately."

Put on the spot, the old man stroked his whiskered chin for several moments, then gave a figure that was lower than Alex expected but higher than Ben thought she should pay.

"You should make a counteroffer," he urged.

"Nope, I don't want to devalue your gift."

"*My* gift?"

"He's the king of the skies," she reminded him as she emptied her wallet to pay the artist. "Show him the proper respect and he'll watch over you every time you take off."

After the seller Bubble Wrapped the kachina and tucked it in a plastic Walmart bag, Ben accepted the gift Alex handed him with a lopsided smile. "I didn't know you believed in spirits."

"Some people call them angels," she answered, shrugging. "Some label them saints or prophets. I'm certainly not qualified to debate the differences," she said as she slipped her arm through his. "But I'm willing to cover all bets if it'll keep you safe."

The simple declaration hacksawed through about a dozen of Ben's tough outer layers. He'd been on his own for so long. Had relied on only himself and his squadron mates and his crew for years. He honestly couldn't remember the last time someone unconnected with Special Ops had thumped him on the back and said they'd keep him in their thoughts, much less their prayers.

The realization that he was now part of a small family circle only tangentially connected with the air force hit like a bucketful of ice water. Christ! Had that runaway cargo pallet crunched his head as well as his foot?

These past weeks he'd focused on easing Alex and Maria into his military existence. Introducing Alex to his boss at the 58th and showing her around the squadron had constituted a first step. Bringing up pictures of his aircraft on Maria's iPad and sharing highly sanitized versions of his missions with her had been another. He'd figured that taking the two of them to the Memorial Day picnic would represent the next phase in their induction to military life.

What the hell had he done to enter their world? Sure, he'd picked Maria up from school a few times. And yes, he'd offered to facilitate Alex's entry into the military sales market. But he'd pleaded work as an excuse to avoid going to church with them on Sundays and had zero understanding of the tenets of their Catholic faith. He knew as much about their basic beliefs as Sox did. The thought both humbled and embarrassed him.

"Tell you what," he said, pressing her arm against his side. "I'll explore how angels and saints and kachinas fit into the spiritual galaxy with you. We might both be surprised at what we learn."

"Deal," she said with a smile that sent warmth curling through him.

Lord! Did she have any idea how that smile lit her up from the inside out? Or the punch it delivered to Ben's chest? He was still feeling its impact when they crossed the plaza to the La Fonda hotel.

The multistory building sported a bronze plaque that designated it as one of the Historic Hotels of America. The brief description below indicated that one of the first

businesses the Spanish established when they settled
Santa Fe in 1607 was an inn, or *fonda*. A *fonda* in one
form or another had existed in this same location ever
since. In the 1800s the La Fonda hotel marked the ter-
minus of the Santa Fe Trail. The Atchison, Topeka and
Santa Fe Railway acquired the sprawling establishment
in 1925 and leased it to Fred Harvey, who operated it as
one of his famous Harvey House Hotels.

Constructed of earth-colored adobe, the facility
boasted a number of expensive boutiques all along its
stuccoed exterior. The French Pasty Shop café occupied
a prime spot in the hotel's north facade.

"Kind of incongruous for a Spanish-style hotel set
smack on Santa Fe's main plaza to house a French bakery," Ben commented as they joined the crowd. "What's
the story on that?"

"I'm not sure. Maybe because there's always been a
sizable French presence in Santa Fe. It was a big trad-
ing center for French fur trappers in the early days, and
I know the first bishop of Santa Fe was a Frenchman."
She nodded to the massive, square-towered church that
dominated the view at the end of the block. "Archbishop
Jean-Baptiste Lamy ordered the construction of that ca-
thedral and established the network of Catholic schools
throughout New Mexico."

They entered the pastry shop and exchanged the increasingly warm outside air for air-conditioned cool carrying the tantalizing scent of fresh baked goods. Ben
was more of a huevos rancheros than quiche kind of
guy but the array in the bakery's glass cases looked
eminently edible. He and Alex placed their orders, then
snagged a corner table that overlooked the plaza. He
was careful to position both his cane and the Bubble

Wrapped kachina on the inside of his chair, out from the traffic pattern. He still felt guilty that Alex had spent so much for the Eagle Dancer and fully intended to reciprocate with whatever piece of jewelry or art that might catch her interest.

"I better call and see how Chelsea's surviving kitten and kid." With a wry grin, she fished her phone from her purse. "They *should* be up by now, although both Chelsea and Maria have been known to sleep past noon."

"I'm betting Sox got at least one of them up."

He would've won the bet. Judging by Alex's side of the conversation, her roommate had some choice words to say about animals that sat on a person's face while other unnamed persons slept blissfully undisturbed.

"It's almost ten, Chels. You need to get her up and moving." Alex listened for a few moments and had to bite her lip to keep from laughing. "You're right. She does give an excellent imitation of a dead dolphin when you try to roll her out of bed. But you can handle it. I know. I know. Okay, I'll call you later."

She hung up, her eyes dancing, and shot Ben a conspiratorial grin. "They're going to the mall. If and when Chelsea can rouse a still-comatose Maria."

Having listened to Alex perform the same Herculean task a number of times now, Ben wished the showgirl luck just as a server arrived with their order.

"Here you go."

To his relief, his mushroom, onion and Gruyère quiche came in a man-size portion. As an added bonus, the croissants were flaky and buttery and the coffee was dark and rich. He left the pastry shop more than satisfied and ready for whatever Alex wanted to do with the rest of the day. When asked, she hesitated.

"I usually roam the Canyon Road galleries when I'm in Santa Fe. They give me a lot of inspiration for my designs. But they're all pretty artsy-fartsy."

"I can handle artsy-fartsy."

Maybe. Ben wasn't quite as confident by the time they reached the start of the historic half mile. Flowering vines, cacti and clay pots spilling brilliant color lured visitors into shops housed in traditional adobe structures trimmed in turquoise and white.

"There are more than a hundred galleries, artist studios, jewelry stores, boutiques and gourmet restaurants along this short stretch," Alex informed him happily. "I promise I won't drag you into all of them, but only if you promise to tell me if your foot starts to ache. Agreed?"

"Agreed."

"Here, let me carry the kachina."

"I've got it," he said, shifting the bag to his right hand so he could work the cane with his left.

He made it through less than a third of the galleries. The sculptures and paintings and lithographs and squash blossom necklaces were all stunning but a guy could only ingest so much dazzling art. He tried to talk Alex into identifying a favorite piece that he could purchase for her. She resisted, insisting she was just there to generate ideas.

He found an unexpected niche in an antiques shop specializing in early Spanish and American military artifacts. Alex left him perched happily on a folding camp stool while the shop owner detailed the history of various service pistols. She returned a half hour later and found him walking out of the shop trying to maneuver cane, kachina and a bulky, brown-paper-wrapped package.

"Ben!" She rushed to relieve him of the package. The

weight made her arms sag, and the musty odor wrinkled her nose. "What is this?"

"A buffalo coat."

"Huh?"

"Trappers wore them to keep warm in the winter. So did US soldiers on the frontier."

"What in the world are you going to do with a buffalo coat?"

"Send it to Dingo."

"Who's Dingo?"

"Blake Andrews. Ex-military cop. You met him at the Cactus Café the night of the Badger Bash."

"Oh, right." She shifted the heavy bundle. "Why does Dingo want a buffalo robe?"

"He doesn't. That's the whole point."

"I don't get it."

"The thing is, I still owe him for..." He slanted her a quick, slashing grin. "Let's just say I owe him."

That cocky grin twisted something in her heart. She didn't have time to analyze what it was before he hooked two fingers in his mouth and summoned the cab sitting idle at the top of Canyon Road with a piercing whistle. Moments later Alex manhandled herself and the clumsy bundle into the back seat. Ben folded himself in on the other side.

The ride back to their hotel took less than ten minutes. Once there, Alex suggested they chill on the patio for a while before entering any serious discussion about a late lunch or early dinner.

"We could do that," Ben agreed. "Or..." He stashed his aromatic purchase in a corner of the sitting room and hooked his cane over the back of a chair. "We could soak away our aches in our own private hot tub."

"Ben!" Alex's face flooded with instant concern. "You promised you'd tell me if your foot started hurting."

"My foot's not hurting," he deadpanned.

"Then what...? Oh!" The worry darkening her eyes shaded into laughter. "You idiot! You scared me there for a moment."

"Sorry. How about I make it up to you with a nice soothing soak?"

Stifling another snort of laughter, Alex let him lead her out to the patio. He took a few moments to reset the hot tub's controls. She used the interval to peel off her clothes. After getting the water bubbling and tinkering with the temperature settings, Ben followed her example. Not for the first time, his muscled shoulders, flat belly and lean flanks stopped the breath in Alex's throat.

"You," she murmured, her voice low and throaty as she closed the distance between them, "are an artist's dream."

"Not hardly," he said on an embarrassed huff.

"Yes, hardly."

She skated her hands from his shoulders to his chest, then teased the fine hair that arrowed down to his belly. His midriff hollowed at her featherlight touch. All parts south went on instant alert.

The involuntary reaction sent a bolt of sheer feminine satisfaction through Alex. The mere thought that she could stir him with just her touch was incredibly intoxicating. Before she could wallow in her triumph, though, he hauled her against him for a kiss and her own body betrayed her.

The muscles low in her belly contracted, hard and fast. Heat raced through every vein. She hungered for this man. Ached to take him into her body and join with him in the rawest, most elemental way a woman could with a man.

Something was different, though. She couldn't pinpoint what, with her senses spinning and desire closing her throat. The heat seared her. The now-familiar hunger gnawed at her. Yet the stop at the cemetery… Her instinctive feeling that identified Ben with the Eagle Dancer… The fact that he was so much more complex, so multifaceted…

When he swooped her into his arms and carried her to the hot tub, her traitorous mind shot back to her conversation with Chelsea yesterday morning. Suddenly, she understood that funny little twist in her heart earlier. She loved this man. Loved his generosity, his quirky sense of humor, his dedication to his job, his easy self-confidence.

And she ached with the sudden, shattering realization that their too hasty, too casual arrangement wasn't enough. She wanted more. She wanted it all.

The thought stabbed into her as he hunkered down on a corner seat and arranged her so they were face-to-face, her hips straddling his. He was as hard as a rock, every muscle in his body taut with need.

"Ben…"

"I know, sweetheart. I know." Grunting, he shifted and slid his hand between her thighs. "Just let me…"

"Ben, wait."

He raised his head, and the sexual haze clouding his blue eyes set her heart pounding. Later, she decided, her breath as ragged as her pulse. She'd tell him later that she couldn't hold him to their casually negotiated marriage. Couldn't hold either of them. Right now, though…right now, she would take everything he wanted to give her. Every kiss, every touch, every taste.

"You okay?" he asked. "Is the water too hot?"

"It's fine. I just, uh, needed to catch my breath."

"Caught it yet?"

When she nodded, the crease between his brows disappeared and his voice dropped to a teasing growl. "Then let's see what we can do to make you lose it again."

Making love in a hot tub, Alex decided during her second immersion in as many days, wasn't all it was cracked up to be. The pulsing jets produced some decidedly delicious sensations but the internal heat her body generated made the water seem too hot against her skin. Ben adjusted the temperature several times but they ended up exchanging the tub for one of the oversize loungers that had done such yeoman duty yesterday.

From the lounger they transitioned to the bed and then, after a long, drowsy recovery, to the sitting room. Fully clothed again, Alex steeled herself for the discussion she hadn't had the nerve to initiate naked.

Curling up on one end of the sofa, she tucked a leg under herself and accepted one of the bottles of chilled water that Ben retrieved from the suite's refreshment center. He claimed the other corner and twisted off the top of his bottle, then chugged about half the contents.

Her fist tight on her dew-streaked bottle, Alex watched the muscles play in his throat. Her own was tight when he lowered the bottle and angled toward her.

"Any place special you want to go for dinner? Since we'll be joining the Saturday night crowd, we should maybe ask the concierge to make reservations."

"I picked the French bakery for brunch. You choose

dinner. But first…" she dragged in a long breath "…we need to talk."

Ben didn't alter his relaxed slouch. He did, however, cock his head and send her a half curious, half wary look. "About anything in particular?"

"Our marriage. Or more correctly, our sham of a marriage."

Again, he didn't change his position. But it felt to Alex as though the temperature in the room suddenly dropped at least ten degrees.

"Funny," he said with careful deliberation, "I've been operating under the impression we'd passed the 'sham' stage."

"Okay, maybe that wasn't the best word choice."

Alex gnawed on the inside of her lower lip. She'd gained enough of an insight into Ben's personality by now to know he wouldn't consider his commitment to her and Maria as anything particularly noble, much less a self-sacrifice. She also knew he seemed perfectly content with their domestic arrangements.

Content might work for some people. Maybe if they were bent and doddering and long past the passion of their youth. Or less concerned about their partner's feelings than their own. But Ben deserved more. *She* deserved more.

Finding the words to tell him so, however, was one of the toughest things Alex had ever done. She dragged in another deep breath and made herself look him square in the eye.

"Do you remember when we talked about…?"

The chirp of her iPhone interrupted her carefully crafted beginning. Not sure whether she was more relieved or annoyed, Alex glanced at the photo that came up on the screen.

"It's Chelsea. I'll let it go to voice mail."

"Go ahead and take it."

"I can get back to her later."

"Take the call," Ben instructed. "I'm not going anywhere."

That sounded more like a warning than a reassurance. Particularly since Ben's expression had grown as cool as his tone.

With a sense that she'd already bungled this conversation badly, Alex hit the talk button. "Hi, Chels. What's…?"

"You have to come home. Now!"

The panic in her friend's voice brought Alex bolting upright. Water sloshed from the bottle still gripped in her other hand. Fear sliced into her heart.

"What's happened?"

Ben reacted to her shrill demand by jerking around to face her more squarely. She barely registered his narrowed eyes or the sudden tautness to his neck and shoulders.

"Chelsea, tell me what's happened!" Before her friend could answer, a cry ripped from deep in Alex's chest. "Is it Maria? Has she been hurt?"

Please let it be a minor injury. Please, please, please, pl—

"She's missing, Alex." Chelsea's voice broke on a sob. "She's missing."

Chapter Eleven

"When? How? Oh, God, how long has she been gone?"

Alex gripped the phone so tight the edges cut into her palm. Beside her, Ben barked a quick order.

"Put the phone on speaker."

Thoroughly panicked, she barely heard him. Her whole being was concentrated on the torrent pouring out of Chelsea.

"Sox got out. She slipped through the front door. Maria and I were leaving to go to the park. We chased…"

"Put the phone on speaker!"

Blindly, Alex stabbed at the speaker button.

"…after her, but she darted up a tree. That piñon next to the driveway. Then she couldn't get down. The tree's not that tall," Chelsea gasped, "but the branches are thick and I couldn't—"

"Forget the tree! What happened to Maria?"

"I went back in the house to get your stepladder. When I came out again, both she and Sox were gone." Her voice broke on a sob of guilt and fear. "I couldn't find the ladder, Alex. Not right away. But I wasn't in the house more than a few minutes. I swear it."

"When did this happen?"

"About twenty minutes ago. All I could think was that Sox jumped down and ran off. I…" Close to hyperventilating, Chelsea gasped for breath. "I figured Maria had chased after her, so I shouted for her. Then I searched up and down the street. The alley behind the house. I pounded on your neighbors' doors, Alex! No one saw her. They're all out helping me search now."

"What about the police?" Ben cut in. "Did you call 9-1-1?"

"Just did. They're on their way."

"So are we," he told her grimly. "We're leaving right now. Keep us posted."

Alex's hand was shaking so badly it took three tries to hit the button. By then Ben was already off the sofa and throwing their few things into their bags.

They didn't bother to check out at the front desk.

"They've got my credit card," Ben said as they rushed for the Tahoe parked in the tiny lot behind the hotel.

The drive back to Albuquerque was the longest of Alex's life. The speed limit on I-25 was seventy-five mph. Ben pushed that to eighty and still it wasn't fast enough for her. Getting them both killed in a car accident wouldn't help Maria. Alex knew that. Still, she had to bite her lip to keep from urging him to go faster.

She was straining against her seat belt, both fists clenched, when Ben pressed the talk button on the

Tahoe's steering wheel and brought up his cell phone's voice assistant via the high-tech communications console.

"Siri," he barked, keeping his eyes on the road, "call Dingo."

The ex-cop, Alex remembered, her heart thudding. She held her breath through five long rings until a laconic drawl came through the speakers.

"Yo, Cowboy. How's it hanging?"

"We've got a situation here, Blake."

The drawl disappeared, and the reply came sharp and fast. "Speak to me."

"Maria, the kid Alex has temporary custody of, has gone missing. It happened about a half hour ago. She and I were up in Santa Fe. Maria was staying with a friend."

"Have the police been notified?"

"Yes. Tell me what we need to give them."

"A photo, as recent as possible," he rattled off crisply. "A detailed description of what she was wearing when she went missing. A copy of the custodial agreement. A list of her friends. Access to her room and any electronics she uses. There's more, but they'll lay it on you once they assess the situation."

"Got it."

"I'm in El Paso. I can have my folks turn our plane around and be there in two hours."

"Thanks." Ben's gaze cut to Alex and the phone buzzing in her hand. "I'll call you as soon as we talk to the police."

"Roger that."

Ben ended his call at the same moment Chelsea's nerve-racked voice jumped out of the speaker on Alex's phone.

"The police are here. They want a picture of Maria."

"There's one on the fridge."

"I gave it to them," Chelsea reported, her voice shaken and wobbly. "And I zapped them the one I took of her and Sox yesterday."

She added that they were now searching places she hadn't thought to check—inside the car Alex had left parked in the garage, under shrubs and bushes, even the crawl space under a neighbor's house.

"They went through the house, too. In case she came home and I missed her. We checked the closets, under the bed, inside...inside the freezer."

Oh, God! Every awful statistic in the parenting books Alex had read about accidental deaths in the home came back to haunt her.

"The police will need a list of her friends," she told Chelsea grimly, "in case she decided to visit one of them without telling you."

"She wouldn't do that...would she?"

"I don't *think* so. But have them contact Dinah Madison and her mom, Pat. And Jason Hernandez. His mom's name is Elena." Alex rattled off their phone numbers, then scrubbed the heel of her hand across her forehead as she tried to remember all Maria's young friends. "I'll scroll through the address book on my phone and call you back with additional names."

"Her school," Ben interjected. "Tell them to contact Maria's teacher. She can give them a class roster."

When Alex supplied the teacher's name, Chelsea confirmed she'd pass it to the police. "I'm also supposed to secure Maria's room. And give them access to any computers or electronic devices she uses."

"She's got an iPad and gets on my computer but only if I'm there to supervise."

Alex gave her the password for each and told her to provide the police anything they ask for. Anything! Then she skimmed the roadside markers flashing by outside her window for a milepost or exit sign.

"We're just passing the exit for Bernalillo. We'll be there in twenty minutes."

They'd covered barely another mile when Alex's phone buzzed again. Unknown Caller flashed up on the ID. Praying for good news, she jabbed the speaker button again.

"Alexis Scott."

"Hey, Lex."

Her brows slashed together. The voice was vaguely familiar but she couldn't pin a face to it.

"Who is this?"

"What, you don't recognize your own bro-in-law?"

It took a few seconds for that to cut through the fear crowding her mind. "Eddie?"

"Got it in one, babe."

She shot Ben a disbelieving glance. "What did you do? Break out of jail?"

"Didn't have to. Bleeding hearts on the parole panel let me out."

"But I thought... My lawyer told me..."

She could hardly breathe through her suffocating fear, but every instinct in her body was now screaming that Eddie's call was tied to his daughter's disappearance. She shook her head to clear the numbing paralysis.

"My lawyer told me your parole hearing wasn't scheduled until next month."

"They got me in early."

Dammit all to hell! The New Mexico Parole Board should've notified her or her lawyer. Summoning every ounce of courage she possessed, Alex asked the question now eating at her soul.

"Is Maria with you?"

"Yeah. Her and her ratty little cat. They're playin' just a little ways away from where I'm sitting."

Alex slumped against her seat. Tears stung her eyes. *Thank you, Lord. Thank you!*

"Where are you?" she asked when she pulled herself together again.

"Not far from your place."

"Where, Eddie?"

"Don't worry. I'm keepin' a close eye on her. More than I can say for you, Lex. I went by your house and there she was. In your driveway, practically bawling 'bout her cat getting stuck in a tree. I got it down for her and was an instant hero. Yep, that's me," he bragged smugly, "daddy hero."

Her vision still blurred by tears, Alex glanced at Ben. His face showed the same profound relief still gushing through her. But it was tempered by a swiftly gathering grimness as her former brother-in-law continued in a too chatty, too smarmy tone.

"Almost didn't recognize the kid," he related. "She's grown so much. A real cutie, too. Takes after her dad. She didn't recognize me, either, till I showed her the picture of Janet and me and her. Then she was all smiles and hugs."

"The police are looking for her, Eddie. They think... We all thought she'd gone missing."

"Yeah? Well, she sure as hell coulda been snatched.

Not too smart, letting a kid her age play outside. All alone. No supervision. You shoulda been watching her."

"We were up in Santa Fe for the weekend. Chelsea's looking after her."

"Well, well. Wonder what Judge Whazisface will think of you leaving my kid in the care of a stripper with big tits and zero brains?"

Alex didn't bother to counter the ugly insult. The one and only time Janet and her husband had visited Alex in Vegas, Eddie had drooled all over the generously endowed showgirl. He'd also hit on her. More than once, according to Chelsea. Mercifully, she'd refrained from kneeing him in the balls. She'd pretty much ripped his ego into tiny little pieces, though.

"And who's this 'we'?" he wanted to know, oozing the sly, tell-me-something-nasty innuendo Alex had despised since the first day she'd met him. For about the thousandth time, she wondered how her otherwise intelligent sister could've fallen for such a creep.

"You shacking up with someone, Lexie? Bet the judge'll wanna know about that, too."

"I'm married, you turd."

"Yeah?" Clearly surprised, he demanded details. "Since when?"

"Since none of your business. Take Maria back to my place, Eddie. Now! Or the police will haul your ass back to jail."

"What for?" he sneered. "I got visitation rights, remember?"

"Those rights were granted before you got busted!"

"So? They're still on the books, aren't they?"

Alex threw Ben a helpless glance. She'd talked to her lawyer about going back to court to revoke the visitation

rights. But with Eddie in prison and the adoption hearing coming up fast, they'd decided not to rock the boat.
She bitterly regretted that decision now.

"Guy gets outta jail, he wants to see his kid," Eddie
continued in the same sneering tone. "That's all I'm
doing, sis. Visiting my kid."

"You're supposed to notify me first," Alex reminded
him through clenched teeth. "Get my permission."

"Yeah, and you're supposed to keep an eye on her.
Seems like you screwed up a lot worse than me. I guess
we could fight it out in front of the judge. Or…"

When he let that hang, she had a sick feeling she
knew what was coming next. She caught Ben's tight-
jawed look and knew he was expecting the same thing.

"Or what?" she ground out.

"We could settle this friendly like."

He let that hang, too, milking every second until Alex
wanted to scream at him to get to the bottom line they
both knew was coming.

"Look, I admit I'm not prime daddy material. With
the right incentive, I might even be persuaded to drop
my objection to the adoption."

"How much, Eddie?"

"Enough to set me up in a new place. A new life."

"How much?"

"Ten grand oughtta do it. In cash."

"I don't have access to that much cash!"

"The hell you don't. Maria says your business is doin'
real good. You gotta keep some backup in your account
to buy supplies and stuff."

"It's Saturday. The banks are closed."

"So make the rounds of the ATMs."

"I can't withdraw that much from—"

The anger he'd banked up to now broke through. Spewing venom, he cut her off.

"I don't care how you get it, bitch. Just get it. Or maybe I should tell the court how close Maria and me got this afternoon. Whaddya call it? Father-daughter bonding or some crap like that."

He pitched his voice to a high, fake falsetto that raked along Alex's nerves like fingernails on a blackboard.

"Oh, Judge, I gotta tell you. When I saw my kid, standing there, all by herself, playing in the street while her guardian was up in Santa Fe getting it on with her new husband, I had to step in. Had to identify myself. 'N' when she walked into my arms, I thought my heart was gonna burst. All that stuff Ms. Scott 'n' her lawyer fed you 'bout me abandoning Maria and her stepmom. Lies. Nothing but lies. The kid loves me and I love her."

Nausea roiled in Alex's stomach. There was just enough truth stirred in with Eddie's perverted recital to tip the scales against her.

"Or maybe," he added, slicing into her chaotic thoughts, "I might take a little trip. Tell you the truth, I'm not real excited about reporting to a parole officer every month. Maria and me might go to Florida. Or California."

"You can't take her out of state, Eddie! That's kidnapping."

His voice hardened. "Get the money, Lex. And call off the cops. Or I promise, you'll never see the kid again."

He was bluffing. He *had* to be bluffing. Yet her mind was so crippled with fear for Maria that she couldn't dismiss the very real possibility he would carry through on his threat.

"Eddie, listen to me. You can't—"

Muttering a vicious oath, Ben yanked the phone out of her hand. "No, asshole. You listen to *me*."

"Who the hell is this?"

"Alex's husband. Maria's stepdad."

"Stepdad?" he echoed on a snort of derision. "You're not a 'step' anything, pal. You're not her blood kin. Neither is Alex, for that matter. And the both of you have zero chance of adopting my kid if I tell the judge how you left her with Ms. Tits while you went off and did the dirty. Anyone coulda walked away with her."

Ben's jaw went even tighter. "Tell us where to meet you. We'll bring ten grand."

A smug laugh came over the phone. "Glad someone's talking sense."

"Where?"

"Call me when you've got the cash and I'll tell you. And come alone," he warned. "One sign of the cops and me and the kid are gone."

Ben hit the off button and tossed the phone to Alex. "Check your Recents and write down the number he called from. Then call Chelsea and have her put one of the police officers on the line. Give him the details and see if they can start a trace on the number."

Alex gripped the phone. They had to involve the police. Her rational mind didn't dispute that. Yet the fear roiling her stomach was anything but rational.

"What if he disappears, Ben? With Maria?"

"If he's stupid enough to think you can withdraw ten thousand dollars from various ATMs in one day, he's stupid enough to sit wherever he is and wait for it."

He shot her a look that glinted with the promise of pure savagery.

"We'll take him down, Alex. Hard."

* * *

The police were waiting with a clearly distraught Chelsea when they pulled up at the house. The seasoned veteran introduced herself as Officer Elizabeth Park. Her partner was a kid who looked like a rookie but both officers impressed Ben with their efficiency.

They'd already traced the number Musgrove had called from to a cell phone purchased yesterday at an electronics store in the South Valley. They'd also confirmed that he'd been released from the Central New Mexico Correctional Facility in Los Lunas the day prior.

"The prison texted us Musgrove's mug shot," Park told them. "We've put it out over the police net, along with Maria's picture. Our commander has also notified the FBI and they're activating a Child Abduction Rapid Deployment team. Luckily, one of the teams operates out of the FBI office right here in Albuquerque. Team members should begin arriving on scene within the next few minutes. Among other things, they'll need to know your custody arrangements and the details of any court-ordered visitation conditions."

"I was granted temporary custody after my sister—Maria's stepmom—died. Eddie was allowed 'reasonable' visitation but that was before he was convicted and sent to prison." Alex's precarious hold on her nerves slipped. "This isn't a *visit*, Officer Park! He's kidnapped Maria. He wants cash to return her."

"That's what it looks like. Did you by any chance manage to record the ransom demand?"

"No, but my husband heard it."

Ben nodded, a feral gleam in his eyes. "The bastard wants us to call him back when we have the cash. We'll get him on record then."

* * *

After that it seemed to Alex that events moved with a combination of agonizing slowness and blinding speed. As promised, elements of the FBI's Child Abduction Rapid Deployment team began to arrive within mere minutes. They reconfirmed the situation with Ben, Alex and a still-shaken Chelsea, then carefully coached Alex on what to say when she contacted Eddie. Her heart thudding, she hit the return-call button.

He answered on the first ring. "Yo, sis. You got the cash?"

Alex ignored the tense, tight circle listening in on headsets and focused every ounce of her concentration on Eddie. "I've got it."

"See, I knew you could get it together."

"Let me talk to Maria."

"She's playin' in the sandbox with her cat."

"Put her on the phone."

"Why? You don't think I'd hurt my little girl, do you?"

"You don't get a cent until I talk to her, Eddie."

"Okay, okay!" He raised his voice. "Hey, kiddo! Grab the cat and come say hi to Alex."

Every listener in the room breathed palpable sighs of relief as Maria's seemingly cheerful voice floated through the phone.

"Hi, Alex. Did Daddy tell you that he climbed up the tree and rescued Sox?"

"Yes, he did."

"He said he called Aunt Chelsea to let her know we got Sox down. Hope she's not mad at me for coming to the park with him. I probably should've told her first, huh?"

"Yes, you should have."

"When are you and Ben coming home? I want to… What? Oh, Daddy wants to talk to you again."

Her heart in her throat, Alex heard Eddie tell Maria to take her cat back to the sandbox before firing off a quick set of instructions. "Guadalupe Park. Bring the cash there. We make nice in front of the kid, you pass me the dough and I'm outta your life."

"Until the next time you're broke and need to score a hit," she said bitterly.

"Just bring the cash. I'll be watching," he warned. "Make sure it's just you."

"It'll be me and my husband," Alex countered quickly. "I need him to drive. I'm too upset."

"Oh, right," Eddie sneered. "The *step*jerk. What kind of wheels?"

"What?"

"Your car, what'll you be driving?"

"A black Chevy Tahoe."

"Okay. I'll be watching," he warned again. "Don't do anything stupid, or Maria and me will take a nice long trip."

The FBI team leader whipped off his earphones. "Good job, Ms. Scott. We'll take it from here."

"No! Eddie needs to see me, see the Tahoe, or he might get desperate and hurt Maria."

"We won't let that happen."

"I can't take that chance. I *won't* take that chance. Ben, tell them!"

"Alex and I will go to the park," he confirmed tersely.

Surrounded by older homes and shaded by centuries-old live oaks, the small oasis of green was located in the south part of the city. Alex's frantic gaze swept the swings and monkey bars, the sandbox, the benches with their peeling green paint. When she didn't find any sign of Maria or Eddie, her glance zinged to the rusted junker parked on the cross street.

She was out of the Tahoe almost before it rolled to a stop. Ben shoved it into Park and was right beside her as she headed for the junker.

Ben's ex-cop pal Dingo always maintained that most criminals were pretty stupid, even the military variety. Eddie Musgrove proved no exception to that general observation. He obviously believed he'd conned Alex into complying with his demands because he made no effort to stop Maria when she hopped out of the car.

"Alex! Ben!" the girl called joyfully. "You're home early."

Hugging Sox to her chest, she darted across the stubby grass. Alex raced to meet her, then swung her up in a fierce embrace that made Maria squeal and the kitten hiss a protest.

Musgrove followed in a saunter. Ben needed only a single glance to peg his type. Too cocky. Too sure of himself. Muscled up, probably from his years in prison, and thick as a stump between the ears.

The ex-con did some pegging of his own. His disdainful gaze drifted from the plastic shopping bag in Ben's right hand to the cane in his left.

"Whaddya do, Alex? Marry a cripple?"

The jeer brought Maria's head around. A surprised frown creased her brow. "Ben's not crippled. He just broke his foot."

"If you say so."

"He did," she insisted, still frowning. "And you shouldn't make fun of people, 'specially if they're sick."

"Yeah, okay, whatever." His derisive glance cut back to Ben. "You got something for me?"

"I do, but why don't we conduct this business in private? Alex, take Maria to the car."

He, Alex and the FBI team had agreed the first single most urgent priority was to remove Maria from any possible line of fire. Although Musgrove didn't appear to be armed, none of them was about to take that chance.

Nor did they want the seven-year-old to witness an FBI team swarm the park and take her father down. No child needed to see that, especially one who had no idea that Musgrove had offered her for sale. The psychologist on the team had promised to help Alex finesse an explanation of that situation later.

"Say goodbye to your dad, Kitten."

The words almost made her gag, but she got them out and managed not to claw her former brother-in-law's face when he flipped his daughter a careless wave.

"I'll see you later, kiddo."

"The hell you will," Ben muttered while Alex transported Maria and her now mewling pet to the Tahoe.

"You gonna stop me, Crip?"

"I might."

"Don't think so," the punk facing him drawled as the Tahoe's engine kicked over. "You're big. I'll give you that. And you look like you got some muscle on you. But you're old and you gotta be slow with that clunky black boot 'n' cane to trip you up. I got nothing to worry about from you, Crip."

From the corner of one eye, Ben saw the Tahoe turn a corner. He and Alex had agreed she'd get Maria away from the park. Ben would hitch a ride back to the house with the police. He had some business to conduct first.

"You want the cash, asshole?" A slow smile curved his lips. "Come and get it."

"Christ, you really think I won't hurt you? Guess again, pal. In fact, I'm lookin' forward to—"

That's all he got out before Ben dropped the cane, tossed the shopping bag aside, and took two lunging steps.

Musgrove swung first. Ben made sure of that. He blocked the wild punch easily, then followed with a vicious right to the midsection that doubled the ex-con over. A left uppercut caught him on the way down, snapping his head back. He sailed backward and slammed into the ground just as police cars erupted from half a dozen side streets and swarmed the park.

Chapter Twelve

Alex drove home, drowning in relief and wanting desperately to shield Maria from the ugliness that almost happened. She also burned with the urge to scream at the girl that she'd better not go off with *anyone*—a friend, a relative, a teacher or even a police officer—before checking with Alex or Ben or, as in this case, the babysitter they'd left in charge. But the psychologist on the FBI team had suggested that Alex hold off any explanations or recriminations until he had a chance to ascertain whether Maria had sustained any emotional, physical or sexual trauma.

Alex's own emotions almost choked her, however. She barely heard Maria chat happily about the ice-cream cone her dad had bought her, said nothing as she coaxed a purr from her kitten. When they turned the corner and the girl saw the squad car parked at the casita, however, her expression slid from surprise to guilty comprehension.

"Did you call the police to look for me?"

"Chelsea did. She didn't know where you were and got scared."

"But Daddy called her." A faint hint of doubt crept into Maria's voice. "Didn't he?"

She got her answer when the front door flew open. Chelsea raced out, her black hair a wild mass of tangles and mascara streaking her cheeks. Yanking open Maria's door, she dragged the girl and her kitten into a fierce embrace almost before she'd unsnapped her seat belt.

"I've aged ten years in the past hour, brat! Don't ever, *ever* do that to me again."

Maria squirmed loose, still clutching her indignant pet. Her face wrinkled with worry, she tried to calm Sox with a quick, nervous stroke. "Daddy said he called you, Chelsea. He told me you said it was okay to go to the park."

"Yeah, well, he didn't. And when I get my hands on that sorry excuse for a…"

Alex stopped her with a quick shake of her head. "Let's go inside, Chels. The police want to talk to Maria."

Thoroughly scared now, the girl clung to her pet with one hand and groped for Alex's with the other. "Are they gonna arrest me?" she asked in a small frightened voice.

"No, sweetie. They just want to make sure you're all right."

The team psychologist was a pro. Tall, calm, his dark hair liberally sprinkled with gray, he gave Alex a card that identified him as Dr. James Silverthorne and introduced himself to Maria as Dr. Jim.

Responding to the doc's request, Chelsea scooped up Sox and disappeared into the kitchen with her. Alex moved a few feet away to provide a status update to the law enforcement officials remaining at the house. Silverthorne settled in one of the living room armchairs while Maria perched nervously on the edge of the sofa. His relaxed manner soon had her explaining how Sox had slipped out and scampered up a tree before either she or Chelsea could stop her. Although she sounded a little hesitant about her dad now, Maria still obviously considered him a hero for rescuing her pet, then buying them both ice cream and taking them to the park. The psychologist didn't disabuse her. And he couched his questions about whether her dad touched her so gently and skillfully that Maria remained completely open and unselfconscious with her answers.

After their chat, he drew Alex aside to say he didn't note any obvious signs of trauma but would need a longer session in a more controlled environment before finalizing his report. He would also, he informed her, interview the father and include that assessment in the final team report.

"When you bring Maria in, I'll be happy to discuss with you how best to apprise her of her dad's hidden motives."

"Thank you."

A stir at the front door interrupted their quiet exchange. Hopping off the sofa, Maria rushed to greet Ben.

"Didya see the police cars?"

"I did."

He scooped her up, cradling her loosely in the crook

of his right arm while he maneuvered his cane with the left—the knuckles of which, Alex noted, were bruised and split.

"They were looking for me," Maria explained, alternating between guilt and a revived excitement. "But I wasn't lost. I wasn't. Really."

"Yeah, I know." He dropped a kiss on the top of her head. "Alex and I were pretty worried, though."

"Chelsea, too. She yelled at me."

The girl's lower lip inched out. Not all the way, since she knew she'd crossed a line, but enough to earn a grin from Ben.

"Guess you better come up with a way to get back on her good side," he advised.

"Like what?"

"I don't know. Help make her a special dinner, maybe? Or put her picture in one of those pretty flower frames on your iPad, like I showed you, and send it to her iPhone."

Maria's face brightened. "I can do that! But I'll put her in a fish frame, since she's gonna be a mermaid in an underwater show."

Wiggling free, she scampered down the hall to her bedroom. Ben watched her disappear, then turned to Alex and the man beside her.

"This is Dr. James Silverthorne," she explained. "He's the team psychologist."

"She okay?" he asked the doc softly.

"She appears to be. I want to talk to her again in a few days, privately. What's the status on her father?"

"He's in custody." A small, tight smile played at the corners of Ben's lips. "The detective in charge is going to swing by the ER before they head downtown for booking. Seems the bastard tripped and hit his jaw. He might've cracked a few teeth."

Silverthorne's gaze dropped to the bruised knuckles, lifted again. "Right."

"I hope you knocked every single tooth in his head loose," Alex said fiercely.

"Not *every* one. He'll be spitting out chunks of enamel for a while, though."

"Good!"

With a nod to Ben, the doc shook hands with Alex. "You have my card, Ms. Scott. Call me if Maria exhibits symptoms of delayed trauma. Fear, anxiety, nightmares, sleepwalking, bed-wetting. Otherwise, I'll have my people call you to arrange a follow-up."

He was on his way out the front door, but pulled up short to avoid colliding with the dust-covered stranger just stepping onto the stoop. Frowning, the doc eyed the man's unshaved cheeks and reddened eyes.

"Can I help you?"

"I'm looking for Major Kincaid. Is he...?"

"I got this, Doc." His boot loud on the tiles, Ben stumped forward without the aid of his cane and pumped the newcomer's hand. "Thanks for coming, Dingo. You didn't need to, though. The situation's been resolved."

"The kid okay?"

"She's fine."

"Thank God!"

The doc departed and the two men came inside.

"I left a message on your phone," Ben said.

"Damned thing ran out of juice right after we lifted off. Couldn't check my messages until... Yowza!"

He broke off, his glance riveted on something just over Ben's shoulder.

"I met your missus at the Badger Bash," he muttered. "Please tell me that glorious creature with her is an unattached and eminently available sister."

"An unattached and possibly available best friend," Ben corrected before he turned to offer introductions to the two women who'd gathered at the end of the hall. "Alex, you remember Dingo, don't you?"

"I do."

To the ex-cop's startled surprise, she rushed down the hall and threw her arms around his shoulders. The tears she'd held in rigid check for the past hours thickened her voice.

"Thank you!"

"You're welcome, but I came too late to the show to be of much help."

"You told us what to expect," she said, gulping. "That helped. More than you know."

"Okay, well. You're welcome," he said again, flashing Ben an SOS.

Grinning, Ben detached his wife and made the second intro. "This is Alex's former roommate, our recent maid of honor and a soon-to-be headliner in Vegas."

"Not a headliner," the dancer protested with a provocative twitch of her full lips. "Yet."

Her ink-black mane was still tangled and she hadn't swiped the mascara streaks from her eyes. But the roll was back in her hips and a smile teased her lips as she sauntered forward.

"First Pink, now Dingo. You and your friends have some interesting handles, Cowboy."

Dingo's arrival helped erase some of the gut-twisting tension of the afternoon. Not all of it. But enough for the adults and Maria to sit down with a semblance of calm to a hurriedly thrown-together dinner of salad and pizza a few hours later.

Alex picked at her meal, trying not to think about whether Judge Hendricks would hold her at least partially responsible for an incident that could've resulted in disastrous consequences. She made a mental note to call her attorney's hotline after dinner to ask for an appointment as soon as possible.

Maria's surprisingly artistic underwater photo montage featuring a silver-scaled mermaid with flowing black hair and laughing eyes had restored much of Chelsea's usual ebullience. Dingo's unconcealed admiration helped, too.

Ben sounded the most normal by entertaining the group with explanations for the treasures they'd brought home from Santa Fe. "We didn't have time to buy you anything," he apologized to Maria, "but we scored some great stuff."

"Right," Dingo drawled.

He'd already been presented with the buffalo robe but both he and Ben had resisted all questions relating to the reason for the bulky, smelly gift. Maria was more interested in the kachina now occupying a place of honor on the living room mantel.

"The artist who carved it said the Eagle Dancer is the king of the skies," Ben informed her. "They're sort of spirit beings who connect humans to the other world."

"I know. We learned about kachinas in our New Mexico history class. There are a bunch of them. Like the corn grower and the bear hunter and a black-and-white-striped clown guy."

"A clown guy?"

"I can show him to you on my iPad."

"Deal. Right after we finish dinner and the troops pull KP."

Maria giggled at the acronym Ben had explained stood for "kitchen patrol."

After the frightening afternoon, the happy, girlish laugh acted like a balm on Alex's lacerated nerves. Still, she was quiet through the rest of dinner and voiced no objection when Ben sent her and Chelsea out to the patio with their coffee while he, Dingo and Maria performed KP.

Alex made a call to Paul Montoya first. After leaving a brief message for the attorney, she requested an appointment as soon as possible. Then she and Chelsea settled at the patio's wrought iron bistro table with its colorful inlaid tiles. The evening air still shimmered with the heat of the day, but the slanting beams of the pergola drenched them in jasmine-scented shade.

Chelsea wrapped both hands around her coffee mug. The first words out of her mouth were another apology for her part in the afternoon's drama.

"I'm so, *so* sorry, Lex. It's all just beginning to sink in, but I swear, I was only in the house for five minutes."

"It's okay, Chels."

"No, it's not. The police report will say that Maria was outside, unsupervised, when her asshat father snatched her." She shuffled the mug around in circles. "How do you think that will play with the judge?"

"I don't know."

The question tapped into Alex's deep-seated worry. She let her gaze drift to the patio doors and the lit kitchen beyond. Ben had his hip propped against the counter, supervising while Dingo carted dishes to the sink and

Maria loaded the dishwasher. Chelsea followed the direction of her gaze.

"All that raw masculinity," she murmured appreciatively.

"Mmm."

"You wouldn't think either one would be that patient with a seven-year-old."

"No, you wouldn't."

The too quiet reply brought her friend's head around. "Doesn't that make you happy? That Ben's so good with her?"

"I guess."

"You guess?"

Alex didn't answer for a moment, her eyes on the three in the kitchen. The men seemed to shrink the compact space with its sunshine-yellow walls and colorful tile backsplash. Dingo reminded her of a lean, predatory wolf, but to her mind Ben oozed more of the raw maleness Chelsea had mentioned. He still wore the jeans and collared black polo shirt he'd pulled on after their lazy lovemaking early this afternoon. The knit shirt stretched tight across his shoulders, and the dark color made the tan on his neck and arms appear even deeper. By contrast, the bandage on his skinned knuckles stood out white and stark.

"Alex?"

"Huh?"

"What do you mean, 'you guess'?"

She chewed on her lower lip for a moment. "Do remember the movie *Jerry Maguire*?"

"The sports flick with Tom Cruise and Renée Zellweger? Of course I do. We must've watched it a half-dozen times."

"Then you remember how Zellweger's character described her marriage. That she'd hooked up with a great guy who loved her kid and really liked her."

"Are you serious?" Chelsea threw an incredulous look across the bistro table. "You really believe that hunk of beefcake in the kitchen cares more about Maria than he does you?"

"Oh, he *cares* about me. And that's the problem. He deserves more than 'care' in a marriage. So do I."

"Whoa!" Her friend flung up a palm. "Let's back up about twenty paces. You proposed to Major Sweet Cheeks, right?"

"You know I did, but…"

"And as I recall," she interrupted ruthlessly, "you told him flat out that sex was not part of the deal."

"Yes, but—"

"Now you're bumping like bunnies every chance you get, correct?"

"We are," Alex returned, a little peeved at her friend's hectoring. "But you of all people know sex isn't the answer to everything."

"We're talking about you, Miss Priss. Not me. And I don't believe for a moment that Ben's going to buy that 'he deserves more' line. Hell, he's a guy. He probably thinks he hit a royal flush when a hot wife and a ready-made family dropped into his lap with zero effort on his part."

"Maybe. But—"

"Would you stop with the buts!" Anger flared in Chelsea's cheeks. "Christ, Alex, the guy's nuts about you. If you'd open your damned eyes, you'd see it."

"Hey!"

"What's more, you're nuts about him. Problem is,

you're so wrapped up in worry about Maria that you can't see what's right in front of your nose. Or won't *let* yourself see," she added with a sudden, shrewd guess.

Head cocked, she studied a now silent Alex.

"That's it, isn't it? You're in love with the guy, but you're so worried about the adoption and feel so damned guilty for fast-talking Ben into marriage that you won't admit it. Just like you won't admit, even to yourself, that he might be in love with you."

"*Might* being the operative word!"

"Oh, for…! Talk to the man, Alex. Tell him how you feel."

"I was going to! Up in Santa Fe. Then you called and…oh, hell. I can't sort it out with him now. After this afternoon, none of us need any more drama."

"True enough." Her brief spurt of annoyance spent, Chelsea sighed and pushed back her chair. "What I need is a stiff drink and a long soak. Oh, and I moved my things into Maria's room. I'll bunk in with her tonight."

"You'll never fit in that girl-size bed."

"I'm a dancer," she reminded Alex with a lofty flick of one hand. "I routinely contort my body in ways that would cripple most folks. Some of which," she murmured as her glance zinged to the brightly lit kitchen, "I might be convinced to demonstrate to Ben's pal."

"Chelsea!"

"Okay, okay." She gave the two men a final, regretful look. "But El Paso's not that far from Vegas, is it?"

When they went back into the kitchen, Dingo was on the phone with a contact at APD. He waited until Maria was out of the room to report that her father was being held without bail pending his arraignment on charges of kidnapping, child endangerment and parole violation.

"They'll keep him until he pleads or goes to trial. Either way, odds are your boy will be heading back to Los Lunas in the very near future."

"Good!" Alex said fiercely.

Dingo checked his watch and grimaced. "Hate to bail on you but it sounds like everything's under control and I need to get back to the deal I was negotiating. I'm in Vegas fairly often," he added casually, his glance shifting to Chelsea. "Maybe we could have dinner sometime."

"Maybe we could," she replied, just as casually.

He got her phone number, then had Ben and Alex walk him to the front door. The rebundled buffalo robe sat waiting beside the hall tree, emanating its distinctly musty scent. Dingo hefted it in one hand and thrust out the other.

"I guess we're even now."

"Guess we are," Ben said, gripping his hand.

"One of you guys *has* to share the story behind this," Alex commented.

"Pry it out of your husband," Dingo replied with a quick, slashing grin. "You'll probably have to get him drunk first, though."

"Sounds like some secrets are just not meant to be shared."

"This is one of them. Text me a copy of the police report," he instructed. "I'll look it over and let you know if I find any holes."

"I will." Maneuvering around the bulky bundle, she planted a kiss on his whiskery cheek. "Thank you. Again."

"You're welcome. Again."

They were just closing the door behind him when Alex's phone buzzed. It was Paul Montoya's assistant calling to tell her the attorney could see her at nine Monday morning.

Totally wiped by the day's emotional roller coaster, Alex showered while Chelsea watched TV and Ben and Maria checked out kachinas on the iPad. Wrapped in an oversize bath towel, Alex was stretched out on the bed and almost comatose when Ben came to check on her.

She heard him come in, felt the mattress dip when he joined her and curled instinctively into his arms. For now, for this moment, her little world was safe and secure and whole. She didn't want to think about how long it would stay that way.

The next afternoon Alex, Ben and Chelsea dropped Maria off at her friend Dinah's house to play while they met with members of the Child Abduction team to review the initial report and sign their statements. Dinah's mom swore fiercely she wouldn't let either girl out of her sight.

The FBI occupied a multistory, sandstone-colored building on Leucking Park Avenue, just off I-25. Although the Sunday afternoon was warm and sunny, the air inside the glass-fronted building was chilly and filled with a quiet hum of energy and activity.

One of the team members met them at the entrance. Alex went blank on the agent's name until she reintroduced herself, signed them in and escorted them through security. When Alex expressed surprise that the initial report was ready so quickly, the agent nodded.

"Unfortunately, we handle more child abduction cases

than we'd like to. We've got the paperwork part down pat, especially when the cases are resolved as quickly—and as satisfactorily—as this one."

"Can we get copies of the report?" Alex asked.

"Shouldn't be a problem. By the way, Dr. Jim left a message for you. He can see you and Maria Tuesday afternoon at three, if that's convenient."

Halfway through their meeting with the team, Ben got a call from his squadron. When they exited the FBI building, he apologized for bailing on them.

"One of the simulators just went down. I need to go in and see what the problem is. Then we'll have to hink the schedule and lay on extra sessions to fill the gap. I'll run you two home, then change into my uniform and get to the base. Sure you can't stay a few more days?" he asked Chelsea as she slid into the Tahoe's rear seat.

"I wish I could but I've got my first aquatic session tomorrow." Her irrepressible smile kicked in. "Is there a water kachina?"

"You bet."

"You might want to say a little prayer to him or her tonight."

"Consider it done."

After they picked up Maria and returned to the casita, Ben made a quick change into his flight suit, dropped a kiss on Alex's lips and headed for the door again.

Alex and Maria drove Chelsea to the airport four hours later. When they pulled up at the curb, she reached behind into the back seat to give Maria a hug.

"Take care of Sox, brat. And don't let her climb any more trees!"

Unfolding her long legs, she emerged from the car

with the grace that seemed to be embedded in her DNA and met Alex at the open trunk.

"Come to Vegas after the adoption hearing," she urged. "You can hoot and holler and stamp your feet when you see me in Cirque du Soleil. Then we'll celebrate. You, Maria, Major Sweet Ass, me."

"And a certain ex-cop?"

"Why not?"

As grateful for Chelsea's unquestioning friendship as she was for her effusive personality, Alex wrapped her in a ferocious hug. "We might just do that."

"You'd better! It's anyone's bet how long I'll last in the show before my lungs explode."

Both women were sniffling now, ignoring the cars that had backed up three deep behind them. When an impatient driver honked, Chelsea untangled.

"Go home," she instructed. "Put Maria to bed and take a long soak. Then slather yourself with that outrageously expensive body lotion I sent for your last birthday. When your man comes home, be waiting for him wearing a smile, that luscious scent and your red lace thong."

She rolled her weekender toward the entrance, paused and shouted over her shoulder.

"Then talk to him, Lex! Tell him you *both* hit the jackpot."

Chapter Thirteen

Taking Chelsea's advice to heart, Alex put Maria to bed, showered, slithered into the lacy thong with its matching bra, and coated her arms and legs with the sinfully thick, gardenia-scented body lotion. Then she waited. And waited. And finally got a call from Ben.

"Looks like I'll be a while yet," he advised. "Once we get the second sim back online, we'll have to reprogram the tracks and rework the schedule. This might turn into an all-nighter."

Swallowing a sigh, Alex smoothed a palm down her just shaved and slathered thigh. "Okay."

"What time is the meeting with the lawyer tomorrow?" Ben asked.

"Nine a.m."

"Paul Montoya, right?"

"Right."

"I'll be there."

"You don't need to come. I can take him the copy of the initial report and brief him on what happened."

"I'll be there."

Ben's prediction of an all-nighter proved correct. He still hadn't come home by the time Alex walked Maria to school. When the girl scampered off with her friends, Alex asked for a meeting with her teacher and the school's vice principal and brought them up to speed on Saturday's incident.

"The FBI has classified it as a parental kidnapping. At this point, though, Maria doesn't know her father demanded a ransom for her return. She thinks they were just on an outing to the park."

"You're going to tell her the truth, aren't you?" the teacher asked with a frown.

"We've got a follow-up appointment with the FBI psychologist tomorrow afternoon. He's going to help us explain it in a way that won't traumatize her."

"Is the father in custody?" the vice principal wanted to know.

"As of yesterday evening, he was being held without bail pending arraignment. I'm on my way to see my lawyer now. Hopefully, he'll give me an outline of what happens next."

"Please keep us posted."

"Of course."

Back at the casita, she backed her car out of the garage and battled rush hour traffic north to Menaul Boulevard. Mere moments before nine, she pulled in to the parking lot of the complex that housed the offices of

Montoya and Associates. The complex was a warren of single-story, Territorial-style buildings in chocolate-brown adobe and gleaming white trim. The receptionist welcomed her with a smile and an offer of coffee. Alex snatched at it gratefully.

"Yes, please. Cream, no sugar. But first, could you make copies of some reports for me?"

"Sure, no problem."

When Alex fished the initial police report and interim FBI report out of her purse, the woman fed the pages into a printer/copier/scanner and whirred them right out.

"I'll bring your coffee. Just go on back. Mr. Montoya's waiting for you."

As befitting the senior partner, Montoya occupied the suite of offices at the end of a long corridor paneled in pale oak accented with framed prints by Native American artists. Alex had walked this hallway often enough that the barefoot women in the R. C. Gorman prints and mounted horsemen by Amado Peña felt like old friends.

The thought humbled her, and made her so grateful for the people who'd gone out of their way to help her since she'd moved to Albuquerque. The oncologist and nurses who treated her sister. The hospice workers who eased her pain those last, agonizing days. The counselors who helped both Alex and Maria adjust to their new relationship. The officer at the bank who walked her through the bewildering process to obtain a woman-owned, small business start-up loan.

And the man who now stepped out from behind his desk to greet her. Short and stocky, with a mane of blue-black hair and caterpillar-thick eyebrows to match, Paul Montoya was one of the most respected family law attorneys in the city. Alex could never have afforded him if he hadn't expressed such genuine sympathy for the losses Maria had suffered in her young life and agreed to handle the adoption petition at what Alex knew was a bargain-basement fee.

He met her with a firm handshake and a lift of one of those expressive eyebrows. "What's going on? The message you left requesting a meeting sounded urgent."

"We had a pretty scary weekend."

Frowning, he waved her to one of the chairs encircling a round marble-topped corner table. "How so?"

"Maria's dad was released early and tried to kidnap her."

"Sunnuva…!" Brows bristling, Montoya bit off the expletive. "He wasn't supposed to meet the parole board until next month. And the prison was instructed to notify us if and when he walked out the gate."

"Well, he did and they didn't."

She gave him a succinct recap and passed him the copies of the police and FBI reports. He was skimming through the pages when the receptionist came in with her coffee.

"Major Kincaid just arrived," she told them. "He said he's part of this meeting. Shall I bring him back?"

Montoya looked to Alex, who nodded. "Yes, please!"

Ben obviously had come straight from the base. He was still in his flight suit and overnight bristles shadowed his cheeks and chin. But he wasn't leaning as heavily on his cane and his grip was sure and strong as it met Montoya's.

"Sorry I'm late. Good to meet you, Mr. Montoya. Alex has told me a lot about you."

"More than she told me about you," the lawyer said drily. "But the pleasure's mine. And, please, call me Paul."

He waved Ben to a seat and resumed his own. When they were settled, he got right down to business.

"Alex has filled me in on the basics. I'll have my people get a copy of these interim reports to Judge Hendricks's clerk right away. I'll also have them check Musgrove's status and text you an update. But we're not going to wait for the disposition of the charges against that bum. I'll call the judge personally and press him to proceed with the adoption hearing ASAP."

"Do you think he'll do it?" Alex asked, almost afraid to hope.

"He will, or I'll file a motion for him to recuse himself and ask the court to appoint a new judge."

"On what grounds?" Ben wanted to know.

"One, he's dragged his feet too long on this case. Two, we have him on record voicing his prejudice against single working moms."

"Except Alex isn't a single working mom," Ben pointed out. "Not anymore."

"Exactly."

Ben leaned forward, his gazed leveled on the attorney. "Before you make that call, you need to amend the adoption petition."

"How?"

"I want my name on it. Alex's and mine, both."

His brows working, Montoya looked to Alex but she was too startled for an instant reply. She stared at Ben for several seconds, her expression moving swiftly from surprise to dismay.

"Ben," she said hesitantly, "we need to talk about this."

"What's to talk about?" His tilted his head, a frown forming. "We're a family, aren't we?"

Alex threw a quick look at her lawyer. No dummy, he took the hint and pushed away from the table.

"I need to make some calls. You folks wait here. Major, would you like some coffee?"

"No, thanks," he said, his eyes still on his wife. "I'm good. Or thought I was," he added as the door closed behind Montoya.

The silence that gripped the room was swift and smothering. Alex forced herself to meet his now narrowed eyes. It took just about everything she had.

"I don't... I don't think we should add your name to the adoption petition."

"Is that right?"

The ice in the tight-lipped reply sliced into her like a serrated blade. Nausea rolled in her stomach.

"Care to tell me why?" he asked softly, too softly.

"Why don't we wait and discuss this at home?"

"Why don't we not."

She could see he wasn't going anywhere until he got some answers. But providing them was so much harder than she'd anticipated it would be. Floundering, she latched on to the same feeble explanation she'd offered Chelsea.

"Did you ever see the movie *Jerry Maguire*?"

"What?"

"The movie with Tom Cruise and Renée Zellweger? About the sports agent who goes all self-righteous and loses his clients?"

His frown slashed deeper. "No, and what the hell does a self-righteous sports agent have to do with us?"

"It's just...never mind. It doesn't make sense if you haven't seen the movie."

"*What* doesn't, dammit?"

"Our marriage."

That rocked him back. Knowing she was making a mess of it, Alex had no choice but to plunge ahead. "These past weeks with you have made me realize you deserve more than a marriage of convenience. So do I."

"I thought we were past the 'convenient' stage."

"We are but... Oh, God! This is coming out all wrong!"

"You think?"

She squeezed her eyes shut, opened them and bared her heart. "Okay, here's the deal. I told you I didn't want hearts and flowers but it turns out I do. I want the romance. The mush. The silly kind of stupid that lasts a lifetime. And...and I want you to have that, too."

He went still. Absolutely still. Then he shoved out of his seat with a violence that sent his chair crashing against the wall. His face twisted in disgust, he planted both hands of the arms of Alex's chair and pinned her in place. She cringed back, alarmed by the fierceness in his face but not afraid. Nothing, she realized in that explosive half second, could ever make her afraid of Ben.

"Let me see if I've got this right," he ground out. "You're saying you want some Prince Charming to come prancing along, kiss you awake every morning and roll you in rose petals?"

"No! That's not even close to—"

"Good," he snarled, cutting her off. "Because you're stuck with me, sweetheart. And I'm not letting you go. Not without one helluva fight, anyway."

Alex's jaw sagged. "But—"

"But nothing."

He leaned closer, blocking her view of anything but

his bristly cheeks and hard eyes. He was still furious, still disgusted, still breathing fire in her face.

"You're right about one thing, though. We need to finish this discussion at home. I'll meet you there."

Her mouth still hanging open, Alex watched him grab his cane, wrap his fist around the handle and stomp out of the office.

With every angry step down the hall, Ben felt his temper boil higher and hotter. Dammit all to hell! Where did Alex get off trying to cut him out of Maria's life? Out of *her* life!

She'd set the ground rules. Right from the start. First, all she wanted was his name on a license. No cohabitation. No sex. No plans to claim her rights as a military spouse.

Then, after Ben crunched his foot, she mandated separate beds and only limited exposure to Maria. All it took was one steamy session in the shower and a few days with the kid for both of those idiotic notions to go up in flames.

Now, after nearly a month sharing a bed and home and a life, she wanted to rewrite the script yet again. Well, too damned bad. He wasn't...

"Major Kincaid?"

Feeling as though he had smoke coming from both ears, Ben pulled up short and glared at the attorney. "Yeah?"

"Is everything all right?"

"Just dandy. *Amend* the adoption petition."

"Ms. Scott is my client. I have to accede to her wishes."

"Ms. *Kincaid*." He jerked his chin toward the office behind him. "That's Ms. Kincaid in there."

"Yes, well…"

"Amend the petition."

It took most of the drive home for Ben to rein in his temper. Even then, anger still simmered just under the surface, most of it stemming from the fact that Alex had completely blindsided him. He'd known something was bothering her. She'd wanted to talk about it in Santa Fe. Then the call from Chelsea pushed everything else off the table.

Even now the gut-twisting fear that call had generated could still spook him. Saturday it had damned near blinded him to anything and everything except getting Maria back safe. He hadn't pulled in a whole breath during that wild ride from Santa Fe back to Albuquerque. How could Alex *not* know he'd take a bullet for her and Maria?

The question honestly baffled him. So much that he stabbed a connect button and issued a curt voice command to the Tahoe's built-in communications center to contact Chelsea via FaceTime. He caught the dancer in full mermaid costume, complete with iridescent scales, inch-long spangled eyelashes and gold glitter dusted across the swell of her generous breasts.

"Talk fast, Kincaid. I go in the tank in ten minutes."

When he gave a quick recap of his frustrating session at the lawyer's office, she snorted. "And you can't figure it out?"

"Figure *what* out?"

"I'll let Alex enlighten you. But before she does, I suggest you channel your inner Tom Cruise."

"Like I know how the hell to…? Chelsea? Hello? Dammit!"

His lip curling, he cut the connection. Tom Cruise? Christ! Desperate now, he instructed the system to pull up another number. It rang six times before Swish's sleep-drugged voice answered.

"For God's sake, Cowboy. It's the middle of the night."

"Where are you?"

Stupid question.

"Never mind. I don't need to know. Just answer me one thing."

"Shoot," she muttered, her voice still thick and raspy.

"Did you ever see the movie *Jerry Maguire*?"

"Are you drunk?"

"It's ten a.m. here."

"Yeah, so?"

"No, I am not drunk. Answer the question."

"About *Jerry Maguire*? Yeah, I saw it. Five, maybe twenty, times."

"Jesus! What's the deal with that movie?"

"The deal," she said on a jaw-cracking yawn, "is that Tom had to take a two-by-four up alongside his thick skull before he realized he was in love with his wife." She paused, letting her silence roll like thunder through the Tahoe. "Well?"

"Well, what?"

"Oh, for…!" The comm officer let loose with a string of colorful expletives. "Have you told *your* wife you're ass over heels in love with her?"

"Yes!" The scene in the lawyer's office pinwheeled through his mind. "Okay, maybe not in so many words."

"You strong, silent types kill me. Later, dude."

She hung up, leaving Ben frustrated and debating between sitting Alex down for a serious talk and pinning her against the wall the moment she walked through the front door. He was still debating the two options when he pulled up at a stoplight and caught sight of a colorful shop window from the corner of one eye.

Hooking his wrists over the steering wheel, he stared at the busy display until an impatient honk from the car behind jerked his foot off the brake. Swearing, he hit the gas and cut a sharp right turn. Moments later, he strode into the shop and slapped his credit card down on the counter.

Alex couldn't quite meet Paul Montoya's eye when he'd relayed Ben's order to amend the adoption petition to include Mr. *and* Ms. Kincaid. Hands folded, he'd then waited for her instruction.

She'd squirmed in her seat. Opened her mouth. Closed it. Ben's fierce assertion that he wouldn't let her go still hammered on her heart. For several moments she'd swung wildly between uncertainty and an irrational, irrepressible hope. Finally, she'd promised to get back to the attorney on that. He acquiesced with only a small lift of those bushy brows and spent the rest of their hour together strategizing how best to present the latest developments to the judge. Alex's main concern was making sure whatever happened in court wouldn't traumatize Maria.

"That has to be our main concern," Montoya agreed. "I'll wait until after her appointment with this Dr. Jim tomorrow before scheduling a face-to-face with the judge."

"I'm scared to death he'll hold me responsible for what happened."

"Not a chance. Hendricks may be a misogynistic old coot but he hasn't completely lost touch with reality. Yet. I'll make sure he gets the full picture."

* * *

Relieved, Alex walked out into the bright, sunlit morning and beeped the locks on her car. She had to wait beside the driver's side door for several minutes before the trapped heat dissipated. While she did, her thoughts kept circling back to Ben.

He'd been so angry when he'd left. So disgusted with her. No surprise, considering how badly she'd mangled her explanation. She'd do better when she got home, she swore as she slid behind the wheel.

The Tahoe was parked in the driveway when she turned onto the street leading to the casita, and a white panel van was just pulling away from the curb. Alex was too far off to catch the lettering on the rear of the van but the mere sight of it generated a dozen wild possibilities, none of them good.

Was that a forensics team from the FBI? From the Albuquerque Police Department? Had they been to the house to dust for fingerprints or confiscate the electronic equipment Maria used? Or…

Oh, God! Was it some kind of an emergency response team? She squinted at the now disappearing van but didn't see a red cross or a caduceus or any symbol indicating a medical emergency. Still, her pulse skittered as she pulled up beside the Tahoe and jumped out of the car. Rushing up the walk, she fumbled her key into the lock. She yanked open the door, took one step inside… and got smacked in the face.

Startled, she jumped back and batted at the object that whopped her. It was a balloon, she discovered in surprise. A heart-shaped Mylar balloon.

One of what looked like a dozen or more heart-shaped balloons, she saw with a swift intake of breath.

Bobbing alongside others in round and triangular and square shapes. All floating at varying heights and tethered by colorful ribbons anchored at the bottom with little weights. They filled the entryway. Spilled into the living room. Sprouted from the hooks on her hand-painted hall tree.

"What in the world…?"

Feeling as though she'd just tumbled down the rabbit hole, she grabbed the ribbons of the closest balloons and tugged them inside so she could close the door. Still dazed, she skimmed the legends on the objects floating all around her.

Love!

You're in my Heart!

Happy Anniversary!

Be My Valentine!

Only after she'd waded through the first battery of balloons did she see the flowers. They crowded every horizontal surface in the living room. Vases of roses in red and pink and yellow. Pots of daisies. Tall, regal irises in a blue so deep it was almost purple. Baskets of mums and little feathery African violets. Sunflowers on their tall stalks, their smiling faces bending her way.

Gulping, Alex spun in a slow circle while the significance of this magnificent, overwhelming, ridiculous display sank in. Hearts and flowers. She'd told him she wanted the hearts and flowers.

"Well?"

The deep-throated question spun her back around. Ben leaned against the archway leading to the kitchen, arms crossed. He'd changed out of his flight suit into jeans and a black stretchy T-shirt. Judging by his whiskerless cheeks and the damp glisten in his black hair he'd showered and shaved, too.

"I bought out two flower shops. Hope to hell that's enough to get the message across."

Alex summoned a wobbly smile. "I got it. I think."

"You think?" He pushed away from the wall and batted his way through the forest of balloons. "Not sure how I can make it any clearer. Except maybe to do this…"

He slid an arm around her waist.

"And this."

When he drew her against him, her heart hammered so hard and fast she thought it would jump out of her chest.

"And this," he muttered, bending to cover her lips with his.

The kiss was hard and demanding and so possessive that Alex's lids fluttered up in surprise. The look in his eyes was dead serious.

"I haven't said the words, Alex. Like an idiot, I didn't even realize I needed to. I guess we just slid into this crazy marriage so easily that I took it—took *us*—for granted. But here they are. Straight from the heart. I love you and I love Maria. You're what I didn't know I needed. You're my family. And I won't let either of you go…unless that's really what you want."

"Oh, Ben!" She was surrounded by bobbing balloons and drowning in the flowers' overpowering perfume but every sense, every thought was focused on her husband. "I think I can speak for Maria and for me. We love you, too, and we don't want you to ever, *ever* let us go."

Chapter Fourteen

After the hectic events of the previous weeks, Alex almost forgot about the picnic hosted by Ben's unit in conjunction with Kirtland Air Force Base's Memorial Day Open House. He reminded her of it when he stopped by her shop after a doctor's appointment early Friday afternoon.

"Well, look at you!" Delighted, she admired the smaller, lighter boot that Ben could maneuver without a cane.

"Better watch out," he warned. "I'm mobile enough now to chase you around the bed."

"I'll keep that in mind."

He glanced around the shop and gave a wave to Terri and Caroline. "Where's the rest of your crew?"

"I sent them home to get a head start on the long weekend."

"Speaking of which… I don't have any official duties tomorrow, so I volunteered us for grill duty. Hope that's okay."

"What grill?"

"At the squadron. You remember… Open house. Balloon hats. Hot dogs."

"Oh. Right."

She couldn't believe she'd almost forgotten. "Good thing I transferred the design for the T-shirts you suggested I make for Maria and me to my computer. I'd better get to work on them."

"I'll get out of your way, then. Want me to pick Maria up from school?"

"Yes, please."

She chose red scooped-neck tees, then stamped the left shoulder of each with the 58th Special Operations Wing's patch. The patch's black background showed nicely against the red, especially after Alex accented its gold border with shimmering crystals. She highlighted Diana's chariot and antlered steeds with amber crystals but relied on Caroline's delicate touch to add drama to the goddess herself.

"Tough-lookin' gal," the young Goth commented as she wielded glue and tweezers with a true artist's skill. Chewing on the unpierced corner of her lip, she detailed the bow and arrows with tiny silver crystals, then added iridescent color to the folds of her short tunic.

"There." Straightening on her stool, she held up the finished product. "Whaddya think?"

Alex studied the patch with a critical eye. As with her unicorn design, she'd opted for a minimalist approach. The effect was glittery and eye-catching but not, in her professional opinion, gaudy or so heavily ornamented it overwhelmed the key design elements.

"Perfect," she pronounced.

Ben and Maria thought so, too, when Alex showed them the tops later that evening. Maria had to try hers on immediately, so Alex modeled hers, as well.

"Better take an order book with you to the open house tomorrow," Ben advised. "You two will be the star attraction."

The next day dawned bright and sunny with the kind of achingly beautiful blue sky that only New Mexico could produce. Alex and Maria paired their T-shirts with jeans, sneakers and red ball caps. Ben wore jeans, too, and a T-shirt with an unsparkly version of the 58th's insignia.

After plastering themselves with sunscreen and stuffing a tote with bottles of water and a woven straw mat to sit on during the air show, they piled into the Tahoe and joined the river of vehicles streaming through Kirtland's West Gate.

Security personnel and volunteers in orange vests directed them to a parking area cordoned off on a stretch of tarmac. Booths and displays occupied another prime stretch between two immense hangars. Knowing Kirtland shared its runways with the adjacent civilian airport, Alex was curious how commercial airlines could shut down operation for the open house.

"This was all coordinated more than a year ago with the Albuquerque Airport Authority," Ben explained as he angled the SUV into position. "No flights are scheduled to arrive or depart during a preapproved window, and the airspace above the base is restricted to an aerial performance by the USAF Thunderbirds and tactical displays by our Special Ops aircraft."

"Will you show me your airplane?" Maria asked when he helped her hop down from the Tahoe's rear seat.

"You bet. Here, Alex, let me carry the tote."

"I've got it."

She kept a grip on the bag. Although he seemed to move easily in the smaller, lighter boot, she wasn't taking any chances. He didn't argue, just took Maria's hand instead. Little flutters of sheer joy feathered through Alex as she watched the seven-year-old skip excitedly alongside the man who wanted to become her adoptive father.

Please, God, she prayed silently. *Please, let it happen!*

The closer they got to the center of the action, tantalizing scents from the various booths curled out to entice them. Sizzling hamburgers, garlicky pizza, spicy Indian tacos combined with supersweet cotton candy and fried ice cream to give the area a festive, almost circus feel.

The displays were strictly military, however, yet still geared to families. Various squadrons from Kirtland's host unit, the 377th Air Base Wing, had set up both static and active demonstrations. Kids clambered aboard fire trucks and posed for pictures in protective helmets. The hospital unit gave CPR demos. Security personnel from the K-9 unit put on a working dog demonstration that drew a huge crowd.

"Wouldn't want to be that guy," Alex murmured as a snarling German shepherd leaped across a seemingly impossible stretch of open air to take down his heavily padded target.

The Air Force Weapons Lab, a major tenant on the base, put on a laser light show that delighted kids and gave adults a hint of the next generation of space technology. And personnel from Ben's wing had turned out en masse to man static displays of the aircraft assigned to their unit. Nub-nosed C-130s were parked alongside tilt-wing Ospreys and several varieties of helicopters.

Maria had no trouble identifying Ben's aircraft. "That's your plane!"

"Sure is. Want to see inside?"

"Yes!"

Maria's eyes rounded as they walked up the rear ramp into the plane's cavernous belly. A curly-haired sergeant wearing a flight suit with subdued stripes and a name patch that identified him as Staff Sergeant Girolandi was acting as interpreter and tour guide for the visitors. He smiled when he saw the newcomers and came over to join them.

"Hey, Major Kincaid. Glad to see you dumped the cane. This your family?"

"It is," Ben replied, shooting Alex a quick smile. "Maria, meet one of the best loadmasters in the business."

"What's a loadmaster?" she wanted to know.

Girolandi squatted down to her level. "We're responsible for everything that goes in the belly of this bird. People. Vehicles. Cargo pallets. We do preflight checks first to make sure the aircraft is good to go, then see that cargo is properly loaded and passengers are settled in. But our main job is to keep everything safe and secure during flight."

"Does every plane have a loadmaster?"

"Every one like this one."

Her brows pulled together. "Then how come Ben broke his foot?"

"Good question," Girolandi said with a grin. "Probably because he didn't have me working that flight." He pushed to his feet and eyed the sparkling patch on Alex's tank. "Cool shirts you gals are wearing. Mind if I ask where you bought them? I'd like to get one for my wife."

"I made them."

"No kidding?"

"Alex operates a business that designs and manufactures specialty T-shirts," Ben told him. "I'm trying to convince her to tap into the military market."

"Well, if you do any more shirts with that design, my Susan wears a medium."

"I'll do one up for her."

"Told you," Ben smirked to Alex as he maneuvered a careful path toward the cockpit. "You'll be swamped with orders by the time we leave."

She was.

She was also sunburned despite all the sunscreen she'd piled on and itchy eyed from the smoke of the giant grill where she and Ben took a turn cooking hamburgers and hot dogs with other couples from his squadron. Maria romped nearby with a gaggle of other youngsters in an inflatable castle, close enough for Alex to keep a careful watch on her.

The position also gave Alex an excellent view of pararescue personnel repelling from a helicopter and parachuting from both high and low altitudes. A slow-flying C-130 then demonstrated low-altitude cargo extraction almost right in front of them. That was followed by the USAF Thunderbirds' incredible aerial acrobatics.

As jaw-dropping as the display of military might was, the tight bond between members of the 58th Wing impressed Alex even more. They welcomed her and Maria with ready smiles and ragged Ben unmercifully for taking so long to dive into matrimonial waters. And almost everyone wanted to know where Alex bought her shirt.

Ben's boss, Lieutenant Colonel Rochambeaux, made a special point of coming by to introduce her husband. As tall and muscled as the colonel was petite and delicate, Pierre Rochambeaux offered Alex a hand the size of a ham.

"Amiée told me Ben done snagged himself *un belle fille* for a bride," he boomed with a Cajun accent even thicker than his wife's. "Now maybe he won't go around all mopey and *boudeur*."

"I, uh, hope not."

The colonel herself was more interested in Alex's shirt. "Love that! Are you going to make it available through the BX?"

"I'm thinking about it."

"Great. You'll have to let me know when it's in stock." With seeming nonchalance she edged Alex a little way away from the others and lowered her voice. "Ben told us about that business with your little girl's dad. Bastard's lucky he got off with only a few broken teeth. He also said you're worried how that incident might play at the adoption hearing. If you need any kind of a character reference—for him, for you—I can line up a couple hundred or so."

Alex felt her throat catch. "I don't think we'll need a couple hundred but I appreciate the offer."

"You're family now. We take care of our own."

The colonel's words echoed in Alex's head when Paul Montoya called three days later. She was at work, wading through the paperwork to get certified as a small business owner and product supplier to the Army and Air Force Exchange Service.

"Got some news," Montoya said when she answered.

Her heart tripped. "Good or bad?"

"Good. Mostly. Musgrove's public defender just called. His client's trying to cut a deal. Says he'll withdraw his objection to the adoption if we can convince the feds to go easy on the kidnapping and child endangerment charges."

"No way in hell!"

"That's what I told him. But I suggested we might be convinced not to press ahead with the contempt of court motion for his violation of the custodial agreement. It's a small sop, essentially meaningless considering the severity of the other charges, but damned if he didn't go for it. I need to make sure you agree before we proceed."

"How will that look to Judge Hendricks?" Alex worried. "Like we bargained with Eddie to give up his daughter?"

"We'll make it clear he offered her up, and we accepted for Maria's sake."

"So you think we should agree?"

"I do. If Musgrove withdraws the objection, I'll press for an immediate hearing. We won't have to wait for the kidnapping charges to be adjudicated and use those against him."

"Okay, I..."

She caught herself just in time. They were a family. Her, Ben, Maria. Decisions this important couldn't—shouldn't!—be made unilaterally.

"I'll get back to you. This afternoon at the latest," she promised. "I just need to run this by Ben and Maria."

"Understand. In the meantime, I'll have my people check to see if the judge has an opening on his schedule. With any luck, we might be able to wrap this up by the end of the week."

Ben's response when she caught him at work came swift and sure. "Tell Montoya to go for it."

Alex presented the matter to Maria an hour later. School was now out for the summer, so she'd enrolled the girl in a fun-filled day camp that included field trips, art projects and plenty of playtime. To Maria's delight— and as a thank-you to Dinah's mom for her friendship and staunch support—Ben had insisted on paying for Dinah to attend the same camp.

Alex rehearsed her approach as she waited in the activity center while one of the counselors fetched Maria. She had to present the matter in a way that didn't destroy the girl's rejuvenated spirits after learning the truth about her father.

Luckily, she'd picked up some excellent tips from Dr. Jim. In his follow-up session with Maria, the psychologist had deftly guided her to the understanding that her dad had violated a court order when he took her to the park without Chelsea's permission. He'd also very, very gently detailed the ransom demand and subsequent kidnapping charges, framing them more as a desperate attempt by her dad to get back on his feet after being released from prison rather than a cold-blooded offer to sell his only kid.

For Maria's sake, Alex was determined to maintain that same nonthreatening fiction. It wasn't all that hard when the girl skipped into the center with the counselor, her eyes bright and her face streaked with finger paint.

"Hey, Kitten."

"Hi, Alex. How come you're here early?"

"I need to ask you something."

When she patted the seat beside her, the counselor left to give them some privacy. Maria settled happily beside her and chattered about her current project.

"It's montage," she said, impressing the heck out of Alex with her newfound artistic vocabulary. "For Ben, for Father's Day. I know he's not my real dad. Not till the 'doption. But I'm going to put my picture on it, and yours, and Sox's, so I think he'll like it."

"He'll love it."

"Can I have some crystals to decorate it with? Purple and green?"

"Sure. I'll bring some from work."

"Don't tell Ben what they're for!"

"I won't."

Alex let out a long, relieved breath. Maria had just given her the perfect opening.

"You may not have to wait for Father's Day to give it to him, though. Your real dad has decided to agree to the adoption. We want to have the hearing as soon as possible...if that's all right with you?"

"Okay, but..."

Maria's brow pulled together in a frown, and Alex felt her stomach lurch.

"You might hafta help me with the montage so I get it done in time. Or maybe Caroline will help. She's really good with crystals."

Relaxing again, Alex ignored that slam on her professional skills. "No problem. You can come into work with me one afternoon."

That thorny problem solved, Maria was more than happy to return to her masterpiece in progress.

Alex sat in the parking lot, her car's air-conditioning blasting through the vents, and gave Montoya the go-ahead.

"Great. I'll have my people hand-deliver Musgrove's agreement to Judge Hendricks. And I'll see you, Ben and Maria in court Thursday at three p.m."

"Thursday! Like the day after tomorrow?"

"Hendricks had an opening. We grabbed it."

"Omigod! I can't believe it. After all this time, all this trouble..."

"Believe it, Alex. We're almost there."

She was still half hopeful, half worried, and so nervous she'd skipped both breakfast and lunch when she, Ben and Maria walked into the courthouse on Lomas Boulevard and took the escalator to the second floor. Montoya had told them that final adoptions were usually joyous occasions, with balloons and smiles and pictures taken with the judge. Alex would believe that when she saw it.

Ben wore his blue service dress uniform, his wings shiny and his ribbons marching all the way up to his shoulder. Alex had gone with the most conservative outfit she owned: black slacks topped by a short-sleeved, dove-gray jacket with tiny seed pearls trimming the pocket flaps and lapels. Maria was in her favorite pink shoes, dress and big, pouffy bow on her ponytail.

With its packed schedule of cases involving divorce, parentage, custody and visitation, child support, domestic violence, adult adoption and kinship guardianship, the Family Court Division kept four judges, five hearing officers and three domestic violence special commissioners busy full-time. The hearing officer assigned to Maria's adoption was already present in the courtroom, as were Paul Montoya and Eddie Musgrove's court-appointed attorney. Dinah's mom was there, too, to lend moral support. So were most of Alex's crew from the shop.

And filling at least five rows of seats were members of 58th, all in dress uniform! Colonel Rochambeaux led the pack, sitting front and center in the first row. Ben took their appearance in stride but Alex was so nervous she almost burst into tears of gratitude.

It was her former roommate's unexpected appearance, however, that started the waterworks. "Chelsea! I can't believe you're here!"

"Ben called," she said, as weepy as Alex. "He had a ticket waiting for me at the airport and said I'd be on his sh— Er…" she zinged a glance at the beaming Maria and made a quick course correction "…on his blacklist if I didn't fly in at least for the hearing and the celebration afterward."

Maria wormed her way in and made it a three-way hug. "I'm so glad you came, Aunt Chelsea."

"Me, too, brat."

They didn't have time for more. A warning from the clerk sent them to their table and they were barely seated before he issued a sonorous, "All rise!"

Alex's nemesis strode in and took his seat behind the bench. She knew from previous sessions that he was short and frail, with a faint tremor in his veined hands. But the power of the court imbued him with an intimidating authority as he nodded and the clerk kicked off the proceedings.

"Special Family Court, Second Judicial District Court, Judge Samuel Hendricks presiding, is now in session. Take your seats, please."

Alex sank into her chair and surreptitiously swiped away the last of her tears before she locked her trembling hands in her lap. Without saying a word, Ben covered her fists with a warm, reassuring palm.

Hendricks slid his glasses down his nose and observed the solid phalanx of blue in his courtroom. Then his glance slid to Alex. "I'll admit I've had you jumping through a few hoops, Ms. Scott."

A few?

"It's Ms. Kincaid, your honor. This is my husband, Major Ben Kincaid."

The judge harrumphed and tipped his nose lower to peer over his glasses at Ben. For a frightened moment, Alex feared he would question their oh-so-convenient marriage. Just as quickly, she relaxed. He could question all he wanted. It was real. It was forever.

Instead, the judge pinned her with a stern stare. "I hope you appreciate that I had only Maria's best interests at heart."

She understood that, but sure didn't appreciate it. She choked back the retort that she pitied the next single working woman who came before him and offered a properly respectful answer instead. "Yes, Your Honor."

Hendricks's glance shifted again, this time to Maria. His expression softened, making him appear almost human.

"Looks like you've found a fine new mommy and daddy, missy. Are you ready for me to make it official?"

"Yes, sir!"

Her answer rang out with such military precision that it raised chuckles from the attendees and a smile from the judge.

"All right, then."

He signed the final decree with a flourish and handed it to the clerk. Then to Alex's surprise, he reached under the bench and produced a stuffed pony with a glittering pink mane. Abandoning his seat, he came around the bench and presented it personally.

"This is for you, missy. Now let's get a picture of you and me with your mom and dad."

The court reporter took a couple of shots with them

and the judge, then several more that included the hearing officer and Paul Montoya. After that, Ben wanted one with the rest of the attendees. The seats emptied and everyone crowded into a semicircle with the judge, Maria, Alex and Ben at the epicenter.

"Wait!"

With that imperious command, Maria darted back to the table and pawed through Alex's purse. She returned a moment later with a green-framed collage.

"This is for you, Daddy. I made it myself. With some help from Mommy and Caroline," she amended with a quick smile for the chalk-faced, shadow-eyed young Goth.

Alex wasn't the only one sniffling when Ben went down on one knee to accept the jeweled montage and a kiss from his daughter.

The celebration that followed at Chuck E. Cheese's was raucous, joyous and the most viscerally satisfying three hours of Ben's life. He'd thought he'd found a home in the air force. He *knew* he'd found brothers and sisters in Special Ops. Yet these two... This laughing, cinnamon-eyed beauty... This happy, squealing bundle of joy... They filled holes in his heart he'd never realized were there.

When he told Alex that—some hours later, after they'd dropped Chelsea off at the airport and tucked their exhausted but still hyperexcited daughter into bed—she went up on tiptoe and hooked her arms around his neck.

"Who could've imagined one wild weekend in Vegas would lead to this?"

"Colonel Dolan would be proud."

When she went blank, he laughed.

"The Badger, sweetheart. The Badger."

He brushed her lips with his. Once. Twice.

"Rumor is next year's Bash will be in Phoenix. We should go…and get Chelsea to meet us. Dingo, too." His hands slid from her hips to her waist to her breasts. "Who knows? Ole Dingo might get as lucky as I have."

* * * * *

COMING SOON!

We really hope you enjoyed reading this book. If you're looking for more romance, be sure to head to the shops when new books are available on

Thursday
28th June

MILLS & BOON

Coming next month

REUNITED AT THE ALTAR
Kate Hardy

Cream roses.

Brad had bought her cream roses.

Had he remembered that had been her wedding bouquet, Abigail wondered, a posy of half a dozen cream roses they'd bought last-minute at the local florist? Or had he just decided that roses were the best flowers to make an apology and those were the first ones he'd seen? She raked a shaking hand through her hair. It might not have been the best idea to agree to have dinner with Brad tonight.

Then again, he'd said he wanted a truce for Ruby's sake, and they needed to talk.

But seeing him again had stirred up all kinds of emotions she'd thought she'd buried a long time ago. She'd told herself that she was over her ex and could move on. The problem was, Bradley Powell was still the most attractive man she'd ever met – those dark, dark eyes; the dark hair that she knew curled out-rageously when it was wet; that sense of brooding about him. She'd never felt that same spark with anyone else she'd dated. She knew she hadn't been fair to the few men who'd asked her out; she really shouldn't have compared them to her first love, because how could they ever match up to him?

She could still remember the moment she'd fallen in love with Brad. She and Ruby had been revising for their English exams together in the garden, and Brad had come out to join them, wanting a break from his physics revision. Somehow he'd ended up reading Benedick's speeches while she'd read Beatrice's.

'I do love nothing in the world so well as you: is that not strange?'

She'd glanced up from her text and met his gaze, and a surge of heat had spun through her. He was looking at her as if it was the first time he'd ever seen her. As if she was the only living thing in the world apart from himself. As if the rest of the world had just melted away...

Continue reading

REUNITED AT THE ALTAR
Kate Hardy

Available next month
www.millsandboon.co.uk

LET'S TALK
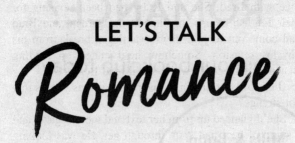
Romance

For exclusive extracts, competitions
and special offers, find us online:

f facebook.com/millsandboon

⊙ @millsandboonuk

𝕪 @millsandboon

Or get in touch on 0844 844 1351*

For all the latest titles coming soon, visit
millsandboon.co.uk/nextmonth

Want even more
ROMANCE?

Join our bookclub today!